Wayne turned her around to face him

"You've been crying. Did something happen to upset you?" he asked.

She shook her head. He had taken a step closer, bringing his body within touching distance of her. At his nearness she felt every nerve ending tingle with a sudden and quite unexpected sensation. A need. She wanted him. She wanted him to hold her.

But she couldn't feel this way! Couldn't let herself. "Wayne, don't!" she protested as he pulled her to him.

"You're trembling," he whispered, ignoring her plea. "Why?" He did not wait for her answer as his head descended, and he found her mouth with his lips. The kiss began slowly, tenderly, but in seconds, as if her body's need had communicated itself to him, inflaming him in turn, the pressure of his lips hardened.

ROSEMARY CARTER

master of tinarua

Harlequin Books

TORONTO • NEW YORK • LOS ANGELES • LONDON
AMSTERDAM • PARIS • SYDNEY • HAMBURG
STOCKHOLM • ATHENS • TOKYO • MILAN

Harlequin Presents first edition March 1983
ISBN 0-373-10575-4

Original hardcover edition published in 1982
by Mills & Boon Limited

CHAPTER ONE

'I'LL take those.'

Eyes the colour of amethyst widened as Teslyn stared at the man whose presence she had not registered until the moment he spoke.

'Thanks, but I can manage.'

Pity she did not have the key in her hand, Teslyn thought; it would have saved her juggling the groceries as she unlocked the door.

'The milk is about to fall out of the packet and the eggs will follow.' She heard the bubble of laughter in the low vital voice. 'I don't know about you, but I'd think mopping egg-yolk from a black stone floor would be a chore I would do without.'

He was a stranger, and girls had need to be wary of strangers in the city, especially in an area which not even the most generous person could class as desirable, yet as Teslyn looked into a face that was rugged and open, she found that her returning smile was involuntary.

'Well, thanks. My key seems to have slipped to the bottom of my bag and I'm carrying a whole week's groceries.'

He took the packets from her. His hands were strong and well shaped, Teslyn noted abstractedly in the moment before she turned her attention back to her bag and the search for the elusive key. They were hands that went well with the firm handsome lines of his face.

'Got it.' She turned the key in the lock of the outer door to the building, slipped it back in her bag and turned to the man. 'Thanks,' she said again, holding out her arms for the packets.

He made no move to hand back the groceries, but stepped instead into the foyer of the building. 'We're going the same way, I think.'

For a moment Teslyn stared at him in surprise. Then she shrugged and began to walk along a corridor where the carpeting was so threadworn underfoot that the floors might as well have been bare. There was not a thing he could do to her, she told herself firmly, as he strode beside her. Why, a really loud scream would bring at least one of the other tenants from their flats.

'You don't live here,' she offered.

'No.'

The question was purely conversational. Everything about him, from the well-cut clothes to the look of easy confidence, suggested money. He looked as if a corporate boardroom would be his natural setting, or perhaps a luxury seaside hotel, for with the rugged face went a tan and an athletic build. Without knowing all her neighbours Teslyn was confident that he was not one of them.

She was very aware of him as he walked beside her through the narrow corridor, aware of a physical closeness, and she wondered why. She did not want to be aware of a man. Not yet. Perhaps never again. In the circumstances it seemed necessary to dispel the feeling with conversation.

'Visiting?' she asked.

'Right.'

They were at her door now. She turned to him, holding out her arms for the packets. 'This is where I live. Thanks again.'

And again he kept hold of the packets. Looking down at her with a smile—heavens, but he was tall, he literally towered above her—he said, 'Visiting you, I think.'

'Me?' Her eyes were suddenly wide and startled. For the first time she knew real fear as it occurred to her that he might actually have been waiting for her on the street. He had seemed all right until now, quite safe and respectable. But she was expecting nobody, and just last week a girl had been molested not half a mile from here. The building appeared all at once even more deserted than usual.

'Oh no.' She lifted her chin in a show of confidence and kept her voice very firm. 'You're making a mistake.'

This time she made no attempt to take the groceries from him. Let him keep them! She would open the door and walk through very quickly, and she would close the door before he had a chance to follow her in. The packets would make him clumsy.

'I've frightened you—sorry about that,' he said, just as if he had read her thoughts. 'My name is Wayne North, and I'm here on behalf of Jim and Mary Morrison.'

The words stopped her in her tracks. As she shot him another look, heart beating, mind racing, he went on, 'I think you *are* Teslyn Morrison?'

'Yes.'

'And may I come in?'

'. . . Yes.' She expelled a breath she had not known she was holding. 'Yes, of course.'

Once inside, she was glad of the perishables among the groceries; putting them away gave her a few minutes to calm herself, to collect her thoughts. He had come from Jim and Mary Morrison. Why now? Why so long after Alec's death had his parents decided to get in touch with her?

'Lived here long?'

She had not heard him approach. Not that he had far to come, for the flat was small, and there was no door to separate the kitchen from the area that combined living-room and dining-room.

'A little more than a year,' she said, thinking that in the three years of their marriage she and Alec had lived in more places than she cared to remember.

'You were living here then before Alec died.'

'Yes.' As always any mention of Alec's death stabbed her with guilt and uncertainty. 'We had three months together here.'

'Long enough,' Wayne North said reflectively, 'to have let Alec's parents know his change of address. But let's not blame the departed, he's not here to defend himself. Why didn't you let them know, Mrs Morrison?'

'I thought Alec would have. . . .' She stopped, staring at him in confusion, and wondering at what sounded like an accusation. A little unsteadily she went on, 'I phoned them.'

'When Alec died,' he agreed.

'When Alec died, yes. I . . . I phoned them . . . spoke to them. . . .'

'An incoherent phone-call, I gather. Just enough to let Alec's parents know that their son had been in a motor accident.'

She turned from the fridge and stared at him, this tall man with the handsome face and the expression that had become cool and polite, and did not know why her sense of uneasiness had increased.

Incoherent? She remembered the call, knew that she had made it, but the details of the conversation were gone from her mind. Mercifully, she often thought, much of that terrible day had been erased from her consciousness. What she did remember was that she had been more upset than ever before in her life. In the circumstances the phone-call could well have been incoherent.

'I'm sorry,' she said simply.

'Jim and Mary Morrison understood your grief. Even through their own grief they understood. They wanted you to come to them.'

'I didn't know.'

'How could you? You said your piece and put down the phone without giving Jim a chance to speak.'

'I didn't think. . . . If I had I would have. . . . But it never occurred to me that they didn't have our address.'

Teslyn ran a distraught hand through shining fair hair that feathered softly away from a piquant oval face. Troubled blue eyes looked a little desperately around the tidy kitchen. The perishables were in the fridge, the task having taken no more than a few minutes, for her needs were fewer now than they had been when housekeeping was for two. If only there was something else left to do. Anything that would allow her to keep her eyes away from the big virile-looking man who was making the tiny space seem even smaller. She could of course put on the kettle, but something in her rebelled at the thought of providing Wayne North with tea.

'Why don't you just come and sit down?' he suggested dryly into the silence that had fallen between them.

In the circumstances it would have been childish to refuse. And childishness, she knew with strange certainty, was a quality Mr North would not find endearing. Nevertheless, as she sat down in the chair farthest from his, she said, 'That sounded like an order.'

An elegant eyebrow lifted. 'Did it?'

'Yes. This place may be humble—it *is* my home.'

'You're right, and I'm sorry.'

Sorry was the one thing he was not, she decided, seeing brown eyes sparkle. He had the look of a man who was accustomed to giving orders—and to having them obeyed. From the start, even through the moments of fear, she had noticed his aura of distinction and authority. Alec had been a follower, a fact he had resented, though he had not known how to change it. Wayne North was a leader.

'So you didn't think of telling Jim Morrison your address.' His tone was deceptively conversational.

'No. I told you, I thought they had it. . . .'

'They didn't.' The vibrant voice hardened. 'Just as they didn't have the previous one. Or the one before that.'

'If only I'd known!'

'Tell me, Mrs Morrison, was there a reason why your husband kept his whereabouts a secret from his parents?'

Were there reasons for any of the things you did, Alec? I thought you hurt only me, that you went out of your way to confuse me and cause me grief. I could have been wrong. Perhaps your behaviour was all just a part of the character which you kept hidden from the world behind the façade of a boyish smile and a handsome face.

She looked up to see Wayne North watching her. In the lean tanned face his eyes were penetrating. With a start she realised that he wondered why she did not answer.

'I don't know why Alec didn't write to his parents. Perhaps he was busy.'

'Or thoughtless.'

Oh yes, Alec was thoughtless. And cruel. But you don't need to know that, Mr North. Whatever happened between my husband and myself is private. A man as hard as you are would have neither sympathy nor understanding.

'And unreliable,' Wayne North added.

Teslyn shifted in her chair, and her eyes sparkled with defiance. 'It was you who said we shouldn't speak ill of Alec.'

'Point taken.' Wayne North paused and studied her face, his expression changing a fraction. 'Whatever his omissions may have been, are you also unreliable, Mrs Morrison?'

Anger leaped inside her, swift and hot. She had been leaning back in the chair, a little bemused still by the unexpectedness of the visit. Now she jerked up straight. 'I've had enough!' she flung at him, voice high. She jumped to her feet. 'I've things to do, Mr North. I'll just see you to the door.'

'I didn't spend all this time tracing you just to be shown to a door that I can see perfectly well from where I'm sitting. Sit down, Teslyn.' He grinned as he spoke her name, and she saw that his brown eyes were lit with flecks of gold. 'Do you know you look a little like an angry kitten getting ready to attack?'

She took a breath, caught more by the smile than the words, and after a moment she did sit down.

'Why did you come here?' she asked, and now her tone was low.

'To take you back with me to Pinevale.'

She shook her head disbelievingly. 'Alec's old home? I don't understand.'

'It's quite simple. Your parents-in-law want you to come.'

'But I can't!'

'They'd have asked you when you phoned but you hung up in such a hurry.'

'That was almost a year ago.'

'It's taken quite some time to find you. When can you be ready?'

I'm not coming, don't you understand? I will *not* go to Alec's parents, to his home, to the place where he once lived. Our life together was a living hell, and I don't want to be reminded of it. I'm only just beginning to come to terms with his death and my part in it. The sight of Alec's parents will open wounds that are better left closed.

'I'm not coming,' she said dully.

'It would mean very much to Jim and Mary.'

'They've never met me.'

'You were Alec's wife.' He leaned forward and two long hands grasped her wrists, covering them. 'Don't you realise that you're their only link with their son?'

All she realised at this moment was that she was shaking. His touch had sent waves of shock through her system. Violently she pulled her hands from his.

'Don't touch me!'

'I'm sorry,' he said, a little oddly. 'I didn't think that after so long. . . . Mrs Morrison—Teslyn, I'd like you to change your mind.'

'No. Please tell Alec's parents how sorry I am that I didn't think to tell them my address, but I can't come. Not now, probably never.'

She had dropped her eyes from a face that was lean and hard and attractive, and found that she was looking instead at long legs encased in well-cut rather tight-fitting trousers. Would his legs be as tanned as his face and his hands? Muscular legs, she guessed, with well-shaped thighs and calves.

The thought had been involuntary. And then she realised what she was thinking and shock hit her once more. Mustering control, she stood up. 'You really must go now, Mr North.'

'Jim and Mary need you.' He was studying her, a strange expression on his face. Almost as if he knew her thoughts. Which was impossible! She was letting herself become fanciful.

'Please go,' she said, a little desperately.

He stood up. Relief—he was going! She could not take much more of this.

But he did not make for the door. Instead he closed the distance between them. Teslyn had no chance to move away as he put his hands on her shoulders. 'What does it take to get through to you? I said Jim and Mary need you.'

He was very close to her, closer than any man had been for as long as she could remember. Certainly closer than she'd been to Alec after the first few months of their marriage had passed. Wayne North was so tall that she could not see his face. It was his silk shirt that was before her eyes, blurring them, as a distinctive male smell filled her nostrils.

'Let go of me,' she whispered. All at once she felt very giddy.

His voice came down to her, his words suggesting that he had not heard her, or if he had, had decided to ignore her plea. 'Does it mean nothing to you that they've tried so hard to find you?'

On the contrary, it means very much. It's a threat. Because if I go to Pinevale I will never be free of the horror I experienced. The little peace of mind I have now, so fragile and so painfully won, could be shattered.

As it is being shattered now with your closeness and your hands on my body.

'Don't touch me!' she shouted.

She thought afterwards that until that moment

Wayne North had not consciously regarded her as a person, a woman. He could have taken hold of her shoulders in a mood of frustration, using the gesture as a means to further his argument. With the violence of her words his manner changed.

'So you don't want to be touched,' he said mockingly, making no effort to release her.

'I'm glad *I've* got through to *you*!'

'Strange for a woman who was married and who's been without a man for almost a year.'

She could feel every one of his fingers through the thin fabric of her dress. It was hard to conceal her trembling.

'I loved Alex,' she lied shakily. 'Get out of my flat, Mr. North.'

'You'll think about Jim and Mary Morrison?'

'No.'

The grip on her shoulders increased. Then he was pulling her against him. The contact, lasting no more than seconds, was enough to let her feel the long hard length of him. He was bending his head, and panic welled as she anticipated a kiss. From somewhere she found the strength to pull her right arm from between them. She was lifting her hand to force it against his mouth when he pushed her away from him.

'Get out!' she ordered through quivering lips.

'I'm going. I wish I could say meeting you had been a pleasure.' His face was a mask of contempt as he went to the door.

'Wrong jacky, Tessy,' someone whimpered.

It was not the first time the words had been said, Teslyn realised as the blur cleared from her eyes and she focused on the small figure before her. Andy Johnson, three years old and head covered with a mop of hair the colour of fading fire, was looking up at her, his eyes wide with reproach.

Kneeling, Teslyn pulled the little boy to her and gave him a hug. 'So it is, Andy dear. Silly Tessy!' Releasing him, she took off the jacket which belonged to another child and replaced it with Andy's own.

'Better,' said Andy, rewarding her with a broad smile before going to the door to meet his mother.

'Feeling okay, Teslyn?' a voice asked when the last of the children had gone.

'Fine,' she said, swinging round to meet the gaze of Linda, one of the other nursery-school teachers.

'Sure?'

'Yes, of course.' And then, as steady eyes continued to hold hers, 'You saw me goof with Andy. Not hard to get the jackets mixed up, they're all much the same.'

'And we all make silly mistakes,' Linda conceded.

'You just think I've been making more than my fair share,' Teslyn said after a moment.

'These last three days, yes. Something on your mind?'

Teslyn hesitated. 'Yes,' she said after a moment.

'Feel like talking about it?'

'Oh no, it's nothing much.' Turning, she began to riffle through a stack of paintings. The children had experimented with finger-paint, dipping their fingers in paint and splotching and trailing them over big white sheets of paper. It would give them pleasure to see their efforts displayed in the classroom the next morning. Decorating the walls would also delay the moment when she would have to make her way back to the quiet flat.

'I'm going to have a cup of tea. Kettle will be boiling by the time you get finished here.' Linda was watching her from the doorway.

Teslyn threw her a half-smile. 'You never give up, do you?'

'Not when my friend starts acting out of character. See you in the staff-room.'

'It's crazy,' Teslyn was saying a little while later. 'This man walks into my life, uninvited, and I spend the next three days in such a spin that I can't concentrate on my work!'

'Is it crazy?'

'Yes, of course—it must be! I met him once, for less than an hour, I'm never going to see him again.'

'Sometimes even an hour can be meaningful,' Linda said with perception.

More meaningful than you realise. He frightened me, shocked me. He awoke in me feelings that I thought were dead, that I never want to experience again.

'Don't you see,' Teslyn said slowly, 'I have no reason to give the meeting another thought. So why am I doing just that?'

'You said he asked you to visit Alec's parents.' Linda had been given the bare details by a girl who thought she had managed to sound detached and amused when in reality her voice had quivered with emotion.

'Yes. He asked me when I'd be ready to leave.'

'I don't blame you for not going then and there, but would it be such a bad idea to think about a visit in the near future? You do have some leave coming up soon.'

Even Linda, Teslyn's closest friend, did not know the facts of her marriage. The charade Teslyn had maintained during Alec's lifetime had remained intact after his death. There were times when she longed to talk about what had happened, when she yearned to purge herself of the guilts and doubts and fears that made her days unhappy and her nights sleepless. But she could not talk, not even to Linda.

'Why don't you think about going?' her friend asked.

'I don't want to. I don't want to go.' Blue eyes, heavy with fatigue, looked up. 'That part of my life . . . my marriage . . . it's over.'

'Can it ever be completely over?'

'Yes. It has to be.' Teslyn was closer to divulging her feelings than ever before. 'I'm trying so hard to make a new life for myself. I enjoy working here at the nursery school—I've always loved children. I planned to have six of my own, can you imagine?' She gave a choked laugh. 'Some dreams come to nothing.'

'And that, my dear, is nonsense,' Linda said firmly. 'You're just twenty-one, plenty of time to have children.'

'Not for me.' Teslyn fixed her gaze on a cage of hamsters. 'I don't intend to marry again.'

Silence followed her words. The ticking of the wall-clock filled the room, and the hamsters made a rustling sound as they scampered on the straw. Teslyn's fingers curled into her palms, then gradually loosened. If Linda intended to pursue the subject she would have done so immediately. Mentally Teslyn blessed her friend's sensitivity. It seemed that Linda knew when to stop.

'I'm sorry,' Teslyn said at last, managing a smile. 'I know you mean well; you don't deserve to have me snapping at you.'

'You didn't snap, and you've nothing to be sorry for,' Linda countered cheerfully. 'If you've finished your tea, let's get the puppets sorted—we promised Nancy to have them ready for tomorrow.'

They worked a while, taking puppets from boxes and sorting them into piles. Teslyn liked the apple-faced ones best. The children had helped make them, revelling in the whole process of drying the apples and then carving features into the wrinkled fruit. 'I'm content here, she thought. I really do love the children and the work. In time I will be happy again.

'What was he like, this Wayne North?' Linda asked.

Teslyn sat back on her heels. 'Autocratic.' Grinning, she held up an apple face of a bewhiskered man frowning indulgently over his glasses. 'Mr Know-all, like this little guy.'

'Obviously you didn't like him, but my golly, he seems to have made quite an impact on you all the same.'

More of an impact than I can tell you. More even than I want to admit to myself.

'There *was* something,' Teslyn admitted. 'Mainly dislike.'

'Why do I get the feeling that he made a pass at you?'

Teslyn drew a breath. 'He—did.'

'Did you mind?' Linda asked curiously.

'I hated it.'

And that's not true. I didn't hate it, at least not altogether. Part of me liked it very much, despite the outrage I felt. Part of me wanted him to kiss me, hard and long.

And that's what I hate. I hate the feelings he aroused in me. I don't want to react to a man. I can't. Not after Alec, after all that happened.

'Let's not talk about Mr North,' she said, without looking at Linda. 'Shall we put the apple faces in the tea-chest and the fabric puppets in the cardboard box?'

It was sunny outside, and so clear that the outlines of buildings were crisp edges against the powder-blue sky. The trees in the small square of city park, normally drooping with dust, looked glad to be alive.

For once Teslyn, lover of blue skies and the outdoor life, was unaffected by the weather. Three nights without sleep had taken their toll of her so that she wanted to get home. The talk with Linda had helped. Not that much had been said in terms of her real thoughts and feelings, nevertheless talking had helped to clear her mind, if only just a little. Even had she wanted to tell Linda the truth, it would have been almost impossible to verbalise the complexity of feelings Wayne North had aroused in her. Teslyn was not sure that she understood them herself.

Despite the violent hostility between Alec and herself, she had grieved at his death as she would have grieved for anyone to whom she had once been close. More than just an ordinary closeness in this instance, for surely there had been a time when she had loved Alec. Or had the happiness at the start been no more than infatuation?

What she did not regret was the end of their marriage. After three years of mounting hostility and abuse, there was no way the relationship could have continued. Had death not ended the marriage bond, it would have been severed by law. And soon. It was that fact which had caused the crisis and brought it to its violent climax. Teslyn shuddered, and she questioned if the time would come when she would remember that dreadful night with any measure of calmness, whether she would ever be free of the doubts and recriminations that tormented her.

She had hoped for so much when she had accepted the job at the nursery school. The work was quite different from anything she had done previously—less money than the desk jobs, more demands on her patience and time, but also more satisfaction. In telling

Linda that she loved the children, Teslyn had spoken from the heart. As she had done when she had stated that she would never marry again.

She stopped at the corner café for milk and bread, then went on. The street door to the building stood slightly ajar—she had noticed a day earlier that the lock seemed in need of repair—and so for once there was no need to juggle bag and packets to get to her key. Fleetingly she thought of Wayne North, only to push him firmly from her mind as she made her way down the corridor. Mr North had made enough inroads on her peace of mind already, he had no right in her home.

For home it was, despite the fact that it was shabby and unpretentious. She and Alec had lived in more places than Teslyn cared to remember. They were places that had varied in comfort and attractiveness with the volatile fluctuations of their finances. This last flat was the least pretentious of all their homes. It was home nevertheless. Especially now.

Yet it was no wonder that the Morrisons had not known where to find their son. Teslyn had thought sometimes that she did not know herself where she lived. All the moves had been sudden, at dead of night often. Alec had creditors to dodge, enemies to evade. He seldom supplied details, and Teslyn did not ask for them. To one move she had objected, for she had loved the small brownstone cottage where the Christmas flowers grew in clusters round the stoop and ivy covered and hid the bleak walls. Alec had stopped shifting the furniture out of the door just long enough to bruise one cheek and spread a gash across the other, and Teslyn had learned not to cross him again. Until the last time. And then the consequences had been more dire than she had ever expected.

In the first days after Alec's death, Teslyn had thought she could not remain in the flat. Her memories were too vivid, too raw. It was one more place to which she had moved under duress, and she had made up her mind to vacate it as quickly as she could.

And then she found that a change was impractical, if not impossible. Obstacles presented themselves at every turn. She could not move the few pieces of furniture herself, meagre though they were, and hiring a removal company would have cost her more than she could afford. As for friends to whom she could turn for help, the only men she knew were acquaintances she had met through Alec, slick bar-room' types, people she never wanted to see again. Assuming even that they would want to see her, for she did not know who of Alec's friends had been in his confidence and whether they held her to blame for the accident.

Even the matter of finding a new place was not easy. With accommodation at a premium, prospective land-lords seemed more eager to take on a man than a young girl, and the rents were more than she could afford. That left the option of sharing a place with a few other girls, but the prospect of flatmates was unappealing, and Teslyn decided to stay where she was.

Surprisingly, it was when she resigned herself to the idea of staying that the flat began to become home. She put out the few lovely pieces that had been her mother's, the china figurines and the crystal vase and the porcelain tea-set, things she had kept safely hidden when Alec was alive and a drunken rage was a constant threat. She learned to make scatter cushions and began to haunt the remnant counters of fabric stores for brightly coloured materials. One day, in an alley, she found an abandoned pot of geraniums, and taking it back home with her, she lovingly nursed the sad-looking plant back to life. Inspired by her success and the satisfaction it gave her, she began to gather cuttings of other plants, and soon every inch of space on windowsills and beside the kitchen sink was taken up with greenery-filled glass jars.

Having put the kettle on for tea and some bread in the toaster, Teslyn sank down into a chair and looked around her. A ray of late afternoon sunshine sparkled on the window and gave the faded rug a warm glow. Oh yes, this was home. Not perhaps the home she had once envisaged, but home all the same.

She had taken a bite of toast when there was a knock at the door. Mrs Thomas, the landlady, for the rent? Surely she was a day early, but then again perhaps she might have other plans for tomorrow and was chancing her luck. Just as well she'd been paid today, Teslyn thought as she went to the door.

But it was not the small form of the landlady who stood in the doorway. Instead Teslyn found herself tilting her head until her eyes met those of the tall figure she remembered from her dreams.

'You!' she gasped on a tight throat, and when Wayne North grinned, 'Oh no! You can't come in.'

Almost without thinking she tried to close the door, and gasped when a sleek-shoed foot inserted itself, lightning-swift, into the space between the door and the jamb.

'You can't come in,' a little unsteadily this time.

'Sorry, honey, but it's what I intend.'

With no effect at all he pushed open the door. Sensing that she had lost that particular round, Teslyn stepped back hastily and let him go past her.

CHAPTER TWO

'I INTERRUPTED your lunch.' His eyes flicked the table.

'I told you you weren't welcome.'

'Toast looks good. And that cheese is just the colour I like it.'

'You're very thick-skinned, Mr North,' Teslyn said, refusing to give in without a token struggle.

'And you, little hothead, have no manners.' Brown eyes sparkled above gaunt cheekbones. 'I wonder, did you have any to start with?'

Teslyn swallowed, stung by the taunt. The subject of manners was one which had meant much to her mother. She would have mourned the situation which had bred a newly-brittle behaviour in her daughter. No stranger in her parents' home, whether there by invitation or not, had ever left it without being shown hospitality.

'Don't you know you're not welcome?' she faltered.

'Tell me something new,' he mocked. 'The tea looks good too.'

'It looks dark and wet and you wouldn't know if it was good unless you tasted it.' She couldn't help a smile.

'Better,' he said softly, his eyes skimming her face with an open approval that brought a flush to her cheeks. 'You should smile more often, Teslyn Morrison. It becomes you.'

'Sit down.' She pretended to sigh, not an easy feat when she felt suddenly, and for no justifiable reason, lightheaded. 'There'll be enough for two.'

He sat down at the table, a tall lithe figure, looking elegant yet at ease in surroundings that must surely be alien to him. She watched him lift his cup to his lips. His hands were long and well shaped—sensitive hands, the words came to her involuntarily as she thought how right the porcelain looked in his fingers. Unbidden came a secret pleasure at the fact that she had decided to treat herself to her good crockery today.

'The tea *is* good,' he commented.

'You were right after all.' Her tone had lost its earlier bite.

'I usually am.' His smile, white teeth wicked against his tan, robbed the words of conceit.

'That must be infuriating for the people you live with. Your wife. . . .'

'I'm not married,' he said quietly. And then, giving her no time to examine the odd feeling of satisfaction, 'These cups are lovely. Forgive me, but they seem a little out of place in this setting.' The glance that swept the room was dispassionate, giving nothing away. 'I think you didn't get these things from Alec.'

'They were my mother's,' she said simply, chalking a mental note of approval to the man who was able to recognise quality where he would least anticipate it.

'I take it your parents are no longer alive?'

'They died in a motor accident, four years ago.' The low voice gave no indication of the anguish she had lived through, of the loneliness which had been so intense that when Alec had come along she had seen in him a prince on a charger which she had been only too willing to mount.

'Family?'

'Nobody.'

'I see,' he said reflectively. 'I wonder then why

you're so against going to Pinevale. You'd have a ready-made family right away.'

Her eyes dropped to her plate. Today he had revealed a quality she had not expected in him. She had seen the warmth in eyes that were deep and brown, had noticed the laughter lines around those eyes and the corners of his mouth, had heard the vitality in his voice. Had he come here merely to continue the argument he had begun a few days ago, and was the niceness assumed?

'I don't want to talk about it,' she said abruptly.

'Why not?' His glance was assessing.

She moved restlessly. 'I just don't want to. Can't you accept that?'

'If I knew your reasons I might.'

If I couldn't talk to Linda I certainly can't talk to you. 'The reasons don't concern you,' she said.

'That's a matter of opinion.' His voice was a shade cooler. 'But the Morrisons do concern me, Jim and Mary. For their sake I have to talk to you.'

So the initial friendliness had been a cover-up after all. The knowledge gave her no joy.

'I think you should go,' she said flatly.

'When we've talked. Mrs Morrison . . . Teslyn, don't you feel that you owe your parents-in-law a visit?'

And have them talk about Alec? Lovingly, incessantly. Would I be able to hold back my feelings, or would I find myself telling them the truth about their son? And about that night? Oh God, that night!

Suddenly she was on her feet. 'Go! Just go!'

'You keep saying that.'

'I wish you'd get the message!'

Blindly she made to head for the kitchen. She hardly knew what she was doing. There was just the compulsion to break the flow of a conversation that was unendurable.

'Teslyn . . .!' He put his hand out to detain her.
'No!'

She did not realise that he had followed her until she was caught by the waist and spun around. Panic welled as she tried to twist away from him, but he was too strong for her, his hands holding her firm.

She looked up at him, blue eyes wide with anger and a very special kind of fear. 'Please, let me go.'

'It's not what you want.'

'Yes!'

There was a strange expression in the eyes that looked down at her, as if Wayne saw something he had never seen before and did not quite understand.

'I think you want to be kissed.'

'Oh no. No!' The words emerged on a sob. 'Please don't—I'll hate it.'

The expression in his eyes deepened. He was so close to her that she could see the long lashes and the laughter lines were separate crevices. His nearness was doing appalling things to her. In spite of her outrage she was achingly aware of him. She knew that if she tried hard enough she should be able to move away from him, but her limbs seemed to have developed a heavy sluggishness while her pulse beat a crazy tattoo.

'You're behaving like an innocent young girl,' he told her. 'Like a virgin. And you're anything but!'

A hand touched her breast, lingering sensuously on it for a moment before she managed to push it away. Her heart was thudding in her chest, and it was difficult to breathe.

'Why are you behaving like this?' He had put her a little away from him now, and was gazing down at her, his eyes narrow. 'You're accustomed to lovemaking—proper lovemaking.'

But I'm not! Oh, I'm not a virgin, of course I'm not,

but I might as well be for the small amount of experience I've had. Sometimes I think I never knew what proper love is at all.

And she did want him to kiss her. She wanted it badly. Just as she wanted to be closer to him, to know the shape of his chest and his shoulders, to know how that long hard body felt against hers. She wanted to feel his hand on her breast again, wanted him to kiss her.

As if he guessed her thoughts he bent his head and found her lips. His kiss was slow, unhurried. At the same time it was also totally possessive. Torrents of fire raced along Teslyn's spine, and for long moments she knew nothing but the joy of that sensuous mouth. Without thinking her lips responded to his. Later she would wonder why, but now there was only an urgent delight.

He lifted his head for breath, and with the contact broken, sanity returned. God, how could she have let this happen? How could she!

She had gone mad. She had allowed the sex appeal of a very dynamic man to breach the defences she had erected against all men. She didn't understand the nature of the madness that had taken hold of her—not really—but she did know that she must fight it. Memories of Alec, of what had happened, flashed through her mind. With an effort she lifted her head and brought focus to her eyes.

'You disgust me!' she spat out.

His mouth tightened, and his eyes grew cold. Then he put her from him, so abruptly that she swayed for a moment on unsteady legs. And then she was pushing past him, making for the haven of her bedroom.

She opened the window and leaned her hips against the sill while she drew gasping breaths of air.

Distraught hands pushed through her hair, pushing it away from her face, fiercely, as if in this way she could erase the events of the past few minutes from her mind.

Already she knew that forgetting would not be easy, if it could be managed at all. Her heart was still beating too fast and her legs were weak. How had it happened? Of course, Wayne had taken her by surprise, had taken advantage of a vulnerability and a need of which she had not been consciously aware. But she could have fought him, for she had been so determined never to let herself be moved by a man again.

Moved! A strange word to describe what she felt. Shaken was more apt—shaken through and through. At this moment it was as if her world, the safe world she had tried so hard to create for herself in this last year, had been shattered. Would she ever be able to put it together again? She did not know, for to her awareness of herself had been added a new dimension. She had discovered a femininity she had never dreamed she possessed; a sexuality that was basic and earthy and primitive; urges and longings that sprang from deep inside her. Could they be suppressed now that they had been unleashed?

With Alec she had never felt like this. Even in those early days of their marriage, when they had shared a bed and what had passed for love, she had never been conscious of a womanhood that was so strong that it was surely the foundation of her being. She had never felt as alive and vibrant as she did at this moment. It had been possible, though unpleasant, to adjust to a hostile and sterile life. She had learned to perform the duties he demanded of her, and to keep her thoughts to herself—for if she did not Alec punished her with his cruelty.

In the months since his death she had tried to make a new life for herself, and to some degree she had succeeded. But this new life had been based on the knowledge she thought she had of herself. Wayne North had shown her that she did not know herself at all. If she never saw him again—and she would not, absolutely not!—her world had nevertheless been thrown out of kilter.

Absorbed in the tumult of her thoughts, she did not hear the door open. Only when he called her, softly, did she spin round. He was in the middle of the room and she had not heard him come in. In a light-grey suit he looked cool and sleek, and so unruffled that she knew that the scene which had shaken her to the depths of her being had meant nothing to him. But his eyes were questioning.

'I didn't mean to upset you.'

She stared at him, eyes wide, and did not know that to him she had the appearance of a small wounded animal. 'Get out of my room!' she snapped.

'In a moment.'

'You've invaded my flat. My . . .' She had been about to say 'life,' but she stopped herself in time. Voice shaking, she went on, 'How dare you barge into my bedroom?'

'I knocked. I don't think you heard me.'

That was likely enough, though she would not let him know it.

'You shouldn't have come in,' she said angrily.

'I wanted to apologise.'

And that was not true. Wayne North had never apologised for anything in his life. If he did so now it was only because he wanted something of her.

'Why did you kiss me?' she asked.

'You seemed to need kissing very badly. Also,' he

added with a softness that brought the blood to her cheeks, 'I wanted to.'

'I hated it!'

'Is that why you kissed me back?' He looked at her a long moment, and a look of satisfaction came into his face at her confusion. 'You did kiss me, Teslyn, I think you know that.'

'Get out!' Confusion gave way to a searing anger.

'When I'm ready to.'

She lifted a chair and advanced on him wildly. 'I've warned you!'

Easily he took it from her. As his fingers closed over hers she jerked, just as if she had come into contact with a live electric wire. The contact lasted no more than seconds, and then she heard him laugh, a husky sound in his throat. 'Careful now, hothead. You might do something you'll regret.'

'How many times do I have to tell you to leave!'

'I will. Just as soon as we've talked.'

'We've nothing to talk about, you and I.' She stopped, looking at him in dawning understanding. 'You're asking me again to visit the Morrisons.'

'Right.'

'I won't go—I think I've made that clear.'

'There's something you must know.' There was compassion in his expression. 'Jim Morrison has had an accident.'

She stood quite still, though inside her every nerve was quivering. 'I don't believe you.'

'It's true. Let's go back into the other room, Teslyn. We do have to talk.'

'You're making this up, Mr North.'

'Wayne. I've kissed you, remember? Besides, since we're going to be thrown into each other company's a great deal in the next few months it seems foolish to stand on ceremony.'

Spoken as if he took it for granted that she would be going to Pinevale.

'Wayne.' She said the name slowly, experimentally almost, and was surprised to find how good it sounded in her ears. 'Wayne, this is some new trickery you've dreamed up.'

'I only wish that were so.'

'You said nothing about an accident the first time you came.'

'Because it only happened yesterday.'

She didn't want to believe him. Yet something in the low steady voice proclaimed the truth of what he said.

'Well then, today, why didn't you come out with it right away?'

He threw her a measured glance. 'I had my reasons.'

'You wanted to trick me into kissing you first!' The words were out before she could stop them.

'I have never had to resort to trickery for my kisses,' Wayne said evenly, his eyes mocking. 'I've always found the women I want more than willing to meet me halfway.'

Over the quite unjustified little stab of pain, Teslyn said quietly, 'Well then, why didn't you tell me right away?'

'I wanted to give you one more chance to come to Pinevale of your own will.'

'Wayne. . . .'

'Let's go to the living-room, shall we? Perhaps you could make a fresh pot of tea. Then we'll talk.'

He was giving her orders, just as Alec had done. And yet it was not like Alec at all. Wayne's quiet voice had none of Alec's threatening bluster, and Teslyn found that she could not resent him.

He was sitting in an armchair when she came back

into the room carrying a tray. His legs were stretched out in front of him, and his face looked preoccupied. He glanced up as she came in, rose to take the tray from her, and put it down on the table—a small courtesy, but one that Alec would never have considered. Careful, she thought. I'm letting him get to me again, only on a different level this time.

She poured tea, and watched as Wayne spread a piece of bread with butter, then topped it with a slice of thin Cheddar cheese. If he was used to finer fare, and everything in his appearance and manner suggested that this was so, then such were his good manners that he in no way showed it.

Lifting her cup to her lips, she took a long steadying sip, then said, 'Tell me about Jim.'

'It happened yesterday. I gather he caught his hand in some machinery. Thank God one of the farm workers was nearby and ran back to the house for help.'

'He's in hospital?'

'Mary got him there just as quickly as she could.'

'Is . . . is it very bad?'

'If I'm to believe what Mary says—and she's a level-headed lady—then no, it's not critical. He shouldn't be in hospital too long.'

'I'm glad,' Teslyn said simply.

'Jim will come home.' Wayne put down his knife and looked up, the brown eyes steady and direct. 'But it will be some time before he can work again.'

'Is there nobody else?'

'I do what I can.'

Teslyn stared at him, wondering why it had not occurred to her that Wayne North was an employee of Alec's parents. Perhaps it was because he had the air of being his own man. Not only his own man, but one who was accustomed to the giving of orders and the handling of considerable amounts of money. And then she remembered that appearances could be deceptive— had she not been taken in by Alec's boyishly charming pose? Perhaps, she decided unhappily, I've never learned to be a good judge of character.

'Then you are at Pinevale,' she said.

Something flickered briefly in Wayne's eyes. 'The fact remains,' he observed levelly, 'that you're needed.'

'I know nothing about farming.'

'You'll learn.'

Teslyn shook her head, finding her voice. 'You're just assuming I'll come.'

His eyes held a challenge. 'Won't you?'

'I have a life here. A job.' Her voice rose. 'I feel very sorry for Jim. Of course I do.'

'You work in a nursery school.'

'Right. I can't just walk out and let them down.'

'You can be replaced,' Wayne said relentlessly. 'You're needed at Pinevale.'

'I'm needed here too.'

His eyes held hers. The last of the afternoon sunlight was fading, and it was growing dim in the room. Teslyn could not read Wayne's eyes, but she thought it was unnecessary. She sensed that they would be steady and assessing and very determined.

'Listen to me, Teslyn,' he said quietly. 'If Alec were alive he would come to Pinevale now. I don't think he was the most reliable of men, but he did know the plantation. I believe he must have loved it. I think he would have stood by his parents when they needed him.'

'Perhaps,' Teslyn whispered.

'There was a time, my dear, a long time, when Mary and Jim wanted you to come to them because you were

Alec's wife. They wanted to meet you, to comfort you. Now, with this accident, there's a new reason. Alec can't help, so you must do so in his place. I think you owe your parents-in-law that much.'

She did not answer him. Instead she stood up and walked to the window. From the bedroom she had seen only a mass of concrete courtyards and chimneypots. From this window she saw the small park that was an oasis of greenery in an otherwise bleak suburb. It was here that the children of the area played marbles and football and tag, where pigeons squabbled for crumbs. It was late now, and cold, and the children had gone. Only an old man still wandered on the grass, throwing crumbs to the birds that swooped about him.

Teslyn was cold too, a numbing coldness that had nothing to do with the late afternoon or the lack of heating in the flat; it was a coldness that came from deep within her. She stood at the window, her arms folded around her, and wished she could still the trembling, for she did not want Wayne North to see it.

It was his last words that had got to her as none of his previous ones had done. Of course she regretted Jim's illness. She sympathised with anyone who was sick. But she had never met Alec's parents, had never had a chance to grow to love them, let alone like them.

But Alec had loved them, surely. Even Alec, rotten as he had been, must have loved his parents. If as an adult far from home he had thought of them seldom— according to Wayne he had communicated with them only rarely—his feelings as a boy must have been very different.

'Did Alec speak of his parents?' Wayne spoke into the silence.

'Not often. But I do remember once....' She stopped.

'Once?' he prompted.

She continued reluctantly, 'We'd gone out to the Vaal River. Alec was fishing and I remember how deft he was with the rod. I asked him who'd taught him to fish, and he said his father.'

'Jim has a fine hand with a rod. Best I know.'

Teslyn turned from the window, and saw that Wayne was watching her. In the fading light his face was a study of gaunt lines and angles. He's a man, she thought involuntarily, a man in the real sense of the word.

'Alec seemed proud,' she said.

'Jim is a man to be proud of. And Mary is a fine lady.'

'He said she made good koeksusters.' Teslyn's own first attempt had been a failure. Alec had tasted one, had been rude about the texture, and with one sweep of the hand had relegated the whole sticky dish to the floor.

'Mary's koeksusters are the best in the world,' Wayne said with a smile.

Which did not give Alec the excuse to behave as he did. Teslyn bit her lip hard and swallowed a comment.

'I feel sure Alec would have come home,' said Wayne.

Would he? I wish I was as sure as you seem to be, Wayne North. Alec was not selfless, as well as I know. He might have gone back to Pinevale, he might not. The point is that I don't know.

'Don't you think he'd have wanted you to go in his place?'

'You're playing on my sympathies, blast you!'

'I hope,' Wayne said with a grin that was clearly visible in the half-light, 'that I'm succeeding.'

Oh yes, you're succeeding—more than you could realise. Because you don't know anything of my guilt.

You don't know that I'll never be certain whether or not I drove Alec to his death. The threats I made that night were justified, God knows, but if he died because of them I can never forgive myself. There's not a day that I don't torture myself with thoughts of what happened.

'Will you come?' Wayne persisted.

I've no option. I owe it to Alec's parents to go to them, because if I hadn't threatened to divorce him he might still be alive. He might not have gone to them, but they would still have a son.

'Well?'

'Yes, I'll go. Give me a day or two to get ready and I'll go.'

'This for you, Teslyn.'

'Oh, Andy, that's lovely!' Teslyn glanced for a moment at the sprawl of damp paint, then bent to hug the little boy. 'Thank you, poppet.'

All morning there had been a procession of small children to the corner where she sat bringing records up to date. One child handed her a few sweet-peas picked from the flower-bed in the garden, another gave her a pretty shell, most came bearing their artwork. Looking at the solemn childish faces, Teslyn was moved almost to the point of tears. Wayne North should be at the nursery school this morning, she thought, then perhaps he would not take her agreement to go with him to Pinevale quite so for granted.

'I also have something for you,' said Linda, when the last of the children had gone, and they were alone together in the empty classroom. 'A going-away gift. Something small.'

'Oh, Linda, thank you!' Teslyn unwrapped the perfume and held it for a moment to her nose. 'My favourite!' And then, turning troubled eyes to her friend, 'These presents—I feel as if you're all saying goodbye.'

'Perhaps we are.' Linda's voice was steady.

'That's nonsense,' Teslyn said fiercely. 'The children don't understand. To them a few weeks is the same as eternity. But *you* know that I'm coming back.'

'I wonder.'

'Linda! How can you even say such a thing! Unless of course you don't want me back,' she finished uncertainly.

'And now you're the one who's talking nonsense. There's a job here for you any time you want it. But perhaps you'll decide to remain in the Lowveld.'

'You're daft, do you know that? Daft as they come.' Teslyn looked affectionately at her friend. 'Jim Morrison will get better. He and Mary won't need me for ever.'

'Wayne North might,' Linda said with unaccustomed slyness.

Teslyn jumped to her feet, the movement sending a sheaf of papers to the floor. She bent to pick them up, shoving them violently back on to the table. 'You know how I feel about that man, Linda!'

'I know how you say you feel.'

'I hate him!' She turned on her friend, blue eyes blazing. 'I can't remember when I've hated a man so much. Except. . . .' She stopped.

'And I can't remember when you've reacted to anyone quite so strongly.' Linda gave an impish grin. 'We'll all be delighted to see you back. In the meanwhile, wear the perfume, it might have a soothing influence on that monster of yours.'

And he was a monster, Teslyn decided later that evening.

'I'm not driving to Pinevale with you,' she told him

when he had finished outlining her travelling plans.

'How did you intend going?' Wayne asked politely, but with a glimmer of amusement warming his eyes.

'By train.'

'Have you looked at a map?'

What was he implying? 'I intend to,' she said warily.

'Let's glance at one together. I have a travelling map with me.'

She watched as he spread the map on the table, the glossy dark head bent, the long tanned fingers smoothing the folds of the paper, and wondered why such details made an impression on her.

'Pinevale is about here,' she heard him say, and with an effort she forced her attention to the map, and saw that he had made a small pencil mark.

'I could catch a train to Nelspruit,' she said, finding the nearest town.

'Sure you could. How would you proceed from there?'

She looked up at him, a little troubled, sensing she was in some kind of trap and not knowing how to get out of it. 'Another train. A bus, perhaps. For heaven's sake, Wayne, there must be a way!'

'There is—a circuitous way at the best of times, and not practical. I'm afraid you'd have to be met in Nelspruit.'

'Well, then. . . .'

'I'd have to meet you.'

She looked at him in dawning comprehension. 'Wouldn't Mary be there?'

'Mary has enough on her hands, with visiting Jim and seeing to the plantation.'

'And you're here—I understand. It's really quite simple. I'll wait a few days, give you time to get back to Pinevale, then I'll come.'

A hand reached across the table to cup her chin. At the touch Teslyn felt a tingle that was not unlike an electric current.

'You're awfully stubborn, aren't you? Come with me, Teslyn. I have the car. It will be simpler for everyone.'

'I . . . I prefer to make my own way.' She tried to move her chin from his hand and found his grip surprisingly firm.

'Is the thought of travelling with me so abhorrent?'

It's frightening. And exciting. And I can't seem to make sense of my thoughts.

'Not abhorrent,' she got out unsteadily. 'But I prefer to go by train.'

'That's not a reason.'

She looked at him squarely. 'Even you can't pretend that we get on together, Wayne.

'That's open to debate, Teslyn, but if it's true it can be changed,' he said softly.

His voice sent a quiver down her spine. 'I'd like to go by train.'

Glancing around the room, he gave a shrug. 'I get the feeling you don't have money to waste. And right now Mary and Jim certainly don't have much spare cash.'

She looked at him, hating him, struggling with her feelings. It was true that even the amount that a train ticket would cost would make an inroad on her meagre budget. Earlier that month she had splurged on a record album she had been wanting for a long time. The outlay had meant less money for food, but at the time she had considered the luxury well worth the while.

'Look at it this way, Teslyn,' Wayne drawled. 'One way or the other you'll end up in my car. What is at issue is the length of time you spend in it.'

'You're awfully sure of yourself, aren't you?' Teslyn observed, lifting her chin. 'As your employers, what would Jim and Mary feel about your manner with me, I wonder?'

Brown eyes sparked with an amusement Teslyn was beginning to know. If Wayne was in any way discomfited, he did not show it. 'We leave the day after tomorrow,' he told her. 'Be ready at six.'

CHAPTER THREE

'EVER been to the Lowveld?'

Beyond the window the veld was awakening to a new day. The goldmines of the Witwatersrand were flat-topped humps against the greyness, and the gum-trees were tall blurred shapes. It was cold in the time before sunrise, and Teslyn shivered as she turned her head.

'Never.'

'You'll find the Eastern Transvaal very different from this southern part of the province.'

In the dim light Wayne was little more distinct than the scenery, but it did not matter that she could not see him clearly, for his features were a sharp imprint upon the screen of her mind.

'I've heard it's different,' she acknowledged.

'Alec must have described it.'

'A little.' Her husband had told her almost nothing, a fact she would not admit to Wayne.

'Know the route we take?'

'No.'

'The map's in the glove compartment. Later you can take a look at it.'

She would do that, she thought. She had not wanted to come on this journey, yet now that they were on their way she was filled with a sense of excitement, almost as if a holiday had started, better still an adventure. Yes, she would study the map; she wanted to know where they were and where they were going.

The sun came up lifting itself from the flat horizon in a translucent shimmer. The sky lightened and the trees took shape. The goldmines had been left behind, and now fields lay on both sides of the road. Teslyn had no need to ask Wayne the nature of the crops she saw. Maize—acre upon acre of maize, stretching to the north and the south, the east and the west. Here and there were kraals, the round thatch-roofed dwellings of the tribal population, and there were windmills, blades glinting dully in the early light.

The sun rose higher in the sky. Teslyn was reaching for the map when the car left the tarred road and turned on to a sandy country lane. 'Breakfast time,' Wayne explained in response to her questioning look.

Teslyn was mystified, but she remained silent as Wayne drove half a mile and then turned again, bringing the car to a halt beside a vlei. The pond was rimmed with willows and waterlilies, and low over the water shimmered a white mist.

'This is where we're having breakfast?' Teslyn asked, enchanted with the small oasis.

'Like it?'

As she turned in her seat she forgot that Wayne was a man to be wary of. Her eyes shone as she smiled. 'I love it.'

Something flickered in Wayne's face, then he said, 'I'm glad. Shall we get out?'

They walked towards the vlei, and Teslyn saw that a duck moved beneath the shifting swirl of mist. The early morning chill was intensified by the nearness of the water. Teslyn, clad only in denim jeans and a cotton shirt, shivered.

Almost immediately an arm went around her shoulders. She stood quite still for a moment, as if the touch that was strong and warm, even through her shirt, held her immobile. And then memory returned—the same dreadful memory always—and she tried to move away from him.

'You're cold,' he said, his breath fanning down to her cheek.

'No.'

'You're shivering.' He made no move to release her. Instead the arm that held her tightened, bringing her closer against him. She could feel the length of his body, the hardness of his hip and thigh, and the curve of chest and arm where she fitted against him.

'You're shivering even more now,' he said on an odd note.

It was her trembling that he felt, and it was not brought on by the cold but by the unexpected intimacy—an intimacy that she did not want, yet craved. There was no logic in the way she felt, she thought a little desperately.

'I have a sweater in the car.' Her voice was unsteady. 'Wayne, please. . . .'

'Are you so frightened of me?' he queried softly.

Frightened? I'm terrified. Terrified because you're strong and vital and sexy, and because I find myself thinking of you at odd moments. There's a part of me that wishes you would kiss me, and I don't want to feel this way—not with you, Wayne North, not with anyone.

His arm was still around her shoulders, holding her fast, but she managed to turn her head. His face was very near her, and she quivered as she was caught by the shock of an appeal that could only be sexual. Above the long rigid line of the jaw was a mouth that was firm yet sensual. His cheekbones were high, the tanned skin taut across them. His eyebrows were dark and winging, and beneath them the watching eyes were lit with intelligence and amusement. 'He knows,' she thought, 'he knows exactly what he's doing to me.'

'Of course I'm not frightened of you,' she said spiritedly. 'Why on earth should I be?'

'You tell me.' Still that same softness, seductive and challenging.

'There's nothing to tell.' Somehow she mustered a lightness she was far from feeling. 'But I *am* cold, and I *do* have a sweater. Let me go, Wayne.'

She had prepared herself for a struggle and was surprised when his hand dropped from her shoulders. As she walked away from him, she remembered what he'd told her once before. 'I've never had to resort to trickery for my kisses,' he'd said. 'I've always found the women I want more than willing to meet me halfway.' Her back and the top of her arm, where he had held her, felt suddenly bare, and she was conscious of an odd disappointment. 'You're utterly contradictory,' she told herself crossly. 'Get hold of yourself now, quickly, before it's too late.'

Opening the back door of the car, she found her sweater. It was angora, thick and cuddly, in a deep rose that complemented her colouring. She had stopped shivering by the time she rejoined Wayne at the vlei. He was busy with a thermos flask. He looked up a moment, his eyes seeming to study her, but he did not speak. He just handed her a cup and indicated that she should hold it while he poured the coffee.

He had brought a rug from the car and he sat down on it. He did not invite her to join him. It was as if it was of no importance to him whatsoever whether she chose to sit or stand. By his side was a packet of doughnuts, they looked crisp and delicious, and Teslyn was hungry. She stood a few moments, sipping her coffee, wanting to sit and yet dreading an intimacy that scared her.

Wayne looked up suddenly, holding out the packet

to her, and as she took a doughnut he smiled. He thinks I'm being silly, Teslyn thought, and perhaps I am. I'll be sitting beside him in the car for most of the day, why not on the rug? Balancing her coffee, she sat down, and saw his smile broaden. And still he did not say anything.

'The vlei can't be seen from the road,' Teslyn said, breaking the silence. 'You must have known it was here.'

'I did.'

'You've been here before, then?'

'A few times. It's a good place to break the journey. Just the right distance from the city for a breakfast pause.'

With whom had he shared coffee and doughnuts those other times? With a woman who was more amenable to his advances, perhaps? Teslyn pushed the thought from her mind and wondered why it had come to her at all.

The mist was lifting just a little, and two more ducks became visible on the water. Near the shore was a clump of lily pads.

'It must be lovely here when the mist goes,' Teslyn remarked.

'It is. Pity we can't wait here that long. But you'll find lots of water in the Lowveld.'

'You've been there long?'

'Five years.'

Five years of working at Pinevale. It was strange, Teslyn thought, that she found it quite so hard to imagine Wayne North in the role of employee. There was a strength about him, both mental and physical, and a sense of sureness and authority, all of which seemed to indicate a man who was accustomed to giving orders rather than following them.

'You seem to get on well with Jim and Mary,' she observed.

'They're a fine couple.'

Is that enough for you? Working for a fine couple? I'd have thought you'd want a farm of your own, that you'd have innovative ideas and progressive ways.

'Have you ever wanted your own place?' she asked curiously.

Something came and went in the dark eyes. For a moment his lips curved slightly upwards, as if he was about to smile, Teslyn thought, and held her breath. But then he straightened and brushed the crumbs from the rug and got to his feet. 'Time to be on our way,' he said.

As the sun rose higher in the sky, Teslyn watched the scenery with interested eyes. She had never been so far out of the city, had never conceived the vastness of the veld. It was flat, and where there were no crops to relieve it the bush was khaki-coloured, and yet, she thought, this countryside had a haunting fascination.

She took the map from the glove compartment and studied it. So many familiar names, yet places she had never seen. Again she was gripped with a sense of adventure.

'I think you'll like living at Pinevale,' Wayne told her.

She lifted her head from the map. 'I don't think I'll be there long enough for that.'

His eyes were on the road, his profile was strong and sharply etched. She saw his lips tighten, and his profile took on a more arrogant look than before. 'I thought we'd settled this.'

'So we had. I'll help out at the plantation until Jim is better.'

He took his eyes from the road, and she saw that

they were cold with contempt. 'And then you'll be off?'

'Of course. What did you think?'

'I prefer to keep my thoughts about you to myself.' His gaze swung aloofly over her face. As he gave his attention back to the road, Teslyn's heart was beating rapidly.

'I had hoped, though,' Wayne said at length, 'that you might turn out to be a little less selfish than your late husband.'

'How dare you!'

'I dare because I saw what Alec's absence did to his parents. Not just a physical absence, that they could have forgiven. What hurt was his lack of caring, his lack of communication. Not that they would ever admit that they were hurt.'

Teslyn could have added to the list of qualities which Alec had lacked, but it would not have been fair to him to have done so. Nor did she want to, she realised. A year ago, before the accident, she could not have imagined herself defending Alec. She could not have explained to herself why she did so now.

'Alec wasn't the way you describe him,' she said.

'No?'

'No.' She set her lips to prevent a tremble. It was right, in the circumstances, to defend him. Yet to praise him, to fabricate, was more than she could handle. 'I'd prefer not to discuss Alec,' she said.

'I have no wish to discuss him. I *do* want to talk about his widow. Have you no feelings at all, Teslyn?'

She had turned her head back to the window and now she kept her eyes unseeingly on the countryside. 'What are you trying to say?'

'Jim and Mary had one son and they lost him. Can't you be a daughter?'

'Oh no!' The protest came from the heart, as she came swinging round to look at him.

'I fail to see why not.' The rugged profile had never seemed more forbidding.

'I don't want to talk about it.'

'But I do.' The hand that left the steering-wheel to reach for one of hers was unexpected. Teslyn grew taut. 'Why are you overreacting, Teslyn?'

So he had noticed. Not that she should be surprised; this man would always notice what others overlooked. She had known she must be wary of him, perhaps she had not been wary enough.

'I don't think I'm overreacting at all,' she said brightly. 'It's just that . . . well, you do keep on about all this.'

There were a few moments of silence, a silence in which nothing could be heard save the purr of the car and the sound of her heart. Could he hear it? Teslyn wondered wildly.

'A few minutes ago you asked me my thoughts,' he said with surprising gentleness. 'Despite what I'd imagined, my first impression of you was one of sweetness, a kind of innocence that I didn't expect.' He paused. 'Was I wrong?'

It was ridiculous that his words should give her pleasure. They didn't mean anything, couldn't mean anything. He was flattering her, just as Alec had done when she'd first met him. She'd been a fool then, but she was wiser now. Besides, this man's opinion did not mean a thing to her. Surely!

'Evidently you must have been wrong,' she said with all the coolness she could muster. 'I could hardly be innocent, at least not in your terms. I was married three years.'

Not for Wayne North to know that she could easily have been a virgin, so little did she know about the ways in which a man and a woman could love each other.

'Just as well the innocence is a façade,' Wayne drawled.

His tone caught her off guard. 'I don't understand.'

'Don't you?' His hand left hers and travelled to her thigh, and the deliberate sensuousness of the touch knocked the breath from her lungs. 'The fact that you're an experienced woman,' he drawled again, more softly this time, 'makes it easier for us to go to bed together.'

'How dare you!' she gasped, when she could speak.

'Don't try the prim virgin act with me again. You said a moment ago that you were anything but that.'

'Get your hand off me!'

The long hand moved silkily over her—audaciously. Through her trousers she could feel his fingers, each one singlely, just as if she wore nothing at all. She was beginning to shake. Any moment Wayne would perceive her distress, and who knew what his re-action would be. With an effort she pushed his hand away.

'You said that you don't force yourself on to unwilling women,' she threw at him bitterly, as the hand went back to the wheel.

He laughed, a husky sound that was fire to jagged nerves. 'You're not unwilling, sweetheart. Your words and actions say one thing, your body says something else.'

So he *had* noticed her trembling. And had mis-understood the reason.

'You seem to forget that I'm a widow,' she said in a low tone.

Wayne turned, and the eyes that met hers were steady. 'I forget nothing. For a healthy normal young girl—because that's what you are, Teslyn—you've mourned long enough.'

'Wayne. . . .'

'We won't discuss it further. Not now. Besides, we've digressed from our original topic.'

His eyes had gone back to the road, and she was thankful for that. 'What was that?'

'Jim and Mary. They would like you to make Pinevale home.'

'Impossible!'

'Why so vehement? You haven't even seen the place.'

'I don't need to,' Teslyn said passionately. 'You live there, that's all I need know. I couldn't bear to live within miles of you. I'll stay for as long as Jim and Mary need me, then I'll be off.'

Wayne did not pursue the conversation. Nor did he make any effort at small talk. Teslyn spread the map over her lap and watched the miles roll by.

The places came and went. Witbank and Middleburg, coalmining towns both, where the surrounding countryside was blackened with coaldust. And after that farmland set in the vastness of the Highveld. Farmland to the horizon and beyond.

Teslyn glanced at Wayne when the car left the tar once more for the sand of a country road. Were they stopping for another meal? she wondered. But if he was aware of her glance, as he surely must have been, he gave no sign of it.

For a long moment she could not take her eyes away from him. Loose and lithe, he sat in the driver's seat, the arrogantly handsome face looking cool and at ease. In the aftermath of their interchange, Teslyn was still churning with tension. Wayne seemed utterly relaxed, and she could cheerfully have hit him.

The car covered the miles of the sandy road, making it obvious that lunch was not what Wayne had in mind. Teslyn opened her mouth to ask him where they were headed, then closed it again firmly. Wayne knew her questions and her uncertainties; she would not give him the satisfaction of putting them into words.

At a pair of wrought-iron gates he stopped the car. He got out, opened the gates, drove over a cattle grid, stopped the car to close the gates again, and then drove further. A white stone on the road was lettered T. Venter.

Another mile or two and they were at a farmhouse. The car was drawing to a halt beside a group of blue-gum trees when Wayne spoke for the first time. 'I've some business to discuss with the farmer, Tim Venter.'

'Fine,' Teslyn said stiffly. The glimmer of amusement in his eyes had not escaped her. Wayne knew the effort it had cost her to remain silent until he chose to speak. 'I'll wait in the car.'

'You'll get out.'

'Another order?' Her chin rose. 'I don't have to fall in line with everything you want.'

'But you will, Teslyn, because yours are similar.' He spoke softly, the seductiveness of his tone making it clear what he meant.

'Wayne, you are. . . .'

'Arrogant and insolent,' he finished for her, laughing at the flush that coloured her cheeks. 'But we're not having an argument now, little hothead. Hear the dogs? The Venters know we're here. They'll be wondering why we don't come in.'

'I said I'll wait in the car.'

'Tim and Marie are old friends of mine. You'll be friendly to them, please.'

Wayne had opened the door as he spoke. As Teslyn

watched him walk around the car to her side she understood that she had lost him one more round.

'Sheba— Tungu! Heel!' A fair-headed man with a beard shouted to his Alsatians as he rode up on his horse. Obediently the dogs stilled their barking and fell in behind their master.

'Wayne! Good to see you, man.' He had dismounted and was thrusting out his hand.

'Good to see you, Tim. Let me introduce you—this is Teslyn Morrison.'

'Nice to meet you, Miss Morrison.'

'Mrs,' Wayne corrected. 'And I'm sure Teslyn would prefer it if you called her by her first name. Where is Marie?'

'In the kitchen if I know that woman of mine,' Tim said fondly. 'Come inside, Teslyn, Wayne. And don't let the dogs scare you, Teslyn. They know now you're a friend, they won't harm you.'

The farmhouse was a rambling building, white-washed and a little untidy, but with a warm and welcoming air about it. Marie, who came to greet them, one baby on her hip and a toddler clutching at her jeans, was not unlike her home, Teslyn thought, liking her on sight. Straggles of hair escaped from her pony-tail, and her shirt emerged from the waistband of her denims, but her handshake was firm and her smile friendly.

'Lunch first, and then you men can go out and look at the machinery,' she suggested. 'Okay, Tim?'

'Okay with me, honey.'

'Let me help you,' Teslyn offered.

'Lunch is about ready,' said Marie, leading the way to the kitchen. 'It's been one of those days, the baby teething and Boetie here feeling his thunder's been stolen. I never did get round to laying the table.

Would you like to do it for me, Teslyn?'

'Of course. Just tell me where to find things.'

It took only a few minutes to lay the table. Marie was at the oven when Teslyn came back into the kitchen. 'What else can I do?' she asked.

'Nothing right now, thanks. Why don't you sit down and talk to me?'

Looking around the room, Teslyn thought how different it was from her own tiny kitchen. It was very big, and splashed with sun. Disorder was everywhere, from the baby-bottles on the sink to the apples that had spilled from the vegetable stand on to the floor. But like everything else she had seen here, the kitchen had a warm family feeling.

'Were you expecting us, Marie?' she asked.

'Of course. Didn't Wayne tell you?'

'I don't think he did.'

'Well, isn't that something!' Marie turned from the stove, a comical smile lighting her face. 'He must have forgotten. Aren't men funny old dears?'

A funny old dear was not how she would describe Wayne North, Teslyn thought grimly. Arrogant and insolent, he'd called himself just minutes ago, and the description fitted. Wayne was easily the most arrogant man she had ever met.

'I was so sorry to hear about your husband,' Marie said.

'Yes. Thank you.'

'How awfully sad for you. I think I would go out of my mind if something happened to Tim. Except that I'd have to be strong for the children.'

'How old are they?' Teslyn asked, taking the chance to change the subject. Marie's sympathy made her feel awkward, out of her depth. Her feelings concerning Alec's death were complex enough without having to pretend to a sorrow she did not feel.

'Boetie is two, and Mikey's nine months. And there's another one on the way—bad timing, I'm afraid.' She grimaced, but it was clear by her expression that the prospect of another baby so soon did not daunt her unduly. 'Are you glad to be going to your husband's old home?'

So the ploy had not worked. 'It will be a new experience,' Teslyn answered truthfully.

'And Wayne will be there. I don't know if it's too soon, but I think he fancies you.'

'What!'

'I saw the way he looked at you. Just after you came in,' Marie said mischievously. 'There was a special look in his eyes.'

There could well have been a special look, Teslyn did not dispute the fact. But it would have been one of warning. One that said 'Behave, or expect trouble.'

'You're wrong,' she said firmly.

'Perhaps not. Mind you, it's usually the women who've gone for Wayne in the past. I can think of a few who'd have gone to the ends of the earth for him. Sex-appeal is one thing Wayne North doesn't lack, but he's a fine man with it. Oh hey, the peas nearly burned! Like to take the stew in for me, Teslyn?'

'Of course,' Teslyn was glad of the diversion.

Lunch was tasty. The lamb stew had a delicate flavouring that went well with peas and a green salad. The bread was crusty and freshly baked, and so delicious that it was eaten in no time. Teslyn wondered how Marie managed to fit in breadmaking with all her other chores.

Teslyn discovered that she was much hungrier than she had realised. Soon, like the others, her plate had a second helping. While Wayne and Tim and Marie did not exclude her from their talk—they did in fact attempt to draw her in—their conversation nonetheless slid into the easy banter of old and good friends. Teslyn was content to be quiet. There was an air of calm in this house that was a welcome relief after the tension-filled hours in the car.

Now and then she looked up to find Wayne's eyes on her. Each time she looked away. It was enough that she must endure his company for several more hours, she did not have to suffer it now. Marie's words came back to her, but it was clear that they were no more than the imaginings of a happy wife who liked people to be matched in pairs. There was nothing in the least bit special, or even affectionate, in Wayne's gaze.

There was pumpkin pie for dessert, and Marie uttered a little cry as she uncovered the dish. 'Golly,' she wailed, 'just look at this pie! It's gone and fallen in on me!'

It was true that the pie did not look as it should. Something had gone wrong with the baking, Teslyn thought, or perhaps in her haste Marie had left out an ingredient, because the surface was marked and uneven. Tim bent forward to look at it, and Teslyn, knowing how Alec would have behaved in similar circumstances, held her breath as she waited for his reaction.

'Golly,' he mimicked laughingly. 'It's fine.'

'How can you say that, Tim? Just see what it looks like. What will Teslyn and Wayne think?'

'They'll think my wife is an excellent cook.' The ruddy face was wreathed in a goodnatured smile as Tim leaned sideways to give his wife a hug. 'Looks are are nothing, *liefie*. It's taste that counts. I tell you our guests will want seconds.'

They did. The pie was as delicious as Tim had

promised, and Marie was indeed a good cook, the pie's surface notwithstanding. But it was not Marie's expertise in the kitchen that was on Teslyn's mind. She marvelled instead at the goodwill she had witnessed between Tim and Marie.

There was an evening that was all too vivid in her mind. Alec had invited a few friends for dinner, and Teslyn, knowing that he liked to impress his acquaintances, had used most of her meagre housekeeping money to buy a roast. The meal was cooked, the table ready, but Alec and his friends did not arrive. They arrived three hours late, having spent the evening in a pub. By that time the roast, which had been tender and juicy, was dry.

There had been hell to pay that night, with Alec ridiculing Teslyn in front of his friends, calling her names and eliciting sympathy for himself—'My wife is a slob. Does nothing all day, and can't even have a decent supper ready for me when I get home!' Later, when the men had gone, he had thrown her on to the bed. She had managed to prevent him from raping her, but the black eye produced by a wild and vengeful fist had kept her from going to work for two days.

Perhaps because the event had been so horrendous the memory of it was so vivid. But there were other memories too. Alec had let no chance escape to slight or humiliate her.

It was a revelation therefore to see tolerance between a husband and wife. Tolerance and humour and understanding. And love. Without meaning to, Teslyn looked at Wayne. He was watching her. He could have no inkling of her thoughts, but perhaps he had seen the expressions that had flitted unguarded across her face as she had relived the horror. Quickly she looked away again.

Lunch finished, the two men went off together; they were going to look at some machinery, Tim said. Teslyn helped Marie to clear the dishes and tidy the kitchen. Marie chattered animatedly as they worked. Her children, her husband, her home, these were the topics evidently dearest to her heart. The ruined pie seemed forgotten as she talked.

They had just finished washing up when a thin cry sounded from the back of the house. 'Mikey,' said Marie, 'I hoped he was sleeping. Excuse me one moment.'

The kitchen had a sunny bay window, and Teslyn went to it and looked out. She was still at the window when Marie rejoined her. Mikey was inconsolable, Marie said, the erupting tooth hurting so much that he was unable to sleep. She was sorry, but she would have to sit with him till he calmed. Would Teslyn like to sit on the stoop and look at some magazines?

'Of coursé you must go to the baby,' Teslyn smiled. 'But what I'd really like is to stroll across the fields.'

'By all means. I'll tell Wayne where to look for you when he comes.'

'What about the dogs?'

'No problem. They're with Tim. I'll just send word that he should keep them with him.'

A breeze was blowing as Teslyn walked down the broad stone steps of the stoep and headed for the western fields. She found a path and took it. Around her the maize was thick and green and high. Strange, she thought, all her life she had eaten maize in its different forms—hot buttered mielies, or the hard porridge called mielie-pap, or the sweetcorn that came in tins. Maize was the staple food of Africa, yet this was the first time she had walked through farmlands and had seen it growing.

She stopped and reached out for a cob. It was a day
for first experiences, she mused as her fingers ran over
the ribbed surfaces of the leaves that coiled tightly
around the cob. There had been the breakfast by the
vlei, and just minutes ago there had been the scene at
the lunch-table.

Walking further, she knew that the mood that had
come over her then was with her still. There was sadness in her, and pensiveness, and underlying it all there
was a great nameless longing.

The breeze grew stronger. It caught at the maize,
sending the cobs moving in long swaying ripples, and
it clutched at Teslyn's hair, pulling it away from her
face. She tilted her head back, enjoying the feel of the
sun on her cheeks while the wind played in her hair.

Continuing along the path she found herself at length
at the top of a small rise, and here she stopped and
looked down. Peacefulness—that was the word that
came to her mind. A great and lovely peacefulness.
The sky was blue and cloudless, and where it met the
land the horizon was a smooth curved line. The fields
dipped away from the rise, stretching toward the horizon in waves of rippling green. In the distance stood a
clump of blue-gums, and near them the blades of a
windmill circled.

To the girl who had lived all her life in cities, it
seemed remarkably still—a stillness that was broken
only by the sound of the wind as it brushed through
the maize, and the chirping of invisible insects.

The feeling of longing grew stronger. Why, Teslyn
wondered, had the scene at the farmhouse table impressed her so greatly? Was it because for a few
moments she had glimpsed a love that was unaffected
by the unimportant trivia of life? The kind of love she
had never known existed. Did the sadness come from

knowing that this was a love she had never known, and would never experience?

Her eyes blurred as she stood on the path and looked down over the countryside, and her throat grew tight with sudden tears. This was ridiculous, she told herself fiercely. She was crying, and she could not have put the exact reason into words. She did know that Wayne had a part in her feelings. Alec too. And she knew that until today she had not known quite how much her marriage had lacked.

'Teslyn.' Someone said her name from behind her, softly.

She stiffened, unable to turn, for he would see her tears, and she did not want that. She could not even lift a hand to her face to dash the tears away, for he would see the action and know what it meant.

'Teslyn,' Wayne said again. And then he was turning her to him, and she was powerless to resist.

CHAPTER FOUR

'You went a long way.'

'Did I?' She kept her eyes down.

'Marie said you'd walked in this direction. I came looking for you, but when I didn't see you I nearly turned back. I was beginning to get. . . .' Wayne stopped. On a new tone, he said, 'Teslyn, look at me.'

She kept her head bent, her eyes concealed. 'I must have walked farther than I realised.'

'I said look at me.'

His hands went to her chin, tilting it. She heard him draw breath, and then both hands were cupping her face. 'You've been crying.' His tone was rough.

There was no looking away from him now, and for some reason she did not even try to. Her eyes were upturned to his, and they were big and blue and luminous, and on the long dark eyelashes were a few tears. In her face was the sadness that had been suppressed in her for so long. There was also the longing—a wild and poignant longing—that had been with her since lunch.

'Teslyn, what's wrong?'

The huskiness in his voice made her throat even tighter. If she talked now she knew she would cry, so she only shook her head.

His hands were still on her face, the fingers buried in the hair that feathered backwards above her ears. He held her just far enough away from him so that he could look at her. His own face was taut, the features rugged and hard, yet the eyes holding a strange tenderness. She looked back at him as if it was suddenly very important that she memorise each one of his features.

'Did something happen to upset you?'

Again she shook her head. Even if she could trust herself to talk, she could not tell Wayne anything of her thoughts. Especially not Wayne, she realised.

'Then what is it?' He had taken a step closer, bringing his body within touching distance of hers. At his nearness she felt every nerve ending tingle with a sudden and quite unexpected sensation. A need. She wanted him. She wanted him to hold her. She wanted to be very close to him, as close as possible.

But she couldn't feel this way! Couldn't let herself. Alec. . . . And what she had done that night. . . . Oh God, don't let me want Wayne.

'Wayne, don't!' She had started to tremble. They were so close now that he must feel the movement, and she wondered if he also felt the hard separate beats of her heart.

'You're trembling,' he whispered, ignoring her plea. 'Why?'

He did not wait for her answer as his head descended and he found her mouth with his lips. The kiss began slowly, tenderly, a very different kiss from the one she had experienced once before. But in seconds, as if the need of her body had communicated itself to him, inflaming him in turn, the pressure of his lips hardened.

Escape—I have to escape. The words thundered through Teslyn's head, and she tried to push away from Wayne. But his strength was greater than hers and as his passion increased, the thundering of her heart drowned out the sound in her head. There was only the joy of meeting arms and lips and teeth, of his hands in her hair, and of the closeness of a body that was hard and lithe. There was a sweetness that was bone-melting in its intensity, and that called forth a need for even greater intimacy.

One hand went to her blouse, and though she felt him open her buttons she did not protest. He found a breast and cradled it in his fingers, the sensuousness of his movements sending a wave of delight through her system. She was no longer thinking rationally as she pressed herself against him, arching her body toward his. When he released her suddenly her legs were so weak that for a moment she swayed, but he put out an arm to hold her. She stared up at him, eyes dazed. What had happened? Why had he put her from him? Why now?

'The dogs.' His voice came to her as if from a distance. 'Do you hear them, Teslyn? Tim's coming to look for us.'

She swallowed hard as her eyes came back into focus. Wayne was bending over her, telling her why he hadn't gone on making love to her. The terrible thing was that the halt had been called by Wayne, not by herself. She stared up at him, and now her eyes were filled with horror. Later, when she was alone with her thoughts of Alec and her guilt, she would try to remember that there was a moment when she had tried to escape from Wayne. But now, with the rugged face so near to hers, and the wind blowing her tousled hair, she knew only how close she had come to surrendering to something to which she had no right.

She could hear the dogs now. She could even hear Tim's voice calling to his animals, and she wondered if providence had sent them down the path at just this moment.

'Tim's calling you,' she said.

'Are you all right?' There was a look in his eyes that she had never seen before. For a moment she felt a new weakness. Then she straightened her shoulders. She could *not* go on like this.

'Of course I'm all right.' And as he continued to look at her, she managed a brightness she was far from feeling. 'My goodness, you don't imagine it's the first time I've been kissed!'

His lips tightened, and his face took on a sudden hardness. 'Far from it. And not only by your husband, I think.'

She curled her nails into her palms. 'Why don't you go on and meet Tim halfway? He must be wondering what we're up to.'

'And drawing the right conclusions, I've no doubt.' Sensuous lips lifted at the corners as Wayne gave a mocking smile.

'You're a bastard, Wayne North!' Teslyn snapped.

'There's a reply to that one, did you know?' He laughed shortly as he saw her hand rising in the direction of his face. 'No need for that, hothead. I'll walk ahead. When you've done up your buttons you can follow at your own pace.'

'I wouldn't follow at all if I had my way,' she muttered on a half-sob as she watched him walk away, and she wondered what Wayne would say if she were to tell Marie and Tim what had happened and ask them for a ride to the station so that she could go back to the city. It was the one thing she would not do, though, for Alec's parents were expecting her, and she owed it to them to go to Pinevale.

Wayne did not look back as he walked. A tall figure, he strode along the path with a step of easy unconcern. When he had vanished around a bend, Teslyn put her hands to her hair. It was even untidier than she had realised. The wind could be blamed for that, she knew, but what could be the explanation for her hot cheeks and her bruised lips? With trembling fingers she did up her buttons. 'Damn you, Wayne North,' she swore softly. 'I didn't want this to happen, not with you, not with anyone.' On a stronger note, she said, 'It won't happen again.'

She began to walk. The wind had grown even stronger, stirring up sand on the path and tugging at her hair with real ferocity, but she did not mind. The mood of longing and sadness had given way to anger, anger at Wayne, but even more at herself, and the wind seemed to fit in with her new mood. The path took a few bends, then straightened. Some way ahead she could see Wayne and Tim, and running in front of them the Alsatians, Sheba and Tungu. As if they sensed her presence, the dogs halted and turned, ears and tails alert. Sheba barked, then stopped at a command from Tim.

These were farm dogs, and they could be dangerous Teslyn knew. But she was not frightened. Tim had his animals under control and would let nothing happen to her. If there was danger it came from Wayne, from the turmoil he aroused in her, from the havoc he had wrought to the little peace of mind she had managed to regain in recent months.

'I shall be very careful of you, Wayne North,' she vowed silently. 'We will complete our journey together. But tonight I shall be at Pinevale, and I shall make it clear to Jim and Mary that I want nothing to do with you while I'm there.'

Marie and Tim saw them off. If they wondered at Teslyn's flushed and dishevelled appearance, they kept their thoughts to themselves.

'Don't be a stranger,' Tim was saying to Wayne. 'Don't take so long to come back for another visit.'

'And bring Teslyn with you.' This from Marie. 'It was good to meet you, Teslyn. *Tot siens.*'

'It's been lovely. Thank you so much.' Teslyn forced

herself to smile back. '*Tot siens.*'

The smile vanished from her face as the car left the farmhouse and took the road back to the gate. *Tot siens*—till we meet again. But there would be no further meeting. For such an event could only come about if she travelled this way again with Wayne. There were few certainties in her world at present, but she did know that today's journey with Wayne North would be the last.

'Tell me about Alec.'

Wayne's words were the first to be uttered between them since they had left the Venters' farm more than half an hour ago. Teslyn turned her eyes from the window. 'I can't believe you're asking me about my marriage.'

The eyes that met hers for a moment were mocking. 'Are you always so prickly? I asked about Alec.'

She shrugged. 'What's there to tell? You knew him.'

'We never met.'

Teslyn sat up and stared at him. 'I don't understand.'

'It's quite simple. By the time I came to the Lowveld Alec had already left home.'

'You talked as if you knew him,' she said accusingly. 'A while back you said. . . .'

'That I know what his attitude did to his parents,' Wayne finished for her. 'I did in fact watch the disappointment of two kind people.'

'Then you never knew each other?' Teslyn asked with a sudden lifting of the heart, and wondered why she should feel quite so glad that Wayne had had no first-hand acquaintance with the man she had married. At least she need not endure his pity.

'Tell me about him.'

'Oh, Alec was wonderful.' Teslyn raised her head, and her voice was animated as she was borne along on a streak of pure recklessness. 'He was fun—tremendous fun. We laughed together so often.' And that was true, up to a point, for in their early days, when Alec was wooing her, they had indeed laughed. 'He was tall and fair and very good-looking,' she went on.

'A good lover?' Wayne interposed drily.

The breath caught in Teslyn's throat. Why am I doing this? she wondered wildly. She gave a little laugh. 'The best—very passionate, very exciting.'

'So much so that he spoiled you for any other man?'

'. . . . Yes.'

Wayne took so long to speak again that she wondered if he meant to speak at all. His gaze was directed forward, his concentration on the road ahead. Teslyn thought she detected a kind of grimness in the firm set of the jaw, and then credited the idea to her imagination.

'I'll have to rid you of that notion,' he said at length, his tone outrageous.

Teslyn's heart did a double-beat. It was a few moments before she could trust herself to speak. 'You won't ever lay a finger on me again!' she threw at him.

'Ever is a long time.' He laughed, the low husky laugh that was becoming too familiar. 'Don't you know yet, Teslyn, that you must be very sure before you commit yourself so far?'

Was there nothing that embarrassed him? No words that could discomfit him? 'If anything, ever is too short as far as I'm concerned,' she said bitterly, and without waiting for a reply to that one she turned again very firmly to the window. She would not look at Wayne again, she vowed, would not rise to his bait. At the most Pinevale could be only a couple of hours away. Until they reached their destination any conversation would be one-sided.

In the event it was Teslyn herself who eventually

broke the silence. They had gone through Belfast, the next place was Machadadorp; that tiny town, Teslyn saw, was a kind of milestone, the place where the Highveld began to give way to the Lowveld. Once out of the town the road started to climb, and as they emerged from a hilly pass, Teslyn found that the scenery was changing. Soon there was a vivid greenness that was very different from the khaki-coloured Highveld bush, and the flatness had gone. This was the beginning of the Lowveld, then, she thought in growing wonder, that rolling land of misty mountains and lovely colours. Almost since leaving the Venters she had looked out of the car window because it was safer to keep her eyes in that direction rather than look at Wayne. Now, as she gazed at the swiftly passing countryside, she was enchanted with a loveliness she had not seen before.

It came to her only gradually that they were on the wrong road. Somewhere Wayne had left the main highway, and the *dorpie*, the hamlet they had just passed through, should not be on their route. Reaching for the map, she spread it quickly across her lap. For a few moments she stared at it disbelievingly, then she jerked her gaze to Wayne.

'We're going the wrong way!'

'We go where the car takes us.'

'Don't be flippant with me. You know this isn't the direct road to Pinevale.'

'It isn't,' he agreed.

'I want to go to Pinevale.'

'So you shall.'

'Direct,' she said imperiously.

An eyebrow lifted. 'I can remember a time when you were not so eager.'

'Don't play games with me, Wayne. Don't you

understand that I don't want to spend even a few extra hours in your company?'

'Then you'll have to resign yourself,' he said in a tone of amused insolence, 'to the fact that you will be spending at least one more day with me.'

She was quite still while the words registered their meaning on her shocked brain.

'You can't mean,' she managed at last, in a choked tone, 'that we won't get to the farm today?'

'I do.'

'No!' Her eyes blazed at him. 'I demand that you turn the car!'

'You're in no position to make demands, Mrs Morrison.'

'Jim and Mary will be furious.'

'They're very glad that I'm bringing you.'

'With an overnight stop?'

'I don't think it occurs to either of them,' he said, and now the insolence was even more intense, 'that their daughter-in-law might be in any kind of danger.'

But I am in danger—awful danger. From you, Wayne, and from myself too. And I don't know how to protect myself. Perhaps because in some far cave of my mind I don't want to be protected.

'Of course I'm in no danger,' she said icily. 'If you tried to touch me I'd put up a fair fight.' He had turned his head to look at her, and her chin rose proudly as her eyes challenged his. 'Besides, we both know how you feel about reluctant females.'

His lips curved. 'Did Alec ever tell you that you're very sexy when you're angry?'

Keeping her face carefully expressionless, Teslyn ignored the bait. 'Why did you lie to me?'

'I didn't lie, Teslyn. You may recall that we never discussed the length of the trip.'

'You said nothing about a detour.'

'No.'

'You misled me deliberately!'

His eyes glinted. 'Perhaps I did.'

'Didn't you think you owed me the truth?' She looked at him with a kind of helpless anger.

'Would you have come with me if I'd told you?'

'Of course not.'

Brown eyes narrowed dangerously. 'There you have your answer. I thought, Teslyn, that it might be a good idea for us to get to know each other a little better. That this trip would be a good way of doing that.'

'You were wrong,' she said tautly.

'Perhaps,' he agreed. He had slowed the car almost to a standstill on the quiet country road, and his gaze moved over her, lingering first on her eyes and then on her mouth, before descending, quite deliberately, to her throat and then to the rounded breasts beneath the cotton shirt.

'Perhaps I was wrong,' he said, 'in thinking that you were a woman, when in fact you're just a girl.'

Alec had said worse things, had hurled insults and epithets at her for no reason, and yet the insults had hurt her no more than Wayne's last words did. 'Why?' Teslyn wondered. 'Why does Wayne have the power to affect me so deeply?'

'That's not fair.' She spoke with a control she was far from feeling. 'It's not unreasonable for a woman to wish to choose her company.'

'It *is* unreasonable, to overreact.' Wayne's eyes went back to the road. 'You've been overreacting from the moment we met.'

It was true, she supposed. The same circumstances but another man, and her behaviour might well be quite different. The fact that the trip involved an overnight stop was not much in itself. She was a girl who had been married. Even more, she was a creature of the late twentieth century, in which overreacting was as much out of fashion as the thought of swooning at a man's touch. Besides, they would have separate rooms. And once more she wondered at Wayne's ability to affect her so intensely.

Soon they stopped—another farm, more gates and cattle-grids, a spread of fields, tobacco this time, with the plants dark and green and lush-looking. Another farming family, by the names of Adams this time, husband and wife and three teenage sons. And, after the business of the men had been concluded, another offer of a meal, which Wayne declined. It was getting late, it was time to go. Throughout Teslyn was wrapped in a kind of frozen detachment.

It might have been interesting to walk around, she realised belatedly when they were back in the car; it would have been fun to see the different barns and kilns and to learn a little about tobacco farming. But tobacco had been far from her thoughts. She could think only of a village somewhere ahead of them, of a hotel where she and Wayne would presumably spend the night under one roof.

'You really are frightened,' Wayne said once, with amusement, and the accuracy of the statement was uncanny.

'Don't flatter yourself,' Teslyn snapped, keeping her eyes on fields where shadows were beginning to form.

The dorp was small—a hamlet comprising a post-office and a station; a concession store that stocked consumer goods ranging from food to fishing-rods; the inevitable corner tea-room, where one could buy sweets and ice-cream and a sprinkling of fruit but almost never a cup of tea. And a hotel—the Highveld

Hotel, the only hotel in the place.

Installed in her single room, Teslyn looked around her. A striped green and yellow bedspread covered the bed, a thin carpet was on the floor. On the walls were two animal prints, the one a giraffe and the other a lion. All of it neat and clean but depressingly uninspiring, making Teslyn wonder what she could do to pass the time until dinner.

She was about to leave the room, perhaps in the little lounge she had seen on her way up there would be some magazines, when there was a knock at the door.

Wayne must have showered and changed since their arrival, for he looked fresh and attractive in dark brown pants, casual yet elegantly cut, and a polo-necked sweater which matched his eyes. Teslyn found herself noting the breadth of the shoulders and the sensuality in the hard mouth and jawline. It took her a few moments to realise what she was doing; when she did, she tore her eyes from him.

Heavens! Only half an hour since she had resolved not to let herself be aware of the man, not to be affected by him in any way at all, and already she was slipping.

'Well?' she said waspishly, and wondered if he knew that her anger was directed at herself.

'I'm going for a walk,' he offered mildly. 'Want to join me?'

'Thanks, but no.'

His eyes flicked over her. 'Suit yourself,' he said, and walked down the passage.

Teslyn closed the door with a bang, then sat down on the bed and looked around her. The idea of finding a magazine had lost its appeal, but there must be *something* she could do. Silly to feel that the walls were closing in on her and that the room seemed even bleaker than before. Nobody, not even a man as vital as Wayne

North, could have such an effect on the atmosphere.

She went to the window and looked out. Below her was the one tarred road, with a few houses on either side. Beyond them, encompassing them almost, stretched the dark green of the farmlands. The room was filled with the heat of the day, yet Teslyn had the feeling that outside the air would be crisp with the approach of night.

A figure came suddenly into view. Tall and uncompromisingly male, he walked along the street, past the houses and toward the fields. Teslyn watched him for a moment, and then she grabbed a sweater from her suitcase and was running down the empty corridor.

'I decided I'd like to walk after all,' she said, a little breathlessly, when she caught up with him.

To his credit he did not mock her for having changed her mind. All he said was, 'I'm glad,' and the warmth in the brown-eyed smile revealed that he meant it. Teslyn felt a leap of quite unjustified happiness.

The air was as crisp as she had anticipated, and filled with a smell that she would for the rest of her life associate with the Lowveld, an indefinable blend of mist and fertile soil and growing things.

In front of them the fields stretched seemingly unbroken, an endless mass of tobacco plants, thick and impenetrable, so that she wondered where there was space to walk. But there was a path, she soon saw, and Wayne found it with sureness.

'You've been here too,' she said, a little wonderingly.

'Many times.' And again his eyes lingered on her face.

They walked on in silence, but unlike the tension-filled hours in the car, this silence was companionable. The leaves of the tobacco plants brushed against Teslyn's legs as she walked, and the sand of the path was thick and a little gravelly underfoot.

The sky was lit with the first colours of the sunset, awash with vermilion and gold. 'Look,' said Wayne, pointing, and Teslyn saw a wheeling bird, its wing-span enormous.

'What is it?' she asked.

'An eagle.'

'A bird of prey?'

'Yes,' said Wayne. 'Farther north-east, in the game parks, there are vultures. Those are the real scavengers. But the eagles take their share of baby animals.'

Teslyn glanced up at him. His face was in profile, as it had been in the car. But now, though she could not see his eyes, his expression seemed to be one of sombreness. He cares, she thought in amazement, he cares about small animals and what happens to them. Maybe he's sensitive in other ways too. It was a new slant on a man she disliked so vehemently, and she did not know why it disturbed her quite so much.

The path twisted, then straightened. Teslyn looked back once in the direction of the dorp, and could not see it. A new smell was in the air, and she wrinkled her nose, unable to place it.

'Woodsmoke,' Wayne told her, and for once Teslyn did not wonder that he knew her thoughts. She was getting used to that.

A little farther, and they were in a clearing, and then she could see the smoke as well as smell it. They had reached a *kraal*, the traditional dwelling of the tribes-people. There were three structures in all, round and clay-walled, with roofs made of thatched straw. The *kraal* was shaped in a circle, and in the centre a fire burned. The women were cooking the evening meal, and the smoke rose thinly in the slight breeze.

The voices of the women were clear on the silent air,

low and sweet and animated. They fell silent as Teslyn
and Wayne came into view, but around them children
continued to play and a few chickens squawked. And
now Teslyn detected another smell too, that of mealie-
pap, the porridge that was made from maize. They
would eat it, she saw, with the long strips of meat that
were being cooked a little way away. The women looked
shy, and not wishing to intrude, Teslyn followed Wayne
farther.

As suddenly as they had come upon the *kraal*, they
came to the river. In a country where water was sparse,
the sight was enchanting. With a little cry of delight
Teslyn bent to paddle her fingers.

'It's gorgeous!' For a while she had forgotten that
Wayne was an adversary, and when she looked up at
him from her squatting position she was laughing.

He had been watching her, she realised. The eyes
that met hers had a look in them that she had seen once
before, and suddenly her heart beat faster. 'Wayne?'
she whispered.

'Come, Teslyn,' he said with a softness that fitted
with her own mood. 'Let's walk before it gets dark.'

Willingly she went with him. As she watched him
lead the way over smooth rounded rocks, she was aware
of a tremulousness deep inside her. Bemused by a feeling that was strange to her, she followed where Wayne
led. She felt as if she could follow him always. Alone in
the bleak reality of the hotel room, she would wonder
how she could have let her emotions get the better of
her once again—there was Alec to consider, how could
she for one moment forget?—yet now, with the farmlands hushed and silent, and the smell of the woodsmoke in the air, and the sight of the tall figure in front
of her she was wrapped in a spell from which there was
no escape. There was not even the wish to escape.

CHAPTER FIVE

THE river made a bend. Ahead of her Wayne stopped, and as she drew alongside Teslyn saw why. A boy was fishing from the rocky bank—a child, not more than eight or nine years, and a member of the *kraal*, Teslyn guessed.

He seemed to have something at the end of his rod, for the line was pulled taut, and his face was a study of concentration. Teslyn moved slightly forward so that she could see better, and as she did so a rock slid beneath her feet. She could not suppress the involuntary 'oops!' and at the sound the boy turned.

Just a moment of lost concentration, but it was his undoing. The rod jerked from his hand and skittered on to the rocks, the line pulling it forward. Teslyn clapped a hand to her mouth, understanding that she had cost the boy his fish, but not knowing what to do about it.

Wayne thought and acted faster than she did. In an instant he made for the child's side. The little boy had picked up the end of the rod and was trying to lift it, to draw it to him. But the line was taut and the rod was heavy, and the feat seemed beyond him. The bones of his face seemed to burst through the skin with his effort, and his throat was a corded mass of straining muscles.

'Careful,' Wayne was saying, 'careful.'

His hands were on the child's hands, extending easily beyond them. For a few minutes they struggled, the two males, one long and powerful, the other small and somehow vulnerable, both equally determined. Tensely Teslyn watched them, gripped with the drama of the moment.

And then the rod was free, and moments later the fish was hauled out of the water. The little boy let out a yell of delight and Teslyn, as relieved and excited as he was, cried 'Bravo!'

Wayne turned. She had known he was tall, but now, from a rock that was higher than the point where she stood, he towered above her. The setting sun had caught his head, gilding it with a sheen of gold. He looked like some pagan giant of old, she thought, the breath of excitement stopping in her throat. No man had the right to be quite so handsome.

'That was fantastic,' she told him.

'Thanks for the acclaim. He laughed, that husky laugh that could melt her bones with no effort. 'But it was our little friend here who caught the fish in the first place.'

'You saved it for him. I'd have felt awful if he'd lost it.'

'But he didn't. Quite a whopper it is too, his family will enjoy their supper.'

They watched a few moments while the child, oblivious of the two adults, busied himself with his fish. Then Wayne motioned that they should start walking back.

Clearly the incident would not be on his mind for long, Teslyn thought, but it would take her longer to forget it. At the start of their acquaintance she had thought of Wayne only as arrogant. Exciting and physically attractive, to be sure, these were qualities she was no longer able to deny to herself. But arrogant and selfish and determined to get his own way at all times.

Today she had seen a new side of him. He had seemed to care about the small animals that might be hunted by an eagle, and he had been concerned enough about a small boy and his disappointment to put himself out for him. Whatever else Wayne North might be, he was also warm and human. The knowledge gave Teslyn a strange feeling somewhere in the pit of her stomach.

Absorbed in her thoughts, she did not notice the loose rocky ground. Sliding, she let out another 'oops!'

Wayne wheeled and saw her sitting wide-eyed on the rock. 'This seems to be an afternoon for oopsing,' he laughed, as he looked down at her. 'Are you all right?'

'Perfect,' she grinned back ruefully. 'Perhaps we'd better get back before I do the third silly thing.'

He bent and held out his hand, and after a moment she took it. She let him help her up, though she knew she could have got up perfectly well by herself. In one movement he had drawn her upright. He did not release her then, but held her against him. She stood quite still, rigid with excitement as she felt the long virile length of him against her. Was he going to kiss her? Bemused, she noticed the little fisherman. At that moment he only made an impression on her as any incidental would have done, an extraneous detail to a scene later remembered.

There was a tautness in Wayne's body. Though his arms were not around her, and she was held to him only by one hand, she could feel the tautness. Involuntarily she let herself lean against him.

And then, gently, he was putting her a little way from him. The child had come almost alongside, and Wayne was calling out a greeting. Of course, Teslyn realised, Wayne would not have wanted the little boy to witness a love-scene of any sort. And now, moments later, with her sanity returning, she did not want it either.

Wayne's hand still held hers. He did not release it as she began to walk, but fell in step beside her instead. She would take her hand away, she decided. It was what she must do. Alec. . . . But a force stronger than memory gripped her, and she kept her hand in Wayne's.

There seemed to be a kind of magic in the walk back to the hotel. Teslyn could not have put into words what it was, but in her heart, in the seat of her emotions, she sensed the components. It was a magic that was contained in the touch of the warm hand with its long fingers, in the brush of an arm and a leg against hers as they walked, in the feeling of sensuousness that emanated from the tall figure so close to her. It was a magic that was also contained in the hush of an African dusk, the aroma of the cooking-fires and the promise of mist.

It was a magic that did not bear careful analysis. Nor did Teslyn wish to analyse. She knew only that she had never in her life felt more feminine, or as close to the primeval elements that exist in all humans. She had never been happier.

She was sorry when they reached the hotel. Out of doors in the mystic time between day and night she had allowed herself to forget Alec and what she thought of as 'that night' for a while. The drabness of the hotel bounced her back to reality once more. Walking through the swinging wooden doors, she took her hand away from Wayne.

'Mr North!' called the receptionist as they came near. There was to be dancing that evening, she told them. A dance-band was passing through; it was spending a few nights at various places in this part of the Lowveld. It could be quite an event in the *dorp* where people used records if they wanted to dance. From all around the district farmers would be coming in for the evening.

The receptionist's name was Sally, and Teslyn had noticed earlier that she was very pretty. Her cheeks were pink and excited and her eyes sparkled as she talked. She addressed herself mainly to Wayne. And no wonder, Teslyn thought, for he was a man who would excite women wherever he went. It had not taken Marie Venter's words for her to know that. Why even Teslyn herself. . . . No! She pushed the thought from her mind, and glanced instead at Wayne to see how he took Sally's merry flirtatiousness. He was smiling back at her, teeth white and wicked against his tan. Obviously he was not immune to her prettiness, 'and that doesn't matter to me,' Teslyn told herself firmly, wishing a moment later that she wasn't quite so pleased when Wayne took her arm and they walked on.

She was very aware of him as they walked together along the narrow corridor. The strength and vitality and sheer animal virility that emanated from him seemed to reach out and touch her even here, in this musty place.

She was glad when they came to the door of her room—his own room was farther on—for she needed time to be alone, to make sense of sensations and emotions that threatened to overwhelm her. Taking the key from the pocket of her jeans, she said, 'I'll see you at dinner, I suppose.'

'Right.' His voice was low and husky in the dimness.

'Yes, well, then,' she said meaninglessly, and a little unsteadily.

She was putting her key in the lock when he took her shoulders and turned her to him. A gentle hand was all it took, for her weak limbs obeyed him willingly.

'Wayne?' It was a whisper.

'Happy you came?'

'Came?' she repeated stupidly.

'With me—this trip. When you could have done the journey in a few hours by train. Well, Teslyn, *are* you happy?'

Happy? I don't know about that. I only know that I've never in all my life felt quite so alive and exhilarated, so aware of being a woman. If that's what happiness is all about, then yes, yes! I'm happy.

'Yes,' she said.

'I'm glad. I thought this trip would be a good idea.' His voice was even huskier now, sending little ripples of excitement shruddering through her. 'I hoped that we'd have a chance to get to know each other.'

His head was bending towards her, she could just see his lips and the glint of white teeth between them, when his words hit that part of her mind that was still rational.

He'd been trying to achieve something. What? Why? She would think about it later. She did know that the behaviour which had almost swept her off her feet— until just a minute ago she had been craving his kisses— had been calculated. Abruptly she jerked away from him.

'Teslyn?' He actually sounded surprised.

'Leave me. Just leave me, Wayne,' she muttered between her teeth.

'Why the sudden change?'

'You don't know me at all,' she said with satisfaction.

'So it would seem. And perhaps you don't know me either. Enjoy the solitude of your room, Teslyn.' Without another word he walked away.

The gong sounded for supper. Would Wayne stop at her room on the way to the dining-room? Teslyn wondered. If he did, she would send him away. She would not share a table with him, would not swallow a morsel of food if she did.

He did not come, and at length hunger overcame her resolve. The walk had left her ravenous.

Mindful of the band and the farming folk who would be coming into the *dorp* for the evening's festivities, she changed from her jeans and shirt into a dress. It was a soft russet shade with a sweetheart neckline and a pleated skirt. She put on lip-gloss and a touch of pearly blue eye-shadow, and then she stood for a moment looking at herself in the mirror. How her appearance had changed in such a short time! The sun had painted her cheeks a soft pink, and on her nose was a sprinkling of freckles. The make-up gave an extra glow to her face, making her eyes wide and sparkling, her expression vivid. Wayne notwithstanding—for it could not be because of him—Teslyn was glad that she was looking her best.

In the doorway of the dining-room she paused. She saw Wayne immediately. He was seated at a table for two. All the other tables were occupied. Here and there were spare chairs, but it would look very strange if she were to ask people she did not know for permission to sit with them when the man she had travelled with sat alone.

Wayne grinned at her as she sat down, a decidedly wicked grin. He knew how near she had been to going without supper, but he did not mention it. As before, Teslyn noticed that he had his own brand of good manners.

There were candles on the tables and the food was very good. The chef must have made a special effort in honour of the occasion. There was prime rib, so tender that it seemed to melt as it touched the tongue, and with it there were apples spiced with cloves and wine, and tiny roast potatoes. Teslyn ate with enjoyment.

Now and then she saw that Wayne was watching her. He was more handsome than ever tonight, in a dark-brown corduroy jacket and a silk shirt of a lighter shade. He looked very virile, and as fresh as if he had just been for a swim. Despite the fact that she now thought of him as a schemer, his appearance caught at her heart. Words trembled on her lips, but she did not speak, and neither did he.

At the table not far away Sally was sitting. Looking that way once, Teslyn caught her eye. On the receptionist's face was a speculative expression. Had she been watching Wayne? Teslyn wondered, for clearly he had made an impact on her. Or was she watching them both and wondering at their relationship? She felt her cheeks grow warm.

Sally was looking even lovelier tonight than she had earlier, a dress of deep coral complementing her vivid colouring. Teslyn was suddenly glad that she herself had opted for a pretty dress and make-up.

At one end of the room a dais had been set up, and the instruments of the band lay upon it. The musicians, identified by their scarlet dinner jackets and bow ties, were enjoying their meal with the rest of the guests.

The meal over, they went to the dais, and the music began—folk music to start with, songs beloved by all. The farmers and their wives crowded the space cleared for a dance-floor, and, watched by the travelling salesmen who were the usual patrons of the hotel, they began to dance—folk dances, the *tickey-draai* and the *vastrap*, South Africa's own form of square dancing.

Teslyn turned her chair so that she could watch. Glad of the excuse to escape Wayne's eyes, she tapped her feet to the tunes she had known since her childhood.

And then the music changed, becoming slow and dreamy, the music of Glenn Miller and Mantovani, melodies that had been danced to by generations. The mood of the dancers changed with it. Burly farmers put their arms around their wives and held them close.

'Teslyn,' the low voice was husky beside her ear, 'let's dance.'

She turned slightly in her chair. 'No, thanks.'

'Don't you want to dance?'

She could see his eyes, they glowed in the candlelight. The lines of his face, normally rugged and angular, were softened. The corners of his lips had lifted, just a little, and she could see the curve of the laughter lines. A throbbing began in her temples.

Yes, I want to dance. I want to be in your arms, close to you, with my cheek against your chest, and your lips in my hair, and your legs moving against mine. That's the trouble. I want it too much—too darned much.

'No,' she said, 'I don't want to dance.'

'If your husband loved you, he'd want you to enjoy yourself,' he said softly.

Teslyn struggled to hide her trembling. She could not look at him as she said, 'You're unspeakable!'

'Look at me, Teslyn,' he ordered relentlessly. When she did not comply he put his hand beneath her chin and forced her round to him. His eyes were perceptive, dark and steady. 'Why don't you want to dance? The real reason?'

Somehow she managed to keep her own gaze steady. 'Isn't it obvious?' she asked in her iciest tone. 'I can't bear the thought of being in your arms.'

Something moved in his face, then was gone. His lips curved again, mockingly this time. 'So be it.' He shrugged, got to his feet and went to the table where Sally was sitting.

And then they were dancing. Sally's arm was curved around Wayne's neck and he was laughing down at her. In a moment he had gathered her to him, and her cheek was against his chest—where Teslyn had longed to rest hers.

Teslyn was totally unprepared for the pain that stabbed her. Blindly, not caring at that moment what Wayne would make of her behaviour, she left the room through a door that led to the garden.

It was cool out of doors, the air headily sweet with the scent of gardenia and jasmine. It was also dark, too dark for her to walk more than a few yards.

She could just make out the outlines of a bench. Sitting down she curved her arm along the back rest and leaned her head against her hand. Her cheeks were hot, she discovered. The pain was still there too, a heaviness in her chest and her forehead.

Jealousy. Though she had never felt this way before, Teslyn was able to put a name to the pain. Heavens, it was awful! She would have to take care never to feel this way again.

What had happened to her? she wondered a little desperately. There had been occasions for jealousy in the past, for Alec had gone much further than dance with pretty girls. He had had affairs, he had never made any secret of them, had in fact taunted her with them. His girls, he had liked to jeer, gave him the satisfaction he did not find with his wife. She had been furious—not so much because there were other women in his life, for the time had come when she no longer cared—but at the humiliation to which she had been subjected. Through all the unhappiness with Alec, Teslyn had not lost her pride, and she had wished he would be discreet about his relationships.

So she had been furious, yes. But jealousy? No, never that. What she had felt just minutes ago, at the sight of Sally in Wayne's arms, was a new feeling, one she had not anticipated. She was shaken by its violence.

Why did she feel this way now? And with Wayne? Why did it matter so much that he might spend the rest of the evening with Sally? That he might very well make love to her when the dancing ended and the guests went to their rooms?

While Alec's affairs had angered her, they had not touched her deeper emotions. It made no sense therefore that just the thought of Wayne and Sally together, wrapped in an intimacy of their own, was a kind of torture. No sense at all. Teslyn did not love Wayne. Love, indeed! She did not even like the man.

But it would be a very good thing, said a small voice that would not be denied, for her to get to Pinevale, to immerse herself in whatever work was waiting for her there. And to keep herself as far removed from Wayne North as possible.

They left the hotel at daybreak next morning. Sally was not in the foyer to say goodbye to Wayne, and Teslyn was glad. As they drove through the awakening veld, dew-laden and misty, she wondered whether he would comment on last night's dancing, and on the fact of her abrupt exit. But he did not, and Teslyn did not speak of it either.

They stopped for a breakfast at a pretty wayside inn where they were served waffles with mulberry jam and whipped cream and strong coffee made from freshly-ground beans. Wayne looked as alert and as virile as ever, and not at all as if the evening's revelries had interfered in any way with his sleep. Unlike Teslyn herself, who had stayed awake long after the music had ended.

'Will you get us to Pinevale today?' she asked, moving her eyes to her plate and away from a face that disturbed her despite her resolve to remain unmoved.

'No.'

She cut into a waffle with unnecessary force. 'Couldn't you try?'

'Only if I were to cut short my business.' She was beginning to recognise the tone of cool amusement. 'I realise that you don't enjoy my company, but since you go out of your way to avoid it'—he paused deliberately, letting the words make their impact—'another day with me shouldn't bother you.'

'I'm glad you understand how I feel about you,' she threw at him burningly, and pushed the waffles away from her, unable to eat another bite.

The day followed the pattern of the one before. Stops at certain farms, discussion with farmers. Two of the farmers' wives were happy to see a new female face and eager to engage Teslyn in talk. At the third farm, where the young wife was in hospital giving birth to her first baby, Teslyn was free to take a walk.

It was so beautiful here, she thought, standing alone in the windswept veld and gazing into distant hills. It was a beauty she would really enjoy if she could but rid herself of thoughts of Wayne.

Pinevale would be a little like this, lovely vistas and sweet-smelling air. She did not know how long her stay there would be, a few weeks perhaps, certainly not more than a month or two. There would be work there for her to do, but there would also be periods of leisure, and she would make the most of that time, learning to enjoy a beauty that did not exist in the city. She would not let Wayne's presence hinder her. He would be at Pinevale, for he worked at the farm, but the claustrophobic intimacy of their trip would be missing. Teslyn would go her way, and she had no doubt that Wayne would be more than content to go his.

It was a little later in the afternoon when they arrived at the hotel where they would spend the night. As before, the *dorp* was tiny, the hotel its only one, and already the concrete car park was filled with the cars and trucks of the travelling salesmen.

Teslyn waited in the car while Wayne went into the office to check in. When he came back outside she thought she glimpsed an odd look on his face as he opened the door for her, but he met her eyes steadily enough.

He took her suitcase, and she walked with him to an annex behind the building. At a room with the number 24 on the door he stopped, and she stopped too and held out her hand for the key. Reaching past her, he unlocked the door, opened it and waited for her to go in. She looked at him and saw an expression she recognised. He'd worn it when he came to the car after checking in. She could not have said why it boded no good, but her spine tingled with sudden apprehension. What was Wayne up to now? 'Thank you,' she said coolly, 'I can manage.'

His grip remained firm. 'I'll take it in.'

With a steadiness she was far from feeling, Teslyn said, 'There's no need.' And then, as he continued to stand by the door, 'I don't want you in my room, Wayne. Not even for a minute.'

'It's our room, Teslyn.' He said it very softly, but there was no missing the emphasis on the word 'our'.

'You're crazy!' she choked.

'No, sweetheart, I'm not. Go inside, please, then we can talk.'

'No!'

'It's all the same to me if we're overheard,' he said mildly, 'but you might not like it.'

The blood was thick in her throat as she strode into the room. She tried to close the door, quickly, so that Wayne could not follow her, but he must have anticipated her action, for his foot wedged in the door and his shoulder humped easily against it.

'You're being very foolish.'

'I won't share a room with you!' She threw the words at him, eyes blazing.

'Calm down.' Putting the case down on the bed, he looked across at her. 'I'm afraid you've no choice.'

He meant it. For a few moments she had tried to delude herself into believing that Wayne was playing a game, that firmness on her part would get him out of the room. But his eyes were steady, and the sensual lips were set in a firm line. She took two steps backwards and found herself against the wall; it was a comforting if unexpected support for legs that were suddenly no firmer than jelly.

'I didn't plan it this way,' he said almost gently.

She cleared her throat, her voice husky. 'In the circumstances I find that hard to believe.'

His expression warmed, as if with understanding. 'I suppose so. It happens to be true.'

She wetted her lips, and then her gaze went from the ruggedly handsome figure to the double bed. 'We can't. . . . I can't. . . .'

'I think we could sleep very comfortably.' His eyes sparkled as they moved over her, dwelling for a long moment on trembling lips and a pulsating throat before moving down over the slim curved lines of her body. 'Pleasantly too,' he added seductively.

'No!' Teslyn's heart was hammering painfully. 'You must know it's impossible.'

'The hotel is full. There's a fair not far from here and many salesmen are headed that way. This was the only room left.'

'There must be one more.' In her distress, the whispered words had the sound of a plea.

'And then I had to be persuasive to get it.' He was unmoved.

'You could sleep in the car.' She looked up, with sudden hope.

'Not in this part of the world. It gets very cold at night, and I'm not equipped for it.' He took a step towards her, and she pressed herself further against the wall. His lips tightened, as if he had registered the small defensive gesture and was displeased by it.

'Resign yourself to it,' he said roughly. His lips lifted briefly. 'It's really not a fate worse than death you know. You might even enjoy it.'

'I'll hate it,' she declared passionately. 'If you make a pass at me, Wayne, I'll have no scruples dealing with it.'

'A well-aimed kick?' He laughed shortly. 'Won't be necessary. Simmer down, hothead. How about going for a walk?'

Remembering the lovely stroll through the tobacco fields the previous evening, Teslyn was tempted to accept the invitation. Yet if she did so, she thought, in some way she would be giving in to Wayne. He would think himself forgiven for this newest outrage, and that would never do.

'No, thanks,' she said icily, and opened her suitcase. As he walked to the door she did not let herself lift her eyes to watch him.

It was very hot in the room, for the sun's heat had been captured in the white walls and after the long hours spent in the car Teslyn felt sticky. A walk in the coolness of dusk was what she needed. But she would not go out now, not even by herself, for the chances of meeting Wayne were good, and he would mock her for her childishness in walking alone when she could have had company. It seemed unavoidable that there would be tension between them later, a tension that might be unbearable. She did not need to add to it.

She would take a bath, she decided. With Wayne off on his walk and likely to remain away quite a while, she could even use a bubble bath, a luxury that seldom failed to lift her spirits.

She sank into the water and the foam was soft and sensuous on her bare skin, the fragrance filling her nostrils. She relaxed and lay back, her head leaning against the wall of the bath, and stretched first one shapely leg, then the other, laughing as she saw her toes emerging from the white bubbles. A walk would have been fun—in different circumstances—but this was fun too.

The bath cooled, and she leaned forward to turn the tap and let in more hot water. Lying back again, she closed her eyes and revelled in a lovely sense of weightlessness.

'Were you never warned about sleeping in the bath?'

Her eyes jerked open. Wayne was standing by the bath.

CHAPTER SIX

SAVE for a pair of white shorts Wayne wore nothing. Even in her fright, Teslyn's eyes were riveted on the bronzed muscularity of his body. Tall, broad at the shoulders with a narrow waist tapering to even narrower hips, he was the epitome of virile maleness, she thought irrelevantly.

'I wasn't sleeping,' she said over the lump in a throat that had gone very dry. 'How did you get in?'

'A water nymph bathed in foam,' he observed seductively, ignoring the question. His eyes ran the length of the bath and though she knew he could not see through the foam his expression suggested that he knew precisely what lay beneath it. She could feel the blood racing in her veins.

'How did you get in?' she asked again.

'The door was open.'

She was silent a moment, remembering that she had not locked the bathroom door, it had seemed unnecessary.

'You had no right to come in here,' she said at last, ineffectually.

'I had no idea I'd find you here. The room was empty, I thought you'd gone walking too. How about showing me a little more of yourself, Teslyn?'

The bubbles were thinning. Looking down, she could see, very faintly, the outline of her breasts.

'You got back quickly,' she accused, wishing he would go.

'I came for my pipe. And once here, I thought I'd

freshen up with a shower.' He knelt down beside the bath. 'Let me see you, Teslyn.'

'No!' Panic welled in her as she tried to stir up more foam with her hands. It was hard to find her voice. 'Wayne, no!'

'Yes, sweetheart.'

He bent over her, and his hands slid along her shoulders, the fingers flat against the bare wet skin. They lingered there a few moments, then moved beneath the foam. Silkily, sensuously, they found her breasts, cupping them, one in each hand, then caressing them, slowly and rhythmically. The blood was like fire in her veins now. She had meant to push him away, but her head and her heart were pounding with such excitement that rational thought became impossible.

He bent lower, never releasing her breasts, but now his lips were touching her face, teasing a path around her cheeks, her throat, then up to her lips. Of her own volition Teslyn turned her head to him, and now his kiss deepened, it was sensual and hard and drugging to the senses.

He lifted his mouth for breath and looked down at her. 'I still can't see you,' he said huskily.

But she could see him. Every rippling muscle in the bronzed shoulders, the taut column of his throat, the small dark hairs curling on his chest. The air of virility that clung to him like a second skin was more concentrated than ever, a basic animal quality that was like fire to her maddened senses. She wanted to touch him as he was touching her. She had never wanted anything quite so badly.

She didn't realise what he was up to when he bent forward, a little away from her, and pushed his hand deeply down through the foam. Not till the water ebbed beneath her and the foam began to subside did she understand that he had released the plug. Half an hour ago his daring would have enraged her, now she was only consumed with an intensity of wanting such as she had never experienced before.

There was a hushed silence as the bath emptied. Even their breathing seemed to have been suspended. When the last of the water had gone and just the residue of the foam still clung to her body, Wayne suddenly groaned, 'My God, you're so beautiful, Teslyn!'

Then he was bending again, one arm going around her shoulders, cupping them, the other sliding beneath her knees. 'Come out,' he whispered huskily, as he lifted her.

They stood together on the tiled bathroom floor, the tall dry man and the small wet girl, and then Wayne's arms were around her, pulling her to him, and in moments his body was wet from hers. He began to kiss her again, exploring the sweetness of her mouth as if he could never get enough of it, while Teslyn, all thought of resistance gone, responded with a passion she had never dreamed she possessed.

Puddles of water gathered on the floor, unheeded, as they stood there, two figures so close together that they could have been one. Wayne's hands were on Teslyn's back, shaping themselves to the curves of her waist and her hips, pressing her against him. In turn her hands were busy with an exploration of their own, and as she submitted to a kiss that seemed to have no ending, she revelled in the feel of hard bone and strong muscle.

He took his mouth away from hers at last. 'Come,' he said raggedly, and lifting her again he carried her into the bedroom. She made no move to stop him, her body wanting the final surrender as much as his did.

He put her down on the bed, then moved to the suitcase that still lay on the covers. Through passion-glazed eyes Teslyn watched him, her gaze travelling over him. His hands were on the suitcase, closing it, for she had left it open. The suitcase! Her eyes focused suddenly. The case Alec had bought at the time of their marriage.

Alec! When last had she thought of him? Certainly not since the moment she had opened her eyes and seen Wayne by the bath. Perhaps not for hours before then.

'Sweetheart, move over.' With the suitcase out of the way, Wayne was at the bed once more. He knelt down beside her, waiting for her to make room for him so that he could lie down beside her. So that they could make love, fully, and with all the passion that possessed them both.

But she could not. With Alec's accident haunting her—as it always would—she could not give herself up to the wonder of this man and what was happening between them. She had slept with Alec and been repelled by his drunken fumblings, yet she had never known the beauty and excitement of real lovemaking. And now she never would. It was her punishment, self-inflicted, for what she assumed was her blame in what had happened.

'Wayne, no!'

He looked down at her, his eyes puzzled. 'Why not?'

'I can't.'

His hands were on her shoulders, the thumbs making a soft trail along her throat. 'I don't understand. You want it, we both want it.'

She tried to push him away. Her body was filled with a heavy and betraying sweetness. She wanted him so badly, but she had to get him to leave her, now, while in some small measure she still had the ability to resist him.

'I can't. Wayne, please!'

His eyes hardened. 'You're not frightened, Teslyn—you're young, but you're not a virgin. You've been married.'

'That's why,' she managed to whisper.

Understanding came into his face, and with it the hardness increased. 'Alec?'

'Yes"

'You can't mourn him for ever. Teslyn, sweetheart, he wouldn't expect it.'

If only he wouldn't keep calling her sweetheart. He did not know what the endearment did to her. Or perhaps he did. And yes, Alec would expect her to stay away from men for ever. It was the punishment he would have chosen for her.

'I can't go on.' Her throat was so dry that it hurt her to speak.

Brown eyes glittered in a leanly rugged face and the thumbs continued their stroking. Please go, she pleaded silently, I can't stand much more of this. As if Wayne had heard her plea, his hands lifted from her throat.

But the respite lasted less than a second. His hands came to her breasts, cupping the fullness, and she could feel her nipples, hard and swelling against his fingers. Her body was betraying her, and there was nothing she could do to prevent it.

'You want me,' he said very softly. 'How can you deny it?'

She turned her head away, and focused her eyes on the curtains so that she would not have to see his face. 'I do want you,' she acknowledged unsteadily. 'But it doesn't mean anything. It's just this proximity. . . .'

And that was not true! She had wanted him before, though always until now she had tried to push the knowledge from her mind. She had been stirred by him, had wanted him to kiss her. Finally she had to admit it to herself.

'Even if it were just a matter of proximity,' he said in a strange voice, 'why can't you let yourself enjoy this?'

'Because of Alec.'

'You still love him so much that you can't be with another man?'

I never loved him. What I once felt was infatuation, and even that didn't last long.

'Is that the reason?' he insisted.

The reason is that I killed him. At least I think I may have been responsible for his death. I'll never know for certain. Until I do, which may be never, I can't let myself be with another man. That is my punishment.

How would Wayne react if she said the words out loud? Would he recoil from her in disgust, or would he understand the horror of her life with Alec, and the circumstances which had led to the events of that terrible night? Would he understand the despair of not knowing if Alec would still be alive today if she had not threatened to leave him?

But Wayne had given her a way out, and she would use it. It was enough that she must live with the truth. There was no reason why he should know it too.

'Yes,' she said, and her eyes were still on the curtains. 'I loved Alec. I still love him. That's why. . . .' Her voice was beginning to break. 'Wayne, please try to understand.'

He did not answer immediately, but when he did his voice was hard. 'It seems I have no option. Pull the blanket up.'

With trembling fingers she did so. Until that moment she had forgotten she was naked.

'As for our sleeping arrangements,' he went on, in

the same tone, 'I'll ask for two chairs and push them together.'

'Will you be comfortable?'

'Probably not. But it's preferable to sharing a bed with a warm and sexy woman who doesn't understand the demands of her own body.' He crossed the room and began pulling on his clothes. 'I'm a normal man, Teslyn, and there are definite limits to my endurance and control.'

They came to Pinevale at noon the next day. Alec had spoken so seldom about his home and his family that Teslyn knew almost nothing of his background. So it was with interest that she looked out of the window as Wayne began negotiating the winding road that led to the homestead.

Pinevale was a timber plantation. A relatively small one, Wayne said, and even that she had not known. The pines rose straight and tall on either side of the road, and here and there were bundles of logs where trees had been felled. In this part of the Eastern Transvaal, the Lowveld, the land was mountainous. To one side Teslyn saw a mountain slope rise steeply from the road, to the other it fell away to a valley. And on both sides the trees grew in abundance, the foliage vivid where the sun slanted through.

Mary Morrison was waiting for them at the homestead. As the car drew up beside the stone steps that led up to the big red-brick house, she came hurrying to meet them.

'Teslyn, my dear!' She was smiling as she hugged her. 'Welcome to Pinevale. I'm so very glad you came.'

Mary too was a surprise, Teslyn thought as she followed her mother-in-law into the house. She was small and wiry, with a tanned and wrinkled skin that spoke of many years spent in the sun, and eyes that were warm and kind. Laughing eyes, and Teslyn wondered how she knew it, for now they looked sad. Mary was not at all the woman she had expected Alec's mother to be.

'How's Jim?' Wayne wanted to know.

They had come into the spacious living-room, made comfortable with plants and colourful floor-rugs and walls hung with handwoven pieces. At one end of the room stood a weaving-loom, on it a piece in progress, though Teslyn guessed it was some time since Mary could have given it any attention. Alec's mother was evidently a woman who loved her home and gave it much care.

Glancing at Mary, she saw that the smile had left her face and that her eyes were sadder than before. 'He's not well,' she said.

'In much pain?'

'A great deal.' The soft voice was low. 'Teslyn, won't you sit down? We'll have lunch in a few minutes. Yes, Wayne, I'm afraid it's quite bad.'

'How did it happen?'

'*Ag*, man, you know how it is. Jim was trying something new—a great experimenter my husband is,' the last in an aside to Teslyn. 'Yes, a new way for cutting. And one-two-three, his arm slipped, or perhaps the machine did, I don't know. Anyhow, by the time I was called Jim was unconscious.'

'He will get better, though?' Teslyn asked with genuine concern, and saw Wayne's eyes go to her face.

'We hope so. He's to have another operation and with God's help it will make a big difference.' She put a hand on Teslyn's arm. 'Jim was so sorry not to welcome you here himself. This homecoming was not the way he would have wished it to be.'

Home. Teslyn was startled at the use of the word. Did Mary really think of the visit as a homecoming?

But there was no time to ponder the question, for Mary was saying to Wayne, 'I hope you'll stay and have lunch with us.' The words were also a surprise, for surely since Wayne worked at Pinevale he took his meals here.

The meal was eaten at a round table in the farmhouse kitchen. As Mary gave a final toss to the salad, Teslyn looked with delight around a room that seemed to have sprung from the pages of an old-world magazine. The kitchen was huge and sunny with walls that were white and blue tiled. Above the range hung a row of gleaming antique copper pots, and in two corners, suspended from the ceiling, were bunches of drying mealie cobs. On the table stood an earthenware jar filled with daffodils.

'Did you have a good trip down?' Mary asked as they started to eat.

'It had its interesting moments,' said Wayne as Teslyn jerked up to look at him, and she saw that he was ready for her; his eyes sparkled with malice and amusement.

Words bubbled to her lips. Her mother-in-law would be very interested—and disappointed—to hear of her employee's behaviour. She turned to her, but one look at the troubled face told her that the moment was inappropriate.

'I hope you weren't bored, dear,' said Mary.

'I didn't have time to be bored.' Teslyn smiled at her, then threw a look at Wayne. Her own eyes were sparkling this time. 'My point, I think,' she challenged him wordlessly.

For a while they spoke of other things. They were finishing dessert when Mary said, 'Wayne, it was good of you to bring Teslyn. I suppose you'll be off to Tinarua?'

'When I've had my coffee, yes.'

'Tinarua?' Teslyn asked, puzzled.

'Wayne's timber plantation.'

'I thought. . . .' Teslyn stopped, and her gaze went back to Wayne once more. He was watching her, his expression lazily perceptive. He was amused, she thought angrily.

'Wayne must have told you about his plantation.' Mary's voice seemed to come from a distance.

'We had other things to talk about,' Wayne said smoothly, and Teslyn wondered if Mary picked up the hint of mockery, but perhaps she did not, since it was directed solely at herself.

'Thank you for lunch,' Wayne went on. He got to his feet and took Mary's hand. 'Don't think me rude, but there are things waiting for my attention. Tell Jim I hope he'll be better soon and I'll be in to visit him.'

'Thank you for everything.'

'No need to thank me, you know that.' His tone with Mary was so unexpectedly gentle that Teslyn was taken aback. He can be human, she thought, not for the first time. 'But not with me. Only with others.'

'I'll be seeing you,' he said to Teslyn.

'Don't bank on it.' The words snapped out without any thought. At the sight of Mary's puzzled face, she qualified the statement. 'I'll be busy, of course—helping here on the plantation.'

'Wayne has offered to show you around.' Mary was frowning slightly, as if at something she did not understand.

'As I said,' Wayne put in, his backward look as he left the table sardonic, 'I'll be seeing you.'

When he had gone the two women sat for a while

longer over their coffee. 'Is Wayne's plantation far from here?' Teslyn wanted to know.

'A few miles. You'll have to see Tinarua, my dear.'

'Perhaps—I'm in no hurry.'

There was a shrewd glance from sun-faded eyes. 'Did something happen between you and Wayne?'

He's rude and overbearing. He's also the most exciting man I've ever met, and he aroused me to a point where I came within a whisper of letting him make love to me.

There were things she had thought of saying to Mary about Wayne. But now, all at once, she could not say them. She shrugged. 'Nothing at all.'

'Yet I get the feeling you don't like him.'

'He's not my type.'

'I can understand that,' said Mary after a moment, and there was sadness in her tone. When she went on Teslyn understood why. 'He's so different from Alec.'

'Please,' Teslyn wanted to say, 'don't bring Alec into this. Don't compare the two men. Alec can only lose in every sense.'

'But Wayne is a fine man all the same,' said Mary. 'A very fine man. He hates us to thank him, yet we can never repay him for all his help.'

Help that Alec should have given. Which was why Teslyn was here. She didn't want to hear more about Wayne, she had to change the conversation to a more impersonal level.

'I think you said Tinarua is also a timber plantation?'

'The best one in the district. When Wayne came here, five years ago, the plantation was nothing like it is today. It had promise, of course, otherwise he wouldn't have bought it. But my word, Teslyn, the progress that man has made in a short time, you wouldn't believe it!'

But she did believe it. All along it had been difficult to visualise Wayne working for someone else. There was a strength and drive in him that would not respond well to authority. Arrogant he might be, but he would also expect only the best, not only from others but also from himself.

'Let me show you to your room,' Mary said.

They walked together down the long corridor of the farmhouse. At a closed door they stopped and Mary turned to Teslyn. 'I've given you Alec's old room. I thought you'd like that.'

Teslyn suppressed a shiver as Mary opened the door and led the way in. Alec's room. Alec's bed. Would the nightmares that had tapered off slightly in recent months become more frequent again? But she could not ask Mary to let her use another room, for her mother-in-law would be deeply hurt.

And then a minute later she realised that the request was in any case unnecessary. Looking around her, Teslyn saw that this was not Alec's room at all, not the Alec she had known. It was the room of a boy who had lived here from babyhood to very young manhood. The signs were everywhere. There was a bookcase with childhood favourites, *Winnie the Pooh* and *The Hardy Boys* and a tattered *Tom Sawyer*. Had the young Alec identified with Tom, living out fantasies of his hero's exploits in the windswept bush of the Lowveld? It was hard for Teslyn to see him in the role, but perhaps here, in this room, she had discovered a new slant to the husband she had never understood.

Everywhere she saw the treasures of a teenage boy. Models of cars and boats, painstakingly assembled. Pennants and posters and an assegai, the hunting spear of the tribal people honed to a fine point. No photos of sports teams, Teslyn noticed, and and was not surprised—Alec did not function well in a group situation—but on one wall was a gun, and beside it the preserved heads of two impala.

'Loved hunting, Alec did,' his mother said, her eyes following the direction of Teslyn's gaze. 'I used to worry myself sick he'd get hurt.'

Did it ever occur to you, Teslyn wondered, to worry about the birds and the animals that would be hurt as a result of Alec's passion? And did you know that Alec would never lose the enjoyment he derived from hurting those who were weaker than himself?

'A real boy's room,' Mary said fondly.

A boy's room, with no hint of the emerging man, save for the gun and the impala heads. The room would give her no added nightmares, Teslyn knew. It was not frightening. If anything, the collection of boyish memorabilia, save for the animal heads, was endearing. It was also impersonal. The boy who had spent the greater part of his life here had long vanished; there was nothing here of the man he had become.

'It's a lovely room,' she said gently.

'Sometimes I think I should get rid of these things. No real point keeping them. Jim . . . Jim says I'm sentimental.' Mary dashed away a tear. 'I daresay he's right. Teslyn dear, you must want a shower and a change of clothes. Why don't you make yourself at home? I'll be on the stoep if you want me.'

Teslyn was thoughtful as she opened the suitcase and began to take out her clothes. She had never understood Alec, had never been able to identify with the way he thought and behaved. Had she tried hard enough? she wondered uncomfortably. And would their relationship have been any different if she had visited Pinevale and got to know his parents while Alec was alive? Thus far nothing had been added to her understanding, if anything she was more confused. Mary did not seem the mother of a sadistic-natured man. Her kind face would suggest to a stranger that she was the parent of a gentle man. Teslyn had not met Jim, but Wayne had spoken of him with affection and respect, and Wayne, she acknowledged with little joy, would be no mean judge of character.

Stop analysing, she told herself, you're not a psychiatrist. Take Pinevale as it comes and concentrate on keeping out of Wayne's way.

When Teslyn came to the stoep half an hour later Mary was sitting in a low cane chair and was sewing a button on to a pyjama jacket.

'Isn't is silly, the things one does under stress,' she commented with a wry smile. 'These pyjamas have been without buttons for ages and Jim wasn't bothered. Now he needs a spare pair and I cringe because I dread what the nurses will think.'

'Give me some mending too,' Teslyn smiled back.

'I never say no to a helping hand. Baking I adore, and ironing is therapy for a tired mind. But mending I can do without. Here's a shirt that's begging for attention.'

The two heads, one fair, one grey, were bent over the sewing when Mary said, 'We haven't talked about Alec.'

Teslyn looked up, eyes wary. 'No. . . .'

'We've talked about everything else, but not Alec. I . . . I wanted to wait until we were alone and at ease.'

If Mary felt at ease Teslyn was as tense as a spring that was coiled too tightly. What could she say about Alec that would not hurt his mother? And if she lied, would this very nice woman with the steady eyes and tired smile not recognise the words for what they were?

'I must know—did he suffer?'

'No. The car hit a lamp-post. Alec didn't feel a thing, Mary. The doctors assured me.'

'Thank God nobody else was hurt.' Mary's voice shook. 'He liked to drive fast.'

So his parents had put the accident down to Alec's love of speed. They were right, of course, for Alec had been going much too fast; the burn marks of the wheels had in fact been thick and black on the road. But speed in itself, though it had frightened her when she drove with him, had never impaired Alec's accuracy; his reactions had been swift and razor-sharp. Anger must have done that, and a despair at what Alec had called Teslyn's insensitivity to all reason.

'Were you happy together?'

The needle jerked, pricking Teslyn's finger. Keeping her eyes riveted on the spot where a tiny speck of blood oozed on to the skin, she said, 'We were married three years,' and wondered if Mary registered the evasion. Even to please Alec's mother she could not have brought herself to say, 'Yes, we were happy.'

'We were so glad when Alec let us know he was married,' Mary went on.

'You were?'

'Yes. Even though we'd have liked to have been at his wedding. I was sad we weren't invited, but then Alec was always impulsive. Once he'd met you he'd have wanted to be married right away.'

That was how it had been. Swept along on a tide of infatuation and excitement, Teslyn had been happy to yield to persuasion. With her parents no longer alive, and Alec noncommittal about his own family, it had not occurred to her that there was reason to delay the wedding.

'I'm sorry,' she said in a low voice.

'No need for that.' Mary touched her hand. 'As I say, we were glad, Jim and I.'

'Why?' Teslyn asked curiously.

For the first time Mary hesitated. 'Alec was not an easy boy—not that we didn't love him.' She said the last words quickly, defensively almost. 'We did, very much. But Alec was restless, always wanting something, never finding it. We never thought he would settle down.'

That sounded like Alec—restless, impatient, quick to pick up new interests, new friends, quicker to drop them.

'The company he kept, we didn't like it. Boys he met in town, girls too. Of course, when he said he was married we wondered about you.'

'Am I what you imagined?'

'Not at all.' There was something like wonder in Mary's tone. 'His other girls were so different. Fast and impatient, like he was.'

And available. That was what had piqued Alec from the start, Teslyn's unavailability. He seemed never to have met a girl who refused to go to bed with him. In a way it was a pity that the standards her parents had given her had been so firmly rooted. If she had slept with Alec he would have tired of her. Certainly there would have been no urgent rush to a commitment from which there had been no easy release.

'You're a gentle girl, Teslyn—not weak, because there's much spirit in your face, but gentle. So different from those others. I can see why Alec loved you.'

Don't go on! The words were a silent scream. You don't know what happened. If you did your sympathies would be with Alec, for despite everything he was your son and your love and loyalty would be with him.

Somehow she had to stop Mary's flow of words. Putting down the shirt that had begged for attention and received it, Teslyn stood up, making a watercolour on the opposite side of the room an excuse to walk away. She needed a respite, however brief.

She stood a few moments before the picture, barely seeing it, then pretended to examine a tapestry depicting a flower scene and sewn in tiny stitches. She was on her way to the bookcase that stood in one corner when she stopped, her attention caught by a framed photograph standing on a small side-table.

'Alec?' she asked, and hoped Mary did not register her disbelief.

'Taken on his sixteenth birthday.'

Eleven years ago. Teslyn picked up the photo. So this was how Alec had once looked—an eager boy on the threshold of manhood. Just eleven years ago, and yet it was incredibly hard to recognise him.

The eyes were the same, the sideways thrust of the head, and the sandy hair. But there the resemblance ended. In the intervening years since the picture had been taken Alec had grown a beard and a moustache, and his face had taken on a wild recklessness that Teslyn did not see here. The Alec she had known had looked nothing like this boy.

It came to her that this was the first photo of him that she had seen at Pinevale. 'Don't you have anything more recent?' she wanted to know.

'Unfortunately not. Jim and I were no good with a camera. We always said we'd get round to it. Now. . . .' Mary stopped.

When was the last time his parents had seen Alec? Teslyn wondered as she put the photo back on the table. Did they know how he had looked as a man, or were their last memories those of a fresh-faced young boy?

Suddenly she remembered the photo in her suitcase. She'd noticed it when she was packing and had decided to bring it along. Alec's parents might be glad to have it.

She would fetch it from her room and give it to Mary. But in the doorway she stopped on an idea. She would say nothing about the photo till Jim came home, she would give it to them then, her contribution to the homecoming.

As Teslyn came back to the chair where the pile of mending still lay, Mary changed the subject. 'You must be keen to see Pinevale.'

'I saw a little as we drove up.'

'There's more—the barns, and the sawmills, the stables. I have arthritis, my dear, and I can't take you around myself. But as I said, Wayne. . . .'

'I can find my own way,' Teslyn cut in.

'Oh no, my dear, you'd find that difficult, at least the first time. Besides, it's all arranged. Wayne's happy to do it.'

Because he felt that only with his guidance could she get properly acquainted with Pinevale? Or because he knew how much she would hate it and the fact would give him satisfaction? Knowing Wayne as she did, the answer would be the latter. Teslyn stifled a protest. It would worry Mary to know that she dreaded the idea of being in Wayne's company.

She would be even more worried if she knew the real reason, the one that had nothing at all to do with Wayne's arrogance, but was solely the result of feelings over which Teslyn had no control. How would Mary, Alec's mother, feel about that? Teslyn curled her nails into her palms and swallowed.

'He'll be here around ten tomorrow morning.'

'I'll be ready,' Teslyn said quietly, resigning herself to what was seemingly inevitable.

CHAPTER SEVEN

IT rained during the night, and Teslyn listened to it. The rain whispered on the roof and a wind stirred the trees that surrounded the house. Lying in the darkness, enjoying the sounds of the storm and the damp earthy smell wafting in through the open window, she wondered if the rain would continue into the morning so that the excursion with Wayne could be postponed.

Some time during the early hours of the morning the storm ended. When Teslyn woke up the room was already opaque with early daylight, and when she went to the window she saw the promise of a golden day. Beneath her the garden was webbed with dew. The air was fresh and smelled of rain and tropical shrubs, and over the mountain slope, where the trees grew thickly, the mist was just beginning to lift.

The house was quiet. A farming day would begin early, at daybreak, she guessed, but perhaps Mary was still sleeping, and at present nobody else lived at the homestead. She went to the kitchen and made herself a cup of coffee, then went back to her room to stand perplexed before her meagre wardrobe.

What to wear? Her oldest jeans and her plainest shirt, said reason. Today was a working day and she was at Pinevale to work. More particularly, Wayne should know that she was accompanying him only because she had to, and and that the purpose of their meeting today was purely business.

Reason notwithstanding, when Wayne knocked on the door of the homestead, Teslyn was wearing a blue sun-dress that made the most of pretty shoulders, and a slender waist. Her hair, freshly washed, swung round her head in a lightly-feathered cloud, and on her lips was a clear coral lipstick. A glance in the mirror had told her that she looked pretty. 'Idiot!' she had accused her reflection fiercely.

An assessing glance, beneath which she made herself stand still and outwardly indifferent, took in every inch of her appearance. Wayne himself was looking ruggedly virile in an open-necked shirt and riding-breeches, and as his gaze lifted from Teslyn's figure back to her face she had to summon all her control to suppress a quiver.

'Hello, Wayne.' The greeting was as icy as the could make it.

'Hello, Teslyn. You look very lovely in blue. But I'm afraid it won't do.'

She lifted her head, wondering why Wayne provoked her whenever he could. 'It wasn't my idea to go out with you today. I'm staying as I am.'

'No, sweetheart, I think not. Mary, hello.' The last words were said with a smile as Mary, looking pale and preoccupied, joined them on the stoop.

'Wayne, I didn't hear you come.'

'How is Jim?' he asked.

'Not well today. I just spoke to him on the telephone.'

'I'm sorry,' said Teslyn, her voice warm with sympathy.

'Ja—well, I'm going in to see him. Wayne, I'm so glad you're here, that you'll show Teslyn around.'

'I was just telling her that she would have to change. Jeans, Teslyn. Unless, Mary, do you happen to have some spare breeches in the house?'

'You're going on horseback, of course. See how busy

I am with my own thoughts—I didn't even think of it.'
Mary studied Teslyn thoughtfully. 'I have a pair that
should be right for you, dear.'

Teslyn swallowed the protest which had risen to her
lips. It would sound very childish if she refused to
change, and this was not the moment to say that giving
in to Wayne riled her every time.

The breeches fitted perfectly. 'Just as lovely as the
dress,' was Wayne's comment when she came back to
the stoep. 'Sexy too.'

'You're incorrigible!' She tried to look angry and
found herself grinning instead.

'I know.' His answering grin was wicked, and
Teslyn's heart beat faster. 'Shall we go?'

'Where's Mary?' she asked.

'Phoning again.'

'Let's wait.'

'She's expecting us to go. Come along, Teslyn,' another grin, more wicked than the last—'you're running
out of excuses.'

They had taken a path east of the house when he
asked, 'By the way, do you ride?'

'No, so there's really no point. . . .'

'I'll teach you.' Brown eyes swept her face, pausing
on lips that had opened beneath his. 'There are many
things I'd like to teach you.'

'I'll hold you back,' she protested, over the thundering in her ears.

'No, sweetheart. You only hold yourself back. Every
time. And you happen to be missing something.'

'I can't go with you.' Her voice was unsteady.

'Nonsense!'

'Wayne, listen to me.' She stopped walking and
looked up at him, her expression urgent. 'I don't want
to go.'

'Why not?' He had turned to her, and his hands cupped her face. The agonising sweetness of it was almost her undoing.

Alec. It was getting harder and harder to summon his image into her mind, but somehow she did it. 'You always bring sex into everything.' Her voice was choked.

'Sex?' he drawled in pretended amazement. 'We were talking about horses and riding all the time—weren't we?' His fingers moved in her hair. He was standing so close to her that she could feel the warmth of his body through her clothes. 'Enjoy the day, Teslyn. You deserve some fun.'

'But, Wayne. . . .'

'Look, there are the stables, behind the trees.'

The stallion Wayne had ridden to Pinevale was in the paddock. Teslyn watched as Wayne saddled the horse that was to be hers. Hands that had moved sensuously over her body, raising her to heights she had never dreamed of, were assured and confident with the saddle. Wayne would never be anything but confident, she thought.

Though she had never been on a horse before, she mounted quickly, before he could help her. Coolly she met his ironic gaze, then looked away. No use pretending that they had been talking about horses on the way to the stables. They both knew what the topic had been. Perhaps Wayne was right, she did hold herself back from him, and she might well be missing something. She *was* missing something, when she dared to be honest with herself she knew it. But there was a reason for the holding back, one which Wayne might or might not understand, but which he would never know for she would not tell it to him.

The thought of riding had not daunted her in the

least, and after a few minutes she discovered that it was even more fun than she had imagined. Toby, a small grey gelding, was a gentle animal, and the rolling motion was enjoyable. The only disturbing feature was the powerful stallion just a little in front of them and the man who rode it. If she could distract her attention from a combination of sheer primitive maleness she would be able to enjoy the outing.

With determined effort she dragged her eyes from Wayne's dark head and broad back, and concentrated instead on the loveliness all around her. In no time she was enchanted. Seeing the forests from a car window was quite different from riding through them on horseback.

The crystal-like clarity of the air was exhilarating, and seemed to endow the forests with a special vividness. Yesterday she had not noticed quite how green it was here. And so many greens. There was a special smell too, a combination of wild flowers and fallen pine needles and damp fertile earth. Wherever in the world she might experience it again, it was a smell which she knew she would always associate with these forests.

'We're so high here,' she observed wonderingly, when Wayne turned in the saddle.

'No higher than you were in Johannesburg. That city is six thousand feet above sea level.'

'But there I wasn't conscious of it. Here in the mountains I am. That slope,' she added, taking one hand from the reins and gesturing, 'it looks as if it's plunging to the bottom of the world.'

'It will stop when it gets to the valley.' He was laughing, and she could see the tiny lines around his eyes and at the corners of his mouth.

'Don't tease!' She put on a show of mock severity, thinking how hard it was becoming for her to be angry

with him. Even at the homestead, when she had said
she did not want to change her clothes, her defiance
had been no more than a token thing—a gesture she
had felt she must make.

'I never tease you, do I?' Laughter bubbled briefly
in his throat. Then he asked, 'Enjoying yourself,
Teslyn?'

The way he spoke her name had the sound of a caress.
High in the forests, with the cool air on her cheeks and
the scent of pine needles in her nostrils, and a man who
was like nobody else on a horse beside her, it was hard
to think of Alec. She looked at him, her eyes wide and
blue and luminous—like buttercups moist with dew,
thought the watching man—and she said, 'Oh yes. I
never guessed it could be so beautiful.'

'There's more—much more,' he told her.

'I want to see it all.'

'I want you to see Tinarua.' He spoke quietly.

The blood drained from her cheeks. 'No!' And then,
realising how odd she must sound, she added, 'I'll be
busy here at Pinevale.'

'I see.' He studied her face a moment, and his lips
tightened. Putting his heels to the stallion, he said,
'Time to go on.'

Some of the joy seemed to have gone out of the
morning as they rode further. Had the outing been
without a purpose Teslyn might have suggested turning back. As it was, they proceeded without conversation, the silence between them broken only when
Wayne paused to point out landmarks or to offer
necessary explanations.

At the sawmill they dismounted. A few men were
clearing logs. At sight of Wayne their faces brightened
and one of them, apparently the spokesman of the
group, approached with a question. Teslyn watched as

Wayne considered the problem, his brow slightly furrowed, his eyes thoughtful. The answer came unhurriedly, given quietly yet with confidence. The spokesman went back to the group, and from their expressions it was clear that the men were satisfied. Their reaction filled Teslyn with pride, and she wondered why.

When he had finished talking to the men, Wayne turned to Teslyn. While she would never hew the trees and bundle them for the sawmills herself, it was important that she know every facet of the running of a timber plantation. Only then could she be of help to Mary and Jim.

While Wayne spoke, Teslyn found herself thinking of Alec. Why had he turned his back on this lovely place? There was so much here; beauty and a sense of peacefulness and the joy of the outdoors. To Teslyn it seemed a life with much more appeal than the rat-race of the cities. I could be happy here, she thought. Even after one morning, I know that I shall miss it when I go back. Yet Alec had hated it so much that he had told her almost nothing about his home. He had always been restless, his mother had said. Always searching for something. A thing that had also eluded him in the city, for though Teslyn had seen her husband in moods of reckless elation, she could not remember a time when he had been truly happy.

'You aren't concentrating,' she heard Wayne say, and she looked up to see him watching her.

'I'm sorry.'

'Where were you?'

'I was thinking of Alec.'

His lips tightened again. 'You seem to think of him all the time.'

She drew a breath. 'Yes. Yes, Wayne, I do.'

They rode on, in silence again. The path narrowed, and Teslyn was glad. She tried to keep her eyes away from the supple figure on the stallion, but it was becoming more and more difficult to empty her mind of the thoughts that centred on him. She was behaving absurdly. As if he meant something to her. Almost as if she loved him. But she did *not* love him, she told herself fiercely. She never would.

Absorbed in her thoughts, she did not see the house till they came to it, and then she stared at it puzzled. For a moment she thought they were back at the homestead, but then she saw they were not. This house was similar to the homestead, as if it had been designed by the same person, but it looked a little neglected and unlived-in.

She looked questioningly at Wayne. 'Two farmhouses?'

'You seem confused,' he commented.

'I am.'

There was no warmth in the eyes that studied her. 'Alec must have told you the set-up at Pinevale.'

Not for the first time she had to defend him. 'Of course he did.'

'Then why the puzzled look in those very pretty blue eyes?'

The barbed compliment gave her no pleasure. She glanced away from him as she said, 'We shared so much. I suppose it's only natural that there are things I've forgotten.'

'Then let me fill you in. Pinevale is owned by two families. When André Morrison died he left the farm to his two sons. Jim was one son, Marius the other. This homestead is the one where Marius lived.'

Teslyn said, 'I haven't met Marius.'

'He died some years ago.' Brown eyes were razor-sharp and relentless. 'His share passed to his son, Joshua.'

'Really?' No point in pretending that these were facts she had known but forgotten. 'Is this Joshua's house?'

'Yes. Though he's in Europe right now. In Paris, living off the profits sent him by his uncle. Jim and Mary have been managing Pinevale on their own for quite some time now.'

Caught by something in Wayne's voice, Teslyn looked up at him. 'You sound angry.'

'I am,' he said shortly. 'I have no time for parasites, Teslyn.'

'Alec wasn't a farmer,' again she defended him. 'Perhaps Joshua isn't one either.'

'Your cousin by marriage isn't averse to enjoying the benefits his inheritance has brought him. As your husband wouldn't have been likewise.'

'Don't judge Alec!' she said hotly.

'All right then, let's leave him out of it. But what about you, Teslyn?'

'Me?' She stared at him.

With a quick movement Wayne brought the stallion closer to the gentle Toby. There was no time for Teslyn to withdraw as Wayne covered her hands on the saddle, his fingers hard and impatient. The two horses were so close together that she could feel Wayne's booted leg against her thigh. Despite the heat she shivered.

'You've mastered the art of looking innocent,' he grated.

She stared at him. 'I don't know what you're talking about.'

'You must have wondered, just once, what would happen to Pinevale now that Jim and Mary's only son is no longer alive.'

Numbly Teslyn shook her head. In the light of

Wayne's previous remarks she could guess what was coming. But she did not want to hear him say it.

'I've never given it any thought,' she whispered.

'The innocent again!' His voice was steel. 'I wish I could believe in your naïveté, Teslyn, because it has its charms.'

'I'm not out to charm you,' she said tautly.

'As I've learned. Well then, to whom do you think Jim and Mary would probably leave their share of Pinevale?'

'Not to me!' In the light of all that had happened the very thought was appalling. But Wayne was wrong anyway, he had to be. Alec's parents hardly knew her. She had never met Jim, had been in Mary's company less than a full day. There was no reason at all, beyond the fact that Teslyn was Alec's widow, and that was not sufficient reason in itself why they should make her their heiress. Wayne was just baiting her. He was angry with Alec who had neglected his parents while he was alive, and now he vented that anger on Teslyn instead.

'I find this conversation distasteful.' Her tone was cool. 'If there's more to this tour, let's get on with it. If I've seen all I have to, then I'd like to get back to the homestead.'

A distraught woman awaited them at the homestead. Mary's cheeks were pale, and her eyes were red-rimmed, as if she had been crying.

All the way back from the stableyard, where Wayne's hands had rested provocatively on her waist as she dismounted, anger had churned inside Teslyn. She would tell Mary all about Wayne's arrogant behaviour and insist that he stay away from Pinevale while she herself were here. However, one look at her mother-in-law's face was enough to rid her of her own concerns.

'Mary, what's happened?' she asked anxiously.

'It's Jim.' The soft voice was choked. 'He's not at all well.'

'He's had a bad turn?' Wayne wanted to know.

'So it seems. The hospital's just been in touch. They want to operate again, this afternoon if possible.'

'I'll come into town with you,' Teslyn offered.

'That's kind of you, dear, but you'd be more useful here—if you don't mind, that is.'

'Of course not. I just want to help.'

'Bless you!' Mary turned to Wayne. 'You showed Teslyn around?'

'As much as I could in a day. Enough for her to get to grips with the basics. I'm available for questions any time she needs me.'

'You've been so kind,' Mary said gratefully. 'What we'd have done without you these last months I'll never know. They want me to stay at the hospital tonight, Wayne—perhaps even longer.'

'No problem. We'll look after things.'

'But there is a problem.' The faded eyes were troubled. 'Teslyn can't stay here alone.'

'I'll be fine,' the girl put in quickly.

'She'll sleep at Tinarua.' Brown eyes flicked Teslyn an unreadable glance before returning to Mary. 'No problem there either.'

'I'd rather stay here.' Teslyn made a small helpless gesture.

'No child, no.'

'But I. . . .'

Teslyn stopped as the telephone rang, and her mother-in-law hurried inside. 'I can't go to Tinarua,' was what she had been about to say. 'Under any circumstances.'

'You will come with me,' said Wayne.

She turned. He was leaning against the wall of the stoop, his legs extended before him. He looked as rugged and virile as always, the maleness he exuded so strong that it seemed tangible. Just the sight of him made the blood race in her veins.

'No,' she protested unsteadily. 'You know how I feel about you.'

'I think,' he said lazily, 'that your feelings frighten you. Perhaps you'd like to sleep in my bed at Tinarua?'

He was so close to the truth that for a long moment she could only stare at him speechlessly. She *did* want to be in his bed. God, how she wanted it! The blood drained from her cheeks, then returned.

'You're the most arrogant person I know,' she got out with a steadiness that surprised her. 'I wonder what Mary would say if she knew how you behave towards me.'

'I trust you'll wait for a more favourable time to find out,' he said dryly.

'I'm not insensitive. But I won't come to Tinarua.'

'Yes.' His firmness made her quiver. 'You will.'

'No!'

'If you refuse you'll be depriving Jim of his wife when he needs her most.'

'I told you,' she said tautly, 'I'll be fine here at Pinevale.

'You can't stay alone. Mary would never allow it.'

'But. . . .'

'It could be dangerous.'

I'm in far more danger at Tinarua. A different sort of danger. The assault on my senses and my emotions will be constant. I thought I could withstand you, Wayne North, but it seems I never knew myself, or my feelings, at all.

'Mary has more than enough worries,' Wayne was

saying, his voice terse. 'Don't add to them.'

Teslyn looked at him. He was right about one thing—it would be unfair to talk to Mary about her own problems. But later, when her mother-in-law had left for the hospital, then Teslyn could act in accordance with her own wishes without fear that she was being unfair to Wayne, for when it had suited him he had been equally unscrupulous.

She hoped her smile passed for one of reluctant acquiescence. 'It seems I have no option.'

The mock compliance brought anger to his eyes. But he said nothing, because at that moment Mary rejoined them on the stoop. One of the neighbouring farmers had called to ask about Jim, she told them. 'People have all been so kind.'

'And no wonder—Jim is well liked,' Wayne said. 'Everything is settled, Mary. Teslyn will sleep at Tinarua. I'll bring her back here in the morning, then fetch her again at the end of the day.'

'Oh, that's wonderful! Such a load off my mind.'

'Let Jim be your only concern,' Wayne said gently. 'It's getting late. Why not leave soon so that you can be at the hospital before dark.'

It was just four o'clock when Teslyn looked up from a ledger to see Wayne standing in the doorway of the farm office. As always her heart skipped a beat at the sight of him, and as always the fact made her angry.

'Ready?'

'Ready?' she repeated innocently.

'To go to Tinarua.'

'I thought I told you—I'm not going.'

She heard him swear beneath his breath. 'What trick are you up to now?'

'No trick,' she answered coolly. 'You knew all the

time I had no intention of coming.'

'That's not what you told Mary.'

'You told me,' Teslyn countered sweetly, 'not to add to her worries.'

Wayne took a step into the room. 'Why did you lie?'

She shrugged. The action was not easy when inside her every nerve was quivering. 'A strange question coming from you.' She threw him a provocative smile. 'Our acquaintance hasn't exactly been noteworthy for your honesty.'

He advanced further into the room. His lips had a slight upward curve and his eyes glittered. He looked like a panther, Teslyn thought, supple and lithe and infinitely dangerous, and she felt the nerves of her spine tingle.

'Ten seconds to get out of that chair,' he said. 'That's all you get.'

She lifted her chin. 'No.'

'Don't say you weren't warned.'

As easily as if she had been a rag doll he scooped her out of the chair and into his arms. Then he was walking out of the office and down the passage that led to the bedrooms.

For a few moments Teslyn tried to struggle. She would not submit to his outrageous behaviour! She balled her hands into fists and pounded them against his chest—without success, because his stride did not falter. It was only when she became conscious of the smell filling her nostrils, a male smell that was so intoxicating that she felt dizzy, that the fight went out of her. Against her cheek Wayne's chest was hard and muscular, and the arm beneath her knees sent a weakness pervading her body. She had been married three years and had thought she understood the meaning of sexual desire. She knew now that until just a few days ago she had never understood it at all.

Gently, very gently, she let her lips rest on the skin exposed by the open V of his shirt. She yearned to slide her lips further, to explore the tantalising ridge of hard muscle. But this contact was as much as she allowed herself. She did not want him to be aware of what she did, and there was the insane hope that her touch was so light that he did not feel her lips.

Inside her room Wayne put her down. 'Pack,' he ordered. She stole a glance at his face and saw nothing in his expression to suggest that he knew what she'd done.

'Quite the masterful man, aren't you?' she murmured.

Unexpectedly he laughed, his teeth very white against his tan. 'I have a feeling, for all you say to the contrary, that you like masterful men. Get packing, Teslyn.'

He was masterful all right, and arrogant and conceited, and she should be furious at the way he treated her. And yet she could not prevent the slight lifting at the corners of her lips or the smile in her eyes. She turned to the wardrobe so that he would not see her face, for the expression would give him a satisfaction he did not deserve.

Half an hour later they had entered the forested lands of Tinarua. At the top of a rise Wayne stopped the car and motioned to her to get out. Together they walked to the edge of the road and Teslyn gasped as she looked down and saw that they were even higher than she'd realised. As at Pinevale, the slope of the mountain fell away from the road, the land dropping to a narrow valley before rising to the next mountain. Everywhere there were trees—tall straight trees, foliage lifting to the afternoon sun. The air was heady with the spicy scent that Teslyn was beginning to know so well.

'It's beautiful,' she said, turning to Wayne.

He was standing beside her, but she had the feeling that his mind was far away, in the forests perhaps, or in the valley where the smoke of the sawmills made a thin spiral in the clear air. She could see his face, and the expression brought a sudden lump to her throat. This was a man who loved the land with a passion that could not be put into words. She did not know why the fact moved her so deeply.

'Mary told me Tinarua is the best plantation in the district,' she said softly.

'I like to think so.' Spoken with confidence and yet not a trace of conceit.

'She said you made it what it is today.'

'The previous owner could have done what I did,' Wayne said abruptly. 'I'll never understand why he let it slide the way he did.

But I understand, Teslyn thought. Had Pinevale gone to Alec he would have let it run down too. He would have regarded it purely as a commercial venture; he would not have given the plantation the extra love and care that it deserved.

'You love this land,' she observed.

'Very much.'

'Have you never wanted anything else?' She was openly curious.

Wayne turned, and his eyes moved over her face, lingering a moment on her mouth before moving to her eyes. 'There are things I want now.' His voice was terse.

A quiver began in Teslyn's spine, she could feel it spreading to her legs, making them weak. 'I . . . we all want things,' she said weakly.

'Sometimes we want the same things.' He stood very

close to her, but he made no move to touch her, and his eyes were unreadable.

'I doubt it.' Her voice shook. And then, needing to change the subject, 'You've been here five years, Wayne?'

'Five years, yes.' His voice had changed, the mood was broken. 'Tinarua is not all I own, Teslyn.'

'There's another plantation?'

'I have interests in hotels and mines. I keep an eye on them, but I have managers to run them. Tinarua is my home. I can't imagine living anywhere else.'

Seeing him here, tall and male and powerful amidst the trees and the mountains that he loved, she could not imagine it either. But this tree-covered slope was only a part of Tinarua. Much as she had not wanted to come here, now she longed to see the rest of it. Wayne's home might tell her more about him, and she knew, quite suddenly, that she wanted to know all she could about him. Even her guilty feelings about Alec could not rid her of the longing to know more.

They went back to the car and drove further. Everywhere there were the signs of activity that Teslyn recognised from Pinevale. Bundles of logs at the roadside waiting to be transported to the sawmills. Once a truck, swaying with the weight of its lumber load. She saw the fire-paths that led through the forests, and the moss and wild flowers beneath the trees. Her window was open, and she took long breaths of the glorious pine-scented air. The city seemed a long way away.

'There it is,' she heard Wayne say, and she turned her eyes to look straight ahead of her.

'The homestead?' she asked when she had caught her breath.

'Yes.' There was a quiet pride in his voice.

Set against the slope of the mountain, the house was built of wood, with huge windows that caught the rays of the afternoon sun. It was a beautiful house, its lines fluid yet strong like its owner, Teslyn thought. Behind it and on all sides were trees, and in front of it was a garden. Shrubs grew in glorious subtropical profusion, poinsettia and hibiscus, and just beneath the window that had to belong to the living-room there was a bed filled solely with pink and white frangipani.

Along the front of the house ran a wide verandah. On it were cane chairs and a round glass-topped table, and pot plants stood on a tall dark cane stand. It would be cool here in summer, Teslyn thought, and a picture came into her mind of Wayne at day's end, relaxing in a long chair with a beer in his hand. Unbidden a new image entered the picture. A woman, sitting beside him, sharing the quiet moments with him. The woman was Teslyn herself.

But that could never be! It was a picture without reality, without a future. With an effort she managed to thrust it from her, glad when they left the verandah and went into the house.

French doors led from the verandah into the living-room—a beautiful room, Teslyn discovered, looking around her. It was big and light, with picture windows on three sides revealing views that were nothing less than spectacular. The room had been furnished in blues and greens, shades that would be cool during the hot summer months of the Lowveld. But it was not an unrelieved coolness, for there were also enlivening splashes of primrose yellow. The furniture was long and low and light-coloured, and though the lines were elegant they seemed to fit in with the rustic atmosphere of the house and its setting. One one side was a lovely

unit holding books and a stereo—she would look at the
books later, when she was alone, Teslyn thought—and
on the walls were some good modern pictures.

'Well?'

She turned around to find him watching her, brown
eyes alert and questioning.

'Hardly the basic bachelor's pad,' she said lightly.

'You like it, then?'

There was no point in sparring with him. Not now,
when the lump that had been in her throat when they
had stood together on the rise had just vanished, and
when her emotions felt raw. Why did she feel like this,
for heaven's sake why? she asked herself, and did not
come up with an answer, at least not with one that was
acceptable to her. What she did know was that she was
in no mood to play games with him.

'I like it very much.'

'I'm glad,' he said softly.

His tone and the warmth in his eyes suggested that
her answer meant something to him. In the face of all
logic that was impossible, but her heart was racing
nevertheless. Whatever she felt for Wayne—and sooner
or later she would have to admit to herself that her
feelings were far from neutral—he felt nothing for her.
At the start, as if she had been in some way to blame
for Alec's neglect of his parents, she had been the butt
of Wayne's contempt, and nothing in his subsequent
behaviour indicated that his attitude had undergone a
real change. True, he had shown her passion, but his
kisses were no more than the physical outlet of a healthy
man. She would be foolish to let herself read more into
them than that.

Besides, even if there was more, if by some wonder
Wayne really did like her more than a little—she shied
away from the word love—there was Alec. Always Alec.

And a guilt that would remain with her till the end of her life.

'Dinner is ready, I believe,' he told her. 'Your case will be taken to your room—I'll show you it later.'

'You have a good cook,' Teslyn commented at the end of the meal, when a dessert made with egg whites and Grand Marnier had melted on her tongue.

'I have.'

'Good managers too. Otherwise you wouldn't be able to leave all your enterprises in their hands.'

'I've always gone for the best people I could find. Money buys service, Teslyn, that's a fact of life.' He fell silent, an odd silence which Teslyn was hesitant to break.

When he spoke again it was in a voice she had never heard him use. 'But there are things money can't buy.'

She was suddenly breathless. 'What do you mean?'

'I think you know.' He reached across the table and took one of her hands in his. 'I want you to stay here.'

Her throat was very tight. 'I am here.'

'I'm not talking about a temporary visit, Teslyn,' he said dryly.

Unable to trust the emotions rushing through her, she could only stare at him. And then some ray of sanity pierced her joy. 'You're still trying to get me into your bed. I won't be your mistress, Wayne.'

The hand that held hers was gentle, but the fingers began a slow stroking that was remarkably sensuous. 'I'm talking about marriage. Marry me, Teslyn.'

CHAPTER EIGHT

THE lump was back in her throat, thicker this time, making it difficult to swallow. Later she would remember that Wayne had said nothing about love. Now there was just the miraculous realisation of a dream she had never allowed herself to acknowledge. She looked at him, and her eyes were so wide, so luminous, that Wayne thought a man could drown in their depths.

'Well?' he asked. 'Teslyn, my dear, don't you want to marry me?'

Of course I do! I want it more than anything in the world. I think I must have wanted it all along.

'Why don't you answer me?' His hand was warm, tantalising. 'You've been a widow long enough. But if you feel you must wait a few months longer I'll fall in line with that. For God's sake, Teslyn, are you holding back because of Alec? If he loved you he'd want you to be happy.'

He didn't love me. He hated me. He delighted in hurting me just because he hated me. But that doesn't remove my guilt, the fact that he was beside himself when I said I was leaving him.

'You can't be feeling guilty about remarrying?' Wayne persisted.

I am guilty. Guilty because if I hadn't insisted on having my way Alec might still be alive. He might not have had the accident.

'You don't know me,' she said, playing for time.

'I think I do.'

'Just over a week—too short a time to know anybody well.'

'We've been together almost constantly. I feel I know you very well indeed.

'You despised me at first,' she reminded him.

He grimaced. 'I'm sorry, and I hope you'll forgive me. I blamed you for Alec's neglect, and that was wrong of me. Teslyn, love, you have courage and spirit. You look at the land and I see the same sort of reverence as I feel myself.'

She shook her head, hoping he'd stop.

'Warmth too—I watched your manner with Mary. Sweetheart, we'd have a good life together. I can give you so much.'

Love is the only thing I want from you, but it's my punishment that I can't accept it.

'Don't go on,' she whispered.

'I'll stop when you say yes.'

'I can't.' Her voice was very low.

His lips tightened. 'I can't accept that.'

'You'll have to.' She looked at him, blue eyes stark with despair. 'Please try to understand.'

He studied her without speaking, meeting her gaze with an intensity that brought a trembling to her entire body. Then he removed his hand from hers and pushed his plate away. It seemed he had lost his appetite. She had lost her own too.

'You haven't seen the house,' he said abruptly.

'I'd like to.' At this moment she didn't care what rooms there were or what they looked like, but it would be a relief to leave the table and the conversation.

The rest of the house was as lovely as the part she'd already seen—a study with an antique desk and beautiful walnut furniture, a rumpus-room with a pool table, then the bedrooms. Teslyn felt herself stiffening as they entered the bedroom wing.

'Your room,' said Wayne, opening a door. He put the suitcase down on the bed and Teslyn just had a fleeting impression of lime and yellow, when he indicated that the tour was not at an end.

She hung back. 'Why don't I get organised?'

'That little case won't take you five minutes to unpack. There's more for you to see.'

His bedroom. And she didn't want to see it. Or yes, she wanted to badly. That part of her mind that she could not seem to control, no matter how hard she tried, wanted to see where Wayne slept, wanted to take in every detail of the room, to touch the bed that she would never sleep in herself. Don't go, a warning voice said, don't go.

'I really think I should unpack,' she tried to say firmly.

A hand closed around her wrist. 'I always know when you're making excuses. Come along.'

There were three other bedrooms before Wayne's. 'Guest-rooms for the moment,' he told her with a wry grin. 'Rooms for our children eventually, I hope.'

So he did not intend to give up easily. Clamping her lips together, she did not give him an answer. From Wayne's expression it appeared he did not expect one.

She steeled herself as he opened the last door. For a moment she stood rigid, unable to move. Then as the hand on her wrist propelled her forward, she took a few steps in.

The master bedroom—a beautiful room, as bright and airy as the rest of the house. Its colours ran the spectrum of the browns, curtains and bedspread in a dusty gold, the thick carpet the shade of rich chocolate. At one end of the room there were two comfortable chairs upholstered in a lighter chocolate. In many ways it was a man's room, and yet it was not masculine. A woman would be happy here, Teslyn thought. *She* would be happy.

Her eyes had taken in, very quickly, the double bed beneath the window, then had skittered away to other details. After a few moments, as if magnetised, she looked back at it.

Wayne had followed the direction of her eyes. 'It's comfortable,' he told her seductively.

'I bet it is,' she said in a choked voice.

'Like to try it?' He sounded as casual as if he was offering her a drink, but when she darted a look at his face she saw an expression in his eyes which was anything but casual.

She wheeled to the door, forgetting that his hand was still on her wrist. 'You don't understand even now, do you?' she blazed at him.

'I do.' His voice was husky. 'That's why I brought you in here.'

It had been a mistake to let him show her this room. She knew it the moment he dropped her wrist and took her in his arms. She tried to get away from his descending head, but that did not seem to matter to him, for his lips found her hair instead. They pushed it back, then found the lobe of an ear and nibbled at it. Teslyn's heart was thudding so hard against her chest that she felt as if it would burst from her rib-cage.

'No!' she protested, twisting her head to look at him.

'Yes, my darling.'

His mouth came down on hers in a kiss that was deep and demanding, the sweetness of it so intense that she gave a stifled moan of pleasure. She could fight him, could tell herself that physical attraction was mere chemistry and meaningless, but the argument became hollow the moment he touched her.

'Relax, darling.' He had just barely lifted his lips

from hers and was whispering into her mouth. 'Enjoy it.'

The order was unnecessary; reasoning took flight as the demands of her body took over. She was not thinking at all as she wound her arms around his neck and pressed herself against him, glorying in the hardness of his body. His own arms tightened, folding her to him. His kiss became even more passionate, and her lips parted willingly as he invaded her mouth, and she returned his kisses with an ardour born of her deepest needs.

His hands began to move over her, sliding from her waist down to her hips, shaping the curves of her body beneath his fingers, moulding her softness against his own hard body. As if they were meant to fit together, to be one person, Teslyn thought wildly.

Wayne lifted his head and looked down at her a moment, his eyes filled with a kind of torment, his breathing ragged. Then he was undoing the buttons of her blouse, the clasp of her bra. Her clothes dropped to the floor, and he was cupping her breasts in his hands, stroking them with a reverence that filled her with awe.

'You're so beautiful. So very beautiful,' he whispered huskily. His fingers had gone to the button at the top of her jeans, and when they too had dropped to the floor, he said, 'Teslyn darling, undress me.'

It was what she wanted. She wanted to be with him, a man and a woman loving each other to the fullest. She opened the buttons of his shirt and pressed her face against his chest, then let her lips taste the hairs that clung to it—unashamedly this time. And then she reached for the buckle of the belt that held up his trousers. There was no shame in her. She loved Wayne, she had known it a long time, but now at last she could acknowledge it to herself. She loved him, and this lovemaking was the most beautiful thing she had ever experienced.

He was breathing fast as he lifted her in his arms and carried her to the bed. Against her cheek she could feel the beat of his heart, and she knew that he wanted her as much as she wanted him. To know that she could affect Wayne in this way was a heady sensation.

He put her down gently, but she could feel the contained passion in his arms. Then he knelt beside her and began to stroke her, his lips following the path of his hands, over her throat and shoulders to her breasts and down to her hips. It became an agony to lie still, and she reached down and pulled his head to her chest.

'You want it too,' he murmured.

She did not answer, her lips were in the thickness of his hair.

He lifted his head and looked down at her, his eyes urgent. 'You do want me.'

She could only nod.

His eyes were urgent. 'I had to bring you here—to this room. At the table I couldn't get through to you.'

'Couldn't get through?' She looked back at him, a little dazed.

'We're right together. We belong together.'

'Wayne. . . .' Memory had returned, and she knew that she had to stop him.

'This is how it will be when we're married,' he murmured, She tried to sit up, but his body, leaning on hers, weighed her down. 'You're a warm loving woman, my darling. We're going to have a wonderful life together.'

Her throat was tight. 'I told you, I can't marry you.' She tried to struggle away from him. Oh God, how could she have let her senses betray her once again to the point where she had almost let Wayne make love to her! 'Let me go. . . .'

His hands moved to her shoulders, pinning her down. Some of the tenderness in his face had given way to hardness. 'Relax.'

'No!'

'I don't know what you're playing at, but you want my love.'

'You don't understand.' Tears were trembling on her lashes.

'Damn sure I don't! You say one thing—in fact "Wayne, don't" seems to be your favourite phrase—but your body says another. You've passion in you, you respond to me every time I touch you. What in God's name is keeping you back?'

'Alec,' she whispered.

He made a sound in his throat. 'You can't keep this up!'

'I have to.'

'No! You're a healthy young girl.' He began to touch her again, his hands on her breasts, coaxing and receiving a response from hardening nipples. 'You have normal needs, my darling.'

She couldn't deny it. He was right when he said that her body spoke for her every time. 'I do want you,' she whispered over tears, 'but I'm not ready for this yet.'

'When will you be?'

Probably never. I want you so badly that I hurt with wanting. But I can't have you.

'I don't know,' she said.

He bent to kiss her, and she had to stiffen her spine to stop herself arching toward him. Somehow she managed to keep from responding to the kiss.

Wayne drew himself up. 'This isn't natural!'

'It's the only way.'

The hands on her breasts hardened, biting into the

soft flesh. 'You're so young, Teslyn. How old are you, twenty-one? You can't go on grieving for ever.'

'Perhaps it won't be for ever,' she lied.

'Alec must have been some man,' Wayne muttered through clenched teeth.

'He was.' At least that much was true.

'I can accept that you loved him, that he loved you— my God, you're so lovely that any man would love you! But were things so special between you that you can never love again?'

Until I met you I never knew what it was to love a man, to thrill to his touch, to ache, to respond to his lovemaking. I never knew it could be so wonderful.

'I don't want to talk about it,' she managed.

For a long moment he was silent. He looked down at her, studying her face so intently that it was as if he tried to read what was in her mind.

'I'll give you time,' he conceded at length. 'You can't remain a widow, and you won't. But I will give you time.'

Standing up, he took his clothes and made for the door of the bathroom. 'I'm going to dress. Do the same, please. I want you, Teslyn, and I have just so much control.'

The next few days were bittersweet. Early each morning Wayne accompanied Teslyn to Pinevale. He could have driven her there, but the weather was fine and it was more fun to go on horseback. Riding through the forests, with the branches brushing her arms with dew, with the early morning sun in her face and the wind pulling at her hair, Teslyn knew that she had never felt more exhilarated.

The days were spent in the Pinevale farm office, attending to the pile of paper matter as best as she could. Now and then she made her way to the sawmills, and the men would ask her questions. It was as if, with Jim and Mary absent, they felt they could turn to her, and she found their confidence touching. Not that she had the answers—after so short an acquaintance with the timber industry it was obvious that she surely knew less than those who had worked in the forests all their lives—but Wayne was always available. When something was urgent she phoned him. Otherwise she waited until he came for her in the late afternoon, and while they rode back to Tinarua he told her all she had to know.

Back at Tinarua she would shower and change and then she would go walking with Wayne. Walks that were spectacularly lovely, for Wayne knew all the best places. He led her through quiet forest paths, where moss and fallen pine-needles were soft underfoot and the scents of the trees and the wild flowers were like perfume in the still air. He showed her views that were like none she had ever seen—panoramic vistas of mountains and valleys, of stark cliffs and tumbling waterfalls. And when she thought she had seen all there was to see, there was always more.

Teslyn knew she had never been happier than she was now, working at Pinevale and spending her leisure time with the man whom she loved more than life itself.

Mixed in with the happiness there was sadness too, a feeling of poignancy. A sense that every hour, every minute, was precious. A knowledge that this life was temporary, that one day it would end. For end it must. Mary and Jim would come back to Pinevale and Teslyn would go back there. Probably soon, because Mary had phoned and said the operation had been a success. And some time, though it was still too early to say when, Teslyn would return to the city. It was true that Alec's parents had wanted her at Pinevale even before the accident, but she had always known that a visit was all it could be.

At Pinevale memories of Alec would be with her always. She slept in his old room, his parents would want to talk about him. Even away from Pinevale she could never forget what had happened, but at least she hoped the time would come when the torment would grow less.

The constant reminders of Alec were not the only reason why she must leave the Lowveld. She loved Wayne. She would always love him. But the thought of being constantly within riding distance of him would pose a special torment of its own. Since the evening in his bedroom he had not tried to make love to her again. There were times when he touched her, a caress on her cheek, a brushing of fingers on her arm. A kiss, nothing more. Teslyn sensed that he was keeping himself deliberately distant from her; that he felt he was giving her time to come to terms with the facts of a new life.

She must enjoy this time to the fullest, she decided, for there would be never anything like it again. At first she had tried to tell herself that what she felt for Wayne was just chemistry. She knew that she loved him very much. There was chemistry, yes, a leaping of the senses when he was near, a sexual desire and awareness that was electrifying. But there was also a deep and abiding love that was a very different emotion from the infatuation she had experienced with Alec. This was the love of a woman for a man, and it would never leave her.

There were memories that she would take with her when she left here. Wayne on his stallion, exerting an easy authority over the powerful animal. Wayne at dusk, when the golden rays of the setting sun caught the dark head and fired it with light. Wayne laughing at something she'd said, his eyes sparkling with warmth, his teeth white and strong against the rugged tanned face. And the moments when he had made love to her. Those were the most precious memories of all. She would cherish them all her life.

On the day that Mary came back to Pinevale Teslyn did not ride to the plantation with Wayne. They went by car, and her suitcase was on the back seat.

A little way from the homestead he slowed the car, and reached for her hand. 'This isn't goodbye,' he said.

She smiled at him. 'Of course not.'

'Nor is it a permanent departure from Tinarua.'

'You don't give up easily,' she commented dryly.

'Not when I want something badly.' The brown eyes darkened. 'I want you, darling.'

'Wayne. . . .' Her hand stiffened in his.

'I've said I'd give you time.' He released her and gave his attention back to the wheel. 'Take all the time you need.'

If only she really could marry him! The days at Tinarua had shown her how wonderful life with Wayne could be. It was not hard to picture marriage—living in the loveliness of the timber plantation, looking after the homestead, working with Wayne for she found it hard to be idle. And at night, lying with him in the double bed in the chocolate-brown room. Loving him. Teslyn choked down a small cry of pain and fixed her eyes to the window.

Mary came down the steps of the house to greet them, and it was like the first time—could it be such a short while ago?—and yet it was not like it at all. Pinevale had become a kind of home, and Mary was a person she liked very much.

'How's Jim?' Teslyn and Wayne asked the question simultaneously and all three laughed. It was easy to laugh with Mary looking so happy.

'Just fine. Raring to come home. Oh, you men,' Mary scolded Wayne, 'you're all the same, bless you—impatient to be back at work the moment you're feeling halfway okay.'

'Teslyn did a fine job while you were away.' Wayne's words were addressed to Mary, but his eyes were on the girl at his side, and at his praise she felt a surge of pride.

'I know, I just looked in at the office. You took a load from my mind, dear—both our minds. Jim can't wait to meet you.'

Wayne was invited to have lunch at Pinevale, but he declined. As Teslyn watched him drive away she felt as if a chapter of her life had ended. No need to feel so sad about leaving Tinarua, she tried to tell herself. After all, if she was sad now, how would she feel when she left the Lowveld never to return? Lifting her chin, she joined her mother-in-law in the kitchen.

There was much to talk about, and Teslyn was glad. In the weeks and months ahead she would have to find a way of coping without Wayne. Just as well to begin now.

'Friday?' she asked, having caught the tail end of a sentence. 'Did you say Jim will be home Friday?'

'Just enough time to get some *melktert* baked,' Mary said happily. 'Did you know that was his favourite cake?'

Shrugging away her sadness, Teslyn smiled. 'I didn't. Mary, do you know you're a different woman from the one I met a week ago?'

Weathered eyes took on added warmth. 'Yes, my dear, that I am. With my Jim so ill I could hardly think straight.'

'You love him very much,' Teslyn said softly, wondering how it must be to live for thirty odd years with a man one loved.

'Very much. That's why. . . .' Mary stopped. When she went on her eyes were thoughtful. 'We've had our ups and downs—who hasn't? Happiness, such happiness. Also great sorrow.' She was thinking of Alec, Teslyn know, and held her breath. 'But it's been a good marriage,' Mary went on. 'Through it all, it's been good.' .

Alec had been the product of this marriage. How was it possible? She would never know, Teslyn understood suddenly. Perhaps if she probed she would find the answer. There could be childhood experiences she knew nothing about, ones that had left permanent scars on a sensitive boy. But she had no intention of probing: Mary and Jim had loved their son and their memories were all they had left of him. She would not add to their grief.

'It will be an exciting week, all in all,' Mary told her.

'Oh?'

'Our nephew is coming back to Pinevale.'

'Joshua?' queried Teslyn.

'Alec told you about him?'

Not a word. Just as he didn't care enough to tell me about his wonderful mother and the plantation that was his home.

'Wayne and I rode past his house.' She doubted whether Mary had registered the evasion.

There was a sudden alertness in Mary's expression. 'And you know the set-up at Pinevale?'

Teslyn hesitated. 'A little. Joshua's father and Jim were brothers, and they inherited the plantation together.'

'Yes, that's right.' Mary looked as if she was about

to say something more, then she seemed to change her mind.

'Joshua was in Paris, Wayne said.'

'Studying art.' A small shake of the head. 'A gifted young man, though what he thought he'd do with art at Pinevale I can't imagine. The important thing is, Joshua's coming back.'

'He's heard about Jim?'

'I phoned him. He understood how hard it is for us on our own, even with your help. My heavens, it will be good to see him again!'

'When is he coming?' asked Teslyn.

'Monday. Joshua is a fine person, Teslyn. I think you'll like him.'

They began to bake the same day. Not only the *melktert* that was Jim's favourite, but also *koeksusters* and scones and *beskuit*, the hard biscuit that was so tasty with a hot cup of tea. Soon every cake tin in the big farmhouse pantry had been filled. With some amusement Teslyn wondered who would eat all this food, but Mary was in her element. Jim and Joshua were coming back home, and the abundance of baked food was a part of their welcome.

Wayne rode over two days later and Teslyn was taut with joy at the sight of him. So much for strength of will, she told herself wryly.

He had come to talk to Mary, to brief her on certain happenings in the timber industry. But there were also a few minutes when he was alone with Teslyn.

'You look pale and fragile,' he told her, his eyes lingering on her face.

She shot him a mock demure look from beneath long curling lashes. 'How flattering!'

A hand stroked her cheek. 'Are you feeling well?'

She could have told him that she had slept very little

since leaving Tinarua, and that when she did he filled her dreams. She could have said that forgetting him was going to be an impossibility, and that the knowledge was painful. Instead she smiled. 'We've been baking. Hard work, Wayne!'

He did not look convinced, but all he said was, 'Tinarua seems very empty since you went.'

Her heart leaped. 'You really are a flatterer.'

'No, darling.' The hand left her cheek and descended to her throat, sliding to the hollow where the pulse beat a rapid tattoo. 'I'm just a man who feels awfully frustrated.'

'Wayne. . . .'

'Wayne, Wayne,' he said mockingly. 'Please, Wayne. Don't, Wayne. I mean to marry you, Teslyn.'

'You know how I feel,' she said in a choked voice.

'Sooner or later.'

'I can't. You know that. . . .'

'Preferably sooner.'

'You're impossible!' she laughed over a sob that she couldn't suppress.

'And you are ambivalent,' he told her. 'You want me as much as I want you, Teslyn. But for some reason you feel you can't let yourself give in.'

'You know the reason,' she reminded him seriously.

'I know what you tell me.' His voice was sombre. 'I respect your feelings, Teslyn, but I won't give up. I promised you time, darling, but I didn't promise you forever.'

CHAPTER NINE

TESLYN accompanied Mary to the hospital. In the foyer several people were sitting, three of them men, and even before she saw the bandaged hand Teslyn knew at first glance which man was Jim. Tall and broad-set, his head was carried at an angle she knew well, and the nose and the shape of the mouth were familiar.

But the resemblance to Alec was superficial, she realised, as Mary made the introductions. Alec had been debonair and sophisticated, a man of the world who liked to dazzle those around him with his wit and charm—and succeeded only too well she conceded rue-fully, remembering how overwhelmed she had been at their first meeting.

But if Alec had been a man of the city, his father was of the country. Even in a suit and on paved streets he would have the appearance of a farmer. He looked placid and stolid, a man to rely on in an emergency. His eyes were kind and his face weathered, much like Mary's, Teslyn realised after a moment. Perhaps it was true that couples who had lived together many years began to resemble each other. There would have to be love in that kind of living, for how else could there be the harmony that linked two souls? It was a harmony that had never existed between Alec and herself, never could have done so.

She thought of Wayne.

'So this is our Teslyn.' Jim spoke in a low slow voice. He looked at her for a long moment, thoughtfully, before reaching for her and folding her in a hug.

'I'm so glad you're better,' Teslyn smiled up at him when he had released her, her throat a little tight from his warmth and his unexpected use of the word 'our'.

'I'm much better, yes, in fact a few weeks more and this hand of mine will be right back to normal.' He looked down at the bandage, then at his wife. 'She's even prettier than you said, Mary. Our son had good taste, don't you think?'

'In more ways than one. Just wait till you hear how Teslyn coped at Pinevale. Come along, old man, let's get out of this place and take you home.'

As she walked with them to the car-park, listening silently while they talked, Teslyn marvelled at the ease and affection that existed between Jim and Mary. An affection that enfolded her too, she understood with amazement. They had cause enough to dislike her, the girl who had spoken to them only once after Alec had died and who had not thought to let them know her address. Yet they accepted her. More than that, they actually liked her.

It was a liking that was based on fraud, she thought unhappily, as she sat in the back seat—she had insisted Jim be in front with Mary—and stared out of the window at the rolling timber lands. No matter what Alec had been, no matter how he had behaved, he had been their son, their only child. They had loved him— she had only to hear Mary speak of him to know quite how strong and unconditional that love had been. Because she had been his wife they had taken her to their hearts with an outpouring of warmth and affection she had never anticipated. How they would hate her if they knew the truth!

Of course Teslyn did not know the exact events of that night. She never would. But what other explanation could there be for the disaster? Alec had always been a fast driver, it was in his nature to enjoy the recklessness and danger of high speed. Yet his reactions had been razor-sharp, his sense of survival strong. It was out of character that he would drive his car into a lamp-post.

'So you really like Pinevale?' she heard Jim ask.

She turned her eyes from the window. 'Very much.'

'It's as Alec described it?'

She could not tell these two very nice people that their son had never mentioned his home. She forced a smile. 'Oh yes, except that it's even more beautiful.'

The two in the front seat exchanged a glance. Then Jim turned back. '*Ja, meisie-kind*, it is beautiful. This place has been our home since we were married and we've never had the wish to live anywhere else.'

The homecoming was a joyful one. Jim was visibly happy to be back at Pinevale. He stared silently out of the window as they came through the gates and drove along the forest road to the homestead. From where she sat Teslyn could see the expression on the sideways-turned face. It was as if every tree was a special friend, she thought, moved. Here was a man who loved his land with the passion that some reserved for women. Wayne looked a little like this when he rode his horse along the trails of Tinarua. Her throat thickened again as she turned away from an emotion that was private in its intensity.

Wayne was invited for tea. His pleasure at seeing Jim well and back at Pinevale was evident. He was able to stay just long enough to taste Mary's *melktert* and Teslyn's *koeksusters*, and to pronounce them both excellent, and then he had to go. This time Teslyn had no chance to be alone with him, and she did not know whether the fact made her relieved or sorry. A bit of both, she decided, deliberately pouring herself another cup of tea.

Every moment with Wayne was precious, but soon she would be leaving Pinevale; it was time she got used to the idea of leaving the man she loved. If she did not it would be almost impossible to pick up the threads of her old life with any hope of success.

'So Joshua is coming on Monday,' said Jim when Wayne had gone.

'Right.'

There was another exchange of glances between Mary and Jim. Then Mary said, 'Teslyn dear, we want to talk to you.'

She looked once more at Jim, then back at Teslyn. 'It's about Pinevale. You know a little of the legal set-up here—that Jim and his brother Marius were equal owners of the plantation. Joshua owns his father's share now. Our share would have gone to Alec.'

Mary stopped a moment, and unbidden a picture came into Teslyn's mind. Wayne on the stallion, outside a neglected farmhouse, his tone sardonic as he hinted at a possibility that she had found unpalatable.

'With our son gone,' Mary went on, 'it will go to you, Teslyn.'

Like one transfixed, Teslyn stared at Mary, then her eyes went to Jim. They were joking—they had to be. She'd thought Wayne was just trying to provoke her with his hints, but Mary and Jim looked serious. Teslyn felt quite cold, as if the bars of a cage had begun to close around her.

She swallowed hard before shaking her head. 'I can't accept it.'

'Can't accept? Why not, *meisie-kind*?' Jim looked puzzled, even a little hurt.

She didn't want to hurt him, she didn't want to hurt

either of them. Yet what they proposed was impossible.

'You hardly know me,' she managed.

'I think I do,' said Mary. 'Sometimes it doesn't take long to know a person. You're a good girl, kind and level-headed too.'

'There must be somebody else?' Teslyn wondered if they sensed her despair.

'Nobody.'

'Family.'

'There was only Alec,' Mary said simply. 'You were Alec's wife.'

'I don't understand,' said Jim. 'You said this morning you love Pinevale.'

'Oh, I do—I do! But I didn't realise your intentions.'

'Weren't they obvious?' Mary wanted to know.

'No. I never thought. . . . And why tonight? You've only just arrived back home, Jim.'

'Joshua's coming back.' Mary gave her the answer. 'In the light of his return we felt you should know.'

You should be prepared, was how the words sounded. Prepared for what? Teslyn had no clear idea. All she knew was that she could under no circumstances become half owner of the plantation that had once been Alec's home.

'You do understand?' Jim asked anxiously.

'Let the child be,' Mary soothed. 'This has been a shock to her. She needs time to think.'

Teslyn was still thinking two days later when Joshua was due to arrive. Thoughts whirled in her head like leaves in a whirlwind. She was in a trap. She had to get out of it, and she had to do so without hurting Mary and Jim.

Mary had intended driving to the station to fetch her nephew, but a neighbouring farmer who had business in that direction offered to bring Joshua back with him.

He arrived a little before lunch, and as he left the car and walked up the steps to the stoep Teslyn had her second shock in a few days—a worse shock by far than the news that half of Pinevale would one day be hers.

For one appalling moment she thought that Alec had returned to her. And then she saw that it was not Alec at all, but a man who looked just like him. The same stocky figure, the same colour hair and bearded face. He could have been Alec's twin.

Her shock was intense, yet by the time Mary and Jim had finished hugging Joshua she had managed to assume at least an outward composure. Though the colour had drained from her face she was able to smile when they were being introduced.

To celebrate Joshua's homecoming there were drinks before lunch. Joshua came up to Teslyn, a glass of wine in his hand.

'I was so sorry to hear about Alec,' he said in a low voice.

'I know, thank you.'

'You'd been married how long? Two years?'

'Three.'

'No children?'

'No.' Deciding to turn the drift of the conversation away from herself, she observed, 'You must have grown up with Alec.'

'Yes. He was a little older than me. We'd hang around together quite a bit, except when he had friends,' Joshua hesitated a moment—'then he was sometimes impatient. Natural enough, I suppose.'

Perhaps, perhaps not, depending on the circumstances. Certainly it would have been natural with Alec.

'We had some good fun, though.' He smiled. 'I remember the time we were chased by an enraged bull—our own fault for having trespassed where we had no right. But you'd know all about that misdemeanour, of course.'

She knew nothing about it. 'Tell me anyway,' she invited.

'We were looking for excitement,' Joshua said, 'and the idea of going near the bull seemed so daring. . . .'

Alec's voice, she marvelled as he talked. Alec's smile. If there were differences, as there must be, they were not apparent because the similarities were so striking. Was it irony, she wondered, that Alec's double had come here to haunt her?

'I didn't know when I came back to Pinevale that I'd find such enchanting company.' She came out of her thoughts to find Joshua looking at her, a male sort of look that seemed to take in every detail of her appearance.

Teslyn tensed. 'I don't think I'll be here much longer.'

It had grown very quiet in the room, and seeing their eyes on her, she realised that Jim and Mary had heard what she'd said.

'We want you to stay.' This from Mary.

'I know.' She looked around her a little wildly, 'But I have a job in the city, a home.'

'We were hoping that this would be your home now, Teslyn,' Jim put in quietly. 'You know that.'

The last thing Teslyn wanted was to hurt Alec's parents. On the other hand she felt as if the bars of the trap had tightened even more in the last hour. If Jim and Mary had never mentioned the inheritance, perhaps she would not feel quite so confined.

'I love Pinevale,' she said gently, 'and I have no intention of leaving while you need me. But I do have a job. . . .'

'I think I know what Teslyn is trying to say,' Mary interrupted. 'We pulled her out of one life and into another, old man. She left obligations behind her, loyalties.'

'You want to settle things.' Jim's face cleared.

No point in carrying the discussion further, in telling them how she felt. Not at this moment. She would cause further pain and she would achieve nothing. Until Jim was quite better—though his arm had healed and he looked well enough, that would take time—Teslyn would remain at Pinevale to help where she could. She owed Alec's parents that much.

Eventually, however, speech would become essential. She would have to make it clear that she could not accept a half share of the farm. After that she would make plans to leave.

She was glad when they left the stoep and went into the dining-room for lunch. Quite naturally the conversation turned away from herself. Joshua had been in Paris more than two years, and his uncle and aunt were keen to hear all his news. Soon Teslyn found herself equally interested. Joshua had a sense of humour coupled with a way with words, so that even the smallest anecdote was absorbing.

The meal ended, Teslyn helped Mary in the kitchen. Afterwards she left the house and went into the garden, avoiding the stoep where Jim and Joshua were once more talking.

She was filled with a strange restlessness, and without conscious thought she took the path that led to the stables. Toby, the horse she had ridden with Wayne, was in the paddock. As Teslyn climbed over the white-painted fence, the horse whinnyed and lifted its head. Teslyn spent a few moments stroking the soft nuzzle, and wished she had thought of bringing sugar or carrots along with her.

At one end of the paddock a stable-hand was sweeping. With the same impulsiveness that had brought her this way, Teslyn approached the man and asked him to saddle Toby.

Fifteen minutes later she was on a trail that led through the forests. As always there was a slight breeze, and as it cooled her hot cheeks and played in her hair she let out an exclamation of delight. Her work at Pinevale kept her busy, but there was always some spare time, especially at the end of the day, before the sun began to set; in future she would use it more often to go riding.

She spurred Toby to a trot, reining in only when the path forked. One way led in a wide circle back to the stables, the other, Teslyn remembered, went to Tinarua. She hesitated only a minute before making her choice.

Wayne was at the sawmills. Most of the men had gone home for the day, and he stood talking to the foreman. At the sound of the hooves he turned. For a moment he looked astonished, and then delight creased his face.

'How very nice!' he laughed up at her.

'You don't mind?'

'What an idiotic question! Don't get down, Teslyn, I was just leaving myself. We'll ride back to the homestead together.'

She waited while Wayne and the foreman finished their discussion, and then the tall figure mounted the stallion.

'What brings you?' he wanted to know when they had

left the sawmills behind them.

'Just riding this way. I thought I'd drop in and say hello.'

'Disappointing. I thought you'd come over to tell me that you'd changed your mind about marrying me.' He was laughing, but when she looked up, heart thudding, she saw that his eyes were intent.

'That's not the reason,' she denied unsteadily.

'Pity. But one day, sweetheart, I hope it will be.' He watched her a moment, his expression alert. 'Did Joshua arrive today?'

'Yes.'

'Shouldn't you be at Pinevale? The return of the prodigal nephew must be quite an event.'

'It is.' She looked away.

The horses were close together, proceeding at a slow walk on the wide stretch of path. Wayne reached across to put his hand on one of Teslyny's. 'Why did you come?' he asked quietly.

'I . . . I wanted to be alone a while.'

'Joshua upset you?'

Terribly. Every time I look at him I feel as if Alec had come back to punish me.

'Of course not,' she said lightly. She took a breath. 'Wayne, I have to talk to you.'

The eyes that studied her, taking in flushed cheeks and a troubled expression, were steady. 'Easier to talk at the house,' he said crisply, and spurred the stallion to a canter.

Leaving the horses at the stables, they walked together to the homestead. While Wayne went inside to fetch drinks, Teslyn stood at the low stone wall of the verandah and gazed across the valley. The late afternoon sun had caught the tops of the trees, making a panorama of green-gold translucence. It was a scene that she had come to know well during her short stay at Tinarua, one that moved her very much. This was like coming home, she thought—only to realise a moment later that Tinarua was anything but home; it was the one thing it never could be.

Wayne came outside with two glasses of beer shandy, and they sat down on chairs that took in the view. 'I'm ready to listen,' he prompted quietly.

She came straight to the point. 'Jim and Mary want to leave me their share of Pinevale.'

'Ah.' There was no surprise in his tone.

'You knew,' she said after a moment.

He looked at her. 'You must have known it too.'

'You once hinted. . . .'

'You said you didn't believe me.'

'That's right, I didn't.'

His expression was more intense than before. 'Even without me, wouldn't you have guessed?'

She stared at him, a sick feeling spreading inside her. 'No. Wayne, did you really think I had?'

His eyes held hers levelly—as if, Teslyn thought, he tried to read the very depths of her soul. And then something changed in his face, and his eyes lit with a warmth that reached to her heart.

'I thought you must have. In the circumstances it was so obvious, but I see I was wrong.'

'I know what you said, but in fact I had no idea.' And then, 'Wayne, did you think I came to Pinevale because I was fortune-hunting?'

'People have done that sort of thing before now.' He said it without expression.

'I'm not like that.' Angrily she jumped to her feet. 'If you don't understand that, you don't understand me at all.'

'I do.'

'No! That first day, when you showed me Joshua's house, you were so bitter.'

'I was testing you.'

She looked at him in disgust. 'You should have known without that.'

'I should have, and I'm sorry.'

Wayne sorry? She took a quick step away.

He caught her hand, drawing her back. 'Don't go. Not yet.'

'I must.' Her blood was racing, but she tried to resist him.

As always, his strength was greater than hers. He drew her down and away from the chair where she had been sitting, on to his lap instead. 'You wanted to talk,' he said, when she was still. 'I have something I need to say too.'

Through his shirt she could feel the warmth of his body, and the sweat of a man who had spent hours doing work he enjoyed. Desire started deep inside her and she longed to press herself against him. It was hard to concentrate on his words.

'There was a time when I thought you were selfish and inconsiderate. Alec had ignored his parents, and after his death, except for that one call, you behaved as if they didn't exist.'

'I know, but I. . . .'

'Hush, sweetheart, let me finish.' She felt his lips in her hair, and as the sweetness spread through her she was content to be silent. 'All that was before I got to know you. But I do know you now. Whatever my prejudices may have been at the start I haven't given them a thought for a long time. You *are* warm and kind. Why do you think I want you to be my wife?'

I'd hoped you loved me, she thought dully. If all you want is a girl who's warm and kind—almost the same words Mary used to describe me—there must be many who fit the bill. In any event, I can't be your wife, so it's just as well you don't love me.

'But you didn't come here to talk about marrying me,' Wayne was saying. 'You're here about Pinevale.'

She pushed herself a little away from him. 'That's right. I don't want that share.'

He studied her for a long moment. Then he asked, 'Why not?'

'It's not for me, Wayne. My life is in the city.'

'I'd like to think otherwise.'

'I can't stay here in the Lowveld,' she protested, a little wildly.

'Did you say that to Jim and Mary?'

'Yes.'

'How did they take it?'

'Jim was upset, and then Mary said the news of the inheritance had been a shock for me, that I needed time to think about it.'

'Was it a shock?'

'Yes.'

'Why, Teslyn, why?'

She couldn't tell him. Not without going into the story of her marriage, and that was the one thing she could not do. Had never been able to do, right from the beginning.

'You wouldn't understand,' she said simply.

He was silent a moment before saying, 'Perhaps I might if you gave me a chance. I have a feeling Alec comes into it, somewhere. Ah, I felt you shudder.'

'I don't want to talk about it any more.' She buried her face in his chest, closing her eyes and letting the little hairs of his body brush against her lids.

He put his arms around her and held her to him, and once more she could feel his lips in her hair. She shouldn't let herself enjoy this, Teslyn thought, and at the same time she wished they need never draw apart.

At length he released her, and putting his hands on each side of her head, cupping her face, he drew her back just far enough so that he could look into her eyes. 'I don't understand,' he said very softly. 'I don't pretend that I do. But you've proved you're not a fortune-hunter.'

'I never have been.' She wondered that it should hurt so much that he had once thought badly of her.

'I know.' He grinned suddenly, the wicked grin that did such alarming things to her nerve-stream. 'Tell me about Joshua.'

I don't think I can stand living at Pinevale now that he's there.

'He seems a nice person,' she said lightly.

'Keep thinking of him as nice.'

She stared at him, caught by his tone. 'Why?'

'You've called me some awful names, Teslyn darling, but you've also admitted that you want me. One thing you've never called me is nice.'

She lifted her chin, her eyes dancing him a laughing challenge. 'You are definitely not nice, Wayne North.'

'Thank God for that. Don't go falling in love with Joshua, Teslyn.'

She suppressed another shudder. 'No chance of that!'

'Good. I'd like to keep you here all night, my darling, and one day I will, no matter how much you protest. But it's getting dark, and I won't have you riding the trails at night.'

She had not noticed the setting sun. When she was with Wayne it was as if he obscured her consciousness to everything except himself.

'You're right,' she agreed, 'I should be going.'

'I'm riding with you.'

He nudged her to her feet, then stood up as well. As

she made to move away from him, he pulled her to him again. His kiss was deep and searching, and as he folded her to him, welding her to the angular lines of his body, her resistance, always low where Wayne was concerned, crumbled. She trembled with longing as she kissed him back with all the passion that was bottled inside her. It was an ardent meeting of mouths and arms, a joyous exploration of which, it seemed, they could never get enough.

When Wayne lifted his head, his breathing was ragged. 'Let's go inside, I'll drive you back later.'

Teslyn thanked God for the sanity that came to her when she needed it, even though it should not have deserted her in the first place.

'My horse——' she began.

'I'll get it back to Pinevale.'

'No.' She put her hands against his chest. 'Wayne, I really do have to go.'

'Do you know what you've done to me?'

'Yes.' Her breathing was equally ragged. 'I shouldn't have let it happen.'

'It's right for us.' He began brushing fresh kisses over her throat and cheeks, working his way to her mouth. Her longing was like nothing she had ever experienced before.

'Teslyn darling, can't you feel this is right?'

It was very hard to retain control. 'It isn't.'

'Yes!'

'No. Not now. . . .' She looked at the rugged face, at the sensuous lips that gave her such intense pleasure. 'Wayne, I have to go.'

His eyes hardened. 'Go quickly, then. Because if you don't I'll have you in my bed notwithstanding your scruples.'

*

Joshua showed signs of wanting to linger in the living-room with Teslyn after Jim and Mary went to bed. She made fatigue the excuse for her own early retiring. More than ever tonight Joshua reminded her of Alec, and she could not face being alone with him. But she spoke to him gently, careful that the excuse should not have the sound of a rebuff—and wondered if there had been times when she could have been more gentle with Alec.

Reaching her room, she found she was not at all tired. The ride back from Tinarua—Wayne had insisted on riding with her—had been exhilarating, and the very last thing she felt like at this moment was bed.

Yet despite the minutes in Wayne's arms, for once her thoughts were not of him but of Joshua. It was uncanny that one man could look so much like another, and the strange thing was that nobody had remarked on the resemblance. But perhaps it was not so strange after all. She knew already that the only pictures Alec's parents had of him were ones taken long ago. It seemed they had never seen him without a beard. Wayne had never known Alec at all.

Suddenly she remembered the photo. She had kept it for Jim's homecoming, meaning to give it to Alec's parents then, but somehow in the excitement she had forgotten. But it did not matter that she had missed her chance, as Mary had a birthday coming up next month; she would give it to them then.

For the first time since coming to Pinevale she felt an urge to look at the photo. It was still in her suitcase, in the pocket of the lining where she had packed it.

Alec, three years ago. About a month after their marriage. Lolling on the grass with the sun on his face. He was laughing, and Teslyn remembered that the friend who had been with them had just made a joke. In the left-hand corner of the photo was the scrawled inscription, 'To Teslyn, from Alec.'

The man in the photo bore no resemblance at all to the boy whose picture stood in the living-room of Pinevale to the teenager who had once inhabited this room. He did look like Joshua.

Her fingers trembled as she put the photo away, not in the suitcase this time, but among her clothes in a drawer of her cupboard. She would see it there, and would not forget to give it to Mary on her birthday.

It soon became evident to Teslyn that Joshua liked her. Jim and Mary seemed to look upon his growing affection with approval, and Teslyn did not wonder long at the reason.

'You're so young, my dear,' Mary said one morning. 'You'll marry again.'

'Perhaps.' Teslyn's reply was noncommittal.

'You like Joshua, don't you?'

'Of course.' She looked disbelievingly at her mother-in-law. 'Mary, you're not suggesting I marry Joshua?'

'You could do worse.'

'But that's absurd!' Her voice was taut. 'My golly, here you're matchmaking, and marriage is probably the furthest thing from Joshua's mind!'

'He likes you—very much, I think.'

'This is ridiculous!'

'Such a marriage,' Mary said levelly, 'would be a good thing.'

Teslyn drew breath as she caught the gist of her meaning. 'For Pinevale?'

'*Ja*. This division of ownership, it has its problems.'

'You're forgetting Alec,' Teslyn said dully.

'No, child, I forget nothing. Alec was my son, how could I forget? But you've mourned long enough. Alec would wish you to be happy.'

And that's where you're wrong, Teslyn thought, as the iciness of horror gripped her and spread through her body. She would never marry again, neither Wayne whom she loved more than she had ever thought she could love a man, nor Joshua who repelled her through no fault of his own.

'I don't want to talk about it,' she said in a low voice.

'I'm sorry, I didn't mean to upset you.' Mary was remorseful, but her thoughtful expression indicated that the subject would not be forgotten.

As they began to talk instead of changes in the timber industry, Teslyn wondered how soon she would be able to leave Pinevale without letting down the two people she liked so much.

The question was even more on her mind when Joshua asked her to go walking with him. He was taking up more and more of her leisure time, and though she could have refused him, she did not. Joshua was nice, she thought, very nice. As with Mary and Jim, she had no wish to hurt him. But more than that, Joshua was symbolic of Alec, and however much she tried to push the memories from her mind, Teslyn knew that she would never understand the extent to which her rejection of Alec had been to blame for his behaviour. The worst rejection had been the last one, for it had spelled finality. And had brought with it a horrible finality of its own that she had not foreseen.

Round and round went her thoughts. Almost a year after Alec's death she had thought that she was coming to peace with herself, and now at Pinevale the nightmare had begun again. If only she could put Alec's home and the man who reminded her so much of Alec behind her—but she owed it to Jim and Mary to stay. At least for a while.

CHAPTER TEN

'PHONE call for you, Teslyn,' Jim called, early one Sunday morning.

'Get your riding clothes on, sweetheart,' Wayne's laughing voice ordered, and Teslyn, who had not spoken to him for a few days, felt her blood race with happiness.

'Why?' she wanted to know.

'Because we'll go riding, you and I. And then we're coming back to Tinarua for brunch.'

And he would make love to her, and this time perhaps she might not have the capacity to resist him. Might not? Would not! She wanted him so much; just the sound of his voice was enough to provoke an anguish of longing.

'Wayne, I can't,' she protested.

'I'm coming for you in half an hour.' His voice was warm and vital and sexy.

'I'm sorry.'

'Why can't you, for heaven's sake?' For the first time he sounded impatient. 'It's Sunday. You're not working. Have you been outside yet? It's a perfect day.'

Too perfect. That was the trouble, Teslyn thought. There were too many complications in her life now—an inheritance which she did not want, a man who haunted her with his appearance. And another man, whom she loved more than life itself, and with whom there was no future.

'I really can't. I . . . I'm going to be busy.'

Silence; a silence that seemed to crackle through the

wire. Then Wayne said on a hard note, 'You're frightened.'

'Don't be absurd!'

'Is it absurd?' he drawled.

'Well, of course.' She clutched the telephone so tightly that her knuckles were white.

'You think we'll end up making love.'

'That is what happens each time we meet,' she responded tautly.

'And you can't handle it.'

'Wayne. . . .'

'I promised you time, my love.' A new inflection. 'That's what you get. But not too much time. I'm a man, darling, and I want you.'

'I know.'

'I want you in my bed and in my house and in my life.'

Her throat was so dry that she could hardly talk. Somehow she managed to say, 'I have to go now, Wayne. Goodbye.'

She started at the telephone as a click sounded at the other end of the line. Had she been very foolish to refuse the invitation? How many more free days would there be before she left Pinevale? Every minute spent with Wayne was precious, and she knew she would always cherish the memories of their times together. The horseback rides through the forests, the walks in the veld, the bathtub with the soap-bubbles sliding away from her; the moments, timeless moments, wrapped in Wayne's arms. These were the memories that would remain with her long after she had left the plantation and gone back to her job at the nursery school. Today, with its promise of happiness, would have been one more memory.

She could phone him back, tell him she had changed

her mind, that she'd be ready when he came for her. Her fingers moved to the dial. And then she straightened her shoulders and lifted her chin and very firmly put the receiver back in its cradle.

From the kitchen wafted the aroma of pancakes, Mary's customary Sunday morning breakfast treat. Normally Teslyn would have enjoyed them, but today she had no appetite at all. Jim and Mary and Joshua were in the kitchen, she could hear the rise and fall of cheerful voices, and knew she could contribute nothing to their conversation.

Blindly she passed the open door and moved on. She needed time to herself. She would go out walking alone this morning, and perhaps by the time she got back she'd have made some sense of the confusion that ravaged her.

She was in the garden when someone called her name, and turning, she saw Joshua. 'Hello.' She tried to smile.

'You didn't come in for breakfast.'

'I wasn't hungry. And it's so beautiful out of doors.'

'That's why I came looking for you. Let's go out for the day.'

She stared at him, wondering if he could have overheard her call with Wayne. 'Thanks, Joshua, but no.'

'And why not?' he coaxed.

'A few things that need doing. . . .'

'Not today. Jim suggested we take the horses, and Mary said she'd fix us some food.'

It was as if they were all conspiring against her, drawing her into a situation from which she could not extricate herself.

And now she really was being foolish, she told herself impatiently. Nobody was forcing her into anything.

'Teslyn?'

Joshua was smiling at her. He looked fresh and attractive in a fawn-coloured safari suit. He was nice, Teslyn thought, not for the first time, and it was not his fault that he aroused revulsion in her. Remorseful at the injustice of her feelings, she gave in. 'Well, all right, just for a while.'

'Wonderful. I'll take along my sketch-pad. I want to paint you, Teslyn. Perhaps I'll be inspired to do some preliminary drawings.'

There was a sense of *déjà vu* as they came to the stables and waited for the horses to be saddled. A sense of having done all this before as they took a trail through the forests. And yet it was not the same at all. Glancing at Joshua, Teslyn felt as if she was watching the re-run of a movie she had enjoyed a few times before, knowing that this time something was different, so that her pleasure in it would be spoiled. The air was fragrant with the scent of pine needles and the motion of the horse beneath her was as lively as ever, yet for Teslyn the exhilaration she had experienced those other times, with Wayne, was missing. More than that, she felt distinctly uneasy.

Reaching a stream, Joshua indicated that they should stop. The horses would be thirsty and the place was ideal for a picnic. Teslyn dismounted quickly, before he could help her. She had a strong reluctance to feel his hands on her waist and hoped he did not notice it.

'Isn't this place idyllic?' Joshua commented, coming to stand beside her at the edge of the water.

'Perfect,' she smiled up at him.

The ground was soft with pine needles and moss, and here and there tiny orchids peeped white and violet heads through the undergrowth. The water flowed fast, rushing over rocks and stones and filling the air with a lovely sound. The spot really was idyllic, and Teslyn was swept with the longing that Wayne could be here to share it with her. Her caution earlier this morning had been absurd, she told herself rebelliously. She should have gone with Wayne and enjoyed the day to the fullest.

Joshua brought the pack with the food, and they made light conversation while they ate. Actually it was Joshua who did most of the talking, but he seemed not to be aware of the fact. He was an easy companion, amusing with his anecdotes of Paris and his struggles to become an artist. Were it not for his resemblance to Alec, Teslyn thought, she might have liked him very much.

When they had finished eating she sat still while he sketched her.

'You're very beautiful,' he told her.

She laughed, 'Flatterer!'

'I mean it.'

'You just want me to sit for you.'

'I want more than that.' Paper and pencil were cast aside as Joshua came to her, his movements so quick that Teslyn, caught off guard, had no chance to get away from him.

'What do you think you're doing?' she demanded as his arms went around her.

'What does it look like?' he countered huskily. 'You're so lovely.'

His head was bending, he was going to kiss her. Every nerve and fibre of her being screamed protest. He could not kiss her, oh God, he could *not*! She tried to twist away from him.

'You don't like me.'

It was the first time she had known him to be petulant. Alec's petulance. Even Alec's words, he had said them so often. You don't like me, you don't love me.

She put her hands over her eyes to shut out Joshua's face. It was all starting again, and she did not think she could bear it.

'Teslyn, please. I want to kiss you.'

Wayne would have asked no questions. He'd have kissed her, deeply and thoroughly, and she would have gloried in it. Joshua's servile petulance made her flesh crawl.

'No!'

'You don't like me,' he said again.

'Of course I like you. I like you very much. It's just. . . .' She stopped, not knowing what to say. Was there something to say?

'I think I'm falling in love with you.' His voice was unsteady, pleading. 'Please let me kiss you, Teslyn. Don't push me away.'

Don't reject me, sounded the words. Joshua didn't want to be rejected—as she'd rejected Alec. A rejection that had cost them both so dearly.

But she couldn't think because Joshua was pulling her into his arms, and his mouth was covering hers. The blood pounded in her head as she clenched her fists and lifted them to push him away—only to drop them again. She couldn't push him away. It would be like rejecting Alec again.

His kisses became deeper, more passionate. And now his hands were moving over her. They were at her buttons, at her breasts. There was a limit to her endurance, she *could not* let him go on, even if he was hurt by her rejection.

She was about to twist away from him when the exclamation rang out—a furious epithet from somewhere above them. Joshua heard it too, for he lifted his head.

Wayne towered over them, standing by the stallion,

reins in one hand. He looked angrier than Teslyn had ever seen him.

Joshua sat back on his heels as Teslyn fell back, her hands covering her breasts where the buttons were undone. For a long moment there was a silence broken only by the rushing of the water.

'So, Teslyn' Wayne grated at last, 'you meant it when you said you'd be busy this morning.'

Joshua recovered his composure before Teslyn did. 'You're disturbing us,' he complained. 'Please leave.'

'That,' Wayne responded, lips curling as he put one foot on the stallion's stirrups, 'will be my pleasure.'

'You don't understand,' Teslyn said desperately.

'I think I do.' His eyes, steel-hard, flicked her dishevelled appearance. 'The reluctant widow was a merry one all the time.'

'How dare you!' She was sitting upright now, her fingers struggling with her buttons.

'I was a fool to think even for a moment that you were innocent.'

'Careful, North.' Joshua's voice was high. 'You're speaking to my future wife.'

Something flickered in Wayne's eyes and his lips tightened, but there was no emotion in his expression. 'You're getting married?' he queried in a tone of icy politeness.

'What's it to you?' Teslyn snapped at him, furious at his contempt. She glanced from the man beside the stallion to the one on the ground, and all thoughts of tact and rejection were forgotten. All she knew was that she had to get away from this spot.

She pulled away from Joshua's detaining hand, leaped to her feet and ran to her horse. Ignoring Wayne's warning shout, she mounted Toby with a speed born of anger. A spurring of heels and she brought the horse quickly to a gallop.

From somewhere behind her came the sound of horse's hooves. She heard Wayne shouting to her, but now the adrenalin was flowing fast and hard through her system, and his orders, far from stopping her, drove her on. After the humiliation of the last minutes there was satisfaction in defying Wayne and Joshua. Mainly Wayne.

The hooves of the pursuing horse grew louder. The stallion was gaining on Toby. Soon Wayne would be beside her, cutting her off. But nothing would stop her now. Nobody. Recklessly Teslyn dug her heels into Toby's flanks, urging the horse to go even faster.

She did not see the low-hanging branch of the tree. It was in her hair before she knew it. She was jerked backwards while the horse, infected by her frenzy, raced on. Teslyn fell sideways. She did not even see the ground as she hit it.

Teslyn opened her eyes and saw that she was in her room at Pinevale. She stirred, then groaned as her shoulder was knifed with pain.

'Teslyn!' a concerned voice exclaimed, and Mary was bending over her.

'What happened?' muttered Teslyn. 'Oh, Mary, my shoulder. . . .'

'It hurts, dear, I know. You fell from your horse.'

'I fell?'

'Don't you remember?'

'Vaguely. . . . Yes!' Joshua's fumbling kisses. Wayne's contempt. The wild crazy ride.

'You hit your head as well as your shoulder, and then you blacked out.'

'How did I get back?'

'Wayne brought you on his horse. Jim and I were

out. You were already here, in your bed, when we got back. We got an awful fright!'

'Oh, Mary, I'm sorry.' Teslyn slid a hand beneath the blanket, her cheeks growing warm as she made contact with a nightie. 'Wayne put me to bed?'

'Yes. He's waiting to see you.'

Teslyn turned her face away. The memory of Wayne's eyes when he'd skimmed her bared breasts was all too vivid. The words 'The reluctant widow was a merry one all the time' rang in her ears.

'I don't want to see him,' she muttered.

'He's in the living-room. He's been there all this time.'

'Tell him to go.'

'I don't think he will, dear.' Mary's voice was troubled. 'He's made up his mind to see you.' She hesitated. 'He's a very determined man.'

Determined, and not accustomed to being crossed. How it must have galled him to be thwarted by a stubborn girl who would not give in to him! Even worse, as the matter must have appeared in his eyes, that girl had been only too willing to give in to another man.

'All right, then,' she said quietly.

As Mary left the room Teslyn drew a deep breath. Let me have the strength to face him, she prayed. She would listen to Wayne's accusations, deal with them as best as she could, and then she would tell him that she would not see him again.

He came into the room and her breathing quickened. He was still in his riding clothes, looking very tall, very stern. Handsome too, she thought with despair, strikingly handsome, and knew that his face would remain imprinted on her mind for the rest of her life. Useless to tell herself that she would forget him, that the time would come when she would stop loving him. She could as soon stop herself breathing.

'I believe I owe you thanks,' she said in a small voice, and, as his brows drew together, 'Mary told me you brought me home on your horse.'

'Skip the small-talk,' he ground out savagely. 'And if you have any thoughts of going coy on me because I undressed you and put you to bed you can forget those too. I've seen you in less.'

'What do you want?' she asked brusquely.

'An explanation.' His voice was as hard as it had been when he'd come upon her and Joshua at the stream.

'You're angry because I stood you up and went out with Joshua instead. Because he kissed me.'

'That's part of it. And I'm not just angry, I'm sickened.'

She stared at him, caught by something in his voice. 'Why sickened?'

'When I was looking through your clothes for a nightgown I found this.' He shoved his hand into his pocket and brought out a piece of paper. Even before he thrust it at her she knew instinctively what it was.

'Alec?'

'Alec,' she agreed, and felt her heart thudding like a metronome against her ribs.

'The image of Joshua.'

'. . . Yes.'

'What the hell are you playing at, Teslyn? I can understand that you loved your husband, but were you so obsessed with him that you could only let yourself love again when you found his double?'

Her throat was so full that she could not speak. She could only stare at him, her eyes big and blue and filled with shock.

'We had something going for us,' Wayne said after a

long moment. 'Something good. It would have been spectacular if you'd only allowed it to be so.'

'You don't understand,' she whispered.

'Another of your favourite expressions. All right, let's say I don't understand, and suppose you explain.' But he went on without giving her a chance to open her mouth. 'You enjoyed my lovemaking, I *know* it, yet at the last moment you drew back every time. You refused to marry me. And your excuse was always Alec.' He was silent a moment while his eyes seemed to ravage her face.

'And then Joshua came on the scene. Till today I'd no idea he was Alec's double. I doubt Mary and Jim knew it either, Mary tells me she never saw her son with a beard.'

Angrily he paced the room, then stopped again by the bed, towering above her. 'Why were you able to let yourself go with Joshua, Teslyn? Did you see Alec in him? Because if you did, that's sick. It's demented!'

'You really don't understand. . . .'

'You want Joshua because you loved Alec so much.'

'Because I hated him!' There was no thought in her as the dam that held her emotions broke. 'I hated him, Wayne.'

He took a step backward. On a new note he asked, 'Then—why?'

'I killed him.' She stared at him, her eyes stark with horror. 'I killed Alec.' And then she put her hands over her face and began to sob.

An arm slid beneath her and Wayne held her while she shed the tears of guilt and fear and frustration which had been bottled inside her for so long. He made no effort to quieten her; he seemed to understand her need to weep.

At last she grew still. Wayne was still holding her,

and she looked up at him through eyes rimmed with wet lashes. 'I killed him,' she said again.

'Tell me about it,' he invited quietly.

She began slowly, hesitantly, but soon the words were pouring from her. She had been silent for so long, too long. It was time to speak.

'Alec never loved me,' she told Wayne. 'He wanted to marry me because it was the only way he knew to get me into his bed.'

Wayne was still as there emerged the story of a relationship which should never have been formed. Teslyn and Alec had never been compatible. She had been dazzled by his charm, his good looks, his recklessness. He had been captivated by her naïveté. It was only later when they were married and living together that the unhappiness began.

'Alec resented me almost immediately.' Emotion made the words emerge bumpily.

'Why?'

'He felt I'd trapped him.'

'He got what he wanted.' Wayne's expression was unreadable.

'He didn't.' Her cheeks warmed under his gaze as she elaborated. 'After a short time that part of our marriage ended.'

'I've always sensed you were innocent,' Wayne said softly. 'As inexperienced as a young virgin.'

Her flush deepened. 'You were right about that.'

Very soon Alec had reverted to the social life he had led before marriage, spending long evenings with his friends and away from his wife. He'd come home drunk, wanting to make love, and Teslyn, sickened, would push him away.

Alec persisted. A few times, in those first months, she'd given in to him, but always afterwards she had been sorry, for the boy who had swept her off her feet with his easy laugh and charming flattery had turned into a man who endowed any physical expression with brutality and cruelty.

'He hurt you?' Wayne looked grim.

Teslyn hesitated. Until today she had defended the husband who was not alive to defend himself. But now that she had begun to talk the words flowed out of her without check, almost of themselves. Having said so much it made no sense to stop. 'He hurt me, yes. It was as if . . . as if he *wanted* to hurt me.'

Wayne's jaw tightened and his eyes became twin points of steel. Teslyn, distraught as she put long-buried experiences into words, did not notice his expression.

The time had come when she had begun to say no to Alec. 'I had started rejecting him.' Her tone was deeply unhappy.

The marriage took a downward turn. Furious at being spurned, Alec became more brutal than before, delighting in humiliating her whenever he could. He embarked on a series of affairs, making no attempt to keep them secret. He seemed to delight in flaunting his women before Teslyn. The liaisons had not concerned her in themselves, for she had been glad to be rid of his physical advances. What hurt was the open derision and pity of their acquaintances.

Divorce entered her mind long before she actually voiced the idea. She had been brought up to think of marriage as a sacred contract, not to be broken lightly. It was only after three years, when she felt she had reached breaking point, that she told Alec she was leaving him.

'How did he take it?' asked Wayne.

'He was shattered.'

'Why? There was nothing left between the two of you.'

Teslyn hesitated. This was the hardest part of the telling; the part where her guilt entered the picture. 'There was no love,' she admitted in a tone that was so low as to be almost inaudible.

'Well then?' Wayne demanded.

'Alec had become dependent on me.' She looked up, noting abstractedly the firm lines of the rugged face, and wondering if someone of Wayne's calibre could understand the totally different nature of a man like Alec. 'He'd made enemies all round. He was a reckless spender with grandiose ideas. He'd go from one venture to another leaving a trail of debts in his wake. Our wake, because we were constantly on the move, always evading the people who were after him.'

'People trusted him with money?'

'He had such charisma. He could make you believe anything he wanted.'

'I see.'

'He was a charmer.'

'He charmed you.' It was said without expression.

'That wasn't difficult. I was young and lonely and so gullible. I think I was looking for someone to love.'

Wayne's eyes moved over her. 'So Alec was dependent on you.'

'I was all he had left. Oh, he had friends, but they were as mercurial as he was—the fair-weather variety always. I was the one person he could fall back on when he was desperate.'

'To abuse,' he pointed out.

'Also to talk to. To confide in when he didn't know which way to turn.'

'He must have known how you felt about him.'

'I was his wife,' Teslyn said simply.

It would be so easy to stop talking, to tell Wayne that she was tired from the fall and that she wanted to sleep. But she knew she had to go on.

'One evening he came home late, the fourth time in a week. The supper was ruined and I was furious. Anyway, I told him I insisted on a divorce.'

'He refused?'

'Yes. We'd had arguments before, terrible arguments, but usually I gave in for the sake of peace. That evening I didn't. I told him I was seeing a lawyer.'

She stopped. Even after so long the memories of that night were vivid. She could see Alec's face, his expression of hurt and disbelief. A tremor ran through her.

'He pleaded with me to give him another chance, but I refused. He said I was being unreasonable, insensitive, that if I persisted I'd be sorry.' Her throat was very dry. 'I told him nothing he could say or do would change my mind.' Again she was silent.

'Go on,' Wayne prompted.

'He ran out of the flat. That night. . . .' Teslyn's voice shook.

'The accident?'

'The police came to tell me. It was after midnight.'

'And you blamed yourself.'

Wild-eyed, she looked up at him. 'There's no other explanation. Alec was a fast driver, his love of speed frightened me. But nothing had ever happened before.'

'Meaningless in itself.'

'He was desperate. His reactions must have been affected.'

'You don't know that.'

'Not for certain. It's a strong feeling all the same.'

'And that's why you can't get married?' Wayne asked at length.

He understood!

'I should have known the state he was in. I'd rejected him so often, but this rejection was too final.'

There was silence in the room that was filled with a teenage boy's treasures. After what seemed a long time Wayne said, 'I have to know about Joshua. Did you think forcing yourself to love him would make up for anything you imagined you'd done?'

'I can't bear the sight of Joshua,' Teslyn whispered.

'Why did you go out with him today, then? You'd said no to me.'

'It's idiotic, I know, but if I'd said no to Joshua, in a way it would have been like rejecting Alec again. I can't stand Joshua, and it's really not his fault. That's why I felt I had to be gentle with him.'

'It *is* idiotic,' Wayne said fiercely.

'It won't happen again. Wayne, about the inheritance—do you understand why I can't accept it?'

'Of course.' He got up and she watched him pace the room a few times. His body was rigid, his face frowning and concentrated.

His expression had not softened when he came back to her bedside. 'I understand many things. I'm going now, Teslyn. Get some sleep, you look exhausted.' He bent, but the kiss on her forehead was perfunctory, with none of the passion she had come to expect.

CHAPTER ELEVEN

EVERY day Teslyn expected Wayne to visit her, but he did not come. She could have phoned Tinarua, now and then she got as far as starting to dial his number, but each time she stopped. Wayne did not want to see her, it was as simple as that.

She remembered his expression when he had left her room after she had finished telling him about Alec. She had thought he understood, that he had sympathy with her ordeal. It came to her only gradually, as the days passed without sign of him, that she was mistaken. Far from being sympathetic to her cause, Wayne had been repelled. Perhaps he identified instead with a desperate husband; felt that Teslyn had been callous not to give Alec the chance he had so badly wanted. One way or another it was clear that she had disillusioned him and that he had no interest in seeing her again.

And that was just as well, she tried to tell herself. Had Wayne been sympathetic and loving it would have made her departure from Pinevale all the more heart-wrenching. If only she did not feel quite so miserable!

The one heartening factor was that Jim had recovered more quickly than anyone had expected him to. Every day he looked better.

'It's back to work for me again, *meisie-kind*,' he told her one morning, smiling.

'No more tricks with the machinery.' She smiled back at him. 'Jim, you're looking wonderful!'

'I wish I could say the same for you.' This from Mary, who was regarding Teslyn with an air of concern.

'My head is much better. My shoulder too.'

'Physical wounds heal quickly unless they're serious, which yours, thank the Lord, weren't.' Mary paused an instant. 'I'm thinking of your eyes, child. You look so sad.'

Teslyn looked at her mother-in-law, and she felt tears form at the back of her throat. 'It's time for me to leave Pinevale.'

'Nonsense,' Jim protested warmly. 'Just because I'm fit for work it doesn't mean you must leave. You know this is your home.'

It was time to be firm—Jim was his sturdy self once again and Mary's worries were over—they could both take it.

'I have to go.'

'But. . . .' Jim began.

'Don't make it hard for me.' The tears were very close.

'It's Wayne, isn't it?' Mary questioned quietly.

Teslyn jerked up to look at her in surprise. 'So obvious?' she asked at last, painfully.

'It wasn't at first. In fact I'd hoped you and Joshua. . . .' A thoughtful look entered her eyes. 'Something happened the day you fell from the horse. I don't pretend to understand, because I don't. But it *is* Wayne, isn't it?'

'Yes. He wanted to marry me.'

'I didn't know that.' Mary looked stunned.

'Don't make too much of it. He's changed his mind.'

'He told you that?'

'He didn't have to. We had a talk.' Alec's parents would never know the topic. 'I haven't seen Wayne since.'

'Well, of course not,' Jim said comfortingly. 'He's away.'

Hope sprang to life inside Teslyn. 'He's not at Tinarua?'

'Hasn't been for a few days.'

'In that case. . . .' She didn't finish the sentence. In that case nothing! The moment of hope was gone. Wayne could have told her of his plans, could have said goodbye. That he had chosen not to do so was a clear indication of his feelings.

'I'll be going myself in a day or two,' she said.

'So soon?' Jim was dismayed.

Best to make the break as soon as possible now that her mind was made up. Procrastination could only intensify the pain of the leavetaking. 'I'm so afraid so,' she confirmed in a low tone.

Mary put a hand on her arm. 'Wayne might not be back by then.'

I hope he won't be. I want to go before he comes. I don't want to see him, say goodbye to him. I might not be able to hide my emotions and I couldn't bear his pity. 'It doesn't matter,' she said aloud.

There was something more that had to be said. Teslyn swallowed hard. 'Mary, Jim, don't be hurt, please—but I don't want you to leave me your share of Pinevale.'

'You're all we have left.' Jim's eyes were clouded.

'There's Joshua,' Teslyn managed. 'Now that he's had his fling as an artist he seems keen to settle down to farming.'

'He's working hard,' Mary acknowledged. 'But we wanted you to have it.'

'I'd make a wretched farmer and an end to the split ownership will be good for Pinevale.' She got to her feet. 'You couldn't have been kinder to me, both of you. And it will be *tot siens*, not goodbye.'

*

But it *would* be goodbye, Teslyn thought two days later, as she took a farewell ride through the forests. She had grown as close to Jim and Mary as if they were her own family—in a sense they were the only family she had left—yet she knew she would not come back to Pinevale. To do so would mean seeing Wayne and experiencing all the emotions such a meeting would inevitably entail. She'd have to be a masochist to put herself through such an ordeal.

There were many lovely trails, but some were her favourites. One in particular, a trail that led to a sunny plateau, she loved most. Tomorrow, very early, she was leaving Pinevale. Her suitcase was already packed, and at sunrise Jim was driving her to the station. The next eighteen hours would be a time for goodbyes, the visit to the plateau just the first of several.

Toby needed little direction. It was as if the gentle horse was so in tune with its rider's thoughts that it knew of its own accord where to go. Reaching the plateau, Teslyn tethered the horse lightly to a tree, then made for a slanting rock with a view over the wooded slopes to the valley.

She sank down in the soft sweet-smelling wild grass and leaned back against the rock, knees bent, her chin resting on her hands. It was very quiet up here. She could hear the drone of a bee inspecting a fallen pine-cone some distance away, and the slight swishing sound of the grass as it moved in an air which was never entirely still.

Turning her head a little to the right, she looked in the direction of Tinarua. It was hard to know where Pinevale ended and Tinarua began, for the tops of the trees showed no demarcation line, but she was sure of the direction, and a long way down, glinting silver through the dark foliage of the pines, the roof of Wayne's homestead was visible.

This view would remain in her memory long after she had left here. Pinevale, the plantation she had grown so fond of; Tinarua, which but for scruples which might well be ridiculous, could have been her home.

Yet perhaps her scruples had not been ridiculous at all. Had she played her hand differently she could have married Wayne without admitting her guilt; could have been mistress of Tinarua, living there with the man she loved. But sooner or later the truth might have come out. How was immaterial—truth had a way of surfacing in the most unexpected ways. What would have been Wayne's reaction? It was not hard to guess. His absence since her confession was bad enough. Living with him, reading his feelings in his eyes, sharing a bed with a man who despised her, would have been an ordeal she could not have endured.

She had told Wayne the truth and had suffered the consequences. Hard as it had been, she knew now that she could not have acted differently.

The sound of hooves impinged only gradually on her consciousness. At first she thought it was Toby, restless at being confined to one spot and pacing this way and that. And then she realised that the sound came from below her. She could not see the horse which was still hidden in the denseness of the wooded slope, but she could hear it, its hooves dull thuds on the fallen pine-needles.

Alarmed, she brought herself up on one elbow and glanced at Toby. There was only one way down that she knew of, and if she took it she would meet the horse, and its rider, head-on anyway. A moment later she chided herself for unjustified panic. The farm workers rarely came this way, for the trees around the

plateau were fairly young and not for cutting this year.
The rider could only be Joshua, and she had no fear of
him. Since the disastrous day of the fall Joshua had
made no further advances, and, with a generosity she
had not expected in him, had shown no ill feeling. Her
own dislike of him had fallen away. It was as if with
her confession to Wayne certain barriers had been
broken down, and she had realised that Joshua was not
another Alec but a person in his own right—a very nice
person at that.

If Joshua was coming up the slope towards her she
could look forward to a pleasant chat, and then they
would ride back together. She wondered why the hairs
rising on the back of her neck told her it was not
Joshua.

As the glossy head of the stallion emerged through
the trees the breath caught in her lungs. A moment
later the rider himself was in full view—bronzed and
male and devastatingly handsome—and she could only
look at him numbly.

The sun was on Wayne's face, hardening the rugged
lines of it, and Teslyn thought he looked unusually
stern. There was no softening as he vaulted lithely to
the ground, no smile as he covered the windswept grass
that lay between the quickly-tethered stallion and the
rock where Teslyn still sat. Not even the formality of a
hello.

And then he was towering above her, and she could
not get out a word as she looked up at him, her throat
dry. He was wearing a cream shirt open at the collar
and rolled up at the sleeves, revealing the deep bronze
of chest and arms; his breeches, fitting snugly at the
waist and shaped at the calves, somehow enhanced the
impression of broad shoulders and narrow hips. He
was angry, Teslyn saw, and knew she had every need to

keep her wits strictly about her—yet she could not control the wild clamouring of her senses.

'So,' he said in a measured tone, 'you're making your farewell round.'

'You know?' she whispered through numb lips.

'That you'd intended leaving tomorrow? Yes.'

The curious word structure did not register on her fevered brain. She could only look at him, willing him to go for her emotions could just take so much battering; at the same time she was memorising every line of the beloved face, for she knew that when she left the plateau she would not see him again.

'How did you know where to find me?' she asked.

'I know so much about you, Teslyn. Guessing that you'd be at one of your favourite spots wasn't difficult.'

Not difficult either to know what he meant. He thought of her as a callous girl who had driven her husband to the very pit of despair. The fact that she had not heard from him since her confession showed just how deep his dislike ran. Blindly she shook her head and turned away from him. She was getting to her feet, about to make for Toby, when Wayne dropped to his knees and seized her wrist.

'Don't try that stunt again. Wasn't one fall enough for you?' And then, giving her no time to answer, he added on a gentler note, 'When are you going to stop running away from me?'

Her pulses were suddenly pounding. 'I wasn't running.'

'Weren't you?' The grip on her wrist firmed, the fingers sliding a little way up her arm, sending a familiar tingling through her system. 'You weren't even going to wait to say goodbye to me. Why not?'

He was so close to her that she felt giddy. Nevertheless she still held on to some remnant of pride. Pulling herself up as far as was possible in the circumstances, she stated coolly, 'You didn't think it necessary to say goodbye to me. You've been gone a week. How do you think I felt, having to hear from Jim that you'd gone away on business?'

'Angry?' he queried softly.

'Furious,' she responded spiritedly, without stopping to think that she was giving herself away.

Wayne laughed, the sound satisfied and seductive, and the fingers on the bare skin of her arm began a slow rhythmic stroking. 'Excellent,' he pronounced.

She leaned back to look at him was startled to see that eyes she had thought would be icy were warm instead.

'You're pleased,' she said after a moment, puzzled.

'Delighted.' His lips had curved into the smile she loved and his eyes were flecked with gold. 'You're a passionate woman, my Teslyn, with real gut emotions. I couldn't have anything else in a wife.'

'Wife?' She gaped at him.

'Wife, darling,' he mocked her gently. 'Why the surprise? You know we're going to be married.'

She began to tremble. She felt panic again, also a wonderful joy. A joy that was surely unjustified but that would not be denied.

'You'd changed your mind,' she got out in a choked voice.

'Had I?' he drawled.

'That's why you left Tinarua without telling me. You were turned off when I told you I was to blame for Alec's death.'

'I was never turned off, and you were never in all your life responsible for a person's death,' he said matter-of-factly. 'Let alone Alec's.'

The trembling increased. 'I told you. . . .'

'I know what you told me. I've a few things to tell you as well.' He leaned forward and drew her against his chest, holding her with a tenderness that brought a lump to her throat.

'Listen to me,' he said quietly. 'And try not to interrupt till I've finished. I couldn't say goodbye, darling, because I'd have had to tell you where I was going.'

Despite the heat of the sun almost overhead, she felt very cold. 'Where did you go?'

'Johannesburg. Teslyn darling, I once spent a long time tracing your movements. This last week I traced Alec's.'

With only the little information Teslyn had let slip to proceed on, Wayne had spent hours talking to people who had known Alec, going to places he had frequented. Finally he had come to the bar where he had spent his last hours. Alec had been with a girl, a girl he had been with many times before.

On the sunny plateau Wayne paused in his telling a moment, and the tenderness in his arms increased. It was as if he was trying to soften Teslyn's pain. But the telling itself could not be spared.

Alec and the girl had been drinking steadily by the time they left the bar. It had been raining and the streets were slippery. The bartender called after them to be careful, but to no avail. The car had taken off at high speed, tyres squealing on the wet tar. Minutes later it hit the lamp-post. Alec had died immediately. The girl, miraculously only badly bruised, had escaped.

'The police said nothing about a girl,' Teslyn said weakly.

'She'd gone by the time they got to the scene. And

afterwards, darling, you didn't bother to make en-
quiries. You could have found out what I did.'

'Perhaps, perhaps not.' Teslyn did not doubt that
Wayne had used an authority she did not possess to get
Alec's erstwhile acquaintances to co-operate.

'Why do I get the feeling you're not convinced?'
Warm breath fanned her ear.

She pushed herself a little away from him. 'Alec was
a fast driver. Always. Why *that* night, Wayne?'

His eyes were on her face, his expression sombre.
'Coincidence, call it what you will, I can't explain it. I
believe he was upset when you told him your plans—
but the accident didn't happen immediately after that.'

He was silent a moment before going on. 'According
to the barman Alec's drinking had got worse and worse.
His temper too. There were fights in the bar. That
night the road was especially slippery. With what he'd
apparently consumed I'd say an accident was inevitable.'

'I'll never know for sure.'

'But you can stop blaming yourself. The question
is—will you?' He pushed her hair gently away from her
forehead. 'Well, my darling, will you?'

Teslyn took a long shuddering breath, but when she
met Wayne's gaze her eyes were steady. 'Yes.'

Wayne drew her to him and kissed her, long drugging
kisses that were as exciting as the first time. When he
lifted his head at length his breathing was ragged. 'Let's
set the date for our wedding.'

She was happier than she had ever thought possible,
and yet a question remained. 'If you hadn't found out
what you did—would you still want me?'

His answer came out firmly. 'I've always wanted you.
Nothing you said made any difference. I went to
Johannesburg because I knew there could never be any

happiness for us until you'd laid your ghosts. No other reason.' His hands cupped her face. 'How could you not know that? I love you, darling. I love you with every fibre of my being.'

The words she had longed to hear. 'I love you too— so much!' Her eyes shone. 'Wayne, we must tell Jim and Mary.'

'I think they know already. And we're going nowhere till we've fixed the date. Tomorrow?'

'What about the day after?' she teased softly through her joy.

'If I have to wait that long I need to kiss you first.' And very thoroughly he did just that.

THE MUSIC OF GLENN MILLER

During the thirties and forties, an entire generation jitterbugged and fox-trotted the evenings away in fabulous dance palaces, serenaded by the music of the "big bands." One of the greatest bandleaders of the era was Glenn Miller, whose orchestra became famous for performing such sweet romantic songs as "Moonlight Serenade," "In the Mood" and "Tuxedo Junction."

Glenn Miller grew up in Oklahoma City. When he was thirteen, he discovered an interest in the trombone. He worked, milking cows for two dollars a week, saving his money until he could buy his first instrument.

In 1926, when he was twenty-two, Miller went to New York City and began working as a trombonist and arranger for several established dance orchestras. But he carried with him a dream—to have his own band. Once again, he began saving his money, and in 1937 he was ready.

Unfortunately, his first orchestra was disbanded a year later. But he soon tried again, and for more than a year he and his group of musicians struggled through a series of one-night jobs, with no one taking much notice. But in 1939 the band played a theater in New York City, and it was there that lineups for the band's performances began. Soon, Glenn Miller's music was being broadcast on radio, and before long his orchestra was so popular it was breaking attendance records at every dance palace it played.

In late 1942 Glenn Miller enlisted as a captain in the American armed forces. He conducted an air-force band, first in the United States and then overseas in London. Tragically, on a flight from London to Paris in 1944 his airplane disappeared over the English Channel. And though his death was a great loss to American popular music, his legacy of great music lives on.

Now's your chance to discover the earlier
books in this exciting series.

Choose from this list of great

SUPERROMANCES!

#8 BELOVED INTRUDER   Jocelyn Griffin

#9 SWEET DAWN OF DESIRE   Meg Hudson

#10 HEART'S FURY   Lucy Lee

#11 LOVE WILD AND FREE   Jocelyn Haley

#12 A TASTE OF EDEN   Abra Taylor

#13 CAPTIVE OF DESIRE   Alexandra Sellers

#14 TREASURE OF THE HEART   Pat Louis

#15 CHERISHED DESTINY   Jo Manning

#16 THIS DARK ENCHANTMENT   Rosalind Carson

#17 CONTRACT FOR MARRIAGE   Megan Alexander

#18 DANCE OF DESIRE   Lisa Lenore

#19 GIVE US FOREVER   Constance F. Peale

#20 JOURNEY INTO LOVE   Jessica Logan

#21 RIVER OF DESIRE   Abra Taylor

#22 MIDNIGHT MAGIC   Christine Hella Cott

#23 FROM THIS BELOVED HOUR   Willa Lambert

#24 CALL OF THE HEART   Wanda Dellamere

#25 INFIDEL OF LOVE   Casey Douglas

SUPERROMANCE

Complete and mail this coupon today!

Worldwide Reader Service

In the U.S.A.
1440 South Priest Drive
Tempe, AZ 85281

In Canada
649 Ontario Street
Stratford, Ontario N5A 6W2

Please send me the following SUPERROMANCES. I am enclosing my check or money order for $2.50 for each copy ordered, plus 75¢ to cover postage and handling.

☐ # 8	☐ # 14	☐ # 20
☐ # 9	☐ # 15	☐ # 21
☐ # 10	☐ # 16	☐ # 22
☐ # 11	☐ # 17	☐ # 23
☐ # 12	☐ # 18	☐ # 24
☐ # 13	☐ # 19	☐ # 25

Number of copies checked @ $2.50 each = $_____
N.Y. and Ariz. residents add appropriate sales tax $_____
Postage and handling $_____.75

                               TOTAL $_____

I enclose_____

(Please send check or money order. We cannot be responsible for cash sent through the mail.)
Prices subject to change without notice.

NAME_____
(Please Print)

ADDRESS_____APT. NO._____

CITY_____

STATE/PROV._____

ZIP/POSTAL CODE_____

Offer expires September 30, 1983   30356000000

Say U Promise

Say U Promise

Ms. Michel Moore

www.urbanbooks.net

Urban Books, LLC
300 Farmingdale Road, NY-Route 109
Farmingdale, NY 11735

ISBN 13: 978-1-62286-556-7
ISBN 10: 1-62286-556-1

First Trade Paperback Printing July 2017
Printed in the United States of America

10 9 8 7 6 5 4 3 2 1

Distributed by Kensington Publishing Corp.
Submit Orders to:
Customer Service
400 Hahn Road
Westminster, MD 21157-4627
Phone: 1-800-733-3000
Fax: 1-800-659-2436

Coldhearted & Crazy:

Say U Promise 1

The Jump Off

How did this happen? How did I get here? Here to this point. These little simple-minded third-generation punks done got the drop on me! Well, I'll be damned, three damn young kids. I swear on everything I love, I can still smell the breast milk on their stankin' foul, immature breaths. Yet, here I lie stretched out in my best suit ready for a Saturday night of partying. I'm covered with dirt. My pants leg torn at the knee and my snakeskin shoes scuffed the hell up. These murdering sons of bitches! They straight caught me slippin'. Why did I come tonight? Why?

In between my coldhearted stares of these pint-sized killers, I see the small dark pools of blood slowly growing from Melinda's gunshot wounds: one in her side, one near her collarbone. My loyal queen was gasping for air as she choked on her own mucus. I grew infuriated seeing her suffer like she was. I had a love so strong for her as well as the love we shared; our bond was unbreakable. Melinda was more than just my wife. She was the mother of my two precious daughters, my best friend, and my road dawg. Me-Me, as I'd always called her, was damn near my everything and because of my arrogant, stubborn ways, the woman who'd birthed my seeds now lies inches away from me, dying, and I can't do anything to help her. How really messed up is that? I mean I really dropped the damn ball this go-around. Make no mistake, this one's all on me.

Why didn't I just wait for my brother like Melinda begged me to do? I really didn't trust these young cats off rip, but as usual I thought I was bigger than the game and the rules didn't apply to me. Stupid me. I'd violated every rule of the game and was now paying the ultimate price. I'd just met these busters looking for a quick come up and was letting them cop from me on the humble. What can I say? My bad! I got greedy and wanted that money. Shit, I ain't gonna lie. It started gettin' good to a guy. Me and mines was eating good, driving good, dressing good, smoking good, and riding good. We were what poor folk around our way considered hood rich and we played our part well.

They say loot will change a person; hell, I can testify to that shit. Flat out, it got me off my square. I fucked up this time. No doubt! How could I believe in any honor among thieves? It didn't exist. How could I have forgotten the basic levels of being in the life? The rules of the dope game never ever change, just the players. Live by the gun, blah, blah, blah, shit's tight now. Time is ticking. I'm not brand new to the streets. I've been around death long enough to realize that my wifey, Melinda, has just taken her last breath in this lifetime and I, as hard as I was fighting it, was undoubtedly next in line for that same fate.

I'll be damned, here it comes. I can't feel my left lower leg anymore. Now the right! The last bullet these assholes let loose caused a burning sensation that ripped right through my flesh, knocking me off my feet and in this ditch. Still wishing for a different outcome, I wanted to beg for them to spare my wife's life, but I had no intention of going out like a straight bitch. I have my pride, and if nothing else but on point and principle, I'm gonna keep it gangsta 'til the very end. Besides, I knew my Me-Me was already gone. The mother of my two daughters was dead, finished, over, and it was my damn fault. Yeah, it's pretty much a wrap, for both her and me.

If I could turn back the hands of time, I still wouldn't change a motherfucking thang. I can't say I honestly regret one minute of it. Me and my girl had a ball doing what we did, living how we lived. Just thinking about slangin' could get my manhood rock hard. From being posted on the corner of Linwood Avenue, taking two dollar shorts on a top side hit of powder to grinding up on my first cake of that good stuff, that shit was real, hell sometimes maybe even too real. My sweetheart, Melinda, was with me from day one. She always had my back. Now here we go again, but this time we won't be able to get high and laugh this one off.

I feel myself getting weaker as the seconds drag by. It's about that time. The clock is about to stop. I know I've done wrong and more than likely the devil has left the light on for me. That's okay though. I earned my spot in hell. But God, if you can still hear me, for Melinda's sake, please take care of our little daughters, Kenya and London; especially Kenya, who has an inner rage and a lust for the streets just like her old man. They're the purest thing that came out of all this madness. Game over, lights out!

From da cradle to the fuckin' grave!

Chapter One

Two of a Kind

Buzzzzzzzzzzz . . . It was a typical morning in the small family household located in the middle of the crime-infested Detroit neighborhood. The digital alarm clock was making what seemed like an intolerable sound, yet there was still no movement from either one of the "different as night and day" teenage twins. The alarm going off on the clock at 6:45 a.m. every school day was a normal occurrence, just as normal as the girls trying to ignore the sound and their grandmother's sometimes annoying voice.

"Get up!" Gran, cane in hand, yelled with a Southern drawl even though she'd been living up North in the city for decades. "Both of you gals get up before you're late!" Every morning was the same routine. She thought, *Lord have mercy, don't let these girls end up like their mother Melinda because if they do, I don't know what in the world I will do!*

Gran had two children of her own. Melinda was her youngest, her baby. Everyone knew she'd tried her very best with both of her loving children, but to no avail; the black-hearted streets had other plans for them. Both had died young living the life she wanted so desperately for them to leave alone. Her son, just barely eighteen, had overdosed on drugs, heroin to be exact; and Melinda, who always thought she was too smart for her own good, was found shot to death in the projects in a ditch with her husband, leaving the girls, her only children, orphans.

Hattie Jean Lewis was a devout Christian woman, who stood tall in her faith and love for the Lord. She used to stay up countless nights and shed many a tear, worrying about her little girl. *Damn, why did she have to meet that low-down, good-for-nothing Johnnie Roberts?* Gran frowned up her face questioning why things had gone so wrong. *Sorry, Lord.* She quickly repeated over and over, *Let thy will be done. If you thought it was best to call them home, I know you know best and only you can help me with these girls, especially Kenya.*

Gran started loudly singing church hymns; that always got the entire household up and going. Not because the twins love hearing them, but the complete opposite. Whenever it came to going to church one of the sisters, Kenya of course, always bucked at the idea. She was considered the wild child of the two and everyone who would encounter the girls could easily tell the difference. Gran didn't care how much Kenya rebelled. God was the head of her household and Kenya, London, and anyone else who stepped foot inside her home was going to follow suit. Gran would drag Kenya to services week after week praying she would soften her heart. From experience, the old woman knew good and well that everyone would need and call upon the Lord one day, Kenya included.

With a "mad at the world" attitude, Amoya Kenya Roberts was the first one of the girls to jump out the bed. The second verse of her grandmother's song was unbearable to the young teen.

"Morning, baby." Gran tried to kiss her on her forehead, but Ms. Kenya, waving her hand backward, was having none of that. Since the twins' first names were so close, everyone called them by their middle names. Kenya was what you would call the most outgoing one of the two. She often joked and kept a smile on her face; that was, as long as she was having her own way, which she often demanded. Having a thirst for being the center of attention, she was most certainly the life of the party. However, just as easy as the jokes, smiles, and laughter could begin, they could be brought to a screeching halt. Kenya possessed a short-fuse firecracker temper that was unbelievable. The teen with a beautiful face, loved by some and hated by others, could and would snap just like that at a drop of a hat. Kenya was truly her father's daughter in every way you could imagine, from personality and demeanor to his hustle by any means to get paid pedigree. And for that reason, among many more, her immediate family worried about her and what unseen tragedies that mentality could ultimately bring to her.

Amia London Roberts was the latter of the girls to get up and start her day. "Hey, Gran." She smiled as she reached out to her granny. Knowing another day wasn't promised to anyone, she hugged and kissed her every chance that she got.

"Mornin', baby. I love you."

"I love you too, Gran." London beamed with joy as her sister came out the bathroom, interrupting their embrace.

"Dang, why y'all two gotta be so mushy all the time? It's too early in the morning!" Kenya asked while turning her lip up, "And, London, why don't you stop being such a butt kisser? I mean dang!"

London paid her sister no mind. She loved her grandmother. They would discus all sorts of important subjects. Prejudice and racism in America and civil rights struggles that had taken place in Alabama and throughout the South. They shared conversations about Dr. King, Malcolm X, and even the Black Panthers organization. Not only did London like to hear about the struggle of her people, she promised Gran one day to be part of the solution. The honor-roll teen loved to read books and would spend countless hours at the library. She would study every chance she got, even at night when the troubled neighborhood she lived in was quiet and still or her sister was chattering away on the phone.

While London spent her nights studying, Kenya would stay posted on the phone. She could often hold a conversation for what seemed like hours on end talking about absolutely nothing of any value. Meeting different boys at the mall and exchanging phone numbers, she'd tell them all kind of things a normal fourteen-year-old had no business knowing about life in general, let alone repeating. Everywhere she'd go, the boys, some her own age and some much older, flocked around

Kenya like bees to honey, but London didn't care one bit. Her only focus was obtaining and maintaining good grades and a high GPA. Their Gran had taught London that knowledge was true power, and with a good education, she could easily write her own ticket in life.

London always daydreamed, wondering if her mother had stayed in school and hit the books as much as she heard that she'd hit the streets getting into mischief with her dad, would she still be alive today. Nevertheless, bottom line, Kenya, not giving a damn about jack shit, was hell-bent on living her young life recklessly and London, determined to make something of hers, studied, wanting to be labeled something other than a hood rat.

Both London and Kenya got dressed for school. They were only fourteen, but each had already developed their own style of dress. Kenya picked out a pair of light blue jeans that were neatly pressed and had a jacket and baby T-shirt to match. She grabbed her new designer bag and belt, throwing them on the bed. After finally pouring herself into her pants, she turned around in the mirror and smiled as she thought, *Both tight and right.*

"Humph, should I were my K-Swiss or my new Air Force 1s?" she then questioned out loud, still checking out her own ass.

"I think you should wear the K-Swiss," London whispered under her breath.

"Did you say something over there Miss Power to the People?" Kenya had a smirk across her face, turning to face London. Kenya loved her sister, true enough, but she knew the girl had no taste whatsoever. "K-Swiss you said, then I know it's the Forces today." They both shared a laugh as London playfully threw her pillow across the room at her twin.

London pulled out a pair of black slacks and a plain black polo shirt. She wasn't into all of those high-priced designer clothes that her sister liked. Why walk around with someone else's name plastered across your chest and behind? Why be a free walking billboard on display? *Free promotion and advertisement for the white man, I don't think so. No way, not the kid,* she thought as she watched Kenya get dressed.

They both had long sandy-brown hair that stretched past their shoulders. Kenya always let hers hang and flow wildly, while London favored hers pulled back off the face in a ponytail. Their features were identical. If not for their clothes and obvious different characteristics, many of their own distant family members and friends couldn't tell the twins apart. With two different agendas for the day, they were out the door on their way to school—separately.

Chapter Two

Kenya

"I hope none of these fake thirsty snakes try to start no bullshit with me today. I'm definitely not in the fucking mood for their messy asses!" Just as Kenya turned the end of the long block she spotted Carmen. She was her girl, for real, for real; her best friend. If ever there was a female who had your back no matter what happened or jumped off, it would be her. Kenya had been in serious physical altercations with groups of jealous girls several times over, and Carmen was always there standing right beside Kenya, if not in front of her, showing their opponents what was really good with them both.

Carmen smirked, tugging down on her skirt. "What up, twin? What's happening?" Carmen always smiled when she said that shit because she knew that it irked Kenya. Her friend always wanted to be known for her own identity. As far as Kenya was concerned London was London and she was herself, twin or not.

"Very funny. Ha-ha, motherfucker, very funny. I been told your ass about that twin shit! I didn't know I had my own personal comedian to walk to school with!" Kenya snapped.

"Damn, girl, is that a new hookup you rocking? That shit is seriously hot to death. I know that ain't no regular off-the-rack shit, is it? You've been straight holding out on this one!"

Kenya was cheesin' from ear to ear, taking in every last one of the compliments Carmen was dishing out. Kenya knew there wasn't a girl from miles around who could fade her style or unique way of rocking her gear. Everywhere she went, people would be on her envious of her wardrobe.

The girls' uncle was always showering them with money, jewelry, and, most importantly of all to a stuck-up Kenya, clothes. The majority of their gear he would get from New York or Cali. Sometimes he'd even have his weave shop owner girlfriend pick out and send garments back from overseas when she'd travel. After his older brother, Johnnie, and his sister-in-law got murdered back in the day, he always tried to look out for his little nieces the best he could. Even when he'd get locked up, which was quite often considering the ruthless lifestyle he lived, he made sure he had his woman continue to hold the twins down. Gran, knowing it was blood money he was spending, didn't like all the expensive gifts he gave the girls, but what could she do? He was their family also: blood. Matter of fact, he was the only one out of the Roberts family who even tried to maintain a relationship with both London and Kenya after their mom died. She knew he truly loved his nieces and would die for them if need be and Gran respected that fact.

Finally, after letting Carmen go on and on with her praise, Kenya, extremely loyal to her friends, told her she would gladly let her have some of the pieces that she didn't want or couldn't fit in.

"Thanks, girl, I love you." Carmen started trying to hug her friend for always looking out even though she didn't have to.

"Urgg fall back, chick! What I tell your ass 'bout all that kissy-lovey shit? Save that for them busters you be dealing with," Kenya hissed, trying to play that hard role.

Carmen looked at her girl and shook her head. If ever there was a person in need of a hug and some affection it was Kenya. Carmen knew that her best friend had major issues with trusting or loving anyone or anything. She didn't know or even care to know where Kenya had developed those feelings, because everyone in their Detroit hood had their own problems and demons to deal with and she and Kenya were no different. Life was hard in the Motor City.

As they slow strolled down Linwood Avenue, the pair encountered all types of ghetto hood antics, the girls loved to fuck with the "common folk" as they called them: "Y'all girls look pretty today, can you spare a dollar? Get an education, do you have a quarter?" or "I'm trying to get something to eat and I need thirty-five cents."

Kenya, immune to sympathy for the next person's bad luck in life, had heard every crackhead, drug addict, and sorry-ass story in the book known to man. Sometimes she and Carmen wouldn't hesitate humoring themselves by making them do outlandish things no sane human being would even consider. She would have them bark like a dog for fifty cents or imitate other farm animals for their own childish amusement. There was no limit to what they could easily encourage a Detroit crackhead to do if the price was right. And since times were so hard and cold in the city, the price was always right.

As Kenya and Carmen passed the liquor store, Daisy appeared. She was a middle-aged woman hard in the face strung out on heroin, who used to be friends with both Kenya's parents and wouldn't let the young teen forget it. No matter where the girls would go in the economically stressed neighborhood of longtime homeowners, they were reminded about their deceased parents' impact on the community and its residents, whether they were fond memories or not.

"Yeah, me, your mama, and daddy used to get our souls proper back in the day! All top side, uncut! That good shit!" Daisy rocked from side to side to the imaginary music that was playing in her drug-infested mind. "I'm telling you, Kenya or London or whichever one you is, your daddy only copped the best shit this damn city ever seen! Oh, yeah! Ol' Johnnie Roberts knew how to play the game, for real!"

Always begging for this, that, and the third, she felt Kenya and London were obligated to give her spare change whenever she asked for it just on the strength that she and their parents shared needles or blow from time to time. Some mornings, this one in particular, Kenya was in one of her moods and cruelly decided to make Daisy dance for a dollar, recording it on her cell phone so she could laugh at it later and post on Facebook. After humiliating her parents' less fortunate friend with not much coaxing, she and Carmen ran off giggling.

"What's so funny, y'all?" It was Allan, their homeboy from around the way. Randomly, he always seemed to appear out of nowhere when they least expected him to. He always walked with the girls to school. "I said what's so damn funny? Why y'all laughing so hard?" He gave both of his friends a stupid look as he repeated his question, not receiving an answer the first time. They girls looked at each other and busted out laughing again.

"Nothing, nothing." Kenya was wiping the tears off her face. "It's just I didn't know that people could be so desperate that's all."

Allan never got the joke and the girls let it go, especially because Allan's mom was a closet head. Ain't no true secrets in the hood and his mother's smoking crack most certainly wasn't one of them. Everything in the dark always comes to light, please believe.

The trio finally arrived at Central High School. While Allan was a junior for the second time, both of the girls were only freshman, but you damn straight couldn't tell by the reception they received. As soon as they cleared the metal detector, it was all smiles and handshakes on their end for the most part. Every guy in the school wanted to get with Kenya if they weren't gay, and of course her ever-present sidekick Carmen came along for the ride. Even the upperclassmen, who usually didn't fuck with crab-ass freshmen, would stop what they were doing to gawk at the girls' asses bounce by in those tight jeans or hooker short skirts that the two were infamous for wearing. But of course as always there had to be haters on deck lurking. You know that bullshit goes without saying. Hell, real talk, haters make the world go round and what school wasn't blessed with them, Central students included, who regularly took hatin' on the next person, in particular her, to the next level on a day-to-day basis.

"They should rename this bitch Hater High but that might be too much like right!" Kenya blurted out loud as she mean mugged a few chicks who were giving her just as much shade and fever as she was giving them.

As much attention as the fellas gave Kenya and Carmen, the other girls would stare them down and often roll their eyes at the pair. Truthfully speaking, there was not one single female who really liked the conceited pair. However, Kenya made it perfectly clear she couldn't care less if any bitch in the entire school liked her or not; they were damn sure gonna respect her. She was settling for nothing less.

"Hey, ladies, I like your outfits." One girl grinned at Carmen and Kenya, while trying to be a real smart-ass.

Kenya peeped that shit out and let the girl have it Kenya Roberts style. "Girl, I like your outfit too. I know I say that every week when you wear it, but it's so cute." Carmen and Kenya gave each other the side eye and snickered as they left the dusty female looking and feeling stupid as hell for even trying it in the first place.

"You crazy!" Carmen was smiling and falling against the locker after Kenya had cleverly checked one of their many frenemies.

"Man, fuck that skank-a-dank low-budget bird! She runs around here, always trying to be slick-mouthed all the time like her own shit don't stank. Imagine that whore trying to come for me!" Kenya huffed, caught up in her emotions. "She should try putting that jaw of hers to better use and maybe, just maybe, one of those losers she fucks with would upgrade that yesteryear wardrobe she be rocking!" Kenya tried to hold her laughter as she gave the girl one more casually fake smile from across the hall as she entered her class. Once she made it inside the classroom and took her seat, Kenya was quickly surrounded by guys wanting a few minutes of her time. After a few moments of her holding court, the bell rang for the start of first period.

London

"I love you, Gran!" London lovingly told her with affection as she left out the front door. *Let me double check. I've got all my books, my homework and my lunch.* London always took her own lunch so she could sit under a tree and study if she found time. As she slowly walked down her block, the compassionate teen always took time to speak to all of her neighbors, asking if each was having a good day. She, unlike her sister, was friendly to everyone, which was why everyone on the entire close-knit block loved London much more than her cynical-minded twin.

At the very end of the street barely stood the house where Amber and her family lived. She was London's best friend ever since she was four years old and came to live with Gran.

Even though she had her sister to play with, Amber made living on Glendale bearable. At first London seemed to miss her old toddler playmates, her own bed, and her own house, not to mention both her parents, but with the love of Gran and the friendship of Amber, she would grow into her new life without any noticeable problems.

"Hey, girl."

"Hey, Amber." London returned her friend's smile.

"Did you get a chance to finish that report in English you were working on?" Amber had a sympathetic look on her face, hoping for the best. She knew all the hell that her best friend London caught trying to study at home; with Kenya blasting the radio half the night and talking on the phone the other half, London fought hard to keep her grades up and her sanity intact.

"Yeah, I got it finished, finally. The teacher wanted at most four pages, but I ended up with six and a half. I tried to cut some down," London said nonchalantly, always known for overdoing it when it came to schoolwork.

Amber grinned, telling London the exact same thing she said after every A paper that London received. "Please don't forget the little people when you become president one day." They both smiled as they continued walking down the same side street they took every day.

"Hello, girls." The old lady who walked her little dog every morning waved.

"Hi," they answered in unison.

They always stopped to talk to old Mr. Phelps. He was practically blind and a lot of kids in the neighborhood would throw stuff on his porch to scare him and always left his gate wide open. He being eighty-one and blind made him an easy target for kids and drug addicts alike who often took advantage of his disabilities. London, known for being overly nice, would sometimes lose her temper, like her sister, and get in the zone falling into the dark side. It didn't happen often, but seeing some of her peers mess with the elderly or people who couldn't stand up and defend themselves was one surefire way to get London up in arms and to prove she was also her father's daughter.

"Hey, Mr. Phelps," the girls yelled up to the porch where he sat every morning. "How you doing? Do you need anything on our way back from school?" they both inquired.

"No, girls, I'm fine, just fine. I'm just getting some of that good morning air, thanks for asking." Mr. Phelps smiled and thought how nice London and Amber both were. He knew those two girls were going to be somebody someday. Especially London, who'd always made sure on Sundays to bring him by a healthy plate that her Gran would cook.

"I hope there's not going to be a science test today," London stated while kicking a can down the street.

"Me too," Amber agreed as the high school came in sight.

Both girls chatted between themselves about school, homework, and other things that teenage girls talked about: boys. Although her sister was the self-proclaimed diva of Detroit's Central High, London went through school practically unnoticed by both boys and girls alike. The only people at school who noticed Amia London Roberts were her teachers. She was the only one in class who would turn in all of her assignments on time, sometimes the only one who turned them in period. They admired her ambition. Yet, some of the least enthusiastic instructors hated the fact that London had a lot more knowledge than they possessed on most subjects and never once seemed to let them forget that fact.

Some teachers just wanted to cash their paychecks, avoid conflict, and go home to their families. However, London was having none of that. She had a thirst for knowledge and made all her teachers earn their salary, each and every penny. Gran used to joke that London had been here before, and many she'd encounter believed her grandmother's assessment to be true.

As London and Amber entered through the doors of school, they went their separate ways. London went in and out the crowds with ease. She didn't want to bump into anyone or call attention to herself. If she were to make eye contact with any of her sister's sworn enemies, she would give them a faint smile and try to avoid confrontation if at all possible. Some days, of course, were better than others.

"Hey, twin," Shannon hissed with a hint of nastiness she was infamously known for.

"Hello, Shannon," replied London nonchalantly, trying not to look up. She knew both Kenya and Shannon equally hated each other and that made Shannon in turn hate London because she looked exactly like her sister. *All this crap probably over some stupid boy,* thought London. "Why are females so one-dimensional? They need to elevate their brains," she mumbled underneath her breath.

"Excuse me, but did you say something over there you want to repeat, Ms. Thang?" growled Shannon as she bucked her eyes out wanting trouble.

Having more self-control than her sister, London shook her head and walked away, not once looking back. She heard Shannon and her girls still laughing as she made her way down the hall, but she didn't care. London scurried up the hallway quickly before the last bell rang, not wanting to be late. As she passed by one of the classrooms, she saw the most popular girl in the entire school surrounded by a flock of boys. She waved at her sister, Kenya, who waved back. London had to get to class. The bell was ringing.

Chapter Three

Bitch, Please!

After three grueling years of high school passed, it was the last week of the term. The twins had made it and were going to finally be seniors next semester. The only thing left before vacation was final exams. Kenya acted as if passing them would be a total breeze. Concentrating on tests wasn't easy for Kenya. The popular teen knew that she needed to study but would still sneak out of the house almost every night doing God knows what with God knows who. London, on the other hand, would study constantly, keeping her head buried in the books. Although they were both smart girls when it came down to it, unfortunately only London would apply herself.

Gran often worried about both her granddaughters' well-being. However, there was only so much she could do or say to point them in the right direction. At some point it would be up to the sisters themselves to make the right decisions and choices in general. The flow of life was starting to take its toll on Gran; she was getting old. In between the grief of losing both of her own children and trying her best to raise two now-teenage girls, she was rapidly losing speed.

The last bell rang and it was thankfully over. The final class for the semester had concluded. Rambunctious and excited student after student poured out the doors of the school building like it was on fire and they had on gasoline attire. The joy of no more class until fall was on their minds, but the true source of their merriment was the anticipation that'd been growing all day, really all year long. Kenya and Shannon, constant adversaries who argued day after day, were about to battle and the shit was about to be on. They were going to fight on the basketball court after school. Everyone knew about it, even the teachers. But they didn't give a shit; their so-called tour of duty was finally over, so to hell with the students and their madness!

"Let them kill each other," London overheard one of the teachers snarl while she drank her coffee. "Their parents are raising little animals so this is the type of behavior I expect."

Walking past, London, who was ear hustling, couldn't help herself and jumped into the otherwise private conversation. "Wow, you're supposed to be adults, teachers no less. We should be looking to you for guidance. You should be trying to find a way to help us end this black-on-black crime instead of turning a deaf ear." London was in rare form as she waited for a sign of remorse from the teacher. "Somebody should report y'all!"

"Well, Li'l Miss Wannabe Harriet Tubman and Oprah rolled into one," the younger of the teachers smugly responded to the teen. "Instead of you being all up in here giving us a black history lesson, don't you think you should be out on that basketball court trying to stop your sister from getting her pretty little teeth stumped out her mouth?" The teacher, not trying to defend her initial proclamation, was rolling her head around and snapping her fingers, just like she was London's equal. "You're in here judging us like your parents weren't out in the streets back in the day destroying the minds of the youth! Girl, bye! We all know the story of your people!"

Hearing her sarcastic statement about her deceased parents and Kenya's impending battle swiftly snatched London back into reality of what was really about to take place. It was true. While she was preoccupied inside being a one-woman martyr for humanity, the here and now was taking place just yards away. She had to get off her soapbox and get outside fast. That no-good, "always got something ugly to say about folk" Shannon had been running off at the mouth all day long about how she was gonna jump on Kenya when school was out. Well, seeing how the last bell had rung over ten minutes prior, London knew time was ticking. "I hate violence, but there's no way I'm not gonna have my sister's back," London said out loud as she ran down the deserted hallway, bolting out of the school's double doors. Immediately eyeing the crowd gathering, swarming around like flies on a pile of shit on the basketball court, London couldn't believe how many people were actually cheering, happy to see two females try to beat one another down. *Why can't Kenya stay out of trouble for once?* she thought, quickly approaching the middle of all the commotion in the field. *It seems like Gran is right. Her temper is gonna get her in big trouble one day!*

"Fake ass!" Shannon brazenly taunted, feeling as if the crowd was backing her up. With her hands on her hips, she was front and center of the small mob surrounded by her so-called clique, which consisted of three ghetto-painted-face females who also took the bus from the projects every day to get to school. However, that didn't mean much of nothing to Kenya at all. Matter of fact, the only thing it really meant was they weren't just hood rats; they were low-budget project rats. To Kenya it didn't matter much if you were rich, poor, black, or white, old, young, boy, or girl. If you came for her, she had no problem whatsoever returning the favor ten times over and coming for you. So if Shannon wanted to feel Kenya's wrath, then so be it, she would. It was on.

"What?" Kenya let her intended victim rant and rave before she had her turn at showing Shannon what was really good in the hood.

"You heard me, bitch! What it do, Ms. Uppity? You been acting like you wanted some all year long, so what's up?" Shannon was straight-up frontin'. Honestly she was scared to death, but she tried her best to not let it show, especially in front of half the student body.

The crowd was geeking it up and that's all Kenya, already mentally prepared to take her opponent's head off, needed to hear. Knowing her DNA bloodline ran deep on her father's side, Kenya didn't crack a smile, showing not one tooth. She was cut from a different cloth than many, and, in her words, they didn't even make that fabric anymore. The west side's known wild child offspring of Johnnie and Melinda Roberts did her best clowning in front of an audience and this was one of her biggest to date. She had a point to prove about hoes running off at the mouth just because they had lips, and school was back in session for Shannon.

Carmen was on her left and London, not truly wanting to fight but would and could, had just burst through the crowd and was loyally posted on her right. Allan, who'd dropped out a couple years back, was also up at the school to hold them down, just in case one of those busters Shannon would trick with flexed and wanted their ass kicked too.

"Fake ass? Come on now seriously, is that what you let rip out that raggedy grill mouth? Girl, look at you, from the bottom to the top you need a clue. Your synthetic weave has been recycled from week to week. Your blouse got a permanent ring around the collar and do your pants even know what an iron is?" Kenya was going ham and the mesmerized crowd loved the show she was giving them.

Some of the guys in the bunch were ashamed that they ever kicked it with Shannon let alone spent some loose change on her. London felt bad for her also, but deep down inside she knew she had it coming. Yet, at that moment, no one felt as bad as Shannon, who had no defense for the slaughter. Her girls had eased away and faded back into the background. It was obvious they didn't want any of the verbal beat down their so-called homegirl was getting, who was staring down at the ground with tears starting to form in her eyes.

"Oh, hell naw, you stankin' trash bucket! Why you got your head down now? With them ran-over shoes! Did you walk over here from Africa?" Kenya still never cracked a smile as she twisted up her face. The girl was cold-blooded, just like her daddy, and wouldn't stop going until she was satisfied in totally humiliating Shannon. "You want it with me for real? Girl, you better get your life!"

Most of the students standing around were almost in tears from the entertainment Kenya was providing. Carmen was begging her best friend to stop running Shannon's name through the mud because her side was beginning to hurt. She, like the many other spectators, just couldn't stop laughing at Shannon's expense. London, cut from the same cloth as her sister on the other hand, was just like her twin, not cracking a smile either. She knew Kenya much better than anyone else and could tell that the girl had "blood in her eyes." *Poor Shannon,* was all she could think at that point.

"All bullshit aside let's tear this court up," Kenya, aggravated, spoke in a cold, callous tone, following her taunting words with a sock dead to Shannon's jaw, who just stood there, speechless, holding her face.

Just then, luckily for Shannon, the school security arrived, breaking up their one-sided battle before things grew worse. The crowd slowly dispersed, including the twins and their friends. As they made their way down Linwood Avenue, Carmen and Allan couldn't stop making jokes about what had just jumped off. They both were taking turns pretending to be Shannon. Even the normally quiet Amber was cracking up. Hell, she and London had been on the receiving end of Shannon's insults time and time again. It felt good to see the bully get a small taste of her own medicine for once.

While the others went on with the jokes, finally going their separate ways, London walked alongside her sister. She placed her hand on Kenya's shoulder, attempting to calm her down. When Kenya got heated, it was hard for her to let stuff go. Luckily, the sisters finally made it to their house without any further incidents. Kenya sat down on the concrete stair and London followed. As soon as they looked at one another they both burst out laughing.

"Dang, girl, you really let her have it. I was trying hard as heck not to laugh all in her face." London giggled. "But she deserved every bit of it. She's a bully!"

Kenya couldn't wait to roast her sister. "What about you? You came bursting all through the crowd like Freddy fucking Krueger! Shiiit, you even scared me."

In the midst of all of the laughter, they didn't even notice Gran pulling in the driveway.

"Hey, Gran!" London yelled out, running off the porch to help her grandmother with her bags.

"Hey, baby, how are you and how was school?" Gran hugged London tightly.

"It was the best day of the entire year!"

Kenya, acting out of character, cut in, actually hugging Gran too. They all walked to the porch arm in arm, smiling. Today they were a happy family, even Kenya, who was for once not being a pain. It's surprising what an ass kicking would do, especially when it's not your ass that got kicked.

Chapter Four

Seniors

"Summer came and went so quickly. I can't wait. We're finally seniors! I hope we have a few new teachers, maybe someone to teach English or math." London was going on and on for what seemed like forever. She loved school, even if it was Central High.

"New teachers, forget all that! Girl, we're seniors now, queens of the school! It's our turn to be running thangs up in there. It's gonna be a new sheriff in that motherfucker!" Kenya was too excited also as she thought about her impending spot as HBIC of the school. She was spinning around with her hands in the air. "I can't wait!" Kenya was cheesin' from ear to ear.

The girls had become a lot closer during the summer months. Gran had suffered a mild heart attack while she was at work and had to stay in the hospital for almost two weeks straight. The twins had to rely on each other much more for everything from moral support to sharing the responsibility of the household. It was then, even more than before, that they learned of the special bond the two shared. A little bit of maturity on both their behalves had settled in. If they ran into a problem, London figured out the solution and Kenya executed the plan, putting it in motion. They now woke up daily on their own and instead of Gran making them breakfast they in turn would cook for her. While the twins still hung out with their old friends at school, for the first time in three years they walked to Central together. Sometimes it was Linwood Avenue, and others it would be the side streets.

As the months started to go by and the seasons changed, so did Kenya. She just couldn't help herself. As much as she was fighting her alter ego, she'd unfortunately slipped back into her old, wild, carefree ways she was so infamous for. School and turning in homework assignments on time had once again become a second priority in her young, reckless life. All of Kenya's grades she struggled so feverishly to get up to par were rapidly falling, and lastly she returned to skipping class most of the time. She was heading downhill rapidly and nothing anyone said or did could seem to slow her intentions of being "not shit" down.

London, disgusted at what she was watching take place and couldn't stop, blamed her sister's spiral on that stupid foolish-oriented boyfriend of Kenya's. London knew Ty was nothing more than a car thief clown who had dropped out of school in tenth grade and ran the streets of Detroit on a nickel-and-dime adventure trying to sell drugs for the next man when he could get put on. Like most young dudes in their neighborhood, he wasn't smart enough or had enough game to have his own sack to risk getting knocked and going to jail for; he hustled to make the next nigga's pockets fat. Ty, in all his ill-witted wisdom, was always busy putting different kinds of dumb, idiotic ideas in Kenya's gullible mind. Kenya always had delusions of grandeur and escaping hood life no matter how she could do it, hook or crook. Engulfed by nothing but getting off Glendale Street and out of Gran's strict and spiritual household, Kenya was starting to cut off every-one in her small circle of friends, even Allan and Carmen. At night she was either on the phone plotting the demise of her current lifestyle situation or sneaking out of the house to meet up with Ty.

"Hey, boo, it's me, baby," whispered Kenya as quietly as she could. "I can't talk long. My sister is bugging out on me about my grades so I gotta at least do some of my homework."

"Why she be all actin' like a book gonna help you eat out in these streets? She needs to be trying to hook up with my boy. You know for some reason he dig her plain-Jane ass! Plus he's paid, I ain't bullshitting!" Ty cleared his throat after choking on some Kush. "He be pulling in major ends almost every day with these hot box cars we been getting off this lot and he got a sack of this good shit I'm blowing on." He coughed once more. "For real, Kenya, seriously your sister needs to wise the fuck up and get some of this bread from ol' boy!"

Kenya was beginning to get irritated and annoyed with his conversation and the disrespectful direction it was taking. After it was all done and said, that was her twin sister he was badmouthing and tripping on. Since she had an emotional attachment to him, Kenya didn't pay much attention when he talked shit about her—she could overlook that for the sake of young puppy love—but fuck him dogging London just because he thought he could. He was going too far with his comments and suggestions and she wasn't trying to hear any more of it.

"Listen, Ty, I already done told you I was on the clock with talking to you in the first damn place! Now I got a bright idea for your dropout-ass to process: why don't you stop riding your boy's nut sack so hard, leave my sister's name out your mouth, and show me some fucking attention? How about that, nigga?" Kenya twisted her face up as she spoke each word like she meant it, and of course she did.

Ty, who always thought much more of himself than anyone else ever did, immediately got caught in his feelings, wasting no time going ham. "You know what? Fuck you, Kenya, and your stuck-up-ass ugly sister. I was trying to turn both you bitches on to some real game, but I see once again your ho ass ain't trying to respect my gangster!"

Before Kenya had a chance to respond to that lame-ass bullshit knowledge he was kicking, he'd already slammed the phone down, hanging up on her. She couldn't help but laugh. True enough Ty was her so-called man, so to speak, but he also was a little punk and just about everyone on the west side knew it. He was scared of his own shadow and here he was trying to go for bad.

Whenever they were at the mall or out to the park, he would always stand mute when this guy or that guy tried to push up on Kenya. Later on when she would ask him how come he ain't say shit, he would make up excuses and try to play that shit off like he wasn't low-key terrified of getting his ass handed to him on a platter. Kenya started to think, *Why isn't he just honest with me and himself and speak the truth? He could have just simply said, "Damn, baby, you know I ain't no gangster.* She almost fell on the floor from laughing so hard at him trying so hard to be a gangster. He'd call back tomorrow, begging as usual. He always did. "Different day, same idiot," she said out loud. When she finally looked up, Kenya saw her sister looking at her, shaking her head.

"I hope that you're still laughing when you get your grades at the end of this semester," nagged London in a maternal tone.

Kenya opted not to let her sister in on the joke she found so hilarious. "Yes, Mom, I got you. I'm about to hit the books now."

The school year seemed to drag on for what seemed like forever and a day. Ironically both girls were growing bored with school and what it had to offer. London, the smartest book-wise, had received the highest GPA semester after semester. She was top of her class in every honor class they offered and that still was not enough to challenge her brain. The devoted scholar often let her mind roam about what the next year would be about and how college campus life would be. London was more than ready to graduate and leave for the university of her choice on a full scholarship. Most of her teachers were incompetent in her eyes and were going to be happy to see her cross that stage. London had this thing for correcting the teachers so much they should have paid her to teach the class. There was no question, hands down, as to who the valedictorian would be that school year: Ms. Amia London Roberts.

Meanwhile, on the other hand, Ms. Amoya Kenya Roberts was also making a name for herself at Central High School. Of course, the self-proclaimed diva was named both homecoming queen and prom queen. That was expected because she was always fly and sociable with her peers. Not to mention after all the flirting she did, every boy at school voted for her, hoping for a date or at least the attention she gave them during the election process. Kenya was also voted "class smile," "class legs," "class body," and what shocked even Kenya was that she, not her academically industrious twin London, was voted most likely to succeed! However, the question that swam in London's mind was, *Succeed at what?*

Chapter Five

Farewells

Graduation day had finally arrived and both of the girls were dressed to kill. The girls' uncle had taken both of them on a shopping spree to New York to get them gear to look perfect for their special day. The twins respectfully had on pink Armani tailored cut suits. The buttons were gold and trimmed in the same pink that was in the fabric. They each had open-toed gator sandals with a small heel on them. London and Kenya, for the first time since they were small children, wore their hair in the exact same style. It was in a French roll tightly tucked with soft sandy-brown curls cascading down across the sides of their faces. Each had also gotten their nails manicured and a pedicure the day before.

Gran, proud as any grandmother could be, had let them sleep in an extra thirty minutes while she made them a breakfast fit for a queen. Lovingly, she helped London get dressed and ready, and tried her best to keep an always-hyper Kenya still. The girls then left Gran at home to get herself together for one of the biggest days of all of their lives.

"I love you two very, very much and I'll see you at the school. I'm proud of you both and promise me you'll never ever forget that." Gran hugged both of her grandchildren tightly and kissed them, before letting the two leave out the door.

The twins made their grand entrance into the packed auditorium, and all eyes were definitely on them. Both were getting mad crazy attention. Everyone, students, teachers, and counselors were all confused as to which twin was London and which twin was Kenya. The girls, each being who they were meant to be, quickly removed all doubt when they opened their mouths and began to speak. That was always a dead giveaway with the twins.

Kenya was loud and off the chain and her sister was notice-ably quiet when it came to anything other than schoolwork. London was more than a little nervous about the speech she was slated to deliver. She had worked hard all four years and rightly deserved to be rewarded standing behind that podium. All of the late nights she spent lying awake reading and the days she stayed in the house studying were all getting ready to pay off for her. London was proud of herself. She had a wide smile plastered on her face and a nervousness shaking inside. The dedicated teen knew her next step was college, then acquiring a degree, making all her dreams come true.

All the graduating seniors scrambled around posing for pictures with their classmates and parents and signing yearbooks. Kenya, vain as always, broke free from the excited, energized crowd, posting up in front of the wall-length mirror backstage. Turning from side to side, she kept adjusting her cap and checking her makeup. There was no one in the world Kenya admired more than herself. She was stuck on herself and knew that she was a straight-up dime. She was feeling herself, even in a cap and gown.

The girls' uncle, his girlfriend, and a few of their distant cousins were seated in the far back row. The twins had saved Gran, the most important person in both their lives, a seat front and center. With love, respect, and devotion they placed two single pink roses on it for her. Gran had fought hard and sacrificed a lot to get them to this point. They wanted her to know when she arrived in the auditorium that this was her day also.

Time was ticking. It was close to eleven o'clock and the principal was yelling for everyone to get in line so that they could march in and begin the sure-to-be long, drawn-out commencement ceremony. It was time to start what the entire senior class had been anticipating for four years ever since they were freshmen.

"I still don't see her, do you?" London held her sister's hand, shaking, still extremely nervous about giving a speech in front of all the boisterous people.

"No, but you know Gran. She probably couldn't find the right outfit to wear." Kenya chuckled while trying to conceal her equal worry for their grandmother's tardiness.

Everyone backstage was hyped, anxious to get underway; however, the girls continued to peek out from behind the burgundy and gold curtains every few seconds, but still no Gran. Trying to find excuses for her absence, each started to think of what could be possibly keeping her, especially on this day.

"The telephone must have rung and, you know Gran, she was probably too polite to rush one of her church lady friends having a problem off the phone. She's almost here, I bet." London shrugged her shoulders. She was almost in tears.

Kenya continued to hold her sister's hand trying her absolute best to calm London down. Little did the distraught twins know that at that very moment in time the phone did ring. Sadly it was God and He had decided to call Gran home. Up in age, the devoted mother and grandmother never completely recovered from the heart attack that she'd suffered the previous year. With the determination of a lion, the elderly God-fearing senior citizen's weak heart barely held on until London and Kenya were both grown. Gran fought a hard fight but was truly tired.

"Ms. Roberts and Ms. Roberts would you two like to join the rest of us, so that we may begin?" snarled the frazzled-minded principal. He was running around on edge trying to stay on schedule but it was not happening. The girls peeked out in the crowd one last time before the ceremony started. They were still holding hands. They both still felt uneasy.

"Well, this is it," they both said in unison, staring at one another for comfort and moral support while each wondered where Gran was at.

"I love you, London."

"I love you too, Kenya."

"Say U Promise!" They each laughed as they dropped hands.

Kenya walked over to the line that was forming and took her spot in line with the other Rs; and London, of course, took her place on stage so that she could make her speech and receive her honors scholarship declarations and hard-earned certificates of merit. The girls smiled at each other from opposite sides of the room. They were overjoyed at the occasion, but solemnly knew this would be the beginning of being their own individual selves, not a twin, as they had been since conception. As the ceremony started each twin wondered constantly throughout, *Where is Gran?*

A day filled with the extreme promise of the future was also a day filled with sadness for the twins. They had struggled relentlessly through guest speakers, awards, and the seemingly endless roll call of the senior graduates, and still no Gran. Dry mouthed, London could barely get through her speech without stumbling over the same words repeatedly that she had practiced for weeks. The haunting sight of Gran's empty seat with the two pink roses lying alone on the chair made her nauseated and sick to her stomach.

At the end of the ceremony, the girls weren't interested in taking pictures. They had no desire to hug everyone and pretend like they would really miss one another. All of the crowd fanfare was of no consequence to either of them. No sooner than they found their uncle did they jump in his SUV and make him drive them home as quickly as possible. They pulled up in the driveway and before the truck could come to a complete stop the two were jumping out and running up toward the door.

When the Kenya and London got the door unlocked, they bolted inside. That's when they received the pain of ten lifetimes combined. They laid eyes on Gran. She was fully dressed and sitting back in her favorite chair. There were two letters lying in her lap. Each had one of the girls' names written on the white envelope.

After all the initial pandemonium broke loose and the para-
medics, police, and the morgue had left with the body, each
twin, feeling totally lost and in denial, sat quietly in a daze
halfway reading the letters their beloved Gran had written.
The letters told each of them to always trust, depend on, and
rely on one other no matter what the circumstances would be.

Both of the twins wept uncontrollably at Gran's homego-
ing service, even having to be ushered out to get some air
and a chance to recompose themselves. Gran in all her glory
truly looked like an angel. The sometimes-tormented, but
always-spiritual loyal woman was finally at peace. She'd left
the house fifty-fifty jointly to both London and Kenya. Each
girl would receive two acres of land down South in Jackson,
Alabama. That was where their grandmother and mother were
originally born before relocating to Detroit. They also were to
receive $20,000 each in life insurance money. Gran, loving
her girls to the end, made sure each would have a fair start at
life.

It had been a little more than two and a half months since
Gran had gone and London and Kenya often spent nights
lying awake missing her in their own special way. September
rolled around quickly and London, who had wrestled with the
idea of accepting the scholarship from State University, was
getting ready for college. Sure the school was also located in
Michigan, but it was up north. It was almost a two hour car
ride from home, and away from Kenya, her twin. London
would have to stay on campus which meant she couldn't keep
tabs on her often out-of-control sister. Miss Kenya, now living
with a little bit of pocket money and no real adult supervision,
had gotten a little wild and untamable, to say the least. Yet,
despite her shortcomings, and most, if not all, of Kenya's
recent decisions and behavior, London could hardly fathom
being apart from her.

"I've got to do this. I've worked much too hard not to push
on." London was talking to Gran's picture as she packed it in
her bag.

Amber somberly came over to help her best friend pack. She was going to miss her homegirl and confidante. "Dang, I wish I was going with you, so that way we could both get out this tired hood. You are so lucky."

"I wished you were going too, so I wouldn't be so lonely up there with all those strangers."

Both Amber and London looked at each other and sighed. Amber, not the smartest person London knew, barely graduated and felt like in all probability she would forever be stuck working in the beauty supply on Dexter Boulevard. They sadly exchanged their good-byes and Amber left, heading up toward Dexter to work.

Everything was all packed and London's uncle was on the way with his pickup truck. As she sat on the front stairs looking around at her surroundings, trying to remember all the flowers and rocks in the street, London closed her eyes. She wanted to make sure she didn't forget the neighborhood. Squeezing them tightly shut, she locked the memory in her brain. London would miss the hood and all the foolish antics that went along with living in it. Crime infested or not, it was her home, and no matter where she went, who she met, or what great things in life she ever accomplished, she'd never forget where she came from or the ethics Gran had instilled in her. Opening her eyes, she soon heard the blasting sounds of jazz music coming down the street and London knew that it had to be her uncle.

Damn near pulling the truck up on the porch with the huge rimmed tires he jumped out. "Hey, baby girl." He beamed with pride of where they were headed and what London was sure to succeed in. "You's about ready to go get this family some higher learning going on or what?" He grabbed London off her feet and started swinging her around. He was so proud of her; everyone who knew Gran was.

"Dang, Uncle, I can hardly breathe, put me down!" she begged as her feet dangled trying to touch the ground.

"Okay, baby girl! Are you all packed? Do you have enough clothes? Do you need to go get more supplies?" He was talking so fast, on a ten, that London had to tell him to calm down.

"Yes, I'm fine, so don't worry." She playfully pushed his arm, smiling. "I have everything I need and what I don't have I can buy up there in the next few days, so stop worrying about me. I'm gonna be good. I promise!"

London had a full ride scholarship: room, board, and books completely paid for. Whatever else London would need, she could easily take from the money that Gran had left to her. Unlike Kenya, she'd saved more than the majority of the life insurance money that Gran blessed her and her sister with. She'd basically purchased a laptop, a new cell phone, some much-needed and wanted books, and banked the rest for the future.

"Well, London, where is your sister?" her uncle suspiciously questioned. "Why ain't her fast, wannabe-grown-ass out on this porch helping you with your stuff?"

No sooner, seemingly seconds, had the words left out his mouth, than they heard the annoying screech of tires turn the corner. Uncle, instinctively from living the street life, reached under his shirt and put his hand on his thriller. He didn't know who was coming down the block driving like a bat outta hell, yet he did know that any clown-ass fool who wanted to get his "big shot on" was gonna catch a few hot ones real quick, fast, and in a hurry. As the car finally came into focus, he and London both shared an expression of disgust. It was Kenya, riding with that foul-ass Ty, nine outta ten in a stolen vehicle.

"Hey, y'all! What up, doe?" Kenya, obviously turned up, jumped out the car looking like who did it and why. Her hair was out of place and her clothes were slightly wrinkled, looking as if she had slept in them.

"What the fuck is your problem?" Uncle never raised his voice or even cursed in front of his nieces, but he had been pushed to his limit and was pissed off. "You look one hot mess! Have you lost your damn mind out here or what?"

London got terrified not knowing what her uncle was going to do, knowing his reputation for violence, but not Kenya. She didn't give a shit what he or anyone had to say about what she did or who she did it with. Not even blinking, she stood tall in her uncle's face ready for whatever. She had that Roberts blood pumping through her veins just like her uncle and his brother, her daddy, did and Kenya feared no man or woman for that matter. Maybe it was that fat blunt that she had for breakfast or the wine from the night before still circulating in her system giving her liquid courage, but whatever it was she started to laugh.

Ty, terrified as his girl's uncle noticed the ignition column of the car broken and a screwdriver on seat, knew better than to try to go up against the seasoned criminal everyone knew was a cold-blooded killer if need be. He wised up real fast and peeled away from the curb as quickly as he had pulled up, leaving Kenya to face her own demons so to speak. Ty knew the twins' uncle only by his ruthless reputation on the streets and knew he wasn't for any foolishness, so he couldn't help but exhale as he made it down the block to the stop sign without a bullet in the back of his head.

"Have you been out all damn night with that lowlife car-stealing bastard?" The twins' uncle roughly grabbed Kenya by her shirt, waiting for an answer.

Kenya's defiant laughter quickly turned into pure shock as he lifted her upward. "Let me go, let me go!" she cried as she tried unsuccessfully to snatch away from his strong grip.

"Listen, little girl! I don't give a sweet fuck how grown you running around here pretending you are! Let's get this straight. I'll kill you dead first and anyone else who tries to lead your ass down the wrong path. Do you fucking understand me, Kenya?" Their uncle was furious as the veins started to jump out the side of his neck.

London, desperate to not have any trouble, came in between two of the only people she truly called family and began crying. "Please don't do this, please. Not on my last day here," she continuously pleaded.

Seeing both of his nieces in tears made their uncle's rage slightly soften, but it was obviously his sentiment, for what he'd told Kenya remained the same and by the evil side eye he gave her she knew to take heed. "Come on, London, let's get your stuff loaded and get going." He grabbed the last few items off the porch and got back in his truck without so much as glancing in Kenya's general direction at all.

"Well, sis, this is it. I'm gonna miss you, Kenya."

"I'm gonna miss you too. First Mom and Pops, then Gran, and now you, but I ain't tripping." Kenya tried to force a smile as her heart broke. "I'll be good holding it down."

"Kenya, I'm only a phone call away. Matter of fact, I'll call you as soon as I get there." They hugged each other as the tears continued to flow.

"If you need me," they both said at the same time like twins often did.

"One love." London smiled.

"*Say U Promise,*" chanted Kenya.

London jumped in the truck and the girls kept their eyes glued to the other one until the truck turned off the block, heading upstate.

Chapter Six

London

Even though they'd left early in the day, after eating lunch it was getting dark by the time they reached the campus.

Overwhelmed, London took a good look around the campus as they drove up. "Wow, it's a lot bigger than what I remember from my visit on the tour we took in our senior year." Taking out a small pack of papers, she was puzzled. "Well, I know I'm supposed to be in Davis Hall dormitory. So let's see . . ."

They followed all the signs posted along the side of each twisted street corner. When finally they found the building, London leaped out the truck and jogged up to the double glass door. As she entered, she saw plenty of new, interesting faces milling around looking just as confused as she was. After standing in a long line at the front desk, it was her turn to give the lady her personal information.

"Hello, I'm Amia London Roberts. I'm trying to check in."

The young lady behind the desk punched her name into the computer and retrieved London's keys, room assignment, and some important information booklets that would make her transition into college life easier. Keys in hand and a huge smile on her face, London skipped back out to the truck, telling her uncle that they could pull around the back entrance of the building and unload. In the company of at least ten other excited families, the pair patiently waited until it was their turn to use the big freight elevator.

"All right then, baby girl, let's get you settled in."

Her uncle was in a much better mood than earlier when he'd had that big blowout confrontation with Kenya, and London was glad. One half of the elated twins started to grab her things up in her arms, placing them on the elevator as other cars, trucks, and vans pulled up, waiting their turns. *He is the best uncle in the world. Thank God he has my back!* London lovingly thought as they carried load after load up to her new dorm room.

After they were finally done, her uncle started to get a sad expression on his face. "I'm gonna miss you, baby girl. I want you to represent for the entire family. Your father and mother would be so proud of you if they were here!" He fought back the tears thinking about his dead brother and the circumstances of his death. "I'll know you'll be the smartest one here. We're all counting on you."

"Don't worry, Uncle, I won't let you down. I don't know about being the smartest, but I promise I'll study hard and do my very best." London hugged him tightly and before he left out the dorm room door, he reached in his pocket, blessing her with five one hundred–dollar bills.

"Uncle, I'm fine. Seriously, I have enough money to get by," she pleaded as she backed away from his extended hand.

"Okay, London, dig this here. I'm gonna tell you what your daddy always told me: as long as you black, you don't have enough money. Now take this and put it up for later!" He then forced the money into her hand, refusing to take no for an answer.

London smiled and told him that she loved him while they both emotionally fought back the tears.

As he was leaving, London's new roommate, unbeknownst to him, was making her way down the long hallway. The struggle she was having was real. The young teen was having trouble with all the bags and boxes that she was attempting to carry and kick down the hallway by herself. Unfortunately many of her belongings were falling out of her arms and onto the floor.

"Dang why did I bring so much damn stuff?" she spoke out loud, not caring who might have overheard her talking to herself.

"Maybe because a real woman needs a lot of personal items to make strange places feel more like home. How about that?" London's uncle beamed as he bent down to help the overdeveloped young girl gather together her things.

"Wow, thank you so much, sir." She smiled and picked up the bag she was carrying, throwing it back over her shoulder. "I'm just down the hallway I think."

As she watched the numbers getting higher and higher, London's uncle, being a man, watched her body and the way it moved like a hawk. *Damn, I need to go back to school!* He couldn't do shit but shake his head as his manhood automatically jumped.

"Hey, this is it here!" Fatima yelled as they burst through the door that was still cracked open. "I made it."

London, who was unpacking, turned around and saw her uncle standing in the doorway with a huge grin on his face.

"Hey, girl! I'm Fatima James, your new roommate." Out of breath she dropped all her things on the floor and blew up in the air.

"Hello, Fatima, I'm Amia Roberts, but please call me London." The two gave each other a short brief hug. "Oh, and I see that you must have met my uncle."

"Your uncle? Well, yes, I guess I did. Well, sort of." Fatima started to trip over her words as she noticed just how handsome her knight in shining armor really was under the bright room lights.

Knowing he had caught the young girl's eye, he reached back inside his pocket, peeling London off another hundred from his rubber-banded stack. "Well, ladies, I guess I'll leave you two to unpack and get to know each other." Of course, he made sure that Fatima was watching as he strutted his older self back toward the door. "Put some snacks in the fridge for both of you." He then winked his eye at his niece and blew a kiss at Fatima.

"We will. Bye, Uncle. Have a safe trip back!" London was almost speechless by her uncle's blatant flirting with her roommate.

The girls started pulling different stuff out of their boxes and bags to add their own individual personal touches and own flair to the room. While London's side of the room had a lot of pictures of her small family, which consisted of Gran, Kenya, and her uncle, reference books, notebooks, and a few stuffed animals, Fatima had snapshots of Africa and pictures of her Muslim parents in various racial and religious freedom marches they had taken part in. Fatima also had a lot of bumper stickers bearing black pride slogans and tons of books about African Americans. London naturally wondered why Fatima didn't choose to attend an all-black school since she was obviously pro-black.

"Wow, you sure have a lot of books. It's like you have your very own library." London flipped though all of the various titles, somewhat in awe of Fatima's interest.

"Yeah, girl, I love me some books. I stay up hours reading." Fatima smiled at her new roommate. The girls knew, right then and there, they would grow to be good friends. "Hey, I am starving. Let's get something to eat. And then we can check out the campus at the same time." Fatima rubbed on her empty stomach.

London eagerly agreed with her roommate. "Okay, but let me try to call my sister first and let her know that I made it here safely." She reached in a box and handed Fatima a picture of Kenya. "This was taken at the park this summer."

"Damn, this is your sister? You're a twin? Girl, I thought that these other pictures were of you at the club or something with your hair down and makeup on!" Fatima couldn't believe they were two different people. Fatima smiled at London. "Go ahead, girl, and make your call to your alter ego. I'll be down in the lobby."

London picked up the phone, dialing home.

Kenya

Kenya slowly walked up the stairs looking back one last time as she saw her uncle and sister fade out of sight. She put her key in the door and started to make her way into the empty, sure-to-be lonely house. Stopping in front of the mirror in the front hallway, she took a good, long look at herself. "Well, it's just you and me now. It's time to do you, get your shit together, and hold yourself down." Kenya said it over and over out loud as if she was trying to convince herself of it being true. Taking a deep breath, she had to smile thinking about London and all she did to make both their lives better since Gran's passing.

The house was clean as a whistle and smelled like it had been scrubbed top to bottom. *Good lookin', sis.* Kenya nodded as she passed by London's graduation picture that was sitting on the mantle next to her own.

Tired from partying from the night before and not having much else to do, Kenya went over to the new couch she'd bought and fell across it, feet in the air. She then reached for the remote to her high-definition plasma television that she'd had mounted on the living room wall. It had so many buttons on that damn remote it would take a brain scientist, let alone Kenya, a year to learn how to use them all. Kenya, almost penniless, against London's advice, had used most of her insurance money Gran left her to freak the house out. It looked like a magazine layout. In between all the mall shopping and a used car that was on its last leg already, the wannabe hood diva was damn near broke.

At this point, especially considering what had just taken place, Kenya knew that she had all but cut herself out of her uncle's bottomless pockets. Luckily the household bills were paid up for a month or so, but Kenya realized she had to get on that money trail and make a few things happen if she wanted to continue to floss wherever she stepped out to.

Never outside the hustle loop for long, Kenya already put up on a quick way to make some fast, easy cash in hand. Ty, with all his schemes and scams, claimed to have the inside hookup, so why the hell not! Shit, she wasn't slow to the game by a long shot, but stripping? Kenya thought about it as she stared at her checkbook that was a few zeros from balancing out. Heads Up was the hottest strip joint up in the D. Everyone knew that it was the spot where real playas would meet and greet. It was no big secret that there was nothing but wall-to-wall loot in that motherfucker, and girls not half as pretty as Kenya, some not built like shit, getting paid out the ass. From flashy hustlers and blue-collar factory workers to plain-style fucking trick-ass niggas from around the way, they all knew that they had to come correct with their paper game to even walk through the doors of Heads Up, not to mention hanging out in the VIP. That was a given, flat out.

Kenya, trying to get in the zone, switched to the uncut video channel on cable and turned the surround sound up on double bump. "Fuck that shit!" She was hyped as she moved around the room as if she was the star of the evening. "I can do all those dances and make my ass bounce too." She pranced in the mirror and turned around to watch that motherfucker move. "I'm the shit, fuck 'em hoes! They can eat shit and die! I'm gonna make my ends up in that place as soon as I get my foot in the door!"

Exhausted from performing for herself, Kenya started to run her bathwater while she continued to get her dance on. When the water was just right, Kenya slowly undressed and eased her sweaty-ass into the hot, bubble-filled tub. Kenya, trying to get turned up as she daydreamed about her new desired profession, lit her blunt of Kush and lay back. *I guess I can call Ty's ho-ass tomorrow and see what's really good with Heads Up.* Lost in her thoughts as she listened to the music still echoing off the walls and got buzzed, the house phone rang twice as she was soaking. "Fuck whoever it is," she mumbled, blowing smoke rings into the air. "I'm chillin' the most."

Kenya, caught up in her own new world, had missed her twin sister's call.

London

"Hey, girl, let's go." London found Fatima talking to a group of other students who also lived in the dorm. They all introduced themselves and talked for a minute or two.

Fatima, having had just met her roommate, could easily tell by the look on London's face that something was wrong. Without reservation, she questioned London. "What's the deal, black girl? Is everything all good on the home front?"

"Naw, nothing much is wrong. I was just wondering where my sister is, that's all. She didn't answer the phone." London then got it in her head that she had to stop worrying so much about Kenya and let her live her life. After all, from this point on she wouldn't be there every day to watch over her. "Hey, girl, come on. I'm hungry, let's roll out." London changed her expression and attitude, while trying to sound cool. "She'll call when she calls!"

The pair of new roomies left the dorm, laughing and joking all the way to a twenty-four-hour greasy spoon on the edge of campus that some of the other students, all upperclassmen, had told Fatima about. After a long meal filled with conversation about both of their lives, including what had tragically happened to London's parents and her beloved grandmother on graduation day, the girls took their coffee to go. Although London really missed Kenya and her best friend Amber, she had a feeling Fatima would stick by her side no matter what.

"So, girl, I see all these pictures of your family, including that fine-ass uncle of yours, but I don't see not one picture of you and your man. What's up with that? You don't strike me as the lesbo type, so spill. What's the deal with that?" Fatima was waiting for an answer as London sadly started to look down at the floor. "Wow, I'm sorry, girl, did I say something wrong?"

"No, not really. It's just that people always ask me that. My sister was the one born with all the style and flair. She has all the good looks and gets the guys. I guess I'm just used to blending in the background when it comes to me and Kenya."

"Oh, hell naw! You must be high or something. Y'all look exactly alike. So how can you think that she's the shit and don't think you are?" Fatima damn near snatched her roommate in front of the door mirror leaning against the wall and pulled the rubber band out of London's hair. "You need to open those pretty eyes and see what everyone else sees. That flawless skin, a pretty smile, and this long-ass hair! Girl, most sisters would pay good dough for a pack of weave this long!"

London felt good for once about what she saw in the mirror thanks to Fatima. Starting now, she would try to have more confidence in herself. London knew that she needed to stand on her own without Kenya and be more assertive, and believing in herself would be the first step.

When they finished unpacking and talking, it was almost close to daybreak. The freshman orientation started at 9:30 a.m. sharp, so the two girls decided to get some much-needed shut-eye. They both wanted to be on time so Fatima set the alarm. For a change, since Gran's death, London didn't have to be the mother hen.

Chapter Seven

Kenya

"Damn, I can't take this. I gotta get some darker blinds in this bitch!" Kenya, peeking out from underneath her pillow, started her day mad. Always having a major attitude, she had the nerve to be pissed at the sun for shining so brightly into her private domain. Lifting her head all the way up, she looked over at the clock, which read 12:15 p.m. Overjoyed that her sister was not there waking her up early as usual, she found one reason to at least crack half of a smile. Eyes still partially shut, Kenya made her way into the kitchen, sliding her bare feet across the floor. "I need a cold glass of juice, maybe then I can wake up."

Sitting down on the couch, leaning her head backward, as funny as it seemed Kenya thought that she could hear the sound of quiet circulating throughout the entire house. But she was alone and lonely in that big, empty house, bored to death, and the truth of the matter was she knew it wasn't going to get any better. All the frontin' she did on a regular basis about wanting nothing more than for people in general to just leave her the fuck alone was catching up to her. "I gotta shake this bullshit," Kenya hissed, listening to the eerie vibrations of her heart beating. Right then and there she decided it was most definitely time to get put on by her dude. Without any more hesitation or delays, she dialed Ty's phone, who picked up on the first ring.

"What up, doe Kenya?"

"You crazy, you."

"What's the deal with you?"

"Just chillin' that's all. I just woke my punk-ass up."

"Oh, yeah?" Ty had just started blazing his second blunt of the day. "Man, I started to call you last night and see if you wanted to hang, but fuck all that!"

"Huh?" Kenya asked, confused.

"Shit, did you see that fucking 'nigga, I'm gonna kill your ass' death look your uncle gave me yesterday? I mean, I ain't no sucker or no shit like that with mines but, well, you feel me."

Knowing that Ty was indeed a sucker with his in every sense of the word, Kenya decided to not call him out on being scared shitless of her uncle because she needed him to do her a solid. "Come on, guy," she started to lie, gassing his ego up. "I know you ain't intimidated by his old ass! Everybody knows my uncle is past tense with that gangsta bullshit he be running!" Kenya was laying it on thick knowing that, truth be told, on any given day of the year, her uncle could beat the dog shit outta Ty with one hand tied behind his back. "But hey, forget about that old nigga. I need to talk to you about some other shit. Remember what we talked about the other night?" Kenya whispered like someone else was in the room eavesdropping on their private conversation.

"Come on, girl, we talk about a lot of shit, what's the dealio? Be more specific."

"Damn, nigga, you know what the fuck I'm talking about! That Heads Up shit!" Kenya yelled at the top of her lungs, rolling her eyes.

"Oh, yeah, hell yeah!" Ty was truly excited at this point. He then bossed up, practically taking over the entire conversation like he was an expert in stripperology 101. "Okay, here's the deal. Amateur night is tonight about ten. If you do good up on that stage shaking that ass, my man Zack will get you all the way plugged in every night." His preaching continued. "Oh, yeah, you should make sure your hair and nails are tight. Oh, yeah, and make sure you shave under your arms. When I see hoes up there swing upside down on the pole with gorilla hair in them pits, a nigga get sick to his stomach." Ty was going on and on, making Kenya madder and madder.

"Hold the fuck up, Negro! You going too damn far with this bullshit you trying to kick! When the fuck have you ever known my shit not to be topnotch and on point, please believe?" Kenya was fed up with Ty's store-bought pimp impression. "Look just call me later!" she screamed out in total frustration, slamming the phone down in his ear.

As she sat there Kenya, now in total hustle mode, started to think about the half-ass naked outfits she had in the closet and a pair of spiked heels just right for driving the average man out his mind. In the zone, it was then that she decided to partake in her regular "breakfast of champions"—a big-ass blunt. Deeply inhaling, she turned the television on. Still on the video channel from the night before, she got her a quick head-banging routine together guaranteed to make some cash.

Nightfall took its sweet time arriving. It was 8:45 p.m. and Ty had just called saying he was on his way to pick her up. Not in the least bit nervous, Kenya excitedly got her small-sized duffel bag together with two "scandalous even in the night-time" outfits she'd picked out, and a towel. Her face was beat, looking just right. She had just got finished applying MAC high-gloss lipstick and her lashes were long. *Damn, bitch, you the shit!* She snapped her fingers in front of the mirror.

Beep, beep, beep.

Kenya heard Ty pull up in front of her house and blow his horn. She quickly reached down, swooping up her designer bag, throwing the strap across her shoulder. Grabbing her keys and cell phone, she took a deep breath. After one last quick glance in the mirror, she was out the door, headed for her new future and hopefully the road to riches. Reaching for the doorknob, the house phone started to ring as Kenya turned back, securing the last deadbolt lock.

London

Exhausted and worn out, both London and Fatima had made their way through a long list of longwinded distinguished speakers, knowledgeable alumni and upperclassmen, teachers, and various presentations. Staying up the night before talking and unpacking was starting to take its toll on the weary freshmen.

"Girl, I can't wait to get back to that bed. I'm so tired I think I'm going to pass out right here on this ground!" London stretched as she yawned, fighting back the urge to go to sleep on one of the benches that lined the way back toward their dorm.

"I know how you feel." No sooner had Fatima barely gotten the last word out of her mouth than she was unexpectedly interrupted by a tall, handsome man with light brown eyes. He extended his arm, reaching out to shake each of the girls' hands as he confidently introduced himself.

"Well hello, ladies, how are you both doing?" He was so smooth with his tone and overall demeanor both girls could hardly move, let alone speak to respond to his question.

London was the first to regain her composure. "Oh, fine, we were, uh, uh, uh . . ." She was stumbling with her words, struggling to get a clear thought, something that she almost never did.

By that time, Fatima, also dumbfounded, snapped out of her trance, coming to her girl's rescue. "Hell, we're both doing well. We just came from the freshmen orientation in the plaza."

"Yes, I know. I was just at the orientation myself. I saw both you ladies over there. I'm Sanford Kincade." His smile was ultra bright and his winter white teeth were perfectly lined. "Matter of fact, if I'm not mistaken, I think one of you young ladies and I will get to know each other very well over the coming semester." Neither girl had a clue as to what their handsome, unannounced stranger was talking about. Each one looked both puzzled and confused. Seeing them speech-less, he could easily tell by their expressions they were feeling lost and out of sorts. "Oh, I'm sorry, ladies, let me start over again. I'm Professor Sanford Kincade. I'm on staff and teach Intro to Political Science here at the university."

Giggling like middle school girls on the playground instead of grown, mature women in college, London and Fatima recklessly fumbled retrieving their class schedules out of their folders, praying that they were the one blessed to have this God of a man for an instructor. As each visibly anxious student searched for that small piece of paper, Sanford

Kincade, conniving in mindset, already knew the outcome. With ulterior motives in store, he'd checked it out prior to introducing himself, as he watched the two of them earlier.

London was the first to find her schedule. "Oh, wow, I guess it's me." She almost felt ashamed for being the lucky one. Fatima, sad faced, was a little disappointed, but happy for her newfound friend nevertheless.

"Well then, Miss Roberts, I guess I will see you in class and, Miss James, see you around campus." As soon as he was out of ear range, both girls started screaming.

"Girl, he was so fine I could barely move." Fatima held her hand close to her chest.

"Yes, he was handsome," London agreed. "But, Fatima, that man is almost old enough to be our daddy."

"Yeah, girl, you right, I would call him daddy!" Both girls, behaving silly without a care in the world, giggled all the way back to the dorm.

London, after settling down, decided to try to call her sister again that night but still didn't get an answer. She also tried calling Kenya's cell phone, but her twin changed numbers like she changed her panties. The concerned twin was starting to worry and wanted nothing more than to call her uncle. She wanted to ask him to go by the house and at least check on Kenya, but she knew that wasn't gonna happen, especially considering what had jumped off the afternoon she'd left. Her uncle was still probably and rightfully pissed about that fool Ty keeping Kenya out all night and Kenya's nasty attitude and disposition to being chastised.

London then called Carmen, her sister's best friend, on her cell phone. Thankfully, she had Kenya's latest number and gave it to her. After the first ring the voice mail picked up. A long song filled with all types of curse words filled London's ears before she heard Kenya's voice. When the beep finally came, London spoke.

"Hey, Kenya, it's me. I tried calling you last night. I'm okay, I just wanted to know if all is well. I know it's been only two days, but you understand. Call me, all right? Don't forget. *Say U Promise!*" She hung up the phone and fell fast asleep. London had no idea that back at home in Detroit, her sister's long night was just beginning.

Tastey

Ty watched Kenya's full, plump breasts bounce up and down as she ran down the stairs. The way that her low-riding track suit fit her ass alone was enough to get him paid. Anticipating a quick come up, he started to daydream about all the money he could get from working Kenya. Greeting each other with a smile and a small kiss on the lips, both of them were anxious about the night and what it would hold. They both had a different agenda for what they felt was going to happen when they got to the club.

"Girl, you look hot! Good enough for a brotha to eat." Ty's dick started to get rock hard. He grabbed Kenya's hand and placed it on his manhood. "Feel what I got waiting for that ass when we get back from making that bread!"

Kenya gave him a fake smirk and told him, "Maybe later," keeping game on pause. She was trying to keep her mind clear, and his "always wanting to fuck and suck for free" butt wasn't helping her pay any bills around her way. Kenya was really straight starting not to feel ol' boy and his nickel-and-dime hustle ways, but she was smart enough to wait until she got her foot in the door of the Heads Up and when she did, he was so over.

Ty, feeling like he was a big shot, pulled up at the club. Trying hard to appear to be a boss, he got valet, trying keep the big fella image up. As they made their way up to the front door entrance there was a gang of trick-ass niggas waiting to give up their paychecks, bill money, or even the loot owed to the next man on a sack.

Hell, fuck going inside the club! Kenya saw how they were eyeballing her; and she could get most of their dough out their pockets by just looking at their grimy asses. Nevertheless, Kenya was on a mission that was bigger than dudes standing on line waiting to be hand searched by security. Johnnie Roberts's daughter was about that life and getting that serious longevity loot. Winning the amateur contest was her only objective so she could secure herself a permanent position and start making revenue on a regular basis. Moving her curvaceous body through the crowd, she saw a pool of strange, desperate faces watching her like she was a precious shipment of gold. There were just as many hands brushing across her ass on the sly like they were getting away with something.

"Okay, how about this! The next nigga who puts his hands on me without paying is getting his shit split to the white meat!" Kenya made it clear for all possible offenders to hear. She wasn't bullshitting one bit and it showed all over her face. "I ain't into fucking charity and ain't shit for free this way! You touch you fucking pay, flat out, straight like that!"

"Hey, Zack." Ty proudly beamed, showing that stupid-ass gap in his dental. "This is my main girl, Kenya." He smiled, sticking his chest out with pride like he was her pimp or some shit like that.

In between the guys in the crowd having to be told what was really good and now Ty acting like he owned her and her hustle, she went ham. "Main girl?" Kenya finally had enough of his ass. "Nigga, what? Please don't coach mines. You got me all fucked up in the game. Fall back and don't play yourself!"

Zack couldn't help smiling as he watched her put Ty's perpetrating-ass in his place. Easing back, letting her do what she did, he thought, *She is much prettier than any of the girls working here and, damn, that ass is banging. Plus, with that spunk, she could double as security.* Zack had to laugh out loud about that shit. He hated to halt the debate, but Kenya had to be informed about the rules for the contest if she planned on participating. Plus Zack knew Ty needed to go in a corner somewhere, get several drinks, and try to recover and lick all of the open wounds that she'd left to his weak mack game.

"Hello, Kenya, I'm Zack. You can follow me up to the office so that I can explain a few things and check your ID out if that's okay with you."

Kenya smiled and turned around to follow, making sure to give Ty's wounded ego the sho'nuff side eye. As she observantly scanned around the club and checked out the atmosphere, she noticed even the ugliest girls on the guys' laps, grinding like there was no tomorrow. She thought, *Shit, I guess pussy don't have a face around this here motherfucker.*

When they got up the stairs and to the office Zack shut the steel door. Amazingly it was quiet as the library that London often would drag her to if she let her. "Okay, Miss Kenya, first things first, let me check out your ID." As Zack looked it over, he started questioning her on other club-related issues. He asked her just what made her want to dance and did she think she could do it. Kenya thought for a second and was going to try to say something sassy, but quickly changed her mind when she saw that he was trying to be sincere.

"Bills, just a lot of bills that I anticipate accumulating real soon. I don't want to fall behind or be late on any payments. That would mess with my credit rating and I ain't trying to do that." Kenya had learned all about finances from Gran and the importance of a high score.

Not expecting that answer in a million years from a female only seconds away from swinging naked on a pole, Zack was truly impressed with her response. *Finally a girl with a little bit of common sense; well, not that much. She should be in somebody's schoolhouse,* he thought, but who was he to judge? He was here to make money and capitalize off of her beauty, not be a life-changing coach. Zack took his time before he spoke. "You right, Kenya, good credit is a must in the white man's world." Even though he ran a strip joint, he still hated to see young girls go down the wrong path and get turned out or, worse than that, strung the fuck out on drugs. But, hey, the ID said eighteen and that made her grown, so she was just that—grown. She was fair game. If he could profit off of her beautiful ass, why not, he thought. "Well, it's like this. You dance two songs when you go on stage, one fast and one slow. On the second song drop your top." Zack watched for any signs of weakness or apprehension, but none showed. "The guys will try to cop a free feel when they slip the money in your G-string. So as long as they don't get to outrageous with the shit, just try to be polite, make your money and move on. The fellas in the house know it's amateur night, so we always got one fool who gets extra and tries to push his hand. Don't worry about him; we got his ass covered. Be nice, but don't give the whole deal away for free. Remember, what one won't or can't do the next will. So don't listen to all that idle chitchat niggas wanna kick. Everything costs in this motherfucker, even conversation, so keep it moving!"

"Okay. Do I get to keep all of my tips?" Kenya eagerly awaited his answer, hoping it was yes.

"Yeah, tonight you do, but if you do good and you like it, you can get on the schedule. Then it's a house fee of fifty dollars a night, a fee for the DJ, and you should always tip Brother Rasul. He's the head of security. My man doesn't drink, curse, or mess around with any of the girls, which keeps him on top of thangs. He's one hard-ass Muslim brother. I think that's what makes him have such a low tolerance for men disrespecting our black queens, even if they choose to disrespect themselves up in here. That's why most niggas don't even try him. Shit, they'd be better off smacking Jesus off the cross than fucking with that guy. So, take care of him. Shiiit, even I tip Brother Ra! That being said you should be good to go."

Suddenly there was a knock at the door. "Enter!" Zack yelled out, looking over at the security camera while buzzing the door.

Walking through the door as if she owned the place was a woman with a long blond and red streaked weave. It was untamed, reaching down to her ass, which was wide as hell, but she carried it well. She was at least forty or so in age, or so the wrinkles around her eyes revealed.

"Hey, baby. We got like eight girls in the dressing room for amateur night and the crowd is growing restless. So are you about ready to start the contest or what?" The older, fashionably dressed woman grinned while rubbing on Zack's balding head with her long multicolored painted fingernails.

"Yeah, in about ten minutes. This is the last girl for tonight. So if anyone else shows, tell them to come back next week. Besides, I think we have the winner right here." Zack winked his eye at the young future contestant.

"I see, I see. Hey, sweetheart, my name is Angela, but everyone around here calls me Old Skool. I'm sort of the house mother I guess."

"Hello, I'm Kenya Roberts, but you can call me . . ." She paused to think all of two seconds before she blurted out the name Tastey, since Ty had said she looked good enough to eat. "Yeah, call me Tastey."

"Okay, Miss Tastey, follow me."

When they reached the dressing room you could automatically tell the veterans from the rookies. While the vets were fixing their hair and stashing their loot, they still found time to mean mug all the fresh-faced, wide-eyed girls who were entering the contest hoping to win the prize money. After all, some of these green hoes had the potential to be their new competition, so there positively was no love lost. Of course, Kenya's thick model-type ass, when dressed and ready to compete, was getting a gang of major hate from both sides of the fence, new and old. Some of the girls couldn't even walk in heels let alone dance, while some of them needed to hit the gym at least five days a week. But even the ugliest females made a little bit of lunch money for the week in a dark, dimly lit strip club.

"Hey, girl, you ready? You about next." Old Skool was hyping Kenya up, whispering in her ear. "Girl, you got this shit. The prize money got your name on it. These other females are terrible!"

"Prize money?" Kenya was shocked hearing about that part of the contest for the first time. *Ty slick-ass ain't shit!* "How much is first place?"

"Two hundred bucks!"

"Oh, yeah, you right. That two hundred dollars is mine. I'm about to wild the fuck out when it's my time to shine!" Kenya needed that cash like a baby needed his bottle.

A girl who the DJ said went by the name Raven was just making her way down off the stage. From where Kenya stood, she was her only real competition. The other girls in the contest were throwing shade on her also, so the two of them kinda stuck close by the other in case they might have to scrap. "Girl, them fools out there are on the nut. Watch yourself," a breathless Raven advised Kenya before she headed up.

"Okay, good lookin'." Kenya exchanged smiles with her, glancing over her shoulder, heading toward the small set of stairs.

"All right now, fellas, ballas, and any of y'all wannabe playas! This next girl has enough boom boom on deck to snap them zippers on sight!" The DJ was out his shit in the zone as he did his thang on the mic, making the energy level in the already-hot, humid club rise. "Take your hands out your pants and put them together for the one we affectionately call Tastey! Make her feel at home and make that shit rain Heads Up style!"

As Kenya entered the stage, you would have thought that she hit the winning homerun in game seven of the World Series. "Damn, girl, shake that shit," was all she kept hearing from the intoxicated patrons who were throwing currency her way. Kenya only saw dollar signs and didn't give a fuck what them fools was saying as long as that bread kept raining on the stage. Kenya, off deep into the loud sound of the speakers and the song she'd requested to be played, made eye contact with Ty just in time to see him abruptly rushed out the door by security. *Damn, I guess his "wannabe slick" and "work a bitch" knew it was over.* She giggled to herself as she moved like a seductive snake across the cash-covered stage.

The contest was soon over and, without a doubt, Kenya had won first place. With $200 plus another $150 in tips it was the best five minutes of her young life. She now had her foot in the door of Heads Up; hell, both feet, for that matter. And it was time for her to grind!

Chapter Eight

London

The first day of classes began and London was more than ready. She had one morning class and another in the evening starting at 6:30. This was a day that she'd been looking forward to her whole life. She was up, dressed, and out the door before Fatima had even turned over. She didn't have her first class until later. No sooner than London left did the phone start to ring repeatedly. The constant noise of the ringer woke a tired Fatima out of her coma-like sleep.

"Yeah, hello," Fatima's voice was groggy and she sounded completely out of it.

Kenya was hesitant about speaking up because she thought she had the wrong number.

"Hello," Fatima said again, this time with a slight attitude from being disturbed by the phone.

"Yeah, can I speak to Amia Roberts?" Kenya finally blurted out.

Fatima was thrown off for a second, when she remembered that London's real name was Amia. She sat up in the bed and wiped the sleep out of her eyes. "Sorry, she's not in. Whom should I tell her called?"

"This is her sister," Kenya spoke in a cold tone.

"Oh, Kenya! Hey, girl!" Fatima greeted her like they were old friends.

Kenya was kinda fucked up that this stranger knew who she was right off the bat. "Yeah, this is Kenya, and who are you?"

Fatima could tell by the tone in her voice that she was the twin who had got all the bad demons floating inside of her. She tried her best to be nice to her roomie's sister and not go all the way out on her for being rude and disrespectful so early in the damn morning. "Hey, I'm her roommate, Fatima James. Your sister told me all about you, besides, your picture is posted all around the room walls in here." Fatima was still trying to be polite, as hard as Kenya was making it.

"Okay then, bet, tell her I called. Peace." Kenya was still being somewhat a total bitch and it came across. With that exchange, she hung up on Fatima.

After finding out that her sister was off to her classes, Kenya decided to get herself some rest; after all, she had just made it home from the club and a long night of getting money.

London

The start of London's second class was full of anticipation. That was the class that Professor Kincade taught. As she entered the room she saw him standing behind his desk with papers in his hands. He looked so handsome. This was the first man she really ever had a crush on. London was always deep in her studies and had no time for the silly boys at her high school. Anyway, they were always interested in her sister, so her even caring about them was a waste of time.

Professor Kincade waited until everyone got seated and greeted all of his new freshman students. He then went in his briefcase and pulled out a huge stack of papers. "Miss Roberts, can you please come up here?"

London was stunned. What did he want? What would he say? When she reached his desk, she could smell the scent of cologne on his shirt as she walked up. "Yes, Professor Kincade?"

She was a nervous wreck and he could tell. Having what some would call classic good looks, he had this effect on most of the female students he'd come in contact with and some of the female professors.

"Yes, can you pass this course syllabus out for me?" With a smooth way about himself, he made sure to lock his eyes on London's, touching her hand as he handed her the papers. For an older man, he swore he had game. Known as a womanizer around campus, he wanted this young girl and was going to have her.

When class was over, he watched her youthful ass sway from side to side. His dick got hard just thinking about riding that untamed, tender cat. A true freak, he couldn't wait to get home so he could fuck his wife with London on his mind. This was his second marriage and even though his wife was only twenty-five, the professor had a taste for some younger pussy every now and then. And this was one of those times.

"Did you see that fine-ass Professor Kincade?" Fatima was just making it in from her own classes.

"Yeah, I not only saw him, he asked me to hand out some papers. I was scared as hell." London had chills as she told the story. "I wish I could be more like my sister. Kenya would have had him shaking in his boots."

Both girls exchanged stories of how their day went. Fatima, socially conscious, told her about some clubs that they could join. All the organizations were based on helping to try uplifting the black man and women as a whole.

"Wow, that sounds like where we need to be then." London was more than excited to attend the meeting. "When is it?"

"It's tomorrow evening at six o'clock at the student union." Fatima was overjoyed that London was interested and cared about helping her race just as she and her parents did.

"Trust me, I'm already there!" London reassured her.

The two roommates looked in their mini refrigerator and didn't see anything they wanted and agreed to go get some food across campus. London and Fatima put on their track pants and hoodies and jogged over to the cafeteria just before it was closing for the night.

"Dang, we just made it." London was out of breath as was Fatima.

Both girls picked out a few of the sandwiches that were on the counter and left. As they were heading back to their dorm room, London saw two students holding hands, walking, and wondered if she would ever have anyone to hold hands with in her life. She was eighteen years old and had never been kissed. She could vote and even go fight for her country, but hadn't found someone to love her. *Why can't I be more like Kenya?* she heartbreakingly thought.

When the two freshman students made it back to their dorm room, they decided to do a little studying and then hit the sack. Fatima and London couldn't wait to see what the meeting they would attend the next evening was going to be about. They talked about what to expect, until they both fell asleep.

Morning came soon enough and both girls took their turns at the showers and got dressed. London took her time picking out an outfit. She knew she would see Professor Kincade and she didn't want to look too corny. After going through almost all her clothes in the closet, she picked out a blue and black skirt with a black thin-material turtleneck and a cute pair of Prada mules that Kenya bought her for their birthday, so she knew they were fly as hell. London looked in the mirror and was satisfied. She was headed out the door when Fatima yelled out to her, "Hey, don't forget about six o'clock tonight!"

"I won't," London replied. "Six o'clock!"

London made it to her first class right on time. She tried to pay attention to the instructor, but found it hard to think about anything other than the next class awaiting her. Time was ticking by slowly, but finally past. *Thank God,* she thought. It was one o'clock and her first class was finally over.

London ate a late lunch and realized it would soon be time for the start of the next class. *I want to remember to check my teeth for any food before I go in there.* When 2:45 came, it was time. London made her way through the door and looked toward the front of the class. To her dismay, there was no sight of him yet.

"Hello, I'm Donyae." It was the guy who sat next to London at her earlier class. "We must have the same major." He was all in her space.

"Yeah, you might be right." London was having a hard time paying attention to him as he tried to kick game. He was trying his best to flirt with London, but her thoughts were on the professor and the smile that she couldn't seem to get out of her mind.

"Maybe we could study together sometime?" He tried to make eye contact with her, which was almost an impossible task since she was watching the classroom door like a hawk.

"Oh, yeah, maybe," she finally stated nonchalantly, hoping he would give her some air.

Donyae was happy to get a maybe, so he sat down. Besides, the professor was coming.

"Good afternoon, everyone." He scanned the room until he saw London, making sure to acknowledge her presence. In class, they took notes on everything that they would be tested on that semester. By the time it was over, every student had a notebook full of information. "Well, that's it for today, have a nice evening." After that announcement, the room started to clear out.

"Hey, now, I was just wondering, can I walk you somewhere?" Donyae waited anxiously for her response, hoping that London would say yes.

"Well, umm . . ." Before London could complete her sentence, Professor Kincade interrupted the two.

"Excuse me, Miss Roberts, can I speak to you a moment?"

Donyae was disappointed that Professor Kincade had blown his rap to London. "Well, I'll see you later." He grinned at her as he left the room.

"Did I stop a future love connection from taking place?" Professor Kincade was smiling when he said it, but was really slightly jealous of the young boy's youth and the body that he once had when he was his age.

"Not really, I just met him today." London blushed at his assumption.

"Well, I was wondering, could we get a cup of coffee and discuss if you would like to be my class secretary?"

London was beaming with pride that he would even consider her for that seemingly important position. She had no idea that he'd made that title up at the last moment. He had to get a hold of that ass before Mr. Young and Smooth had a chance to. The professor was on a mission and didn't want to take any chances. Grabbing his briefcase they walked across the grass until they reached his car.

"Where are we going?" London felt strangely scared. Not really scared of him personally, but scared she would not know what to say to him in a one-on-one setting. London's heart was pounding. "The student union?"

"Oh, no, I forgot the paperwork in my office. It's right at the edge of campus. Come on, jump in. I don't bite." Professor Kincade coaxed her inside his car.

After a short ride filled with jazz playing on the radio, he pulled up at an office building. He quickly ran in and returned with a look of total confusion on his face, giving London a sad expression. "I'm sorry, the office is such a mess that I couldn't find them and I didn't want to keep you out here waiting." The professor was definitely running his game. Real talk, he'd gotten just what he had come for and had it tucked discreetly in his pocket until the right time presented itself.

"Oh, that's okay. I have to go to a meeting in about an hour or so anyway." London was somewhat relieved because she was at a loss for words.

With the chances of his plan unraveling, he had to think quickly. "Hey, I promised you a cup of coffee. I know a place nearby." Turning right, then left, he pulled up to a little cafe before London had time to protest. They took a seat near the back area even though it wasn't that crowded inside. London wanted to sit on the front patio outside, but he claimed he was recovering from a cold. In reality, the wolf in man's clothing really had no desire to be in the front on display to the other patrons. He needed to be low-key; after all, he was a married man, and, besides, it would not fit into his cynical plan.

The teacher and young student continued to chat about this and that. Soon London checked her watch, and although she was having a good time, she revealed she would have to leave soon. It was already 5:15 and she didn't want to be late. Fatima would be waiting for her and she had no desire to let her new friend down. No man was worth losing a friend over; at least that's what Gran had taught her and Kenya. Sadly, she told the professor of her prearranged plans as she excused herself to go to the ladies' room.

Moments after she left out of sight, he reached in his pocket and pulled out a small vile: the same vile he'd gotten from his office earlier when they stopped. He put three small drops in her coffee and stirred it up, placing her spoon back in the same position. When the naïve teen returned and drank the rest, it seemed to be only minutes before she looked a little out of it.

"Wow, I feel kinda dizzy." London was starting to slur her words. She had never even tasted wine before so she had no idea about what she was starting to feel. The room was starting to spin and she felt confused and tired.

The professor sat back and watched London transform before his eyes. His dick started to get harder and harder as he thought about what was getting ready to take place. *It's show time.* For everything to go as planned, the scheming older man had to walk her to his vehicle before anyone else noticed her being tipsy and out of it.

The professor got her inside his car and locked the doors. As they drove down the road London was in somewhat of a trance as the road started to vibrate and her eyes rolled toward the rear of her head. Taking full advantage of the skirt she had on, Professor Kincade roughly shoved his hand in between her legs after moving her panties to the side. London was soon totally passed out cold and couldn't feel the blunt force of his fingers pounding in and out of her virgin insides. The professor slowly licked his fingers, tasting her moist juices as he pulled them out of her.

My dick is so fucking hard I can't wait, he sinisterly thought. *This freshman is finer than all the ones in previous years!*

After a short drive they pulled up to his destination and London's unfortunate fate that was awaiting—the North End Motel.

Chapter Nine

London

It had been a little more than six hours since London had called Fatima to come and help her. In distress and disoriented, London woke up with all of her clothes torn off. There was blood on the sheets and every part of her body had been terribly violated. She needed a few stitches and the doctors at the hospital wanted her to call the authorities and report the sexual assault. London, embarrassed and ashamed, would have no part of the police. She didn't confide in anyone except Fatima the true identity of who she knew had drugged and ultimately violated her.

When London revealed to Fatima the rapist's name she was pissed all the way the fuck off. When she went to get London's class drop slip signed from the professor's bitch-ass, Fatima spit directly in his face, daring him to do or say something. Knowing he'd get undoubtedly fired or, worse than that, arrested and thrown in jail if the news of his dirty deed surfaced for all to know, he remained silent. He knew at this point, with Fatima's saliva dripping down his face, it was true; he couldn't say or do anything for fear of any police involvement. The professor, usually in total control of his antics, didn't know how he'd let shit get so out of control this time. Lowering his head in shame, he just signed the withdraw slip and wiped his face off with a napkin.

London, after a short time recuperating, made her way to the rest of her classes that semester, and, although she was mentally stressed, maintained fairly good grades all things considered. Wanting to forget the entire tragic event, she finally made it to a few of those socially conscious meetings that she'd missed that night six months ago.

When Thanksgiving came, as well as Christmas, London had gone home with Fatima. It was nice being around a family, a real family, with people who loved each other. Fatima's family were Muslim and didn't celebrate Christmas but they still got together for a big dinner so they could all bond and catch one another up on their current activities. London, engulfed in the atmosphere of family, could tell where Fatima got her caring ways.

Besides a few calls here and there, it was like she had cut herself off entirely from her own small-sized family. Her uncle had his woman still send her money every now and then when she could, even though her man had gotten knocked again and was serving time. This bid unfortunately was for more than just a few months. He was doing a few years on a probation violation so any direct contact he had with London was limited to none.

It would soon be spring break and London would be going home for the first time since school had begun the previous year. Although she enjoyed college life despite what had happened between her and the professor, she did miss her twin sister Kenya. Sure they talked on the phone sometimes, but nothing could take the place of seeing her twin face to face. She needed to see her other half and make sure she was safe and sound.

Kenya

Kenya was doing it big at Heads Up. Ever since her first night of slinging that ass, she was getting more money than any other female in the spot. She was a topnotch dancer at the club and had multitudes of regulars who'd wait to give their money to her and only her. A lot of the other girls were mad jealous of her pole and twerking skills, but Kenya didn't give a shit. She was there to make cash, not friends. Only her girl Raven was rolling with her in that motherfucker. The two of them were tight and got paid no matter what.

"Hey, girl, you making that money tonight!" Old Skool was sitting at the bar with Kenya, nursing a drink.

"Yeah, and you know it. I gotta get some new shit in my crib, maybe some heavy-duty steel doors or something like that." Kenya was being careful and big on security. She knew that crackheads back in the hood knew that she was getting that dough.

Zack walked over to his two favorite ladies in the club and kissed Old Skool on the cheek. "What you two over here scheming on?" Zack smiled as he attentively watched Raven up on the stage under the lights, wowing the crowd.

"Well, apparently Miss Tastey here needs to step up her paper game." Old Skool put Kenya's business out in the street.

"Oh, yeah, okay, what's the problem, Tastey, what you need?" He focused his attention back to them.

"Well, I think I need to switch up a little bit. I don't want to get played out." Caught up in the club life of mutual respect for a hardworking dancers' world, she walked over to the stage and gave her girl some love. "Damn, why don't you ho-ass niggas get ya panties out ya ass and tip a bitch?" She was going off on everyone within ear range who was gawking at Raven instead of throwing dollars. "What's the problem? Did y'all losers leave your purses in the fucking car?"

The DJ even had to laugh at that shit as Zack, Old Skool, and Brother Rasul, who just walked up, stood by, watching Kenya go hard.

"Maybe we should think about putting Tastey on," Zack pondered as Brother Rasul listened, not saying a word. "Kenya's kinda green, but it might work if we work it right."

Having a special place in his heart for the way she would carry herself nightly if she felt she was being disrespected, Brother Rasul always looked out for Kenya since day one. Kenya was a true hustler, not like most of the dick handlers in the club he'd watch sell their bodies for an extra dollar or two. The young girl was all about the money and the business that came with it. Brother Rasul shook his head and walked away, not wanting any part of what Zack was about to do. Zack was his boy and all, but he hated the way he took advantage of some of the girls.

Zack decided he would speak to her next week about what he and Old Skool had planned. Kenya was going to

take a few days off to take care of some personal matters she claimed to have pending. He had no idea whatsoever that Kenya had a sister, let alone a twin. No one she
worked with or for in the club knew about London. That
was her life outside the strip club. They were two different
worlds and Kenya planned to keep it that way for as long as
possible.

After her long double shift had ended, it was finally time to
get off of work. Kenya, worn out, but elated, couldn't wait
to see her sister.

Reunion

*Damn, I gotta hurry the fuck up and get all this stuff put
away. There ain't no way in hell I can have this place on the
nut when London gets home. She might bug out and kill a
bitch if she saw the mess that been piling in this house since
she left.* Kenya had taken time off from the club to initially
clean the house and spend some quality time with her sister.
London was coming home for spring break and the two hadn't
seen each other in months.

After hours of washing dishes and cleaning top to bottom,
Kenya was tired as shit. No sooner than the last dish was put
away did she hear London's key turn at the door.

"Kenya!" London yelled as she made her way inside the
front hallway.

Kenya jumped from around the doorway and started
smiling. "Girl, you know Gran told your butt not to yell in this
house with your rude-ass!"

They both ran to each other and hugged for what seemed
like forever. Tears were flowing from both twins' eyes. "I
missed you so much," they both said at the same time. "Me
too." Once again they said it together. It was like they were
reading from a script or something. It was one of the things
twins were famous for and these two were no different.

When they finally got all of London's bags in the house, they
got a good look at one another and noticed some changes.
Kenya didn't have on her makeup and was dressed in sweats.
Her nails were still manicured perfectly, but she just seemed
so much more slowly paced than London had remembered.

Being on display at the club ten hours a day made Kenya just want to relax more at home and take life easy. She learned how to love to be plain ol' Kenya instead of flashy, flamboyant Tastey: queen of Heads Up.

London, on the other hand, was different as well. There were a lot of huge visible changes. She had started wearing her shoulder-length hair down and wore clothes that were more suited for a girl her own age than someone's grandmother. London wasn't always outspoken, but now she was sure of herself and held her head up when she would speak. She was even downright loud as hell if need be to get her point across. Between Fatima's coaching, her club and organization meetings, and that creep foul bullshit that Professor Kincade did, she'd become a much stronger individual. London was a new person with a new attitude, and it showed.

"Okay, now tell me everything that has been happening around since I left. How are Carmen and Allan? Where is that no-good Ty? Tell me everything!" London was excited to be home as she plopped down on the couch, kicking her shoes off.

Kenya was almost knocked off her feet by her sister's newfound bubbly personality. "Damn, bitch, slow your roll!" She was laughing like crazy by this time and so was London. It was like old times when they were kids, but the tables had turned. The difference was now London was holding court and Kenya was sitting back enjoying the show.

London told her sister all about Fatima and how she always had her back at school, how well her family had treated her on the holidays, and how she even had called Fatima's mother "Mama James."

Initially Kenya was slightly jealous hearing about Fatima, but she had her own little family at the club so she understood where her twin was coming from. Her, Raven, Zack, Old Skool, and Brother Rasul were just like family at Heads Up. Shit, Old Skool had even cooked a gigantic Thanksgiving dinner for them and all the dancers who didn't have or were shunned from their biological family. Even if they did eat it at the club at the same tables they'd shake their naked asses on, it was still all good. They were together and to Kenya that meant something.

London begged Kenya to promise not to get upset when she confessed to her about the brutal rape and the physical and mental condition it had left her in. By the time London bravely finished the story, all hell was about to break loose. She had to beg her sister to slow the fuck down. Kenya was screaming about calling someone named Brother Rasul to kill Professor Kincade and his whole generation by nightfall or as long as it took to drive back up to the university. After nearly fifteen minutes of trying to calm her twin down, London finally got a chance to ask her sister one question, which was, "Who in the heck is Brother Rasul?"

That opened the door for Kenya to tell her about her job and her new friends. Kenya explained to her sister how her new friends were a little different than a traditional family, but they all cared about each other. She explained to her how Brother Rasul taught her about Islam and how she told him about what the Bible meant to her.

London, who learned about the Islamic faith from Fatima, listened with an open mind as Kenya went on to tell her how Zack taught both her and Raven about accounting, so when they started their own business, no one could cheat them. London also soon found out that Kenya was even godmother to Raven's infant son, Jaylin. Kenya said she loved Jaylin just like he was her very own flesh and blood. She wanted the very best for him and even paid for his daycare when Raven would be short.

Though London might not have agreed with her sister's choice of work to make a living, she was glad that she had love in her heart for someone other than herself. London was happy to learn her twin had thankfully got rid of that self-serving Ty and even happier to learn that Carmen and Allan had gotten a place together on the east side of Detroit and were in school trying to get degrees.

"Okay, what about Amber? Where is she? Have you seen her lately?" London was worried about her best friend. "Last time I called her number a recording came on saying it was disconnected. I called her job and they told me she got fired."

Kenya hated to tell her what she really knew about Amber, so instead she put on her shoes and had London walk to the store with her. When they reached Linwood Avenue and turned the corner, London glanced around, and surveyed the neighborhood. She could tell that much had not changed.

"Same blight, same drunks, same crackheads. We need to do something to help our people," she sadly remarked.

No sooner than those words came out of her mouth did they run into what Kenya didn't want to say: it was Amber. She looked torn the fuck up! Her hair was nappy and she smelled just like a real shit bag!

"Oh my God! What happened, Amber? What happened?" London cringed at the sight of her friend and started to cry.

Kenya couldn't do anything but stand mute and let her sister get that shit out. When she first saw Amber tricking in the alley, she was shocked too. That pipe had taken complete control over Amber's young life and was now running things.

Amber glanced over at London and then focused her eyes toward the litter-filled ground. All she could do was be ashamed. She kicked her dingy and battered shoes against the curb as she tried explaining her new life to London. "After you left, I started hanging with Chuck and 'em. One night we was drinking and I decided to just try a little. I swear I can stop, girl!" Of course, Amber was lying to London and herself; she was too far gone to stop just like that.

"Well, okay then, walk back to the house with us!" London pleaded repeatedly. "Let me get you some help!" She wanted to put her arms around her best friend and reassure her that everything would be all right, but between the terrible smell and the open sores on Amber's face, London couldn't bring herself to do it. Amber was too far gone on that glass pipe to be turned around, at least not today. She and the drug were in a committed monogamous relationship, deeper than any marriage.

"I'll be around there later, I promise." Amber licked her dry, cracked lips as she tried to fix her hair. At this point she was telling London anything that popped into her mind because that ten dollars she had just sucked dick for in the vacant house was calling her to get a rock. Amber looked at London one last time, embarrassed, as she started to cry, and ran off down the street to get high.

"Kenya, I can't believe that mess. Why didn't you warn me?"

"Girl, what you want me to say?" Kenya was giving her sister a look that would kill. "That your friend is a li'l crack ho? Is that what you wanted to hear?"

London openly sobbed, trying to get some answers. "Why didn't you try to help her Kenya? Huh? Why?"

"Now wait! Hold the fuck up, don't get it twisted. That's your girl, not mine! I don't have time to be chasing a head all around town! Plus, oh yeah, I heard what you said, and don't be having her all up in my fucking house!"

"Kenya, how can you say that? She needs help. And don't forget, it's half my house too!" she replied, feisty.

"Well, okay then, when we get home, take a good look around, London. Everything that's worth stealing in that son of a bitch is mine, so fuck the dumb shit and recognize! That crack ho ain't never stepping foot in that motherfucker, so you can take that shit how you want it, half yours or not!"

Over the next few days that followed the twin's reunion, they realized just how much the two had changed. London had stepped her game up and now was a vocal leader around campus. She was about to branch out and help start an organization that would target the problems of black youths in school who had come from drug-addicted households. Seeing people being messed up by drugs, and now Amber, was eating away at her. Whether or not Kenya wanted to admit it, drugs had killed both their parents, leaving them orphans.

"After I saw Amber the other day, I made up my mind that it was time. I've put this off long enough. It needs to stop." London was up on her soapbox again as Kenya tried her best to ignore her.

"Dang, girl, stop all that loud talking!" Kenya was tired of her sister being all caught up in her feelings. "I know what you're saying and all and I'm proud of you for real, but damn why you gotta be so high-pitched and shit? Shut the fuck up, damn!"

"I'm sorry, I just can't understand what made Amber go that way. Your boy Allan grew up with his mother using drugs and made the decision to not follow in her footsteps."

"Well, that's life in the big city, London." Kenya walked to the kitchen and looked in the empty fridge. "Let's go out to breakfast."

"All right, let's go," London easily agreed, and thought that she would try to press her luck. "Why don't we go see if Amber wants to go? Maybe we could talk to her."

"Listen here, girl, we fam and all, but you bugging if you think her ruthless behind is rolling out with me! She smells like something crawled up in her ass and died! Come on now, London, be for real! Do you really think I'm going out like that?" Kenya laughed at her sister. "Girl, ain't no stopping a head!"

London knew her twin was right, only on the fact that Amber would feel out of place. "Well, all right then, I'm ready." London knew better than to try to change her sister's mind.

The girls jumped in Kenya's car and rode about ten minutes before they reached the Black Bottom Cafe. It served the best breakfast around the D and at night it turned into a showcase where folks could show off their poetry skills. After a short wait to get a table, the girls were seated near the back in a booth. They checked out the menu as the waitress brought London the cup of coffee that she ordered as soon as they sat down.

Kenya was the first to really bring up their beloved Gran. They both seemed to avoid any real deep conversations about her so, they wouldn't cry. "I see Gran still got that ass drinking coffee." Kenya was shaking her head, placing the menu on the table.

London grinned, shrugging her shoulders. "Yeah, I drink it like water."

"I'm glad you came home, London. I need to talk to you about a few things. I have felt this way for a couple of months, but didn't know how to bring it up."

"What is it? We're sisters, we shouldn't keep secrets." London put her cup down and waited for her twin to speak.

"Well . . ." Kenya looked in her sister's eyes. "I think we should try to sell the house."

"What house? Gran's house? Are you crazy?"

"You mean our house, London. Gran is gone!" Kenya blurted out with no remorse for her sister's feelings. "It's ours, London, you and me."

"I know she's gone, but damn, she worked hard to keep that house!" London was now slightly raising her voice.

"I know, but it's so big!" Kenya pouted as she folded her arms and continued, "Big and lonely. You're at school. You're gone, living your life. I gotta keep that bitch clean. I'm the one who has to keep the snow shoveled, the grass cut, and leaves raked. Pay all the utilities."

"Look, I understand what you're saying, but that's our childhood in that house," London insisted, hoping to change her twin's mind.

Kenya was tired of all that back-and-forth bullshit. She was the only one holding that house down. She was going to come at London with the only thing that she seemed to now understand and embrace: struggle.

"First of all, London, the taxes and the water bill are due this month. You got half? Next, the homeowners insurance; once again, do you got half on that? And then, sorry, I had almost forgotten about the heating and light bill that are being shut off. Let me get out a pencil and paper and total your part." Kenya was pissed by that point and was now raising her voice.

London was totally thrown off by her sister's callous outbreak. She totally was speechless.

Kenya didn't let up. "You see the neighborhood, London. You see how it's changing. Even your own girl, Amber, is setting people up. Our hood is off the fuckin' hook.

London knew her twin was telling the truth about the state of the neighborhood, and even Amber; although, she still knew that Gran wouldn't want the house sold to strangers. "You know I need all my money to pay for extra school expenses next year. Kenya, I can't spend it!"

"Oh, I get it, so you think it's all right for me to spend all of my damn money? Well news flash: the money Gran left me is gone. And now I gotta get mines how I live. I hustle, London. I live day by day, no doubt. Some nights, I'm scared to come home to my own house because of the damn crime, so fuck what you talking about."

London got her thoughts together and finally spoke. "Listen, Kenya, just let me think about it. Let's just eat our breakfast and talk more about it at home."

"I'm sorry that I threw you off your square, but I don't know what else to do. You know I got love for you." Kenya and London smiled at one another and decided to change the subject. That one had run its course for the moment.

When the waitress brought the bill to the table both girls reached for it at the same time. "Let me get that. I know how you 'need' your money." Kenya laughed as she excused herself to go to the bathroom.

London watched her sister walk through the restaurant like she owned the place. *Some things never change!* London thought.

"Hey, Tastey, I missed you last night, with your fine self. You know how I get when I can't get a 'taste'!" A strange guy appeared at the table. The man was leaning all in London's inner space. "Here, baby, let me take care of your bill." He pulled out a wad of cash and peeled off three twenty dollar bills. "I'll see you this weekend, baby." He made sure to touch her hand when he put the cash on the table. London had a flashback of Professor Kincade and was in a frozen trance. He then smiled and went back to the other side of the room to sit with his friends, who were all staring.

Kenya returned to the table, putting lotion on her hands. She saw the money on the table and shook her head at London. "Listen, Ms. Goody-Goody, I told you I had it," she said, and slid the loot back over to her.

"I didn't pay for it, Tastey!" London rolled her eyes. Kenya immediately looked puzzled when she heard her sister call her by her stage name. "Some guy over there thought I was you, or should I say 'Tastey,' and paid for it." London pointed toward the group of desperate-looking men.

Kenya just shrugged her shoulders and nodded her head at them. "It's all part of the game! Life in the hood! Some of us can't escape!"

It was then that London decided to agree to put the house up for sale. She didn't want her sister to have to live right in the mix. Even as soft as everyone thought she was, she knew that you didn't shit where you slept.

Chapter Ten

Tastey

It had been a little over a month since the girls parted ways. They decided that over the summer they would indeed sell the house, and started to pack up most the stuff they wanted to keep. London would be home from school then and would have time to spare. Kenya was spending a lot of time at work. Being both Kenya at home and Tastey at work would sometimes get confusing. Kenya was now starting to turn into her stage name even at home. She was living and breathing the club and all the club life had to offer. It seemed like her government name was starting to become almost nonexistent.

"Hey, Zack, what's good?" Tastey was in great spirits and it showed.

"You, baby, you know that," he replied with his normal charm and swag.

"Look, I need to talk to you later." Tastey had a game plan in mind. "But, I gotta make this paper right now. One of my regular customers just came in and I don't want to keep his trick-ass waiting."

"Do you, baby girl. I'll be posted here all night." He loved to see her in action, getting that dough. Tastey made his club outshine all the others in the city. Zack was glad that she wanted to talk to him. All about a scheme, he also had a few things to discuss with her as well. He wanted to first run his thoughts by Old Skool and see what she thought he should do. A friend and confidante to all the dancers, she would know the right way to come at Tastey concerning his proposition. He knew that the young girl was a little streetwise, but was she street ready?

"Hey, darling, you needed me?" Old Skool came out of the dressing room as soon as she got the message that Zack wanted to speak with her.

"Yeah, I need to see what you think about that shit we talked about last month." Zack leaned back on the barstool.

"What shit? You know a bitch catching years!" Both her and Zack laughed she looked deeply in his eyes. They went back, way back, when Old Skool was considered "young game."

"I'm talking about that traveling thang, remember?"

"Oh, yeah, that. I'm with that! I think Tastey would be able to pull the shit off. Matter of fact she's perfect. Raven is still a little green. Plus, she has a son and might not be able to roll that easy." Old Skool always thought ahead when planning anything.

"Well, I'm trying to figure out how to break on her without scaring her or running her out the club, you dig? She's my best moneymaker in here. Tastey makes all the other girls hustle more." Zack was in full scheme mode at this point.

"Yeah, you right, but I think she's trying to save money to get her an apartment anyhow. I think the crib where she lives at now is going to be sold soon. I overheard her and Raven talking."

Not only didn't Old Skool or Zack know that she had a twin sister, they had no idea she owned a house as well. They thought she was just another dancer renting a spot. They were used to all young girls who danced having nothing, not a pot to piss in nor a window to throw it out of. Tastey was different and Zack thought back to the day they first met. That's why he had to come at her just right to avoid her possibly going ham.

"You know what? I think I'm just gonna be real and take my chances. The game is served cold, like a bowl of ice cream, and I'm gonna give it to her just like that." Zack was on the money trail. His last hook up had been fucking up on the count and that just wouldn't do in his shady world.

Old Skool listened and was in total agreement with Zack. She watched Tastey from across the room while she was giving one of her regulars a lap dance. "She has game, I'll give her that much."

Game Face On!

"Damn, baby, you like that? Tell me you like how all this ass feels on your dick." Tastey was spitting game on Shawn. He was one of her regulars. "Oh, daddy, your dick is so hard. Is all that for me?" Grinning all in his face, the young temptress was careful to keep her eyes glued on him, knowing eye contact would keep him hypnotized. His manhood was rock hard so Tastey knew to ease up on the grinding. She didn't want him to bust a nut on himself. Well, not at least 'til she got four or five dances from him. At twenty dollars a pop that would be at least a hundred. By the time the fifth song was beginning, Ms. Tastey decided to let loose on him. She knew he was about at his spending limit and wanted to make sure that he was satisfied with the dance. She never wanted to make a customer of hers have to get another girl for a good time. "Please, let me turn around and ride you, daddy!" She was licking her lips. "I want you to watch me cum on that big black dick!"

Shawn was all in as he grabbed a hold of Tastey's waist. "Yeah, that's it, make daddy cum!" was all he could get out his mouth before Tastey filled his face with her breasts. She was moving back and forth and talking cash shit in his ear.

After a few more seconds, the song was over and Shawn had a huge smile on his face. As she was trying to make it back into the dressing room to freshen up and change her outfit, a familiar hand reached from nowhere, grabbing out for her arm.

"Damn, motherfucker, what the fuck . . . ?" Before she could finish her sentence she realized that it was Ty. She hadn't really spoken to him since the night she started working at the club. He'd called, leaving a few threatening messages about her owing him for putting her on, but that didn't stop her from getting her money.

"Oh, I guess you just said fuck me and shit. It's like that? You dirty, rotten bitch!" Ty was drunk and slurring his words. "I'm the one who put your cum-catchin'-ass on in this mother-fucker. You owe me. Why don't you come over here and give a nigga some of that famous head I've been missing out on?"

"Oh, you trying it! Listen, Ty, I don't owe you jack shit. You got me all the way twisted in this piece!" Tastey was pissed and aggravated as she put him in his place. "And don't come all up in my job trying to front!"

"Oh, wow it's like that? You a beast now, right?" He was on the nut and about to try to cuff her up by her throat, when out of nowhere a huge arm wrapped around his neck. Brother Rasul was choking the dog shit out of Ty as he struggled unsuccessfully to breathe. He was turning beet red and tears were flowing out both eyes. Zack, seeing the commotion, came running over just as Ty was getting skull drug out the door. "I was just . . ."

Ty couldn't get his explanation out good before Zack also started in on him. "Let me show you how real D-town ballers ball!" Zack reached under his shirt and pulled out a shiny black nine. He put one up top and put the gun in Ty's mouth. "Pay attention, Tastey or Kenya or whatever you choose to call her is family up here, all right! If you ever fucking choose to disturb her well-being again, I'll blow your dental out the back of your neck! Now get the fuck out my club before you get me all the way off my square. That's my word! We clear?"

Zack stuffed his gun back in his rear waistband and left Brother Rasul and the rest of the bouncers to do their thang. Tastey was feeling somewhat bad for Ty, but she felt strangely loved by Zack and the rest of her club family and felt a sense of loyalty to them for coming to her aid.

Old Skool, wanting to put her two cents in the mix, came in the dressing room and wanted to know if she was okay. "Hey, girl. You good or what?" She rubbed sympathetically on the young girl's back.

"Yeah, I just hate when someone tries to put a bitch's business all up in the street. It's all good though. I ain't tripping on it though."

"That's good. Don't let these fools front on you." Old Skool made her feel much better. "When you get dressed Zack wants to talk to you." Tastey gave her a worried look, hoping her job wasn't in jeopardy. "Girl, don't worry. He ain't bugging about that bullshit. He said you wanted to talk to him about some stuff you had on your mind."

"Oh, yeah, damn, I did. I almost forgot!" Tastey was relieved. She didn't want to lose her job. She needed the money and, besides, she had no other friends except her girl Raven and the rest of the club family. Emotionally drained from dealing with Ty's over-the-top antics, she decided to be done for the night. She pulled her hair up in a ponytail and put on a track suit and her sneakers. She was getting herself prepared to meet with Zack.

Tastey made her way into Zack's office and took a seat on the couch. He was on his cell phone, talking a lot of shit as always. After a short while of listening to him boast about this, that, and the third, she got up and started to look at all of the different framed pictures he had on the office wall. There were a few of girls and some of cars, but most of them were nightclub shots from way back when. Judging from some of the outfits he and others had on, he must have been collecting them for a long time. In some of them, Zack's pimped-out-ass was even sporting a Jheri curl and bell-bottoms. As she walked along the wall, one picture shockingly jumped out at her. Tastey moved in extra close to get a better look, thinking her eyes might've been playing tricks on her. "Oh, fuck naw, oh, shit!" Her sudden outburst caused Zack to glance over at her and start to wrap up his conversation.

"What's up, baby girl? Sorry about that. You know how I am when I get to runnin' my mouth. I damn near forgot you were here you were so quiet." He was making his way toward her as he was talking.

Tastey made sure to move away from that particular picture so he wouldn't ask her any questions about her reaction to it. "Don't worry. I kept myself busy looking at all your pictures, especially the ones where you're busting that curl!" Kenya was laughing at Zack, trying to play off a bad feeling that was stirring inside the pit of her stomach.

Playing the role, he started acting like he was fixing his curl in the mirror. "You don't know nothing about this! I was Grand Daddy Caddy, Macaroni Tony!" Zack teased before getting down to the reason for their meeting.

After they sat down and got themselves together it was time to get to it. Zack thought it would be better to let Tastey start and get whatever it was that she wanted to say out in the open before he broke on her with his game plan.

"Okay, this is what I was thinking." She adjusted her body in the chair, praying his response would be positive. "What if we had feature dancers and showcases every week here? You know, some shit where the top moneymakers got put on full blast? I was talking to Old Skool and she told me she used to be a feature dancer at different spots around the city." Tastey took a break in the presentation she was making, to try to peep Zack and see if he was buying into her new hustle.

"That's what's up! I'm glad to see you're thinking of more ways to make the club and yourself extra revenue." Zack had to make sure to give Old Skool some extra cash and some of his dick that she always craved. She had perfectly laid the groundwork out for his plan and he was overjoyed. This was just what he needed to hear. Zack could manipulate Kenya into thinking that it was her idea and he came up with his part of it at the tail end, spur of the moment. "I think we can do that and even a little bit more."

Zack told her to get relaxed and pay attention to what he was about to say next. This was going to be the part of the plan that would make or break the whole deal. "All right, Tastey, here's the real thing that I'm talking about. I got a gravy-ass hookup with a couple of cats out West in L.A. and down in Texas. And we got sorta what you would call a partnership. You see, I got my hands on a lot of, should we say, product, and they're interested in helping me get rid of it." He was rubbing his hands together as he spoke, hoping to lure Kenya on his team. "First, we can do some smaller things in Ohio and other places closer to home, then move up to a bigger scale."

"Are you talking about moving cocaine, raw, or trees?" Kenya was attentively sitting straight up in her seat, taking in all her boss had to say.

"Hell naw! Now just what the fuck you know about all that?" Zack was more than amazed that she had come on him just like that, flat out with it. He was both shocked and relieved all at the same time. The expression on his face told it all.

Tastey could see that he was staring at her strange, so she took over the conversation. "Come on, Zack, you act like I don't be around people. You must think I'm not from the hood. Who the fuck ain't got a head in their family? And, shit, weed is the third creation. Everybody knows God made the heavens, the earth, and then the 'trees.'" Tastey held her hands open and looked toward the sky like she was smiling up at the Almighty Himself.

"Girl, you know you a fool!" It was then that Zack knew that his plan would work out perfectly. The scheming pair talked for close to a hour before Brother Rasul came to the door informing him that a guy was out front looking for him needing a face to face. He was claiming his business was very important and extremely personal, meaning that what he had to say was for Zack's ears only.

"Okay, partner, let me go up front and see what all this is about and I'll talk to you tomorrow, cool?" Zack reached over and grabbed Tastey's hand, shaking it, signifying they had a deal. "Be easy, baby girl, and clear your mind, you about to make some major paper."

As Zack and Tastey left out his office, he saw Old Skool sitting at the end of the bar and blew her a kiss as he stroked his dick. She knew that she would get paid tonight in more ways than one. Old Skool then told Tastey to have a good night as one of Brother Rasul's team walked her out to her car. Seeing something stuck underneath her windshield wiper blade, she took the half-folded paper out. Quickly realizing Ty had left the note, Kenya angrily balled it up and threw it out the window without so much as reading one single solitary word. *Fuck him and all that drama he be bringing with him!* As she pulled out the parking lot still thinking about the picture she'd seen on Zack's office wall, she drove home for the night.

Zack

"Young Foy, my nigga. Man, when did you come home? We missed you in the D." Zack gave his man a play and a short hug. "You did a real little bid this time around didn't you? Do them crackers up north know they done let a straight-up fool loose?" Zack laughed so loudly that some of the girls were alarmed thinking it was more trouble like what had jumped off earlier.

Young Foy was tall and had the build of most career inmates. With a hood mentality, he was a straight-up troublemaker, no doubt. If anything was being sold on the far west side of town he had a piece of the action, even if he had to strong-arm his way on the ticket. The seasoned criminal's temper was on a hairline trigger much like Kenya's. He would fly hot on that ass at the drop of a dime before you knew it. However, being in and out of prison never seemed to stop him from having his ear to the streets. Young Foy, although 100 percent thug, was always spitting rhymes and singing. He needed to get into show business and stop running in the streets before he got killed like most of the dudes he'd come up with. All he needed was a chance and someone to bankroll his dream.

"Hey, guy, I wanted to stop by and check on you. See what you had popping for a brother. You know a nigga fresh out and trying to come back up." Young Foy was running his game down. Playas in the hood knew he was a man of his word when it came to getting that money. "Let a nigga get some work! You know I straight need it!"

"I tell you what." Zack's mind was beginning to work overtime; besides, he knew when it came to Young Foy he'd have to cut him in or cut it out all together. "Stop by in the next few days and I can most def put you on. In the meantime, welcome home!" Zack dug in his pockets, respectfully pulling out two hundred-dollar bills, giving them to Young Foy.

"All right bet, bet, good lookin'." Young Foy then paused remembering the other reason he'd made a trip to see Zack as soon as he touched down. "Damn, dawg. It almost slipped my mind your boy Stone was locked up with me. He wanted me to make sure to come by and tell you that he needs you to come see him and shit as soon as possible."

"Yo, why didn't he just call the phone or drop a nigga a few lines? Do he need some dough or something?" Zack quizzed.

"Come on, killer, what I look like, Ms. Cleo?" Young Foy saw one of Zack's phat-ass freaks walk by and that was all she wrote for their conversation. He was on ho patrol. "Man, I'll holler. Just go get with dude! He acted like it was urgent." And with those words he was out.

Old Skool came over to Zack and put her arms around him. She couldn't wait to get to her house and get her hands on Zack's dick. "Hey, it's almost three, let's have Brother Rasul shut it down."

Zack agreed, kissing her on the lips. "Yeah, okay. Let's be out. After all, I owe your ass a little something-something and you know I hate owing a nigga." Old Skool gave him a yard of tongue, while he ran his hand across her thirty-six DDs. "We'll see you in the morning." Zack patted Brother Rasul on the back as they left for the night. He trusted him with his club and his life.

Chapter Eleven

London

London had been back in school for just a few days when she and Fatima decided to go ahead and really start the organization they'd been discussing for months and months. After plenty of late-night talks they each found out they'd both had drug addicts in their families or, in London's case, Amber. They both came to realize that drugs were tearing down neighborhoods and tearing families apart. They stayed up long nights after studying, coming up with a lot of key points that they wanted to cover in their meetings.

"I think we should make sure to focus on kids who don't get the food they need because their parents are on crack."

London was writing down both her and Fatima's ideas.

"Girl, I think we should try to shine the light on all the crime that senior citizens are subjected to by addicts trying to get money to cop." Fatima was on a roll with things to add on also.

London started to think about her friend Amber and came up with the last thing to put on the list. "Why don't we try to make the main focus on the youth, like kids in between nine and nineteen? If we can try to catch them, maybe we can make a difference. Tell them about another way to make it out the hood. Look how many of us are up here in school and can't look out or protect our little brothers and sisters from the dope man."

Fatima looked at London like she had just invented apple pie. "That's it! For real, for real. I think we just found our hook." Both girls were hyped up but decided to get some rest and get ready for a busy day.

Morning came quick enough, and the girls hurried to get dressed. "You ready, Fatima?"

"Yeah, almost, give me ten more minutes." London heard her say that and immediately thought about Kenya. She was always good for telling Gran that same line almost each and every morning.

Fatima grabbed her dorm room keys and the two were off. After a short walk across the campus, they cut across the football field, finally ending up at their destination. The girls made it to the school's media outlook building in what had to be record time. They were going to print out fliers to post all over the campus. London hoped that at least they would get ten or eleven people to show up at the group meeting that would be held on the weekend.

The day soon arrived and the girls were excited. "It's three o'clock. We have thirty minutes before everyone starts to get here. I'm so nervous." London was walking back and forth from the window to the door.

"Girl, we got this. I been hearing a few people talk about the fliers in class and in the computer lab." Fatima seemed to always know how to calm her friend down. "Just get up there and do the damn thang! Your ass is good at talking shit!" Fatima smiled as she hugged her roommate.

The meeting was about to start and, to the girls' surprise, it was standing room only. They had the dorm conference room packed to capacity with students. Some of their faces they knew on sight, and some of the people London and Fatima didn't even know attended the university.

"That flier must have been all kinds of powerful!" Fatima whispered to her soon-to-be partner in raising some hell.

London shook her head, agreeing. "I know, but I really think it just hit home with a lot of us. Let's get it started."

Fatima looked at London and knew her girl was gonna be definitely on point.

"Hello, everyone. My name is Amia London Roberts. I'm a freshman here and I have a few issues that trouble my mind at night. Hell, sometimes during the day." London had sparked some of the crowd's interest in what could be bothering such a pretty and well-spoken young lady. "It's my neighborhood at home. It's my little cousins and their friends, the ones who used to look up to me for guidance and even sometimes protection. Let me clarify: not protection from the physical side of the street, but the mental. The seemingly never-ending cycle of being hungry because Mom sold all of the food stamps for the month. The embarrassment of having to wear dirty or worn-out clothes to school, that is, if you ever had the encouragement to go." London was truly on top of her game and the entire room was hyped. "Look, I know many of you come from what we call 'the hood.' I bet you have brothers and sisters you worry about while attending school. We were lucky. Most of us had somebody in our lives. That one person who unconditionally cared about us and helped us, sometimes made us, make it through the tough times. All I'm saying is that just like we had that one shining beacon to guide us, it's time we stood up and let them pass the torch to us."

The crowd was on its feet. Fatima looked over to London and decided that she would not even speak. She knew that London would be the group's number one spokesperson from here on out.

The meeting went on for nearly two hours as each and every person gave their own story and personal account of what their issue was. Each one seemed to be worse than the last. At the conclusion of the first meeting, they decided on a name for the newly formed organization. It would be called People Against Illegal Drugs.

In short, PAID was formed and was officially ready to raise some hell for the youth. In London's words, it was time for change and the time was now!

Tastey

"Life is good as hell!" Tastey was feeling herself as she fell back on the bed in her hotel room surrounded by stacks and stacks of dough. Sure, most of it belonged to Zack, but a small cut of it was hers. She'd been stashing dope in the bottom of her dance bag for a little over a month now and getting paid. That meeting in Zack's office that night was paying off big

time for her. Tastey had been stacking her loot from hustlin'
and living off the tips she made from dancing. Her girl Raven
went on the road with her from time to time whenever she
could get a babysitter, so it was double the fun. The two of
them would fall up in whatever strip club in the circuit they
had to make a delivery to and practically take over that bitch.
New girls, fresh meat as they were called, always made much
more money than any of the regular girls on the roster. Tastey
and Raven both were sexy as hell so snatching all the money
wherever they went was never a problem. They knew how to
give a nigga his money's worth. They were true showstoppers.

Zack, on the other hand, was starting to get nervous. Things
were soon going to come to a screeching halt when his used-
to-be longtime friend Stone got released and came home from
prison, and he knew it. Stone stayed deep in Zack's pockets
on an old debt Stone would never let him forget. As Zack sat
down behind his desk, he looked at the pictures on the wall.
One in particular stood out. It just so happened to be the
same one that had jumped out at Tastey months earlier. It
was like it was somehow calling out to him. Zack had no idea
whatsoever what Stone had wanted was so important that he
had to send word by Young Foy to come see him in person. He
often thought back to that day he fucked up, causing Stone to
want to kill him dead. It would come to haunt him daily.

*It was close to a three-hour ride up north to the peniten-
tiary where Stone was housed. Zack went through all the
normal procedures that it took to visit a friend or loved one.
"Damn, this is some degrading bullshit!" he said out loud.*

*The guards just went on with their jobs. They were used to
every type of verbal assault known to man or beast. Finally
he got in and took a seat at a table. He then waited for what
seemed like hours. The gate at the prisoner entrance finally
cracked and Zack saw his old friend Stone bend the corner.
Stone was looking hard faced, but that wasn't anything
new to Zack; matter of fact that was how he originally had
gotten that nickname: being stone-faced. They had grown
up together in the same neighborhood and Stone barely
smiled then either so Zack really made nothing of it at that
point. As Stone got close to the table, he sat down. Obviously*

having something serious on his mind, he didn't bother or waste time even giving his boy any love.

"What dude, no dap, no love, what's up?" Zack was confused by this time. Each and every time his boy would do a bid, which was often, he would always accept his calls or send him some money on his books. He'd constantly looked out for him and his woman no matter what.

"Man, I ain't gonna even front with you or spend no time with all that yang, yang. Dig this here! You know a young cat named Ty, a small-time car-thieving motherfucker from DLA area? He 'bout twenty or twenty-one." Stone's face, being as it was, showed no signs of emotion as he spoke.

"Yeah, I know him. He ain't 'bout shit," Zack eagerly chimed in. "I know his bitch-ass wasn't showing no form of disrespect to you, was he? Because we stumped his ho-ass out awhile back for some bullshit."

"Naw, not him! It's you, playa! You the one violating!" Stone was mean mugging Zack like a motherfucker by this time, wanting to damn near smack the fire out his mouth. "See that little punk was locked up here for a minute, doing a short stay. Ol' boy was talking mad shit about you, your boy Brother Rasul, and that rotten cat house your slimy ass run with Old Skool."

Zack was fucked up at the reckless way his boy was talking to him. Matter of fact he was straight-up offended. "Damn, man, it was all good when you wanted to hang in the bitch. It keeps the bills paid on that phone you blow the fuck up and the money on your account. Where's all this hate from, dawg? I thought we was better than that."

Stone was boiling over with anger and could hardly stay in his seat. "You right, flat out, guy! I thought we was better than that too. That's why I'm all fucked up. Please tell me that the ho-ass little nigga was lying and just trying to keep me from chin stumping his ass."

"Come on, Stone, what you talking about? I'm lost." Zack was looking his longtime comrade in the face and waiting for some sort of explanation for his explosive anger.

Stone swallowed hard as hell and finally let it out. "Dude, dig this here, I know you ain't got my little niece working in that joint, swing from no fucking pole?" You could almost see blood in Stone's eyes. Infuriated and enraged, his jaw was locked tight as he waited for a response to his question, or more like an accusation.

"Niece! What niece?" Zack was stunned not knowing who or what he was talking about. "What the fuck are you talking about, man, and who the fuck?" The entire visiting room was starting to look over at the two of them as their voices rose.

"Ty told me you had my little niece Kenya up on stage showing her ass like some common tramp from around the way!" Out of his seat yelling at this point, Stone was ready to kill. "That's some foul-ass shit, nigga!" You could see the veins in his muscular arms start to swell, resulting in the guards quickly rushing over, trying to contain the commotion.

Zack was busy trying to explain to Stone that he had no idea that Kenya was his niece. "Oh, shit! Damn, nigga! I didn't know that she was your family, I swear! I put that on everything! I'm sorry!"

Stone wasn't buying it and the guards had to drag him out the visiting room shouting the entire time. "I'll be out soon and on my brother Johnnie's grave, it's on, you feel me? You got his baby girl up there like that? You don't wanna see me, nigga, you don't want that!" The door slammed on Stone as he was still yelling, making a scene. Zack was left sitting at the table in shock over what he had just heard.

The phone started ringing, waking Zack up out of his trance. Daydreaming about that visit to the prison consumed most of his time. Haunting him, Zack also reminisced to back in the day when Stone had come to him needing some information about some young cats he'd turned his brother Johnnie on to. Zack didn't know that the guys he had just met that night were into sticking people up. They were flashing money around, claiming they were looking for some dope. How was he to know their true intentions? Even though Stone never came out and said it, Zack knew that a small part of him blamed him for his brother Johnnie's and his sister-in-law Melinda's heinous murders. After all, he did introduce them all. Whenever Stone would come around and bring up his deceased family members, Zack would automatically go in his pocket.

The guilt of what Stone had told him was killing his spirit. And now not only did he have his niece shaking her ass on stage, she was running dope, too. Zack prayed nightly that Stone would not make parole anytime soon. He knew that his now-former friend would be on a rampage and show little or no mercy.

"Hello." Zack had gotten in the habit of looking at the caller ID before answering the phone. Stone had him spooked. He was looking over his shoulder every moment, not knowing what to expect.

"Hey, Zack, it's me. It's all good my way." Tastey was still looking at the money that was thrown across the bed. She wished that all that cheddar belonged to her, but she had made her ends and was satisfied.

"Come on home, baby girl. I need to talk to you about something."

"About what?" she quizzed Zack, sensing a weird tone in his usually chipper voice.

Zack immediately cut her off. "You know I don't head bust about important shit on the phone. I'll just see you sooner rather than later."

"Okay, bet. No worries. I'll be home sometime in the early afternoon."

Zack had never mentioned his trip to the prison to visit Kenya's uncle. Vying for time, the money-hungry opportunist was trying to find another drug mule with as much street game as Kenya had, who could be trusted. He was putting together a big deal that could bring him a huge payoff and then he could cut Tastey off and maybe pay Stone some major bread to stay off his ass. He would hate to see her go. It would be hard, but for his own personal safety there was no other way. Greedy, he knew he was already pushing his luck. But, the girl could hustle in the club and make shit happen in the streets. Realizing she was Johnnie Roberts's daughter, he knew she had that "get money or kill a nigga dead" DNA flowing in her bloodline. However, like it or not, the clock was ticking to let her go, and time was definitely not on his side.

Chapter Twelve

Tastey

It was about 1:45 in the afternoon when Kenya pulled up in the club parking lot. Heads Up had a lot of cars in the valet area, so she had to pull around to the side door. She called inside and had one of the guys on security have the door open. Kenya had more than $25,000 in her bag and didn't want to risk any fuckups by thirsty fools looking for a quick come up. She'd heard stories from old family friends about her parents slipping up that one time resulting in them getting murdered. Kenya, true to the streets, always tried to be on top of her hustle, no matter what it was.

"Hey, Young Foy! What's good?"

"Nothing, Tastey, just playing this work thing for a minute. You know how it is. A nigga still trying to get his music thang together and off the ground."

Young Foy let Tastey in the side entrance and personally walked her up to Zack's closed office door. On the way up the stairs, he mentioned to her that her ex-boyfriend Ty had been repeatedly calling up to the club asking for her.

"Man, fuck his ass. He ain't talking about shit I wanna hear! Last time he was up in here trying to front on a bitch, he got his shit split to the white meat!" Tastey was shaking her head from side to side, in true ghetto fashion, as she talked that talk.

"Yeah, I feel you, ma. Ain't no problem. I was just putting you up on it." Young Foy really liked Tastey, but he knew the upkeep on a female like her would hurt his pockets something serious. He knew a nigga on a budget couldn't keep a steady bitch, especially a bad bitch like Tastey. Young Foy left her to handle her business and made his way back on post.

"Hey, Old Skool. Hey, Zack." Tastey strolled in the office smiling and in good spirits as always.

"Hey, girl, we missed you around here." Old Skool ran across the room, hugging her tightly as if someone died.

Zack was both happy and sad. He knew if Tastey didn't go for this last big run, he'd be fucked in the game. Praying for the best, he smiled, hugging Tastey also.

Having had enough of the emotional couple, she placed her bag up on the table, opening it up. Old Skool went to lock the office door so they wouldn't be interrupted doing the count.

Tastey was beaming with pride. "It's all there. I didn't even take my cut out yet. I just counted it to make sure those niggas in Columbus ain't try no short change stuff!"

"I know you on top of it, baby girl. That's why I love your ass so much." Zack was happy to have that money in his hands. He knew that every trip was like a roll of the dice when it came to transporting, especially across state lines. Automatically, he slid Tastey three grand. Add that to the $850 she made dancing at the strip club she made the drop off at, and she had close to four grand. That was a hellava good night's work.

Tastey gathered her pay and was about to make tracks, when Zack stopped her. "Hold tight. I needed to discuss a proposition with you. I know it'll be worth your while."

"Well damn, let me take a seat. I've been driving all morning and still haven't eaten." Tastey, overly cautious, had to make sure to drive the speed limit and watch out for the state boys.

"Let me get you something from the kitchen. Sit your ass down and chill. You know I got you, baby." Old Skool listened to Tastey's order and took it down to the kitchen. It would give Zack time to hopefully work his game.

"Look, I'm gonna give it to you straight, like I always do. That trip you just came back from will more than likely be the last road trip I need you to make for me."

Tastey was tired as hell, but that statement from Zack woke her all the way up. "Dang gee, dude, why you saying that?"

"Girl, you've been on the highway making the same trips every few weeks. And I don't want them troopers to get familiar with seeing your face. I was thinking about letting the new girl, Spice, do her thang and make some extra money.

She seems like good people." Zack could see the angry look on Tastey's face. "Look, sweetheart, I ain't trying to stop your flow. I'm only trying to look out."

"Yeah, I know, but I need to stack a little bit more loot." Tastey knew that the house that she and London jointly owned would hopefully be sold soon. When that happened, she wanted to have enough money to buy herself a little crib out in the suburbs, maybe even out of Michigan. To accomplish that, Kenya needed all the cash she could make, legal or illegal.

"I do have something else popping. It's kinda different from the driving thing."

Tastey was all in and Zack could tell. "Tell me what it is and what exactly I have to do."

"Well, first of all, are you scared to fly?" He leaned back in his chair, folding his arms.

"Naw, my people used to take me on trips when I was younger." Zack knew that she was talking about her uncle, his boy Stone. He got a chill when he even though about his name. "I ain't scared at all!" she blurted out like a G.

Zack explained to her that his buddy Deacon and his boy Storm had opened up a new strip club down in Texas named Alley Cats and he was trying to get a few girls from Detroit to bring some flavor to his place. Zack also went on to tell her that Deacon and Storm needed some product to move, so that they could finance some major remodeling they wanted to do.

"All you have to do is fly out there once, maybe twice, and it's a wrap. I'll pay you $5,500 for each trip."

"Damn, how much shit is it? I mean how much do I collect from Deacon, Storm, or whoever?" Tastey was all for it, but she had to see exactly how the program itself was supposed to play out.

Old Skool came back with her food and they all chopped it up, devising a solid game plan for Tastey. After talking and eating, Tastey headed home to take a long hot bath and think. She also was going to call her twin to check in on her. For some reason, the girls seemed to always miss the other's calls. London was submerged deep in her new life and Kenya wasn't hating. She was truly happy for her.

***

"Hey, Fatima. How you doing, girl?" Kenya was over all that silliness of being jealous of her sister's friendship with her roommate.

Fatima was also happy to hear Kenya's voice. She knew that London was starting to get worried about her twin because the two hadn't spoken in over a week, which seemed abnormal even in Fatima's eyes.

"Hey, Kenya, girl, we've been wondering where you been hiding out at. Let me run and get your sister. She's at the end of the hall, passing out some fliers for the upcoming meeting. You ought to come up and see your sister throwing down on her speeches. A lot of important people are going to be there. She's gonna blaze the stage, for real!"

"I ain't know ol' girl was getting at they heads like that. You make her sound like a li'l London X."

Both Fatima and Kenya giggled as Fatima waved down the hall to her roommate, holding the phone up. "She's on her way now. You grew up with the chic, you know she gotta get her last words in." Kenya was in total agreement with Fatima.

"Hello, this is Miss Roberts."

"Oh, damn. I ain't know we was all formal. Excuse the fuck outta me!" Kenya, teasing, was sounding uppity, snapping her fingers.

"Oh my God! Fatima didn't tell me it was you. She just handed me the phone, started smiling, and left out. Where in the hell have you been?"

"I've been around, here and there, Ohio, Chi-town, and a few days in upstate New York." Kenya was trying to play that shit off, but in reality, she thought she was Big Willie, low-key.

"I thought you fell your behind off the face of the earth. Don't you ever check your messages?" London wasn't going to let her twin sister get away with avoiding her calls without an explanation.

Kenya went into detail about Ty's visit up to her job and all the times that he called her house and the club. "Sis, I don't even listen to them crybaby messages he be leaving. I just push delete and keep on stepping. That crazy fool even left a letter on my car. I tore that shit up and threw it in the street, fuck even reading his bullshit. That nigga been a liar since conception!"

"Dang, what did you do to him? He seems like a stalker. You need to press charges against him or something." London was concerned for her sister's safety first and foremost.

"Yeah, you right, but forget his trick-ass. He got dealt with proper. Anyway, I heard you up there doing the damn thang." Kenya was hyping her sister up.

"Yeah, I guess you could say I'm doing a li'l somethin'-somethin' as you say!"

Kenya was glad to know that all was well with London and she was doing big things. "So, I heard you got a big rally next weekend?"

London sighed. "Hey, why don't you come up and spend the whole weekend with me? I miss you."

"I wish I could, London, but I'm going to be in Texas and I don't know exactly when I might be back." Kenya hated disappointing her twin but business came first.

London was understanding of the situation, telling Kenya to do what made her happy. However, she had no idea that her sister was being a drug mule for the man their uncle considered partially to blame for their parents' untimely death. Kenya was part of the system that London was trying so hard to endlessly fight. London hated drugs and everything and everybody affiliated with them. Drugs made her and her sister orphans as far as she was concerned, and this was the outlook that she kept in the back of her mind whenever she made a speech.

"Well, London, I'm about to go to bed. I'm so tired that I'm about to fall asleep on this phone."

London hated to let her sister go, but was happy just to hear from her. "Hey, before you go, have you heard from Uncle lately?"

Kenya was apprehensive about talking about their uncle. Ever since she saw that picture of him in Zack's office, she had been avoiding his collect calls. Between him and Ty, she got used to turning the ringer off and pushing IGNORE. "He tried to call a few times, but I wasn't home. But if he calls you, tell him I still love him."

"Okay, then. I love you, Kenya."

Kenya lay back and smiled. *"Say U Promise!"*

Tastey

"You got everything packed just the way we planned?" Zack was a little more than anxious about what was about to take place. With more than $65,000 worth of raw dope on the line, he took his time to go over the game plan repeatedly. "Listen up, Tastey, this is some major shit about to take place and we don't want or need any mistakes. Your freedom and my credibility is on the line. It took me and my people more than a week to negotiate on this deal. My people wants to take delivery of this shit almost as bad as I want to move it."

Tastey was trying her best to ease Zack's mind. "Be easy, I remember everything you said. The shit is twisted extra tight and double wrapped in triple plastic. Old Skool put cotton around it and then we put two more pieces of plastic. So chill, damn!"

"I ain't gonna be easy until your ass call me from the hotel telling me you made it." Zack was sweating, like he had to get on the plane with the dope his motherfucking self. "Matter of fact, I won't be happy until you meet up with Deacon and Storm and get my cash. I love them niggas like brothers and everything, but fuck the dumb stuff. I wanna see my money in hand. You feel me?"

"Listen, Zack, if you keep talking, I'm gonna miss my flight. You starting to mess with my good karma I got going on. Don't fuck my mind up. I need to be straight-up focused." Tastey was giving him a crazy look like, "Negro, please shut up!"

"Let her go. She's got her stuff together. You know that. When has she ever let you down?" Old Skool jumped in as she patted Zack on his back. "Relax!"

Zack watched Tastey and Brother Rasul pull out the parking lot and he wiped the sweat off his brow. In between letting that much dope out his sight and his conscience kicking his ass constantly about crossing Stone even though he knew the consequences, he was sick to his soul. Zack was losing weight and staying paranoid at the world and anyone in it.

***

After a long ride on a traffic-filled highway, Brother Rasul reached the airport. Tastey and he talked all the way there. "When I first met you, I knew it was something different about you, Sister Kenya."

Tastey was kinda thrown off because, it was the one and only time that he'd ever addressed her by her true real government name.

With conviction, he looked her in her eyes and spoke from his heart. "Have pride, young sister. Don't let the planted seeds of evil entice you from your true mission in life. Remember, I always got your back, even when you think I don't!"

Tastey grabbed Brother Rasul's hand and reassured him before she got out the car that this would be the only time that she'd be doing something this dangerous.

"Be safe, little sister, be safe." He headed back to the club to get ready for a long night filled with several reserved spot parties booked.

As Kenya made her way in the terminal at Detroit Metro Airport and checked her suitcases, she felt like all eyes were on her. Although she was used to being a star up on the stage, this was much different; her freedom was on the line.

"Now boarding at gate twenty-two, nonstop flight to Dallas," the lady on the loud speaker announced, causing a line to form at the gate.

Damn, that's me. This is it!

Tastey boarded the plane, found her seat, and got situated. *I wonder if they can tell I have all this shit stashed on me.* Her eyes followed everyone who got on the plane. Kenya got out a copy of a schoolbook and pretended to read, just like her and Zack planned. Getting even more into character, she even had on her State University hoodie that London had given her. If she could keep her cool, it would be all good.

After a bumpy ride and truly getting caught up in the banging novel, the plane finally landed and Tastey got off after gathering her belongings. She couldn't believe that she'd gotten away with it. She had even gotten so relaxed during the flight she took a nap.

I've got to find my luggage and get a cab. As she moved through the crowds of people, she felt at ease. The nervousness she was feeling earlier had passed. When she made it to the taxi stand, she thought, *Zack's boys must be some cheap-ass bastards. He could have sent a limo or something to pick me up,* not thinking that she could have drawn attention to herself.

Kenya got in the cab, telling the driver the hotel she had reservations at. The driver, claiming he made good time, made it to the hotel in less than twenty minutes. After paying the fare and tipping him an extra five, Kenya registered, got her key, and got to the room. She reached inside her purse and pulled out her cell phone.

Stone

Not more than ten minutes after Tastey bravely boarded the airplane heading to Dallas did her once-incarcerated uncle arrive back in the city after miraculously making parole. Young Foy, out in the streets checking his traps, saw Stone on the block as soon as his woman drove up to their house, and immediately stepped to him.

"Stone, my dude! What's good, God? When you touch down?" Young Foy gave his former bunkie some love while Stone's woman opened the trunk, grabbing the bag with her man's personal property in it.

"Just now. You know they can't hold a real hood warrior down. As hard as the white man put his foot down on my neck, the stronger I get." Stone stuck his chest out with pride, beating his clenched fist on his heart. "Real talk, I'm gonna go up in the crib, get some grub, take a bath, and hit these streets running." Stone headed up toward the door, focused on revenge. "I'll holler at you later. Oh, yeah, and good looking on delivering that message to Zack for me. That was right on time."

"You know how we do, nigga! We family first and foremost! And if you need a li'l something in your pocket, I ain't got much, but you always welcome to half of whatever!"

"That's real, young blood, but I'm set. I'm 'bout to hit off some paper in a few! So, I'll holler!"

Young Foy looked at Stone's girl's ass swaying up the stairs behind Stone, and thought, *Fuck hittin' the streets. I'd be hittin' that ass!*

When Young Foy got to Heads Up to start his shift, annoyed, he saw Zack and Raven plotting over in a dark corner of the club. Young Foy, usually a player, had been spending a lot of time with Raven ever since he'd started working there. Surrounded by half-naked women nightly, he started kicking game to the single parent dancer, after he realized that he couldn't have Tastey. Raven, impressionable and loyal, was deeply in love with Young Foy; but he, on the other hand, wasn't exactly sure where his heart was truly at. Used to being classified as a dog, he was brand new when it came to the love game in general. All he knew for sure was music, slinging dope, and hustling; anything else was foreign.

"Hey now, Zack, what's the deal this evening, guy?"

Noticeably, his boss had a worried expression on his face. "Nothing, Young Foy, just seeing if Raven can text message Tastey for me about something." Without question, he was going to give himself a heart attack waiting to hear from his drug mule.

"Dig that," Young Foy responded, feeling uneasy about Zack being so cozy with his girl, boss or not.

Zack, having got Raven to text, then excused himself. "Well, let me go to my office. I have some things to take care of. I'll see you two in a minute." As Zack turned to walk away, Young Foy unknowingly threw some salt in the game, asking him if he was going to block off a VIP section for his old friend Stone.

Dry mouthed, Zack quickly turned white as a ghost. "What you mean, block off for Stone?" He was sweating bullets, waiting for Young Foy to answer the question.

"Come on, dude. I know you knew your man was coming home, didn't you?" Young Foy gave him a strange look, wondering why Zack was acting so shocked.

Zack tried to play it off, not wanting to seem like he was out the loop as he pumped him for information on the sly. "Yeah, um, I did. Have you heard from him yet?"

"Yeah, actually, I just ran into him and his girl around the way. He was just touching down."

When Zack heard that Stone was released from prison, his heart started to pound extra fast. Interrupting their conversation, his cell phone then suddenly started to ring and scared the shit out of him. He looked at the screen and ran up to his office to take the call.

"Damn, what's up with that?" Raven asked Young Foy as she kissed him softly on the lips.

"I don't know what's up with his ass. That guy been bugging out for the past few weeks now." Raven and Young Foy laughed together as Zack entered his office, slamming the door shut behind him.

Tastey

"Hey, Zack, I'm here! What took you so long to answer the phone?" Tastey was kicking her shoes off, getting ready to take a long bath and relax her nerves.

"I was down in the club handling some business. Is everything okay your way? Did you have any problems? Are you at the hotel?" Zack quizzed her as if he was conditioning a full-scale interrogation.

Tastey was not trying to get stressed the fuck out by his worrying and overthinking shit. "Listen, I'm here in the hotel. It's room 1369 and I'm tight!"

Zack had to think quickly, considering the bad news that Young Foy had just given him. Naturally he didn't want Tastey to come back to town with all his money in tow and Stone was out walking the streets, possibly running into her before he had a chance to explain his side of what happened to her parents that God-awful night. Zack was confused, to say the least, knowing damn well it was just a matter of time before Stone, who was out for blood, would be paying him a visit. "Dig this here, Tastey. It's been a slight change in plans. My boys Deacon and Storm have to hustle up on a little bit more loot. So I need you to chill in Dallas one more day, on my pockets, of course. As soon as they get their situation together, you and them can bump heads. Oh, and by the way,

I don't want you to call me anymore until you three meet. I don't want any phone traces back here from the police or something. The next call you should get will be from one of them; Deacon or Storm." Zack had to buy himself some time to try to reason with Stone, and keeping his niece under wraps would have to do for now.

"All right, Zack, not a problem. I guess I could go to the mall or catch a movie. I'll be fine. Don't worry about me. I'm good. I'll wait for the call and take care of that. Talk to you in a few days." Tastey hung up the phone and placed it on her charger. Happy to spend on someone else's tab, she ran her bathwater and took out an outfit to wear to the mall.

Zack called Brother Rasul up to the office, informing him that he wanted extra security in the club for the next few days.

Brother Rasul, sensing his crooked boss and friend had once again dug himself deep into a twisted weave of bullshit, suspiciously rubbed his chin. "All right then, but what's wrong? I can tell you've been acting strange the last couple of weeks or so."

"Listen, Ra, you been with me since I first opened these doors. You already know I trust you with my life, so I got you. Just let me try to figure a few things out and I'll fill you in later. For now, just beef shit up a little—quick."

Zack knew Ra was his boy and would be up on top of having his back; he always was. Brother Rasul was probably Zack's only true friend he had left in the world, even though he didn't deserve his friendship or loyalty. Zack put on a good front, but he was a real snake, low-key, and everyone who came in contact with him knew it.

Chapter Thirteen

Brace Up

Tastey awoke from the nap that she had taken when she got out the tub. Slipping on a soft pink sundress and a pair of sandals that showed off her perfectly polished toes, she stashed the bag containing the dope and pulled the door closed, hanging a DO NOT DISTURB sign. After stepping off the elevator, she made her way through the lobby feeling like she had life by the tail. All the men turned their heads to watch her ass bounce from side to side with each step. The cab ride was interesting, as she saw a lot of different sights. Dallas was a lot different from Detroit. Being in a brand-new environment made Kenya yearn for a change in her own.

As she entered the mall, the air conditioning in the building was on full blast and you could see her hardened nipples poking through the thin cloth of her dress. A seasoned veteran in shopping, her first stop was the Versace boutique. Normally aware of her surroundings, she didn't notice two guys on the men's side of the shop staring at her. The brown-skinned taller man of the two was mesmerized by her swag.

Kenya took her time browsing through the rack and saw a navy blue suit that was calling her name. She struggled with her bags as she held the outfit up to her body, staring into a floor-length crystal-framed mirror.

"Hello, miss, I'm Nyasha. Would you like to try that on?" The saleslady was very polite and wanted nothing more than to make a commission on the sale of a $950 suit.

"Yes, please." Tastey replied as she entered the dressing room. After carefully fastening the buttons and zipping up the skirt, she exited the fitting room, hoping for a reaction. Once again, all eyes were on Kenya just as she thought. The two guys who had been watching her were both in awe, as well as several other customers.

"Wow, it fits you perfectly. Not everyone has the body shape to pull this suit off like you do." Nyasha wanted to make the sale and nine out of ten times would lie to make it, but this time it was no lie. Kenya was killing it in the suit.

"It is pretty, isn't it?" Tastey turned around in the mirror several times before returning into the fitting room to change back into her sundress. After looking at the price tag and realizing that it was way too much to pay for an outfit that she'd probably never get to wear, she felt sad. It was too much of a classy outfit for her lifestyle. Hesitantly, she handed it to the saleslady over the shuttered door to restock, and finished getting dressed. Making her way back up to the counter to thank the lady for being so helpful, all of a sudden the saleswoman asked her to sign the receipt.

"What are you talking about? I'm sorry. I'm not going to buy the suit today," Kenya insisted, throwing her hand up. The saleslady giggled as she saw one of the guys who were watching her customer approach them.

"You don't have to buy it, pretty lady. I already purchased it for you!" the handsome guy boldly interrupted.

Kenya, knowing you could never get something for nothing, was in shock and of course suspicious of his motives. "I'm sorry but you don't even know me. Why would you do something so random like that? What's the catch?"

"Well, I can easily fix that. My name is Tony Christian." He reached out his hand to shake hers. "And it ain't no catch. I just wanted you to have it! Is it wrong for a man to give a woman a gift? Is that a crime?"

It was then when she noticed his iced-out watch and ring. He had a linen outfit on and gator sandals to match. By the way the generous man's clothes fit, it looked like he worked out every single day. Kenya was in a daze staring at him. She shook herself together and took his hand. "Hello, my name is . . . Kenya." She decided that this wasn't the club, so all that "Tastey" shit could be ceased for the time being.

"Listen, can we go have lunch and talk for a while? I noticed that you didn't have a ring on your finger."

Kenya was impressed with his smooth demeanor. "Yeah, I guess so. I am kinda hungry," she blushingly accepted the invitation and the two left the store. He signaled for his boy to come over to where he and Kenya were standing. "Kenya, this is my little brother O.T." After Tony made the introductions, they all walked toward the food court. He couldn't take his eyes off her. "I would take you somewhere a little bit more upscale, but I know you might feel a little somewhat uneasy, seeing how we just met and all." Storm was used to going first class or not going at all. He knew if given a chance he would really take Kenya out on the town and floss.

They talked for almost an hour before O.T. excused himself and left. He made sure to tell his brother to call him later because they had a meeting to attend. O.T. liked Kenya, she seemed cool, but he knew his brother was acting all in. O.T. could tell by the look in his eyes that he wasn't going to let this female go. Shit, besides, Mr. Christian was already $950 in the hole being a cake.

"So listen, can I take you out for a real meal tonight?" Storm knew he was pressing his luck, but he felt like he'd known her forever.

Kenya, strange as it seemed, had the same vibe about him. She had flown to Dallas for strictly business, but in a matter of minutes, it got extremely personal. "Well, I think that can be arranged. After all, you are the only person I know in town." Kenya told him a quick lie and led him to believe that she was in town to interview for a job.

Tony's cell phone kept ringing. "I'm sorry, Kenya. I have an important meeting to attend and I can't be late. Can I drop you off at your hotel? You have my word, I don't bite." He smiled and melted her young soul.

They gathered the bags and made their way through the mall and over to the valet entrance. Tony handed the guy his ticket, as he and Kenya both stared into one another's eyes until the valet attendant pulled up with his car.

"This us, ma!" He put her bags in the back seat and like a real gentleman he held the door open for Kenya.

"Damn, what the fuck?" she whispered softly under her breath. "This nigga pushing a Benz CLK55, buying $950 hookups, and buying a bitch dinner later, this guy is straight-up ballin'!"

After a short ride, she was in front of the hotel. Tony pulled out a big knot of money and peeled off a twenty, paying the doorman for holding the door for Kenya. He then smoothly leaned over, opened the glove compartment, and pulled out a card. "Take this number and call me when you get ready."

Kenya scooted over and kissed him on his cheek like some old junior high bullshit. "Thanks again for the outfit."

"Don't thank me, just do the right thing and call me!" He winked his eye, blowing her a kiss.

As she walked away Kenya made sure to put a little bit extra in the way she moved her hips.

Damn, I got to have her! His dick immediately got hard as he drove away caught up in his emotions.

Chapter Fourteen

The Plan

"Hey, man! Thanks for coming over on such short notice to have a nigga's back." Stone greeted a couple of his boys he'd hooked up with during one of his various bids in the penitentiary. Charlie Moe and B-Rite were both ruthless criminals with no conscience for wildin' the fuck out. When Stone called, they were more than happy to show up and show out for their comrade. The three men had formed a bond after beating down a snitch on the prison yard. They beat the guy within an inch of his life. No one in or out of the joint liked a snitch.

"Whatever we can do. You know I'm ready to ride." B-Rite raised his shirt up, pulling out his gun. He took the clip out and checked the bullets one by one. Charlie Moe followed almost the same routine, as he yanked his shit out of his waistband.

Stone gave both his boys a dap and started to explained the situation to them. "Let me tell you what the deal is. A bitch-ass nigga named Zack, who first got my brother set up and murdered back in the day, got my young niece showing, spreading her legs open up in his spot. I'm through tolerating his foul-ass!"

"Dawg, let's stretch his ass proper!" Charlie Moe was hyped to tear some shit up. With him killing was never a problem, but more like a hobby.

Stone instructed both his friends to meet him inside of Heads Up at about 7:30 p.m. and come ready to put in that work. "Y'all make sure to wear your Muslim garb so that way you can get your heaters in. The cat at the door is all about Islam, and nine out of ten times he would never disrespect you by asking to search your garments."

The trio went over the game plan as they downed a couple of forties that Stone's woman had brought in from the kitchen.

Zack

"Hey, baby!" Old Skool greeted Zack as he made his way inside the club doors. She was sitting at the bar, watching Young Foy eat the dinner that Raven had cooked for him. She couldn't help but wish that she and Zack could go back to the time that he was in love with her, but he'd made it perfectly clear on more than several occasions his feelings had changed. However, Old Skool was still in love with him and that feeling would never die. "I said hey, baby! What's the matter with you? Didn't you hear me?"

Zack stopped, giving her a slight hug. "Oh, I'm sorry, my bad. I got a lot on my mind." He wanted to tell somebody about just how fucked up he was really living, but his pride wouldn't let him. He wanted to announce he'd been looking over his shoulder, terrified to breathe all day long, but couldn't. "Look, I'm gonna go up to my office. I'll be back down later. I need to make some calls and handle a few things." Zack held his head down as he walked up the stairs.

Brother Rasul, doing what he did, came over to get the roster of girls who would be working that night, so he could post his best security around the big moneymakers. The club had two bachelor parties booked and he wanted to make sure that everything went smoothly on the shift.

"All right, fellas! Let's give this next lady some love. She has enough shake in the ass to make a blind man see! Enough junk in the trunk to a make a crippled man walk, and even bring Tupac out of hiding!" The crowd erupted in laughter at the DJ. "I'm looking for the one they call Raven!"

The club was full, energy level on bump, and the crowd was hyped. Both bachelor parties were in full swing and everyone there were getting their drink on. Having double-checked to make sure Kenya, aka Tastey, wasn't working at the club that evening for sure, all systems were go in the plan Stone laid out. B-Rite and Charlie Moe had both easily gotten into the club without being checked. They even stood at the front door, kicking it with Brother Rasul for a good ten minutes or so about where they prayed at and mutual friends they shared. Him being able to recognize them meant nothing at this point in time, because nine outta ten, Charlie Moe and B-Rite knew Brother Rasul; if he chose to step up and go for bad, they wouldn't live to see daybreak anyhow. They didn't give a shit what Muslim renegade group he was affiliated with. They also had their boys posted throughout the club and made sure that they'd handed off pistols to each one of them, having all angles covered when the festivities of revenge started.

Zack walked over to his office wall and snatched down the picture of Stone, throwing the snapshot in the trash. *Fuck being scared! Stone don't want none with me! Let me get this call over with!* Zack was trying to be brave and think positive, but he wasn't even fooling his own self. Zack sat behind his desk and dialed Deacon's cell phone number and waited for him to answer.

"Hey, dude, what up, man? I've been waiting for you to hit me up." Deacon was anxious to get started in their impending venture and new-formed partnership. "Me and ol' boy are about to meet up in a few minutes. We're definitely ready!"

Zack had to get the tradeoff over and get his money home as soon as possible. He was a nervous wreck and hadn't slept well in days. This shit was taking a serious toll on his health. His hands shook as he held the phone. "My people are already in town. Dial this number and ask for Tastey. You two can decide on the drop-off location. I don't need any short shit, Deacon! I got a lot riding on this!" Zack added extra bass in his tone as if he could really reach out and touch someone.

Deacon reassured Zack that their revenue was right and he had his best people on top of it. The two then went over a few minor details before they ended the conversation. Zack then went inside his private bathroom to splash cold water on his face before he went downstairs to play host for the evening. *It's all good. I ain't fazed,* he repeated relentlessly in his mind, still trying to convince himself of the lie.

Mayhem

It was 7:25 p.m. and Stone was getting out of his girl's car. He was more than ready to confront Zack on the grimy shit he'd done once again to his family. This was the day he'd been waiting for ever since Ty put him up on the disrespectful situation concerning Kenya. He'd been trying to call Kenya every day for over a month or so and couldn't get an answer to hear her side of the story. Stone didn't want to send his woman to handle his family business. That just wasn't his style. He also had no idea that Ty, too, had been trying to get in touch with his niece to warn her about him finding out. Ty, just like Stone, had been leaving message after message with no response.

Nevertheless, it was time for Zack to finally shake hands with the devil. Stone reached the front door and cracked his knuckles before he opened it up. He could hear the loud music and the sounds of the crowd, laughing, cheering and having a good time. *All this hee-hawing 'bout to cease when I get up in this joint. That's my motherfucking word!* Stone entered the club trying not to look suspicious. His first sight was Young Foy, who, luckily, was working the front door. It was right then and there he knew that getting his gun inside would be no problem at all.

"What's good, God? I told that nigga Zack that he should've blocked you off a VIP section." Young Foy leaned in and hugged his friend. Automatically, he felt Stone's gun on his hip, but thought nothing of it. After all, he knew Stone was Zack's homeboy from way back when, and always received special treatment whenever he was on deck wherever he went.

"Oh, naw, I'm tight on that. I'm just gonna grab a seat at the bar, get a quick drink, then bounce."

Stone stepped all the way inside door. He stood at the front of the club quickly scanning the crowd. He first saw B-Rite in a corner booth, followed by one of his crew posted by the stairway. After making eye contact with them, he walked past Charlie Moe and two other cats nodding at them. They all were in place and the shit was going as planned. The only holdup was Zack's punk-ass. He would be the star of the show tonight, not the half-naked strippers. Stone ordered a rum and Coke and waited for the shit to go down.

Old Skool was sitting at the far end of the bar with Brother Rasul counting the number of girls and who hadn't paid the house fee yet. It was a busy night, which always led to plenty of confusion.

"Let me get back on post. Do me a favor and send some juice over to my Muslim friends who came in. They're sitting over there in that booth waiting to meet up with some people." He pointed over toward B-Rite and Charlie Moe.

Brother Rasul had no idea that they were not friends and hadn't come in peace. Although their presence in the club bothered him, he wasn't representing Islam to the fullest by being there either. The entire night so far was leaving him uneasy for some strange reason. The usual strong-minded individual was a little thrown off his square. Between worrying about both Tastey, who was out of town, and Zack hiding a secret, his mind wasn't focused. This job was taking a toll on him and his spirituality.

Old Skool never looked up as she replied, "All right, Ra, as soon as I finish the count I'll have the juice sent right over." She had her mind focused on collecting from every dancer that night; no more weak excuses. Some of the slick, ghetto-raised females were starting to fall off of paying and it was her job to be on top of it. Old Skool never liked to let Zack down. She knew that her longtime lover worshipped money and she always wanted to bless him with as much as she could get.

As the evening got into full swing, there was a growing crowd of fellas at the entrance waiting to get inside. Per club policy, each one had to get patted down and searched for any weapons or bottles they'd try to sneak inside. Heads Up was almost at capacity level. Brother Rasul went back up to the front door to switch spots with Young Foy, who was more than happy to get back to the floor so that he could watch his woman Raven handle her business. Some of the guys who were with the wannabe white bachelor party were getting a little rough with the dancers. The out-of-control few were ordering bottles of champagne and acting wild, breaking all the strict house rules they felt they could get away with. Several of the bouncers had already argued with them, warning of the consequences. The group of drunk and disorderly men was well on their way to getting thrown out of Heads Up for the night, which was fine with Young Foy.

"Hey! Whoa! Please don't grab me like that. You're hurting me!" Raven was trying to reason with the man from the group she was giving a lap dance to. He was yanking at her long weave and trying to feel in between her legs.

"Look, I'm giving you twenty dollars for a few minutes' worth of work. Now stop your annoying bitchin', you uneducated little slut!"

The man possessed a sinister look in his eye. Young Foy was getting pissed off as he angrily stared at them. It was at that moment in time he realized just how much he really did love Raven and her small son. Feeling some sort of way, he decided he would tell her later that night. Young Foy was ready to settle down, and he was sure Raven was the one. However, his blood pressure was shooting straight up as he watched the older man disrespect his woman. *This nigga got one more minute before I say fuck this job, and beat his ho-ass!* Young Foy thought as he rubbed his hands together and his heart raced.

Zack cracked opened his office door and heard the sounds of people spending money. *Damn, I gotta get downstairs and play host. Time for me to shine!* In spite of being sick from worry about Stone making good on his promises, he still had a club to run. After all, he was the boss and had to keep his fronts up no matter what the price was.

Getting it together, Zack fixed his tie and headed down the stairs, trying his best to overcome his fear. With the eye of a hawk, he looked across the entire club for any signs of anything abnormal. As far as he could tell, it was packed. Everything seemed normal and everyone appeared to be having a good time. That meant he was making money, so he was happy. But like they say, all good things must come to an end. Well, this was about to be one of those times in Zack's otherwise perfect life.

Stone sat inconspicuously perched on a barstool on the other side of the room. Feeling unstoppable, he saw Zack, dressed in a suit and tie, make his way slowly down the staircase. His blood started to boil. Stone could feel his heart pumping overtime as he also watched some of, if not all of, the dancers degrade themselves like he knew Kenya was doing as well. As the clock ticked, his adrenalin rose. This would be his ultimate revenge for having his niece whore herself out for a few dollars, and his long-coming payback for both her parents' murders. Stone swallowed the last bit of his drink he was nursing and stood up, brushing his pants off. That was the signal for Stone's crew that it was getting ready to go down. Zack was his, and any wannabe heroes, on staff or not, his cohorts who were riding with him would deal with. It was on! It was showtime!

"Hey, Old Skool, sweetheart. How's the count on the girls and the door going? How we looking?" Zack was so engrossed in finding out about the dollar amount that he didn't observe Stone creeping up behind him. Old Skool noticed Stone first and smiled. She knew all of Zack's boys.

"Hey, baby. I was wondering when you were coming down to join us. When did . . . ?" Before Old Skool could finish greeting him, her smile quickly turned into her jaw damn near dropping to the strip club floor.

Zack, already nervous and jumpy as a cat, saw the expression on her face. Praying first, he eased his body around just in time to see Stone push his newly shined 9 mm pistol dead in his face. Zack, terrified, wasted no time with being humble, trying his best to cop a plea. "Let me explain, Stone. Hold up! I can pay you! Wait! Please don't do this!" Zack was begging for his life knowing the pedigree of his longtime associate and what he was capable of if pushed to it.

Stone, not caring about the multitudes of witnesses, had to laugh at his former friend, Zack, who always tried to go for bad every chance he got. "Don't do what, motherfucker? You ain't shit but a store-bought pimp. Look at you! You fuckin' little pussy! You thought it was okay what you got my niece doing up in this motherfucker?"

"Niece?" Old Skool puzzled with tears in her eyes.

"Shut the fuck up, Old Skool. This murder about to take place right here is between two grown-ass men!"

Zack was paralyzed with fear as he faced his future. It was certain death as Stone nudged the barrel of the gun to his temple. "Naw, man, please hold up! I told you I didn't know Kenya was Johnnie and Melinda's daughter! I told you that!"

"Please don't, Stone!" Old Skool begged for mercy, shocked at who Stone was claiming Kenya truly was. "Please don't! For old time's sake don't!" All the nights the three of them spent in the club drinking meant nothing to Stone at this time. He was in a zone of his own.

"Shut the fuck up, you ancient, sagging-titty bitch! I done told you this is between me and this ho-ass nigga here!" He spat directly in her face, leaving her stunned. Stone was hyped and drunk with power as he humiliated his prey. Zack had tears in his eyes and warm piss was running down his right pants leg. "Now straighten your tie and boss up!" Stone laughed out loud and, without a second thought about the crowd of shocked onlookers, ruthlessly pulled the trigger. "Damn, my nigga! Ain't no fun when the rabbit got the gun. Is it, bitch!" Stone emptied his entire clip into Zack's body. Feeling smug with no remorse, he then watched his former friend collapse onto the floor. "You already suited and booted for a funeral, casket ready, so it's whatever!"

Old Skool had blood splattered across her dress and face. She screamed over and over again as she held Zack's limp and lifeless body close. "No! No! No!" she sobbed uncontrollably in the middle of what had become chaos.

At that point, all hell broke loose and shots were fired from every direction possible. In the midst of the pandemonium, Brother Rasul pulled both guns out, which he always carried, ready for war. Fearlessly, he ran into the crowd of hysterical people toward Zack's assailant, Stone. B-Rite, being the loyal goon he was paid to be, saw the direction his Muslim brother was headed in and let off several rounds. Good with his aim, three bullets hit their mark, knocking Brother Rasul off his feet and into the side of several chairs. On the other side of the club Raven, terrified like the rest of the innocent dancers, was trying to get off of the disrespectful man's lap she was giving a dance to. Using all her strength, she fought, struggling to get away and to safety, but couldn't. The man was cowardly holding Raven close to him like a shield from the gunfire.

Young Foy, having the heart of a lion, was jumping over chairs to rescue Raven from harm's way. He made it less than two feet from her when a parade of more shots recklessly rang out inside the strip club walls. Shockingly he saw one of the bullets tear through Raven's back. All of her movement and attempts to break free from the man's hold abruptly stopped. The customer who was holding Raven coldly let her limp body fall to the broken glass floor without so much as a second thought. When the spineless man looked up to make his escape from any more stray bullets that were flying, he was face to face with Young Foy, who raised his pistol and made the coward meet his Maker. The street-born and raised youth made sure the older dude, who had just proven himself to be less than a man, was sure to have a closed-casket funeral. Young Foy felt his heart break in two as he looked at Raven, knowing she was gone. He then laid his body on top of hers, shielding it, to make sure that she didn't get hit again.

All of Stone's crew had made it safely to the door and he was almost there also. People, not know which way to go or turn, were screaming, taking cover in every corner of the bar they could hide. Charlie Moe yelled out to Stone to hurry the fuck up. He knew that the police would soon be on their way and no one on the team wanted to go back to prison, at least not tonight. Stone dumbly had used all his ammunition laying Zack down and was now at a total disadvantage to defend himself. Bullets were flying in every direction and sheer panic and pandemonium were taking over the club. When Stone finally reached the door, he was suddenly stopped by a hot, burning sensation rushing throughout his entire body. Everything started to move in slow motion to him. He was getting weak and felt dizzy. Stone fell to the ground and looked up to see Old Skool standing over him with a smoking gun at her side.

"Why? Why did you do it, Stone? I know he was a snake, but I loved him!" Tears were streaming down her face, causing her eye makeup to run down her cheek like a sad raccoon.

Old Skool screamed out loud in anguish and shot Stone once more, ripping a gaping hole in his chest. *What else is left?* she thought before turning the gun on herself, choosing not to live life without her man.

Chapter Fifteen

London

London had been working on her speech for the entire week, wanting to make sure it was perfect. Tonight would be her first time speaking in front of a packed auditorium, filled with not just students, but most of the professors, the deans, and a few politicians, all who wanted to attach themselves to the fast-growing antidrug movement Fatima and London founded. The media was set up on the side of the stage and the lights beamed brightly. The crowd was constantly growing, as they were all anticipating London's inspiring, heartfelt words. She already had a loyal following who related to the message she and her organization were trying to get out.

"Girl, I can't believe all these folks are out here. I know we wanted a big turnout, but dang!" London had to try to calm herself down. It was a little bit overwhelming for an orphaned twin from the ghetto to grasp.

Fatima asked one of the people backstage to please get London a glass of water. "Listen, London, you got this. We've been passing out fliers and cards for close to two weeks now. Everyone is excited. Everyone is motivated. And last, but not least, everyone is tired of drugs ruining their neighborhoods. Go do your thang. They're waiting for you!"

After listening to Fatima give her a pep talk, London was motivated, ready to move the crowd. "Ladies and gentlemen, students, professors, and distinguished guests, I want to welcome you to the first ever 'Take Our Kids Back' rally, sponsored by PAID!" The crowd started to clap and everyone was hyped as London continued, "For those of you who don't know what PAID is, it's an organization that was formed by a group of students, such as myself, who are sick and tired of getting phone calls from our parents about the trouble that our little brothers and sisters are getting into. We're tired of our family not being able to walk to the candy store without being harassed!" London took another drink of water. "Smoking crack, shooting dope, or sniffing cocaine, whatever their choice of high is, is certainly not our choice. We want to be left out of the world that these people bring to our children. Kids don't deserve to live in poverty and total despair!" The audience was in a trance of total agreement as they listened to London speaking. "Black-on-black crime is at an all-time high, because most of us only know destitution. It's a complete injustice to children, of all races and nationalities, to be continuously subjected to being hungry, being scared to walk to school, being ignored by their drug-addicted parents, and feeling like no one cares!" Every one of the people in attendance was standing on their feet and cheering.

Fatima was holding London's bag and couldn't turn off her cell phone, which kept ringing. After about three times of the phone ringing, back to back, she finally answered it. Fatima was having trouble trying to hear what the caller was saying, so she went out the side door of the building where it was somewhat quieter.

"Hello, hello." Fatima listened to the caller speak and instantly began to panic. "No, this is her roommate! Oh my God! She's on stage!" Fatima was almost in tears in the middle of the conversation. "As soon as she walks off I'll have her call you right back. Is this the number where you're at?" Fatima, frazzled, waited for the woman on the phone to respond and then closed the phone up. She ran back in the auditorium, just as London was finishing up her speech.

"I don't have the luxury to have a lot of money. I can't just pick up and move to what people say is a better block or neighborhood. Let's not move. Let's take back our kids and our community!" London took another sip of water and continued. "I ask every person here today to get involved. Write to your local politicians and demand that legislation be passed to help our kids. Start policing your own community. PAID is going to start chapters at each and every campus that we can. Please pick up the literature at the back tables, and thank you for coming out."

The cheers from the crowd could be heard from outside of the building and all over campus. Some of the people in the audience were moved to tears. The excitement and waves of emotion from them filled the air. As London walked off the stage making her way through the many people congratulating her on the speech, she spotted Fatima running toward her. She had tears in her eyes that London quickly noticed as Fatima got closer.

"What's wrong with you? What happened?"

Fatima quickly pulled London out the side door so they could have some privacy and talk. "Listen, while you were on stage you got a phone call. There's been an accident and we've got to get you home!"

"Accident? What do you mean, accident?" The first thing London thought about was Kenya and that club. "Is she all right? Is she okay? I knew that club wasn't any good and would get her in trouble!"

Fatima saw that London was bugging out and tried her best to calm her down. "Slow down, London, and pay attention. It's not Kenya. She's okay, I assume. It's your uncle, Stone. He's been shot. We gotta get back to Detroit as soon as possible! Now hurry, come on!"

London stopped dead in her tracks. She was confused. "My uncle? But what are you talking about? He's in jail. How did he get shot in jail? Did he try to escape or something?" London was holding her head by this time, in utter shock.

Fatima gave London the number where she could reach the woman who had called with the tragic information. After London dialed the number and spoke to her uncle's woman, they rushed back to the dorm room, gathered some things, and jumped in Fatima's car, heading to Detroit. No soon had they gotten on the highway than London pushed in the numbers to Kenya's cell phone, praying that her twin sister would answer and hopefully shed some light on what was going on at home.

Tastey

Kenya was happy to be back in her hotel room so that she could try on the suit that Tony purchased for her. She closed her eyes while remembering the smell of the cologne he had on and the his soft cheek. It made her want to run to the phone and tell him to turn back around, come up to her room, and fuck the shit out of her. It had been more than a minute since the last time she had gotten some and Tony's athletic body had the potential to be just what the doctor ordered. Kenya was getting wet just imagining.

Deacon had just hung up the phone. He and his partner Storm had been anticipating Zack's call for days. It was finally time for them to start to really blow up on their own, independent of any local connect who was cutting the product off jump. Deacon was small-time hustling since he was a teenager and had to spend every dime that he'd saved to open up his new club. His hope was to make Alley Cats the most popular strip club in Texas. Deacon didn't have any cash left in his stash when almost complete with the project, so his boy, a boss in his own right had his back. Deacon wasn't broke, but his cash flow was tapped out; that's why he needed Storm to come in on the deal.

When Zack got in touch with him with what was a deal of a lifetime, he and Storm had to jump on it. Storm, just like having his back for extra revenue for the club, still was holding hard. He was making some major chips and Deacon knew he was one of the only dudes in the city who had that type of cheese readily available. He knew that Storm would definitely want in on the deal. He was all about making money.

"Yo, my nigga! I was just wondering when you would show up. Your brother got here about a half hour ago. He told me you was out chasin' that cat." Deacon had a huge grin on his face as he let his boy inside the door.

"Never that guy. I don't chase cat, cat chase me. Fuck what you heard!" Storm was holding his nuts, while both Deacon and O.T. made fun of him. "Y'all busters up in here fooling, hell, I might just make ol' girl wifey. Why you bullshitting? Ask O.T., that guy seen her ass. She's right with hers!" Storm was serious and they could tell. He was putting a deep bass in his tone as he spoke. "Deacon, I'm telling you, she's badder than any of these cum-drunk broads you got pole slanging up in this bitch!" He continued to campaign on Kenya's behalf, until he saw that all he was getting in response was laughter. Storm then grabbed the darts that were on the bar and started throwing them extra hard at the board.

"Listen, guy, I ain't mad at you. Do what you feel, but a nigga like me gonna keep a ho selling my half of the pussy! Matter of fact her half too! Ask my girl Paris, she'll tell you. I'm about that bread!"

All three of them fell out at O.T.'s crazy wannabe pimp-ass. Ready to handle business, the trio sat down, counting up all the money Deacon and Storm had put aside for their impending deal with Zack. When they made sure the count was correct, Deacon reached over the bar, getting the cordless phone. "Let me make this call and set this thing into motion." Deacon dialed the number Zack had just given him and waited for someone to answer. After three rings, a sexy-sounding female answered.

"Hello." Kenya saw the area code on her caller ID and knew it was the call that she was waiting for.

"Yeah, can I speak to Tastey?"

"This me. Who is this?" She automatically got into gangsta mode.

"This is Deacon. Can we meet up soon?" He started to pace the floor, anticipating making money. Storm and O.T. went behind the bar and each grabbed two beers, waiting for Deacon to get the tradeoff location.

"Damn, I wonder if she is tastey." O.T. licked his lips as he opened his bottle.

Tastey suggested the mall and Deacon quickly agreed.

"I'll tell you what. I'm gonna send my man Storm to make the exchange. Let's say about eight thirty this evening. It will be real busy at that time with folks buying last-minute hookups for the night."

Tastey thought about her dinner date with Tony and wanted to make the drop-off sometime tomorrow. Yet she also knew, first and foremost, she was in town for business, and Zack's worrisome-ass would bug the fuck out if she messed this exchange up. "All right then, eight thirty. Have him sit on the bench in front of the pizza stand in the food court. Put the cash in a shopping bag. You and Zack supposed to go way back, so he says, so there's no need to count it. He trusts you!" Tastey made her words sound like a threat. Deacon had mad respect for Zack because of his successful strip club experience and would never try to dick him. Besides, where would he go? Zack's grandma knew his grandma out there in Detroit.

Ending the call, Deacon gave his boy Storm the details of his and Tastey's brief talk. Deacon put the money in the bag, like requested, and gave it to Storm. As he parted ways with them, Deacon and O.T. prayed for the best.

Storm hoped Kenya wouldn't call him until he finished taking care of his business. Taking a hot shower he got dressed for the night. Planning on taking her to dinner at Lady Fee's Place, Storm was intent on showing her a good time. It was a jazz cafe that only cats with deep pockets could afford to take their girl to. Lady Fee's only sold the whole bottles of wine, not a glass. The smallest steak was forty-five dollars and that didn't include an entire meal. That was just for a sandwich.

"This female is something special. Fuck what them busters talking about. I want her ass bad!" Storm was talking to himself as he checked the mirror before leaving his condo.

Meanwhile, across town, Kenya was thinking almost the same thing. *I hope this dude Storm be on time. The sooner I get rid of him, the sooner I can get with Tony.* She put on her lipstick and checked her hair one more time before she left the room. To make sure that they were on for later, she took Tony's number out her purse and picked up the hotel phone. "Hello, may I speak to Tony please?" Kenya was twirling the cord around, blushing as she talked.

"Hey, ma. This me." Tony saw the strange number and knew it was Kenya. He was of course overjoyed she called.

"I was just calling to see what was up. Were you still gonna spend some time with me later?" She tried to sound sexy.

He loved the way her voice purred already and his manhood was getting harder by the minute. "You know I ain't trying to let you get away from me that easily. I just need to make a couple of runs then I'll be ready. Give me to about nine thirty and call me back, cool? We can get something to eat and check out some jazz at a little spot I know." Fingers crossed, he hoped that she would agree with his plans.

"Oh, that's cool with me. I just woke up anyhow," she automatically lied. Kenya was happy about the time he picked because she had to make a run also. "I'll be here waiting." She was lying again, but what could she do? Tell him she was a drug mule from Detroit and was going to make a transaction before they met up? With her game face on, she went downstairs and got into one of the cabs that were posted in front of the hotel. It was time for her to get into "Tastey" mode.

Storm pulled the low-key piece of shit he was driving into valet. He got out and tossed the attendant the keys. Even if he was riding foul, he wasn't gonna be walking all far from the door in his $1,000 gators. He looked like a businessman trying to return a package for his wife, or something of that nature. Anxious to get this over with, Storm sat down on the bench and checked his diamond-filled watch for the time. *This bitch, Tastey or whatever, better be on time!* He got out the slip of paper that Deacon had given him with the bitch's 1-800 cell phone number on it and had it in his hand.

Tastey entered the mall at the other end opposite from the food court. She wanted to peep out her surroundings before she met up with ol' boy. There was no way she wanted to get set up and possibly killed. All the stories she'd heard of her parents' murder jumped back into her head. As the out-of-towner tried to appear casual, Tastey cautiously approached the bench. She saw the back of the guy's head and a shopping bag beside his leg. Knowing that must've been the guy she was supposed to meet, her heart started to beat fast. When she got closer, she shockingly realized that it was, of all people, Tony. She forgot all about the drugs she was carrying and immediately got a serious attitude. Kenya ran up on him and let her bloodline-inherited rage take over.

"Damn, is this your little run? You picking up one of your little bitches from work and got me waiting?"

He was in shock. He was at a loss for words. "Where did you come from, Miss Lady? I thought you were supposed to be at the hotel waiting for me."

Storm was starting to get nervous because he knew that Tastey was due there any minute and didn't want Kenya to get the wrong idea. "Listen, Kenya, sweetheart, slow your roll. It ain't nothing like that." Liking her "fuck the world" mentality, he liked the fact that she set tripping, acting jealous. It made him know that he wasn't the only one who, crazy as it seemed, was catching feelings so soon.

"Is this your li'l bitch number? Let me call the trick and tell her that she's been fucking canceled for the evening!"

He had forgotten that he had Tastey's name and number in his hand. Kenya, feeling disrespected, like she ran the world, had gotten beside herself and snatched the paper out his hand. Furious, she hated for any nigga to try to play her.

Storm, seeing things were quickly going south, held his head down because he knew that all hell was about to break loose when she read that name. *Please don't let this chic Tastey show up right now and set ol' girl off even more, please!* he kept repeating in his mind over and over.

"Oh, hell, fuck naw!" Kenya rolled her eyes, shaking her head. "Ain't this some crazy shit," she hissed while sucking her teeth.

"Listen, baby. I'm trying to tell you it ain't like that. It's just business!" He was trying his best to take a cop like they'd known each other for years. "I don't even know the stankin' bitch. I swear!"

Kenya looked into his eyes and saw that he was starting to look hurt and decided to let him off the hook. "Damn, baby, why I gotta be all that? Tell Deacon he needs to teach you some manners. So, Tony, they call you Storm, huh?"

Storm stood up, giving her a dumbfounded look. "Is that why you in town? You're Tastey? Oh my God! You right! Ain't this some shit?" He had to smile too at the irony of the situation.

After about ten minutes of tripping on what they were obviously there to accomplish, the couple decided to split up and meet after they finished both their business. He walked her to the taxi stand at the mall and kissed her. This time it was a small peck on her lips.

"You know this is a sign, right? We're supposed to be together." Storm wanted her even more. He knew that she had game and would have a nigga's back in the streets if need be.

"Okay then, I'll meet you at nine thirty in front of the hotel. And don't keep me waiting!" She blew a kiss to him as the cab pulled off away from the curb. Storm wanted to drive her back himself personally, but having drugs, a gun, and a lot of money in the car didn't mix no matter which way you calculated it.

Within minutes of Kenya getting back in her room, her cell phone rang again. "Yes, baby!" She answered it without checking the caller ID, assuming it was Storm.

"Hey, Kenya, is that you?" It was her twin sister and it sounded like she was crying.

"What's wrong, London, why you crying?" Kenya was instantly frantic, hearing her sister moan.

London started crying harder and couldn't get the words out, so Fatima took the phone out of her hand. "Hey, Kenya. This is Fatima." She focused on driving while preparing to deliver her roommate's sister the tragic family news. "Girl, you need to come home. There's been an accident. Your uncle has been shot. We're on the road now on our way to Detroit."

Kenya was full of questions, just as London was when she first heard the news. "I thought he was in jail."

Fatima was trying to drive and talk and had to cut the conversation short. "Listen, Kenya, I know you're out of town, but you need to catch the first flight back. We'll see you when you get here."

Kenya quickly packed her shit up and stashed the money in different suitcases. She checked out the hotel and rushed to the airport. There was a flight leaving in eighty-six minutes and she planned to be on it if at all possible. On the ride to the airport, she tried to call Heads Up, but didn't get an answer. It constantly went straight to voice mail. She then decided to call Storm and explain to him what she'd just heard and had jumped back home. "Hey, baby, I'm not going to be able to have dinner with you. I'm on my way to the airport."

Storm could tell that she was upset. "What happened, why?" Storm was truly interested as well as disappointed they couldn't have dinner. He turned the radio down in his car so he could give Kenya his full, undivided attention. He was really feeling Kenya. There was something special about her that he liked.

"I want to stay, but I just got a call. My uncle had an accident and he's the only family I really have." Kenya was crying on the phone like her sister was doing less than thirty minutes prior.

"Listen, Kenya, I'm sorry to hear that. Have a safe flight and please promise me that you'll call me as soon as you get a chance. I wanna still take you to dinner one day even if I have to fly to Detroit to do it."

Agreeing to stay in touch, they both hung up the phone.

Chapter Sixteen

The Aftermath

FIVE DEAD AND ONE CRITICALLY INJURED was the headline in Saturday's morning edition newspaper. It was also the top story on every single television channel in Detroit. All three—Kenya, London, and Fatima—sat almost as still as mummies as they watched report after report flash across the flat screen mounted on the wall.

"This seems like a nightmare. I can't figure it out. How did all of this happen?" Bewildered, London was almost in shock as she shook her head.

Kenya's eyes were close to being swollen shut from all the tears that she had shed, and she was just as confused, losing more than one good friend in the melee.

Fatima, being supportive to the twins, went into the kitchen to get some tea for all of them. Fatima then came back in and turned the television up. It was the top of the hour and the girls were waiting to see if they could get some accurate additional information about what went down at the club that night, since the police were being so hush-hush about the details of the case.

"Good morning. I'm standing in front of Heads Up, known as a notorious popular gentlemen's club, located on the far east side of the city. This location was the backdrop for one of the most senseless, vicious, fatal shootouts in recent times in Detroit. It was inside of this very building, shortly after seven thirty p.m., that shots rang out. Needless to say pure terror erupted. The callous gunmen fired aimlessly into the crowd, striking several people and causing injuries to others who were trampled by innocent bystanders trying to escape the line of gunfire." The newscaster was shaking his head. "On the screen we have the pictures of the deceased."

The girls' eyes continued to be glued to the screen.

"They are, Zack Carter, forty-one, the club owner, Monique Peterson, nineteen, a dancer and mother, Angela Sims, forty, the club manager, Jason Roberts, thirty-nine, who was paroled from prison just hours before the shooting, and Professor Sanford Kincade, forty-three, who taught political science at State University. Another person is listed in critical condition. He is identified as Rasul Hakim Akbar, thirty-five, who is the head of security at Heads Up."

The reporter's face looked agitated as he continued with the grim accounts of the previous evening. "For several years now people have being trying to get this strip club shut down. Now, with the owner being gunned down inside of his own establishment, some might just get their wish granted. The police are still looking for two or more gunmen. They have no motives as of yet for these murders. Anyone with information is asked to call Homicide. This is Marcus Randal, reporting for channel seven news."

"Did you see that shit?" Fatima, in the midst of the gloominess that was consuming the room, was falling over laughing.

"Oh my God, yes! I can't believe it. What was his slimy-ass doing down here?" London was still sad, shocked, and visibly shaken because of her uncle's death, but like Fatima she was also full of glee at the news report.

Kenya watched the two of them and finally blurted out, "I don't get it. Can one of you bitches fill me in, please?" Kenya was getting annoyed.

Fatima took the honor, explaining the reason for their amusement. "Kenya, Professor Sanford Kincade. That name doesn't ring a bell to you? Think about it. He teaches at our school!"

All of a sudden Kenya jumped up. "You bullshitting! I know that ain't that coward motherfucker who raped you?"

London was over being ashamed about what had happened to her and used it for her strength. "I guess it's true what they say: God really don't like ugly, does He?"

They all three had a good laugh as they continued to mourn Stone and Raven.

***

The twins went to their uncle's funeral. Kenya cried extra hard after listening to the entire backlog of messages that Stone left her. Sadly she realized that he was dead for trying to protect her. Ty even showed up at the services and he and Kenya made their peace. He explained to her that he was trying to get in touch with her so bad because he owed her uncle a favor. Stone had kept some guys in jail from kicking his ass and in return he promised to get his niece to answer her phone.

After seeing her uncle's picture on Zack's wall, Kenya realized they'd known one another years prior. Yet, she didn't know that Zack had also known her parents and Stone blamed him for their deaths. Kenya, feeling some sort of way, didn't attend Zack's or Old Skool's funeral services. She was pissed off at both of them for hiding their true identity from her, even though Old Skool in reality didn't find out who Kenya was until the end. Not that it would do any good or really matter who knew what and when, but it would be like a smack in her uncle's memory to go mourn them. *Fuck him and her!* she thought. *It's all good with me now anyway!* After all Kenya did have that cash that she had gotten from Storm and Deacon in the transaction. It was hers now, all $65,000.

She spent a little bit of the money on Raven's funeral service. Kenya knew that her family didn't have any income. Raven's mother was a junkie and got high every chance she got. The only good thing to come out of Raven's dancing in Heads Up was meeting Young Foy. He had really stepped up to the plate after that fateful night, and took Raven's small son, Jaylin, to live with him. Kenya gave him $5,000 to get on his feet and get a two-bedroom apartment for him and his new son. Young Foy promised her he would be dedicated and get off into his music, showing Jaylin a different way to make money. She also gave her twin $15,000 for school and put the rest in a safety deposit box.

London and Kenya, knowing it was time for a change and new beginnings, cleaned out Gran's house, putting a lot of stuff in storage. It was hard going through all of their childhood memories, but it was time to try to put the past behind them. The only things left were beds, a dresser, and an old couch.

"The last load is on the truck. Let's go!" Kenya was calling out to her twin sister. "We need to drop this stuff off at the storage trailer and get back. I have a plane to catch!"

Kenya had been talking to Storm every day on the phone since she'd left Dallas. They had truly fallen in love over the phone and Kenya was moving out there to be with him for a while to see how she liked Dallas. She hadn't even had the dick yet and she wanted him. They talked about a lot of stuff, but, for some reason, she didn't tell him she had a sister, let alone a twin. London hated drug dealers, so she chose not to bring it up, ever, but Kenya knew that forever was a long time to keep a secret, especially one as major as that was.

"Okay, sis, here I come." London was checking for any last-minute boxes that had to be stored before they left.

Fatima had gone back up to school to stay on top of PAID. Since London's speech, the night of the horrible shooting, the little organization was starting to really blow up and spread. A lot of East Coast schools were interested in starting chapters as well as the West. They wanted London to come and speak at their campuses and hopefully motivate their students to make a change and take a stand against illegal drugs and all the woes associated with them.

When the two girls reached the storage bin, London pulled out her set of keys and opened it, so that the guys they had hired could load it up. Kenya, trying her best to avoid any further work, went to the front desk to pay the bill up for an entire year.

"Yes, I'm here to pay the bill on bin 316." Kenya kept checking her watch. She didn't want to miss her flight.

The desk clerk got out his folder. "Yes, are you London Roberts?"

"No, I'm her sister Kenya. She's around back with the movers. I just want to pay the rental fee up for the year."

The man was happy to hear that and gave her the computer receipt. "Please sign the account holder's name."

Kenya signed London's name and put her copy of the receipt in her purse. With that exchange she was out the door.

***

"I'm gonna miss you so much. I love you." London was starting to cry as her sister was about to board the plane to start a new life in a new place.

"You know I'm gonna miss you too. We all we got. I'm not gonna forget that, London, even in Texas." Kenya hugged her twin tightly.

"I'm proud of you, Kenya. I always have been even though I might not say it much. You're strong and I've always envied and wanted to have that quality."

Kenya had tears streaming down her face. She was the one always proud of London.

"Give 'em hell out there, Ms. Roberts!" London smiled as Kenya boarded the plane.

Chapter Seventeen

Kenya

"All right, fellas. I gotta be out. My girl is flying in today and I don't want to be late." Storm was excited as hell that Kenya was finally on her way back to him.

"Take your henpecked-ass on then, nigga!" O.T. was still bent down, rolling the dice as he talked shit to his brother. Deacon and the rest of the guys who were in the back of the Alley Cats shooting dice laughed at O.T., who was clowning as usual.

Storm didn't give a fuck. Nothing could knock him off his square today.

By the time he stopped to pick up some roses and get his car detailed, it was time to pick Kenya up. Storm got inside the terminal hoping to see her face. She looked more gorgeous than he remembered. She had on the suit that he bought her and some sling-back pumps to match. Her hair was hanging down across her shoulders. Kenya, excited as well, ran into his open arms.

"Hey, daddy, I missed you." She closed her eyes as the two kissed for the very first time. Storm held her close and stuck his tongue in her mouth. She felt her legs getting weak.

"I missed you too, baby." They both were elated as they went to get her luggage.

"I think we gonna need something like a buggy. I've got eight bags. They made me pay extra for all that shit." Kenya was going on and on.

Storm couldn't do anything but smile. He was happy that she had a lot of bags. It showed that she really was gonna stay with him and try to make what started off as their long-distance relationship work. "You could have a hundred bags and it wouldn't matter. I'm just glad to have you here—with me."

Storm had to pay a taxi van to carry all of Kenya's bags to his condo, which was not a problem. When they pulled up, Storm gave her the keys and pointed out the door. "Go ahead and open the door up, sweetheart. I'm gonna help my man with these bags."

Kenya opened the door to her new life and stepped inside. It smelled just like jasmine and wildflowers. The living room had a huge plasma screen, a few big throw pillows on the floor, and a plant that looked like it hadn't been watered in months. She went toward the kitchen and saw that it was clean. Everything was in its place. It had a long marble countertop and the dining room had a card table and two chairs in it. Before she could go upstairs, Storm stopped her.

"Hey, we got all the bags in the front hall! I know it's empty down here, but up 'til now it's just been me. After you get settled in, you can go get living room and dining room furniture. We probably need new dishes, pots, pans, towels, and whatever else you want or think we need. How about you just make this condo all about you? I want you to be happy. This is our home now. It just needs a woman's touch."

They started to kiss again. Only this time it was much more intense than at the airport. Kenya could feel Storm's dick getting harder.

"Hold up, baby, I want our first time to be special. I want to take you to that dinner that I promised you. I want you to know that I love you and always will."

"I love you too, Storm."

They went out to dinner at Lady Fee's Place, just like he had planned months ago. Tonight would be the night that they had both dreamed of. Any- and everything on the menu was being showcased to the young couple in love. After devouring a fantastic meal, Storm and Kenya were soon almost finished with their desserts. The two had drunk almost the entire bottle of wine as they ate their meals and talked. Kenya took her shoe off, seductively running her foot along the side of his leg. Storm's eyes grew wide when Kenya finally reached the hardness in between his legs.

"Baby, you know you wrong for doing this to a brother out in public."

Kenya smiled and continued rubbing his manhood with her foot until she felt it damn near ready to bust out through his zipper.

The waitress came to the table, asking the pair of soon-to-be lovers if they needed anything else. Storm, feeling self-conscious, had to readjust himself in the seat so that she wouldn't notice the bulge in his pants. "No, thank you, just bring the bill. We're both about ready." He paid the bill, then left her a nice, fat tip and they were out the door.

"I'm glad to see you act like you have some class and tip like you're supposed to. I hate when guys don't tip."

Storm held her close and whispered in her ear. "Don't worry about that shit anymore. You're with me now. You're my girl. That means you want for nothing!"

As they made their way home they couldn't keep their hands off each other. From the time they made it through the condo door, it was on. Storm grabbed Kenya and covered her mouth with his. His tongue was moving in and out fast and deep. She held her head back as he seemed to devour her entire neck with light nibbles that were sure to leave passion marks. Storm's hands were exploring her body. Kenya, light-headed and dizzy, felt his hands roam across her breasts and then squeeze her shoulders, never once removing his tongue from her skin. His dick was rock hard and Kenya could feel it throbbing through his pants as he pressed her body hard against the wall.

"Do you know how bad I want you? Do you understand just how much I need you?"

She could feel his hot breath in her ear as he started to caress her skin softly, sending chills throughout her whole body. A single tear started to fall from Kenya's eye and Storm quickly kissed it off of her face. He kissed both her closed eyes, the tip of her nose and called out her name, both quiet and loud at the same time.

"Let me make love to you." He took his hand and raised her face to meet his. "Feel this." Storm placed her hands on his shaft and made her fingers squeeze his dick as if she was massaging it. "This is yours, tonight, tomorrow, and forever. Let me give it to you."

Kenya could barely catch her breath. Her mind was confused. She had been fucked before, but not once had a man made love to her. The room was spinning and wouldn't slow down. Storm, with the strength of a bull, carried her up the stairs and into the bedroom. It was the only furnished room in the condo, but it was done up right. Not missing a beat, he laid her trembling body across the king-sized bed and started to undress her slowly. Storm, eager to make her totally his, kept his eyes glued on her. It would finally be time for Kenya to be the prey instead of the predator. Storm had gotten her down to her thong and a matching white lace camisole and finally felt the need to speak.

"Damn, baby, you look good as a motherfucker. I gotta have you—forever."

Kenya watched his every move as he took his belt loose and unzipped his pants. When they dropped to the plush carpet beneath him, she could see his big black dick standing at attention, curving to the side. Kenya tried to resist, but couldn't help herself as she crawled over to the edge of the bed where he was standing, and let her mouth take his dick inside. Storm moaned from pleasure as she took control of him. He heard the sweetest sounds known to man as she slurped and sucked him hard.

Storm instinctively grabbed a handful of Kenya's long hair and twisted it in between his fingers. The head of his pole was pounding. He could feel it easing its way down her throat. As if a porno king state of mind took over, he started fucking her in her mouth hard, so hard that he had to slow down and control himself before he came. Kenya, not complaining about his sudden rough demeanor, was moaning as much as Storm was. He didn't want to cum in her mouth, so he pulled back and took her hands in his. Slowly he pushed her back onto the bed and tore her thong off, tossing them over his shoulder. Storm went to work and her pussy was full of his tongue. She was filled with love and tried to wiggle free from the grip he had on her hips, but that, of course, only gave him more pleasure.

"Let daddy give you your present!" Storm got on top of her and slowly slid his love inside of her. It filled Kenya's moist, waiting box, hitting all her walls, tickling each spot. Kenya closed her eyes as he made love to and fucked the shit out of her at the same time.

They made love most of the night until they both fell asleep. When they woke up the next morning, it was on again—round two.

Ticktock

It had been a few months since Kenya and Storm began their new lives together. She'd just finished remodeling the condo the way that she wanted it. She had a lot of new friends and was happier than she had ever been in her life. Since Storm and his brother O.T. were so close and always together, it made her and O.T.'s on-again off-again girlfriend, Paris, kinda cool. They would go shopping and talk shit about the fellas for hours on end. Paris and Kenya were both fly as hell and didn't take any shit from either one of the brothers. They put one another up on any bullshit that the two siblings would try to pull, especially O.T. And truth be told, Paris was the only one that O.T., a straight-up fool, would halfway listen to.

Kenya really liked her new job. Storm got his boy Deacon to let her manage the bar. In reality, she was doing him a favor. She had a lot of strip club experience from dancing at Heads Up, not to mention the fact that she knew how to balance the books. Zack had taught her that much. She knew that one day it would come in handy and it did. Kenya even had all the girls in check, making money and not focused on silly bullshit that could and would occur when a gang of females got tighter under one roof. Storm was always impressed at Kenya's people skills, as well as Deacon, who knew she was trained by Zack, once his hero in the nightclub business. Alley Cats was now the new blazing hot spot in Dallas just as Heads Up was in Detroit. From NBA players, musicians, and doctors, to the average nine-to-five guy from down the block around the way, they all came to hang out at the club, have a great time, and, most importantly to the bottom line, spend money. Dudes and females alike would party inside together with few incidents. They had a slamming menu and the most exotic-looking dancers in the entire city on deck nightly.

Deacon and Storm were both making money hand over fist. They agreed that after six more months of slinging dope, they would retire from the game and open another club, go legal. They had a new supply pipeline from across the border and were getting their product at a bargain price. The more they would buy, the sweeter the deal was. However, Deacon and Storm weren't the only crew that was getting money in the city. A yesteryear player, Royce, and a couple of other older guys had been doing their thing for years across town. They were more laid back than Storm and Deacon, but stayed in their lanes unless it was necessary for them all to cross paths.

Royce

"Hey, Deacon, did you read today's paper?" Storm came in the club with the newspaper tucked under his arm.

Deacon was pissed. "Yeah, I read that bullshit! We gotta slow this shit the fuck down. The cops are running up in all the houses that are on the north side. It's getting wild out there like it's an election year or something!"

Storm poured himself a shot of Remy. "Yeah, I feel you. We need to try to sit down with that old, wrinkled nigga Royce and figure some shit out that can help us all. I know that he gots to be hurting just as much as we are, shit, probably even more."

Deacon knew his partner was right. He had an idea that might smooth things out for both crews. "You know what, I'll send one of the girls over to the spot where Royce and his crew hangs out at, and ask him to come to the club for dinner, drinks, and discussion. We gotta slow these motherfucking police raids the fuck down! This shit gotta stop!"

It was Thursday night when Royce and three of his main men decided to take Deacon and Storm up on their invitation for a sit-down. They were all suited and booted acting as if they were going to a funeral or some cornball shit-bag-ass job. That's how Royce and his boys rolled every day everywhere they went. Most of his crew were younger and rarely dressed like their boss, but some were desperate to fit in and possibly raise in the ranks, so they followed his lead, dressing like men three times their age.

"Look at these old players, players who done escape from the museum." Storm nodded in the direction of the door and Deacon glanced over to see what his boy was talking about.

"Well, baby boy. Let's do this shit!" Deacon patted Storm on his shoulder, reassuring him that his idea to meet with

Royce would have a good outcome. When they started to walk over to the table, Storm stopped one of the shot girls and asked her to bring over a bottle of Hennessy VSOP and several glasses for the special guests.

After all the talking and trying to peep each other out, the two rival crews had come to an agreement. Both of them hardcore, not wanting to be the first to blink, were reluctant to give any sort of solid guarantee, but would try to stop any more unnecessarily outrageous violence in their zones. It would be hard to promise a 100 percent total truce, because they were at war. And with war, there were always casualties. That was a given. But for now, the police and the everyday snitches were common enemies they could beef with together as a unit.

"Why don't you gentlemen enjoy the rest of your evening? Of course, everything is compliments of Alley Cats." Deacon then called a waitress over, authorizing her to put everything on his book. "Tell the girls to take care of my friends here. I'm going to take care of their fee. Dances on me!"

Royce stood up to shake both Deacon's and Storm's hands. "Listen, young brothers. I respect both of you as men, and I wish you well. You try to handle your end and I got mine. Thanks for the hospitality. My crew and myself appreciate it to the fullest."

For a Thursday night, the bar was off the hook. Kenya had booked a featured dancer from back east, who was also an XXX porn star. Cum4u was on stage performing the most erotic, nasty, and shocking dance routine ever seen to man or beast. She'd not only captured every one of the males' attention, but the other dancers, the wait staff, and Kenya, who thought that she had seen it all; but this ho was a master at the craft of entertaining a crowd. She was bending like a pretzel and licking every part of her own body. The crowd loved it as they watched, spellbound.

"Damn, Kenya! Where in the hell you get her from?" Deacon was also amazed as he lusted for the flexible young dancer on stage. "That ho wifey material!"

"Come on now, you know a chic like me got skills and contacts. Look around. Everyone is buying drinks and spending money. I'm about that life." Kenya was doing her thang and knew it.

Deacon patted Storm on his back while looking at Kenya. "Damn, girl, tell me you have a sister, a cousin, even a close friend anything like you. You know how to make shit really happen. Plus you fine as hell!" They opened a bottle of Moët and toasted to the club and making money for the rest of their young lives.

"Just like me?" Kenya laughed out loud to her inside joke. "Naw, sorry, Deacon. I'm an original, besides, what the fuck would y'all do with two of me running around?"

Deacon, Storm, and Kenya were finishing up the bottle when Royce and his crew, done taking advantage of Deacon and Storm's offer of hospitality, were leaving, heading toward the door. Royce, old but not blind, couldn't help but stare lustfully at Kenya. Alley Cats had some bad bitches swinging from poles and grinding in laps on the payroll, but Kenya was the finest of them all, and she had all of her clothes on.

"Damn, fellas, where did you have this one hiding at all night? She the real showstopper!" Royce was looking her up and down, from foot to fro, licking his lips, imagining what he'd do to her given the opportunity.

Making sure Royce knew what was really good, Storm wrapped his arms around Kenya's small waist. "Hold tight, this here is top shelf, cat daddy! This all me!" He started kissing her on the neck while Royce marveled at the young man's eye candy.

"Damn, I can respect that. Let me just say, you're one lucky man." Royce envied him as he grinned.

As Royce and his crew left out the door, Deacon and Storm were overly amused at his game, or lack of it.

"Old players kill me. They just don't know when their time in the sun is over! Shit, it's our time to shine bright!" Storm gave Deacon a dap and they continued drinking the rest of the night.

Chapter Eighteen

London

Within the few months of London returning to school, a lot of things had changed. The first thing being that PAID had blown up far beyond her dreams. The days following the big meeting she'd spoken at got a lot of people motivated. Both students and politicians alike were starting to get involved in the newly formed movement. Not only was her campus fired up, so were schools all across the East Coast. Different schools were forming chapters of PAID and were getting London to speak on their campus.

"Wow, I never thought we would be getting this much mail!" Fatima was going through all the correspondence that the organization was receiving.

"Girl, I know what you're saying. This entire thing has us so busy, it's getting hard for me to study. I need some sort of a break."

Fatima smirked as she spoke. "Well, stop getting folks so damned geeked up with your speeches and maybe you can get some rest."

London sat back on her bed, wondering what her twin was up to. It had been more than a hot minute since the two had talked on the phone and she missed at least hearing her voice if nothing else. She hoped that Kenya's new life was everything that she wanted it to be and more, but still secretly prayed for her to move back home. London tried calling Kenya a couple of times, but her cell phone always went straight to voice mail. She knew her sister and knew Kenya would get back to her in her own time.

Fatima, who'd been acting somewhat peculiar since the night of the shooting at Heads Up, was looking in the mirror, fixing her hair. Strangely, she'd been making a lot of trips to Detroit over the last few months for reasons London couldn't quite figure out or put her finger on. "Hey, girl, I have to make a short trip to your city. Do you want to roll with me so you can check on the house or visit some of your old neighbors or friends? For real, not trying to get off into your business, but you and Kenya should accept one of those offers and close that chapter in your life so you can start a new one." Fatima, outta nothing but love, was always concerned about her roommate's well-being.

"Naw, girl, I'm tight on all that travel. I think I'm gonna just try to fall back, get some rest, and study this weekend. Besides, I know how you like dumping me off somewhere in the city while you take care of your secret stuff you got going on." London playfully pushed her roommate's shoulder, teasing.

"Stop playing. You know I don't have any secrets I'm hiding from you, soul sista. I'm just doing some volunteer work, that's all."

"Yeah, right, stop it! Way in Detroit?" Fatima and London giggled and talked about a lot of different stuff before the two went to sleep.

Morning came and Fatima was up, dressed, and ready to hit the highway early. "Are you sure you don't want to ride?"

London was sitting on the side of her bed, rubbing her eyes. "Girl, go do you. I think I should read a few more of these letters from other schools and respond. There's even a few from out on the West Coast trying to organize. This thing is a monster!"

With an exchange of hugs, Fatima hit the road while London started to read and reply to the letters by e-mail.

Storm

Storm was pissed the fuck off. He never really got upset, but when money was involved he turned into a pure maniac. "Son of a bitch! When is this bullshit gonna cease? My pockets are starting to feel this shit. For real, for real I'm over it!"

Storm and Deacon were getting a lot of complaints from their workers on the block. It seemed as if a lot of do-right organizations were starting to form all along the West Coast hell-bent on slowing down if not attempting to stop altogether the sale of drugs in certain low-income areas.

Deacon was heated as well as he cracked his knuckles. "I know that nigga Royce is pissed off too. I saw him and his boys out at the mall and he was complaining about getting his hard."

Storm and his brother O.T. were shooting pool and trying to come up with a new game plan as Deacon paced the floor, almost wearing a hole in the carpet. After about an hour or so, they decided to set up another meeting with Royce. They knew he got all his dope from the same connect as they did, an old man in the Islands named Javier. If both crews could hopefully arrange a sit-down with the "elusive of the law" kingpin, maybe they could slightly lower the ticket and be able to stay above board until the heat of whatever was taking place would slow down and it could be back to business as usual.

"Real talk, I'm gonna call his phone and see if he wants to bump heads on this shit." Deacon went to get the number and make the call. "I know he sick right now just like we is!"

"Yeah, do that, while I finish tapping your boy's ass on this table." O.T. laughed as he put chalk on his cue. "Ain't gonna be nothing nice, son, know that!"

Deacon soon came out of the office with a big smile on his grill. "I talked to Royce. We're gonna meet at the football game two weeks from now. He said he got some tickets reserved for all of us." Storm gave Deacon a stupid look and O.T. took over from there.

"It better not be any damn nosebleed seats up high. You know them old motherfuckers are broke as a fuck."

"Man, shut your young-ass up!" Deacon was shaking his head, laughing at his comments.

O.T. continued to clown, having such an easy target to talk shit about. "I ain't playing. That ancient Negro gonna make me catch a case up in that bitch if them seats is foul. That's my word! Don't nobody wanna be sitting damn near in heaven watching the game with the angels!"

By that time Storm was falling out too, holding his side. "Man, I'm out. I gotta get to the crib. Kenya is cooking dinner and I don't want to be late." Storm grabbed his jacket and headed toward the door.

"Yo, give her a kiss for me." Deacon gave Storm some love and went over to the pool table to give O.T. a much-needed lesson in losing.

Kenya

Storm and Kenya were sitting down at the table and finishing up the meal she'd prepared for them.

"Damn, baby, that shit was on point. You've got the total package, beauty, brains, and you can cook like a motherfucker. How did I get so lucky?"

Kenya cleared the table off and poured each of them another glass of wine. "I love you so much, Storm. I swear, you're my entire world." She went and sat on his lap, resting her head on his chest. "When you gonna marry me?" As soon as the words came out of Kenya's mouth, she couldn't believe that she had said that shit. She had a look of embarrassment on her face. They hadn't been together a year, but it didn't matter, she was all in.

"Baby, let me take care of a few projects and I plan on doing just that, make you my wife. I want to make sure that I can buy us a house first."

Storm asked Kenya if she would go in the floor safe in the guest bedroom and bring all the money down. He wanted to get an accurate count and see just what he was working with as far as cash on hand. Kenya had been putting his money in the safe both from the streets and his cut from the club almost nightly. He let her handle the cash because she was good at balancing shit.

"Baby, this money is our future." Storm spread all the money on the floor and started to count.

While he was doing that, Kenya decided to check her messages from her cell phone. It said that she had seventeen new calls. After checking each one, she went upstairs to call London. It had been months and Storm still didn't know that she had an identical twin sister living back in Detroit. Maybe it was London's strong opposition to drugs: the one main thing that paid her and Storm's bills and would ultimately pay for their new house. Whatever her reason was, Kenya felt the strong need not to tell him—at least, not yet.

"Hey, girl, I missed you." Kenya shut the door behind her for some added privacy.

"I missed you too. I've been trying to call you ever since last week. We got a good offer on the house and I want to take it." London was ready to let go and move on just as Fatima had suggested. "What do you think? Unless there's a chance you might move back home!"

"All right, London, you set up the meeting with the real estate agent and I'll catch a flight out there. Just give me a couple of weeks. I seriously don't think I'll be moving back and if I do, I wouldn't want to stay in that neighborhood."

Sad to hear Kenya's final verdict about relocating back to Detroit, the twins chatted a little bit more about all the hell that London was causing on the entire East Coast and of course how Kenya's new life was going in Dallas. When they hung up the phone Kenya made her way back downstairs. Storm was almost done counting all the cash and asked Kenya to run him some bathwater. When the water was just right, they both got in the tub and before even five minutes had past, they were making love. Storm's strong hands were firmly gripping Kenya's waist as her body took on a total sense of relaxation and pleasure. He pulled her wet hair as he slowly eased in and out of her. After repeating the calculated stroke motions over and over, Storm and Kenya both moaned out in passion as they started to climax together.

The two of them remained embraced in the water, talking until the water grew cold. Storm got out first and brought his woman a huge white fluffy towel. He picked her up out the tub and wrapped her up like a baby. Storm then carried her back to their bed and slowly started drying her off.

"Do you know how much I love you? You're my queen!" Storm kissed her hands and started sucking her fingers one by one.

Kenya was on cloud nine and confused. Anytime Storm touched her, she still trembled. She closed her eyes trying to stay focused. Kenya had to think of a lie and fast. She finally told him that she had to fly back east in a few weeks for her godson's birthday. Anytime she mentioned him, Storm would melt just as she did. He truly loved Kenya for her loyalty to the little boy despite not being blood related. She hated lying to her man, but what else could she do? Tell him her twin dope-dealer-hating sister and her had business to tend to?

Chapter Nineteen

Storm

As always, time flew by and Storm, Deacon, and O.T. went to meet with Royce at the football game. Just as O.T. feared the seats were terrible. Also, just as equally as they were feeling the pain of the new antidrug movements being formed on the West Coast, so was Royce. Most of the conversation was filled with different angles that they could use to push their products and gain more revenue. All parties involved felt that selling dope was a game to be run and operated like a Wall Street firm. They had strict rules to follow and sometimes a guy had to check his ego at the door if he planned on being profitable.

Although the two crews were rivals in Dallas, they both understood that it would be advisable for them to join forces with one another, cooperate, and try to set up a face-to-face with Javier. Both of the crews' pockets were suffering and at that present point in time neither wanted to relocate their business dealings in an attempt to start all over again, possibly ending up with the same headache. The two rivals joining forces could be the final deal-breaker in coming up or the final nail in their coffins, much depending on Javier's answer.

Royce and Deacon jointly made the conference call to Mexico, making the travel arrangements with a reserved but open-minded Javier. If things went as planned, all the parties involved could get back to business as usual—making money.

Kenya

"Baby, you know that I'm gonna miss you while you're gone. I wish that I could fly out east with you and meet your godson." Storm was covering Kenya's face with kisses. He loved her with all his inner being. It was the first time that he truly opened his heart up to a woman. She was the one he'd waited for his whole life. He felt like the sun would rise and set on Kenya.

"I love you, daddy! You know I'm gonna miss you too, you and this dick." Kenya started to rub on his pants and his manhood instantly jumped to attention.

Storm held Kenya tightly in his arms and hugged her like there was no tomorrow in sight. "Before you get on that plane and fly away from me, I want you to take this with you and promise me that you're gonna come back to me!" Storm reached in his pocket, pulling out an engagement ring and slipped it on to Kenya's finger. "Will you marry me?"

The room grew silent as Kenya stood in shock, weak in the knees.

"Well, is that silence a yes or a no?"

"Yes! Yes! Yes!" Kenya, ecstatic, jumped up and down.

Storm and Kenya made love in the middle of the floor until it was time for him to take her to the airport. Kenya felt guilty for lying to the man she loved about her secret life back in Detroit. Admiring the ring he'd just placed on her finger, she made a promise to herself that when she got back to Dallas she would tell him the truth about everything she'd been hiding, especially London, and let the chips fall where they may. She prayed their love was strong enough to overcome whatever.

Storm

Storm had just returned from dropping his new wife-to-be off and had to get ready to meet Deacon at the club. He, Deacon, and Royce were flying out in the afternoon. The meeting with Javier was set and they hoped that it would go well. O.T. was going to stay behind and run things at the Alley Cats until Storm and Deacon returned. It was going to be a few days of terror at the club, because O.T. was a straight-up fool and everyone on staff knew it. Deacon had to leave a detailed list of do's and don'ts for him to follow. He was a clown, but with Kenya out east, unfortunately he was the next in line to run the place.

"Damn, it's getting about that time." Storm looked at his watch. Kenya had packed his bag for him and had everything neat as hell. Storm looked at the picture of both of them on the dresser and threw it in his bag for good luck. He missed her smile already. *I just need to put this cash up. Damn, why didn't I remember to get Kenya to put it in the safe before she left?*

He went to the guest bedroom and went into the closet. After moving all the clothes and boxes that Kenya had stacked up over the floor safe, he opened it, tossing the money inside. As he started to throw all the stuff back like he'd found it, a box fell down, almost hitting him in the head. The contents were scattered across the floor. It was a gang of papers that obviously belonged to Kenya. They were mostly old bills and receipts from what he could tell. Without paying much attention, he stuffed them back into the box, until one of them stood out.

"Motown Storage Units" was on the top of one of the paper printouts. It was dated the day that Kenya had flown out to be with him. He knew that she had a few things still out there that she couldn't bring on the plane, so that wasn't the big problem. The problem was the signature on the receipt. *Who in the hell is London Roberts?* He had seen Kenya's ID when they signed some insurance papers. He recognized Kenya's handwriting. He knew Amoya Kenya Roberts was her government name for certain, but who was London Roberts and how was she related to Kenya? Time was flying and he had to go pick up Deacon so they could catch their flight. He put the paper in his wallet and would ask Kenya about it when she got home or the next time they spoke. He trusted Kenya and knew that there was a good explanation for it.

Storm arrived at Alley Cats just as Deacon was giving O.T. the rundown on things and last-minute instructions as to how he wanted things done in his absence. Deacon and Storm were only going to be gone two or three days tops, but a lot of shit could happen between then and now, especially with O.T. running things. After they were totally convinced that O.T. had it down, they headed to the airport. Storm darted in and out of traffic and they made it to the terminal in record time.

"Damn, I was just out here. I should have just stayed out here, had a couple of drinks, and met you at the gate." Storm and Deacon walked past the terminal that Kenya's plane had just departed from.

"Man, when is Kenya coming back?" Deacon wished that she had never left. Leaving O.T. at the helm made him a nervous wreck. That club was his whole life and he knew Storm's little brother could run it into the ground almost overnight.

"Relax, guy. She should be back in a few days. Just chill, ol' boy got you."

After a minute or two they saw Royce and his boy turn the corner. They had their suits on and looked like some played-out car salesmen desperate for a deal. Deacon told Storm that this was sure to be the longest trip in history. Storm just laughed, knowing his best friend was about right this time even though he was busy missing Kenya. Royce and his boy greeted the two of them and waited for their plane to be ready to board.

"Where is that fine-ass woman you always have on your arm?" Royce questioned Storm, referring to Kenya.

"She had to fly out east to take care of some business. Plus she's not just my woman, she's my soon-to-be wife!"

Royce, his boy, and even Deacon all looked shocked at his announcement. They all congratulated him and jokingly told him to make sure to turn in his player's card before he got home.

The flight was a little bumpy, but it wasn't that long before they landed. A luxury car met them at the obscure airport and drove them all to a private airstrip at the edge of town. There they got on a smaller jet and finally reached Javier's exclusive villa. It was like a small paradise inside of a paradise. All of the small-time hustlers, compared to Javier's apparent wealth status, were impressed. When they got inside, a small-framed woman showed them to their individual deluxe suites. Each one was decorated with items that were obviously worth more than they ever hoped to afford in several lifetimes. With a welcoming spirit, she gave them fresh towels and informed them that Mr. Javier wanted them to relax, enjoy, and partake in his home's vast amenities, and he would meet with them the next day.

The Twins

Kenya's plane landed on schedule and London and Fatima were both there to meet her.

"Hey, girl, I missed your ass!" Kenya was screaming as she hugged her sister.

"I missed you too. Look at you, still looking all fly as always." London was also elated to see her twin. Fatima had to practically pry the two apart so that she could get a hug from Kenya. They gossiped and giggled all the way back to the hotel where Kenya was staying.

"We have the meeting with the real estate agent set up for the morning. Can you please wake up and get ready by ten a.m.?" London smiled as she messed with her sister. "I know how you do!"

"Yeah, yeah, yeah, girl, I can make it up by then, I guess. My husband-to-be gets up early and runs a few miles every day and I make him breakfast!" Kenya leaned back in the seat, waiting for a response.

"What do you mean, husband-to-be?" London did a double take at her twin sister, raising one eyebrow. She and Fatima were in shock as Kenya waved around the big rock on her finger that they had failed to notice. "Oh my God! When did all this happen? When am I going to meet him?" London was full of questions as she examined the size of the center stone.

"Don't worry, when I get back home I'm going to set something up, I promise."

Fatima had to go on one of her famous top-secret missions and then make a trip up to the school, so she left the sisters alone. The twins sat up all night talking and having fun. They missed each other and by the way they carried on it showed. The conversation started on Storm and the new life Kenya was leading, to London and her organization spreading across the United States.

"Girl, you are going to love Storm. He treats me like gold. It's just like being a little kid in a candy store. Whatever I want or dream about, he makes possible." Kenya was going on and on about her happiness.

"I'm so very glad for you both. As soon as this semester is complete, I'm going to visit, if that's okay. He sounds wonderful. What does he do for a living?" London quizzed her twin, trying to gain more information about the man who had her sister so wide open.

Kenya wasn't prepared for any of London's often judgmental statements, so she quickly flipped the script, changing the subject. Of course, Kenya was the queen of manipulation. It worked and the two were soon discussing London and her love life or lack of it. The back-and-forth conversation went on for hours.

The Meeting

It was a bright, sunny morning on the private island. Storm regretted that he didn't have the love of his life, Kenya, to share the gorgeous sunrise with him. As he got dressed, he looked at a picture of them that he had thrown in his bag, and as corny as it seemed he kissed it.

Storm and Deacon got to the patio just as Royce and his boy did. It was 10:00 in the morning, on a tropical island, and Royce was still wearing a suit, even though it was damn near a hundred degrees in the shade.

"That nigga gonna rock that suit bullshit to the end!" Deacon laughed as he drank a glass of juice. "That hot-ass fabric is a damn heatstroke waiting to happen!"

Storm, like all the other invited guests, was sitting back thinking about what it would be like to be as rich and prosperous as Javier. Just then, two huge men entered the area. A matter of seconds later a short, balding old man joined them. Although none of the men had actually met their host, they could tell from the amount of respect shown by the staff that this was indeed the infamous Javier. He soon introduced himself and removed all doubt of his identity. He poured himself a glass of juice and then began to speak.

"I am, as some may say, a man of few words. Let me start by saying that I do appreciate you all coming to me like men to try to find a solution to your problems, and not trying to locate another supplier. I already know what your main obstacle is, and I have already put one of my best men on top of it. His name is Swift and he is already in the States. He will be sure to make all your problems go, should we say, away. I believe in cutting the monster's head off and that's what Swift will most certainly do. My people are passing around a picture of the source for you to see the face of the so-called Big Bad Wolf who's causing you such a great loss of money and grief. A silly little girl!"

Royce got the picture first and stared at it long and hard. His eyes were almost jumping out of his head. He leaped out of his seat and asked Javier if he could see him in private.

"Please, sir, I mean you no disrespect, but this is urgent!" Royce looked as if like he had seen a ghost.

Javier remained calm as he spoke. "Mr. Royce, we have no secrets here around this table. Feel free to speak your mind, no harm will come to the righteous, I can assure you of that!" Javier stared intensely at Royce, who was turning paler by the seconds. Storm and Deacon were watching him also.

Royce finally spoke. "I think these two are undercover police or something!"

Deacon and Storm both jumped out of their seats and couldn't believe what Royce had just blurted out alleging. "Man, what in the fuck are you talking about?" Storm, immediately infuriated and insulted, barked. "Are you fucking crazy, old man?"

"I'm talking about this bitch right here! Your woman is out east now ain't she? I mean that is what you told me!" Royce threw the picture across the table at Storm, who picked it up and started shaking his head, confused, in disbelief. Royce then started calling Storm a fucking snitch-ass rat who couldn't be trusted.

Javier sat back and watched the heated exchange take place among the three men. He told Royce and his boy to give him some time to sort this unfortunate mess out. Royce was asked to enjoy the rest of the day on the island relaxing and that he soon would be rewarded for his loyalty. After carefully observing Storm's and Deacon's responses to seeing the picture, he then reacted when dealing with them. Showing his power, the old man waved his hand and had his men remove both Storm and Deacon from the table and lead them to a back room.

Storm was totally speechless and in shock. He couldn't understand what he had just seen.

Deacon was terrified. "Damn, man, what the fuck is Kenya off into? I knew that bitch was too fucking good to be true. I can't believe this shit! What did she say she was flying out east for anyway?" He asked Storm question after question, knowing their lives were on the line.

"Listen, Deacon, I swear to you, guy, I don't know what the fuck is going on. Maybe these old cats are trying to test us or something? Besides, it was your boy Zack who turned us on to her in the first place. So stop pointing fucking fingers at me, okay?"

They were confused as hell and scared of what the outcome might be if this tangled web of deception wasn't straightened out fast. The two friends paced the floor as they tried to think of an explanation for the shit they were now in. After about an hour or so of being locked in the room, they heard footsteps approaching. They both started to sweat, as they watched the doorknob start to turn. The door was swung wide open and a group of men rushed inside, followed by a slow-paced Javier. As he entered the room, he focused all of his attention on to Storm. He had the picture of Kenya and Storm dangling from his hand. Javier had his men search Storm's luggage for any clues or evidence linking them to the mystery woman in the picture and what Royce had claimed to be true. They easily discovered the picture, along with a piece of paper, in his wallet.

"Okay, you men have your orders." Javier gave his crew a slight nod. Some of his men grabbed Deacon by his throat, dragging him out of the room. He was begging for his life as he struggled to breathe. His eyes were bulging out his head. "Don't beg! It shows no pride. Be a man," was all that Javier said in a nonchalant manner while still watching Storm, who two other men were holding back. Deacon didn't take Javier's advice and could be heard screaming as they took him in the basement. Javier seemed cold and unbothered about what was obviously about to take place. Deacon was undoubtedly on his way to heaven or hell thanks to an awful misunderstanding.

"Please, Javier! I don't know what's going on. I swear to God!" Storm was panicking, wanting the men to release Deacon before it was too late. "Listen, I know it looks bad, but it's not like that. That female in the picture can't be my girl. It doesn't make any kind of sense. My woman is down for me. She loves me! Something ain't right! She ain't no damn police! Trust me, she's not!"

Javier's men threw Storm in a chair and tied him up. He was still trying to explain, even though he didn't understand himself. Even though he was facing death, he couldn't grasp why or how his beloved Kenya could betray him like it seemed like she'd done. "It's not her! It must be a mistake! Let me call her! She can explain!"

"Please don't play with my intelligence, young man. The way you looked at that picture was a dead giveaway of your guilt and if I wanted more proof, you yourself provided it to me. So please stop with the lies." Javier held the picture of Storm and Kenya up next to the picture that he'd passed around earlier at the table. As he lit a cigar, he asked Storm once again, "Do you care to try to explain?" Storm just shook his head and looked toward the ground. "I didn't think so," Javier mocked, blowing smoke rings in the air.

Storm was in shock. The girl in the picture looked just like Kenya, only without makeup. How could this be? Storm was lost in his thoughts. How could this be his Kenya, but how could it not be? The final nail in the coffin came as Javier held up the paper that he had gotten out of Storm's wallet. He read the words that headlined the page. It said "Motown Storage Units." It was the same receipt that Storm found in the closet and wanted to ask Kenya about himself.

Javier read off the name that was at the bottom of the page. Storm heard the name and couldn't believe what he heard. His mouth dropped open, remembering the name also. "I guess that you still don't know who London Roberts is, do you?"

Storm was heartbroken. Not because he knew he was about to die, but because he believed that Kenya had betrayed him. Javier motioned for his men to take Storm away. They untied Storm and snatched him up from the chair. Unlike Deacon, he didn't scream, fight, or negotiate as he was led away to the unknown. Javier and his men couldn't hurt him any worse than he believed that his once-cherished Kenya had already done.

Chapter Twenty

The Twins

It was 10:30 in the morning and the twins had just come back from signing the final papers on the sale of the house. They both cried at the real estate office, but knew that it was time to move on. It would take some time for the people to close on the house and the girls were happy. It gave them time to sleep at the house a few more nights, just for old time's sake. Although the pair had most of their belongings in storage, they still had their old beds there. The girls knew that they wouldn't have any use for twin beds in their new future endeavors. They were both grown and leading different lives. As soon as the two entered the house, they felt a sense of calm. It was almost as if Gran was watching over them, telling them it was okay and she approved of what they'd done.

Hearing a car horn blow outside, London ran over to look out of the front window. "Hey, that's Fatima! Let me go see what's up with her." London went out onto the porch and started to talk to Fatima.

Kenya took that opportunity to call Storm and check on him. He hadn't checked in with her since she had left Dallas. On the first ring, his phone went straight to voice mail. *Maybe it doesn't pick up in Mexico?* She decided then to call O.T. and see if he had heard from either Storm or Deacon. O.T. answered the phone on the fifth or sixth ring.

"Hello, hey, O.T. Have you spoke to the fellas yet?" Kenya was sounding cheerful.

"Naw, girl. And what fucking time is it anyhow? And why you calling me all early and shit?" O.T. snapped.

Kenya had forgotten all about the time difference. "Dang, bro, I'm sorry. My bad. Call me when you get up and tell Paris hello." She hung the phone up and peeked out the window. Kenya watched her sister and Fatima talk shit about a march that they were going to participate in, and smiled. She was proud of her twin and the woman she'd become despite all the obstacles that were thrown in her way.

While Kenya was watching the two of them, she had no idea that she wasn't the only one. Swift had been following Fatima around all morning since she had left the school and knew that eventually she'd lead him to his intended target: London Roberts. Smugly, he sat back in the car with her picture on the front seat.

Bingo! I knew that bitch would get with her girl sooner or later. Swift stared at London and Fatima as he licked his lips.

Finally, after twenty minutes of them talking, Fatima had to leave. She promised both girls a big surprise later when she returned. "Tell Kenya to be dressed and ready when I get back. The surprise is for both of y'all."

London assured Fatima that they would be ready and went in the house to take a nap. Swift sat in his car and waited for nightfall.

After about a half hour passed, another car pulled up in front of the house. The young guy driving the car got out and helped a little boy out of the rear seat. All of a sudden Kenya bolted out the door and grabbed the little boy up in her arms. It was her godson, Jaylin, and Young Foy. She tightly hugged them both.

"I'm so happy to see you guys. I think about y'all each and every day." Kenya kissed Jaylin on his jaws.

"I'm so proud of the job that you're doing with my godson. Raven would be proud too. You know she loved your crazy-acting ass!"

Young Foy blushed and reached into his car. "Here, this is for you. I'm about to do the damn thang!" He gave Kenya one

of his new CDs that would be released soon. They talked for a
short time before he had to leave. Young Foy and Jaylin said
their good-byes to Kenya and were off.

As she waved to them on the edge of the curb, Swift took
notice of her shape and beautiful facial features. He couldn't
help but think how much better his intended target looked
with makeup on than earlier.

Nevertheless, when nightfall finally came, she'd be dead
just the same, with or without makeup even if she gave up the
booty. Swift had a job to do—silence London Roberts for good.

Double Trouble on Dat Ass!

It had just gotten dark and the girls were getting ready to
get dressed to go out to dinner with Fatima. She'd promised
them a surprise and London could barely wait. She was the
first to get in the shower and start to get herself together
because she knew that Kenya would take practically all night
getting dressed. While London was in the shower, Kenya took
her cell phone off the charger and tried calling Storm again.
Still, she got no answer. Once again it went straight to voice
mail. Kenya looked at the clock before calling O.T. again and
decided to call Alley Cats to see if he had spoken to his big
brother yet. Something was wrong and she felt it. This wasn't
like Storm not to call and check on her.

O.T. answered the phone after several rings. Between the
loud noise of the club and him holding conversations with
everyone else, he gave Kenya the response that she hated
to hear. "Sorry, Kenya, nope, still no word. You know them
dudes probably lying back on the beach, chillin' with some
hoes! Naw, I'm just fucking with you." He tried to lighten the
mood she was in. "Don't worry, girl, that sorry lovesick Negro
you got is all right with his soft bitch-ass! They just probably
somewhere teaching Royce how to dress!"

O.T. started to tease her and she felt much better. He even
put his woman Paris on the phone, who also made her laugh.
Paris let Kenya know that everything was running smooth at

the club and she was keeping O.T. in order as well as Alley Cats. Kenya, still concerned, felt a little better when she hung up the phone, but her women's intuition wouldn't let her stop from worrying.

London got out of the shower and went into their room. "All right, girl, you next, and please don't take long to get ready. I don't want to be late. Fatima is always punctual."

Kenya got up and saluted London just like they were kids again. They both laughed.

While Kenya jumped in the shower, London started blow-drying her hair. With all the noise going on, they didn't hear Swift jimmy the lock on the back door and come inside the house. He was both quick and quiet. That's where he had gotten his nickname from. Swift paused in the kitchen and listened carefully. Making sure the rest of the house was empty he crept into the living room. There he overheard noises coming from upstairs. Taking a deep breath, he ran his tongue over his teeth and headed in that direction. With the picture in his hand, Swift looked at it one last time, kissing it for good luck as he put it in his jacket. That was a habit that he started on his first murder-for-hire assignment and this was no different.

Swift reached in his inside pocket, removing a hit man's best friend. With expertise, he screwed the silencer on his pistol and slowly eased up the stairs. He took his time on each one. The age of the old house caused each one to make a creaking sound with every footstep. He finally made it to the top and was headed toward the direction of the sounds of the blow dryer. He was ready to do what he'd come to do, when all of a sudden the noise of the dryer stopped. *Damn!* Swift froze in his steps. Confused, he heard the bathroom door open and saw a shadow move out the side of his eye. Swift remained perfectly still as he gripped his gun tightly.

Kenya started talking. "See, sis, I told you that I wasn't gonna take all day. I was in and out!"

"I see. That's a first. What's the occasion?" London yelled back to her sister while checking to see what part of her hair was still damp.

Swift glanced around the dimly lit hallway as he thought, *Fuck it, two bitches for the price of one.* He'd been parked out front all day and he never saw her friend come in. He thought for sure that London was home alone. *I must be slipping, but oh well!* Swift questioned himself. Just then Swift heard one of the girls ask the other if she could come and help her with her hair. In a matter of seconds both girls were standing in the hallway and looking Swift dead in his face. *Well, I'll be damned!* He had his gun raised and pointed at the sisters. Both of them, stunned, screamed loudly, not knowing what else to do.

"What the fuck?" Swift looked back and forth over and over and was confused. "Damn, it's two of you bitches!" He started to laugh and let his guard down. "Ain't this some bizarre shit!"

That's when the twins attacked him at the same time. It was another one of those situations where twins were famous for sharing the same thoughts. It took no words being passed for them both to react as one. Swift was trying his best to hold his own, but the girls had a lot of their father's blood in them. They were like wildcats. London and Kenya were definitely getting the best of Swift. The girls were filled with intense rage and it was on; fists being thrown, faces being socked and scratched, balls getting kicked, and eyes being gouged.

Swift's gun had fallen on the floor and was kicked across the hallway into the darkness. All three were yelling and screaming as they struggled. The fight seemed to go on forever, when all of a sudden Swift's body jerked backward and went limp. He was motionless. The twins turned around and saw a huge figure in the corner with Swift's pistol in his hand. Kenya and London eyes grew wide as they awaited their fate. They then heard footsteps running up the stairs.

"Are you two all right? We knocked at the door and you didn't answer so we walked around the back and saw that the door was open. We heard yelling and rushed in. Are you two hurt? What happened?" Thank God it was Fatima. She was crying and so were the twins. She was overjoyed that her friends were both safe. "I guess you two couldn't wait until dinner to get your big surprise could you?" Fatima wiped her eyes and smiled.

It was then that out of the shadows the man who had saved their lives appeared. London looked puzzled as she tried to focus on the massive-sized man. Kenya, relived, jumped to her feet. She ran over and embraced their savior.

"Oh my God, Brother Rasul, where did you come from? How did you get here? Never mind the questions. I'm so glad to see you! He was gonna kill us!"

Brother Rasul held her close and told her, "Remember I told you that I'd always have your back? Well, now you know it to be true." Kenya, out of breath from the struggle, had tears of joy streaming down her face. "I keep my word, no matter what!"

Fatima went to help London to her feet and introduced her to her big secret, Brother Rasul. He hugged London and told her that he was finally glad to meet her. Kenya and London were both dumbfounded and in shock at the fact that he was hooked up with their friend. The questions quickly began. Fatima explained to the twins that she met him in the hospital the day that their uncle was shot. She saw some of his family reading the Qur'an to him and joined in prayer with them. After that she and he became closer and closer.

Brother Rasul came and stood in the middle of the girls. "Excuse me, ladies, I hate to break this up, but we do have a dead man lying here I need to deal with."

The girls looked over to the other side of the hallway and hugged one another. The sight of Swift's curled-up, broken-neck deceased body caused them to have chills and turn away in utter disgust. Joining Brother Rasul, all the females went downstairs and sat down on the floor to regain their composure.

"We should call the police!" London yelled, not knowing what else to say. "We need to get that thug out of Gran's house!"

"Naw, London. We can't do that," Kenya chimed in. "We need to stop and think first."

"Yeah, that's right!" Fatima agreed. "We don't wanna get Rasul in any more trouble. He's already on probation from the shootout at Heads Up!"

"Not to worry!" Brother Rasul spoke again. "Calm down and let me use the phone. I got this!"

Now What?

The girls were all sitting close to each other as Brother Rasul's friends removed Swift's body through the back door. They had wrapped him in some old sheets that were in the basement and put him in the trunk of a car. As they pulled off, Brother Rasul approached the girls and showed them what he had found in the dead man's jacket. It was a picture of London. It apparently was taken at a PAID meeting. All three of the girls sat there with their mouths wide open not knowing what to think or say. They thought that the man was just a regular burglar who had broken in.

"That man was a professional hit man. Someone hired him to kill you, London!" Brother Rasul was trying his best to keep the girls calm, but at the same time he had to keep it real. This was serious, a serious matter. It wasn't over and he knew it. Just because Swift hadn't succeeded meant nothing. Whoever had paid him could probably easily afford to pay others. "Listen, little sister, I'll do all I can to find out who could have sent him, but in the meantime you need to lay low. That means no more meetings or school for the time being."

Kenya and Fatima both agreed with Brother Rasul. They trusted him with their lives; they had no other choice. Kenya wrapped her arms around London. "Why don't you fly back out to Dallas with me? It's no way in hell that they would look for you out there! You can stay with me and Storm in our guest room." Kenya had no idea that she was leading her sister straight into the belly of the beast.

After a lot of tears being shed, a distraught London lastly gave in and decided they were all correct. It would be in her best interest to take a break from school and go out west with

Kenya. She needed a break anyway from all the limelight of PAID. Fatima promised to pack and send London's things to her as soon as she got back on campus and temporarily sign her out of all her classes.

Fatima and Brother Rasul drove both of the girls to the airport so they could catch a late flight. They said their farewells at the gate and sadly boarded the Texas-bound aircraft.

"Don't worry, London. You'll be safe when we get to Dallas. Storm and his boy Deacon have got that town on lock! We gonna be good!"

Kenya was trying endlessly to ease her sister's troubled mind, while she herself was a hot nervous wreck. When they landed and got their luggage, Kenya tried calling Storm's cell phone but unfortunately once again it went straight to voice mail. Needless to say she was starting to get beyond worried.

"Damn, why isn't his ass answering? He'd better not be fucking around with one of those island bitches!" Kenya slyly mumbled under her breath.

"Is everything all right?" London asked her sister as she looked directly in Kenya's face. She could tell that it was a problem. Even Ray Charles could.

"Yeah, I was just trying to call Storm. He must not be back in town yet, but it ain't a big deal. I'm straight!"

Kenya didn't know how she was going to break the news to him about London. After all, she had been lying. Well, sort of. He always thought her uncle was the only family she had, but bottom line it was time for her to face the music. Storm didn't have a choice in the matter. He would have to accept London and she in return would have to accept Storm and his crooked lifestyle.

Kenya tried not to worry as the pair took a taxi to her and Storm's condo. When they drove up, Kenya noticed all the lights on inside the house. She then made a mental note to curse Storm out for leaving all the lights on. He was, after all, the main one complaining about the bills.

"Well, this is it! I can't wait for you to see how I decorated it!" Kenya excitedly leaped out the cab, stretching her arms.

"So this is it, huh?" London looked around the quiet street that her sister had been calling home.

The driver set the bags on the curb, waited for his tip, and pulled off into the darkness of the night. Kenya and London picked them up slowly and made their way up to the door.

"Wait 'til you see it, London. It is nice as hell. It's everything I've ever dreamed about." Kenya stuck her key in the door, strangely discovering it was unlocked. *He must have really been in a rush.* Confused as to why Storm had carelessly left without securing their home Kenya pushed the door wide opened and stepped inside the entranceway. *What the fuck!* She couldn't believe her eyes and what she and her sister were faced with. "Oh my God! Oh my God! Oh, nooooo!"

Kenya almost collapsed to the floor as London held her chest in utter disbelief. The karma that Kenya had put out in the universe had just come back to bite her dead in the ass!

Ruthless and Rotten
Say U Promise 2

Chapter Twenty-one

OLD NEWS

Welcome Home

Kenya and London stood in somewhat of a daze. It was like looking at something out of a movie. London was totally confused, while her sister was completely shaken up. "Oh, my God! Oh, my God! Oh, shit!" a stun-ned Kenya repeated in a loud, panic-filled voice, standing in the threshold. "I'll be damned! What in the hell happened in this place? Storm! Storm! Oh my God. Storm—where you at?"

"Wow—what happened here?" London quizzed, dumbfounded and astonished.

Kenya yelled out her fiancé's name once more, as her twin sister London's jaw fell open, almost dropping to the ground. "I can't believe this bullshit!" Her eyes were stretched open wide and soon filled with tears as she quickly glanced around her once-perfect, gorgeously designed living room. "Storm! Storm!" she shrieked, still standing frozen in the doorway with her knees weakening by the second and her lips trembling from fear. "This is a nightmare, London. I'm confused!"

"Kenya, what went on in here? How did this occur?" London wondered, interrupting her sister's apparent emotional breakdown. "This is awful. I mean—wow!"

The pair couldn't believe their own eyes, let alone stomach the nauseating, eye-stinging stench that caused them to almost throw up. London, not knowing what else to expect, reached over, grabbing her sister's hand tightly as they hesitantly made their way completely into the high-priced condo. Leaving the custom-carved wooden door unlocked and open just in case they needed to make a quick escape, they each prayed for the best. Considering what the pair had just been through back home in Detroit and the overall condition of the room, neither Kenya nor London knew what to expect with each passing step that they took.

It was burning hot inside the condo. Kenya raised her hand to the thermostat, turning off the heat that was strangely on full blast, like Miami. The temperature had caused the walls to sweat and each girl to immediately become drenched in perspiration. As the seconds past, it was becoming painstakingly clear something was drastically wrong. First, all the lights in the house being left turned on, then the heating system on the nut, and of course, her living room destroyed. What else was next? What else could possibly go wrong? Kenya was beyond terrified and needed her man by her side, not her scary cat and judgmental sister.

"Storm! Baby, are you here?" she pleaded repeatedly, hoping for a response. "Are you at home? Please answer me, baby—please!"

London darted her eyes around her twin's supposedly new home. She looked at the huge painting hanging over the fireplace that was crooked and peeling away from the frame. Next, she focused her sights onto the obviously damaged wine-colored leather furniture, as well as the completely destroyed, crushed coffee table. Despite the terrible mildew odor that filled the room and the mess that surrounded them, London could tell that Kenya once had the condo organized and magazine worthy, but now was not the time to complement her on her style or flare for fashion.

The newly laid, plush wall-to-wall white carpet was now soiled with debris. It was soaked with filthy water turning some areas dark brown. The soles of the girls' shoes were wet, submerging deep into the carpet, making squishing sounds with each step. Sections of the ceiling were caved in, exposing the floor support beams of the upstairs rooms, along with a constant stream of water still causing chaos.

"Listen sis, seriously, from the look of things it seems as if your so-so brain-challenged, brilliant boyfriend must have left the water running somewhere in the house. He must be the smartest man alive. Kenya girl, you are so lucky to have a man like him." London snickered at her twin, shaking her head. "We need to at least get the water turned off!"

"Damn London, college did teach ya li'l behind one thing!" Kenya put her hand on her hip, definitely not in the mood. "To be a real smart-ass!" She wiped the dripping sweat off her forehead, rolled her eyes, and waved her hand in London's face. "And FYI, he's not my boyfriend! Remember the ring! Remember this here ring, heffa! My man put a ring on it for real!"

The tension that was originally felt when they walked into the condo was broken briefly by the girls clowning on one another.

"Okay, 'Miss I Got The Ring', why don't you go upstairs and see where all this water is coming from. I'll try to open some of these windows and let some fresh air in here. I can hardly breathe in this palace of yours."

"You mean you want me to go up those stairs all by myself?" Kenya pouted with her lips stuck out. "You must be insane or something! I don't know what's up them damn stairs!"

London laughed at her sister. "You so big and bad all the time, thinking you can beat the world! Why don't you go by ya dang-gone self? Who stopping you?"

"Stop playing around so much and come on." Kenya yanked her sister by the shoulder. Arm in arm, they both slowly headed toward the staircase.

The closer they crept to the top of the condo stairs, they could clearly hear the sounds of water running. The floor on the upper level was much more damaged than the downstairs, causing the twins to lean on each other for support so they wouldn't slip or fall. The horrible smell that'd taken over the living room was getting worse. The water that drenched the carpet was more infested with debris than the bottom of the condo.

"It must've been the fish tank that overflowed," Kenya finally reasoned with herself, trying to calm her nerves. She started feeling somewhat relieved at the thought all this bullshit she'd been met with on her return home was nothing more than an unfortunate accident. "That's the only water that could be flowing from that direction. Maybe the pump broke or something. That has to be some of Storm's dead fish or something like that." She waved her hand across her nose.

"Yeah, you're probably right, Kenya. That's got to be it. I mean, that's the only reasonable explanation for this ratchet smell." Using the collar of her shirt as a mask, London rolled her eyes. As they got to the edge of the slightly cracked den door, pushing it wide open, the odor worsened. The smothering heat that was trapped inside rushed out and hit them smack dead in the face. "Oh, dang gee! It smells like not some, but all your fish are already dead." London twisted her face, turning up her lip. "God it smells bad! *Urggg*, I wanna throw up! Yuk!"

"All right girl—damn! Stop with all the dramatics and carrying on! I know it stank bad as hell, but listen, I'm gonna run in my bedroom and get the telephone number to the condo management so they can send someone out here ASAP. You go in and at least see if any of them are still alive." Kenya tightly placed her hand over her nose and mouth, hoping to stop the overpowering stench from filling her throat. "I'll be right back. Shit! Storm is gonna be pissed the hell off. He put a lot of dough into that freaking aquarium." She left her sister standing in the hallway as she disappeared into her bedroom.

This is so dang-gone gross, London thought, walking into the unfamiliar room, searching the wall for the light switch. She felt the side of her tan Payless loafers being filled with water she could only assume was contaminated. Carefully, she bent down to roll up her pants legs that were dragging along the floor, making each step much grimier than the last. "Kenya, you is gonna replace my shoes! Cheap or not—I just bought these!" She angrily barked out, hoping her sister heard her declaration. The fish tank was located over on the far left side of the spacious room. It was making a terrible piercing, grinding sound. She wanted to place her hands on her ears to block some of the annoying noise, but would have to stop using her collar as a mask. At this point the smell was worse than the sound, so she chose to endure the lesser of two evils.

London slowly headed over to investigate the huge fish tank and hopefully solve the source of the problem.

Kenya made it to the side of her and Storm's king-sized bed. Disgusted at what kind of cleanup she was facing, she sat down on the edge of the mattress. Opening the nightstand drawer, she grabbed the business-card flyer with all the condo management's contact numbers on it. As she quickly scanned down the list, she overheard the sound of more water flowing from one of the adjoining bathrooms.

The two baths that were connected from the master bedroom were designed differently to fit both her and Storm's own individual taste.

I know Storm's crazy self ain't leave the water on in his precious bathroom! He better not have! Kenya huffed, thinking to herself as she leaped to her feet, bolting into the bathroom. *If he did, then that's his ass! I swear on everything that's in his pockets! He got my entire house on the nut smelling and looking like God-knows-what!*

When Kenya ran inside, she immediately lost her balance from all the water spewed across the marble floor. Not able to catch herself from falling, she slid, scraping her arm and shoulder on the way down. "Ain't this a bitch," she mumbled angrily, soaked to her skin. "Now my clothes are ruined and shit! He's gonna straight-up replace my outfit! Trust and believe! Who does this—who? First, he leaves the heat blasting on hell, lets the fish tank run over, now this! Where they do that at?"

Sure enough, she quickly realized the water was indeed turned on full speed in the tub and had overflowed. The room smelled just like raw, dirty rotten sewage. Kenya, nauseated, was almost in tears again as she tried getting up and slipped back down in all the muck. Instead of attempting to walk over to shut the water off, she wisely decided to crawl. At this point, it would be much easier than trying to stand up. So, on her hands and knees, drenched, slimy, and covered in God-knows-what, Kenya cursed the love of her life as she tried to maintain her composure through the turmoil.

"I'm gonna flat-out kill that fool Storm when I see him. How could he be so careless? This is ridiculous!"

London cautiously neared the corner of the room. Not able to move, she started to hyperventilate at the sight of the huge aquarium and what was seemingly inside. Her entire body was shaking uncontrollably and she became light-headed. She opened her mouth to yell out her sister's name, but no sound was coming out. Terrified, London grasped for air, holding her chest while backing up slowly.

"Kenyaaaaa! . . . Kenyaaaaa!" she stuttered loudly, finally getting the words together. "Come here quick! Hurry up! Please hurry!" London's heart was pounding and seemed as if it was going to jump out her body. With her adrenaline racing, the once naive-to-life college student bolted out the room. Fighting to make sense of what she'd just seen, she stumbled into the debris-covered hallway. Her system broke all the way down. She couldn't hold back any longer. Disgusted beyond belief, London threw up all over herself and the already filth-soiled carpet. "Kenya! Kenya!" Gagging, she continued to call out while wiping her mouth with the sleeve of her shirt.

London's repeated shouts of fear were interrupted by a constant assault of Kenya's high-pitched screams. Desperate to reunite with her twin, she followed the sound of her sister's voice down the hall, in the bedroom, and lastly into the bathroom. "Kenya! Kenya! Please—you have to hurry and come with me," London shouted loudly. "You need to see this! Matter of fact—we need to get out of here!"

Focused on revealing what she'd seen, London rushed inside the bathroom. Painfully, she had the same misfortune as Kenya, sliding across the floor past the sink and toilet, landing flat on her back. London, still frightened, half out her mind, was now next to a sobbing, also scared and in shock, Kenya, who couldn't do anything but point her trembling finger. Placing both hands down on the cold, dirty, and wet marble floor, London sat up and reached for her twin. "What is it Kenya? What are you trying to say? What is it?"

No words came out her otherwise tough-natured sister's mouth as she continued to point. Not knowing what to expect in this surprising house of horrors, London took a deep breath, preparing herself for more of the unknown. Leaning over, she bravely peeked over into the bathtub, taking a long, hard stare. Astonished once again, London felt as if she and Kenya were costarring in a bad, low-budget scary movie, considering all the bad luck that was following them around.

Chapter Twenty-two

Oh, Shit!

"Who is this, Kenya?" a shocked London demanded to know after seeing a body floating in the tub. "Do you know this man? Kenya, is this your boyfriend? Is it?"

Kenya was hysterical and trembling. In a trancelike state, she seemed not to comprehend anything that her sister was asking. The unthinkable was now happening to them all over again: another dead body at their feet. After crawling through the toxic mess and leaning over to turn the knob, London found the totally nude, dead, decaying, bloated body ass-up underwater. And to make matters even more horrible, it had been decapitated.

"Please, Kenya. Listen to me!" London grabbed her twin's shoulders, shaking her hard. "Kenya, do you hear me? Listen—you've got to snap out of it! It might be somebody still in here. We need to get out of this place and call the police ASAP! Kenya—listen!"

London was getting no response from a zombielike Kenya and could only think of one thing to do. So, with one of her wet hands, London raised back with all her strength and knocked the cow-walking shit out of her. *Smack!* The sound was so loud it instantly woke Kenya up out her trance. London rubbed her stinging hand and repeated her first question. "Now, is this Storm? Is this your boyfriend?"

"Naw, sis. Naw, that's not him. Oh my God—I'm not sure who that is!" a red-faced Kenya screamed, somehow making it to her feet and running out the bathroom, back into the bedroom. Instinctively she rushed over to the closet, getting one of the many guns that were stashed all around the condo.

Wanting to protect herself as well as London, she put one up top. "I don't know what the hell is going on. I need to find Storm! He'll know what to do! This is crazy! This whole thing is crazy!"

London was hot on her sister's heels and kept the questions coming one after another. "Kenya—we should get out of here! We should call the damn police! And are you sure that isn't Storm?" London stared at Kenya, waiting for the answer.

"Dang, what in the hell is wrong with you? Are you crazy? I just said that ain't Storm in there!" Kenya was getting pissed about this nightmare she was caught up in and all the unanswered questions that were coming along with it. "Don't you think I know my own man, London, head or no head?"

"Well?" London replied. "What are you waiting for? We need to call the police!

"Forget calling the damn cops! You must be out ya rabbit-ass mind! And just how would we explain this bullshit, a mysterious body floating in the tub with the freaking head missing?"

Pulling her by the arm, London forced her angry, now gun-carrying twin out the bedroom, down the hallway. "Come with me, Kenya. I need to show you something that might help you figure out exactly who that could be floating in your tub."

As the pair cautiously walked into the den, Kenya, urged by her twin, gradually eased over to the noisy fish tank and got a good look.

"What the—! Oh, hell naw!" The once—strong-minded female was standing face-to-face with a head submerged in the corner of the aquarium. Its eyes were half eaten and mutilated by the few larger-than-normal fish that were still alive, swimming in and out of its mouth. Weak in the knees, Kenya was seconds away from passing out. A familiar letter-A, custom-designed yellow diamond earring was barely glistening through the dirty water. She recognized it immediately as one of three that she, Deacon, and Storm wore religiously to represent their club, Alley Cats. Kenya clutched her chest, falling back over toward the doorway and falling into her sister's arms. Confused, she shivered with fear and total, chaotic uncertainty. "Why? Why? I don't understand!"

"Do you know him, Kenya—do you? Is that Storm?" London once again coldly drilled, talking over the piercing sound that still filled the air. "Is it?"

"Damn bitch! What the fuck is wrong with you?" Kenya snatched away, ready to attack her own blood. "Naw, that ain't no motherfucking Storm! Now stop asking me that dumb shit and acting so stupid!"

London knew that Kenya was in shock, so she let all of her disrespectful comments go without firing back her own round of insults. "Well, who is it, then? Do you know? Can you recognize him?"

"Yeah, I know." Kenya's face was full of sorrow and regret. She remorsefully dropped her head down, holding the huge gun tightly in her small hand. "It's Storm's best friend—his boy Deacon. They were supposed to be together when they left town." Kenya started to let her tears pour. "But if they left town, why is Deacon here? And where is Storm?"

"Wow!" London shook her head in disbelief. "Listen, sis, enough of this bizarre madness we going through. We need to first get out of here and secondly call the police!"

"I'm scared, London! I'm really, really scared!"

London hugged her twin, trying her best to console her. "We need to call the police, Kenya." She placed both hands on her sister's shoulder, looking her dead in the eyes. "We need some help. I mean, seriously, what kind of folk do you know in this awful town who would do something so heinous like this? And are you sure they're not coming back or worst than that, still in here somewhere! What kinda people you deal with?"

"Yeah, right!" Kenya judgmentally looked at London with a dumb expression and replied. "Probably the same assholes who were trying to get at you for that PAID bullshit you so insistent with organizing! That's the only people I can think of. Now, how about that?" Kenya still found it hard to believe this was happening to her; to them. "But who would do something as treacherous as cut off a human's head? What have you done? Who you done pissed off with those speeches of yours?"

"Yeah, all right, maybe I do have some enemies, but I don't understand. What in the world would your boyfriend's friend have to do with me and my personal business?" London fired back, folding her arms.

"Who knows?" Kenya wiped her tears away, trying to regain her composure. "But one thing is for sure. It's no way in hell we can call the cops to find out that answer. We definitely can't do that!"

"Okay then, Kenya. What's the game plan? We gotta do something—I mean, it's a dead body in your bathtub and a head over there! I vote for calling the damn police!"

"Look, I'm gonna call O.T. He'll know what we should do and hopefully he's heard from Storm."

"Who is O.T.?"

"That's my man's little brother. He's running Alley Cats for Deacon and Storm while they're out of town."

"And what in the world is Alley Cats?" London quizzed as things grew weirder by the moment.

"That's the strip club that Deacon and Storm own. They're partners."

"Well, sis," she pointed at the aquarium that was still loud before pulling the plug out the wall socket. "I guess you mean the club that Storm owns now. Don't you?"

"Damn, London, that's some real fucked-up shit to say right about now!" Kenya glanced at the bedroom door, getting chills thinking about Deacon's headless floating body, as they passed on the way downstairs. "But, yeah, I guess you're right. It is Storm's now."

London shrugged her shoulders, following her sister out onto the front porch. They moved their luggage to the side of the door and sat on the bottom stair. Kenya, praying for the best, pulled out her cell.

"I've gotta make this call to O.T., so we can get some damn help!" Kenya nervously fumbled with her phone.

"Okay, I know he's Storm's brother, but what is he, a detective or something? I mean . . ." London questioned her twin, wondering what was coming next. "Can he help with a headless corpse in a tub? Just what kind of people are you out here affiliating with?"

"Damn, London, damn! Stop asking me all of them questions and let me make this fucking call! Damn!"

"Okay, okay, sorry to annoy you! Go ahead and call him."

With her heart beating overtime, Kenya nervously dialed O.T.'s number. After about four or five rings, Storm's grumpy-voiced brother answered.

Chapter Twenty-three

What Da Hell

"Yeah, speak on it!" O.T. was angry and pissed off by being disturbed from his sleep. "And you better make the shit quick, fast, and in a hurry with your words!"

"Hey O.T., this is Kenya."

"I know who it is," he barely mumbled. "What you want so damn early in the morning? A nigga like me just got in the bed good and shit."

"I was wondering, have you talked to Storm yet?" Kenya held her breath, waiting for his response. She prayed to God that he would say yes.

"That's why you called me?" O.T. shouted through the phone, loud enough for London to hear. "You blowing up my phone because you can't catch up with dude? You set tripping like that? Come on now, Kenya, that's straight-up foul!" He was fed up with her and her constant calls.

"O.T., listen, I swear I'm sorry to wake you up, but this is a real emergency. Now, have you spoken to him or not?"

Sensing the seriousness in her attitude, he finally answered. "Naw, girl I ain't. What's wrong? What's the deal? I ain't talked to him or Deacon since they left."

"Oh my God!" Kenya closed her eyes, crying softly as she lowered her head.

"*Oh my God* what?" O.T. sat up in the bed and started to panic. "What the fuck is wrong, Kenya—what?"

Kenya's voice was cracking as she spoke. "I need you to come over here as soon as possible! I mean right damn now! For real, O.T., now!"

"What the fuck is wrong, Kenya?" he repeated, putting bass in his tone. "Stop playing around with me and let me know!"

A sound-asleep Paris, under the thin blanket lying next to O.T., immediately jumped up, startled by his loud, boisterous demands. "Who is that?" she mouthed the words. "What's going on? What's wrong? It better not be no bitch!"

"Chill on all that. It's Kenya! Something is wrong and shit!" O.T. was fuming as he shook his head at his girl and her always jealous behavior. He quickly turned his attention back to the phone conversation with Kenya. "Listen, can you cut the games out and give a brother a damn clue? Do I need to bring some fire over there or what? What's the deal?"

"I can't tell you over the phone," Kenya hysterically whined. "I need for you to just come over here now. Hurry, it's on a nine-one-one tip—real talk!"

"Okay, dig that. I'm on my way, Kenya! Just sit tight!"

Asking God for strength, she closed her cell phone, dropping her head once more. The reality of the situation was setting in for Kenya. This was a living nightmare she was trapped in. O.T. had just confirmed that Deacon and Storm had indeed left town together. Now she couldn't get in touch with her man, his brother hadn't heard from him, the condo was destroyed, and poor Deacon was dead as a doorknob. Whatever the explanation was could only mean trouble.

O.T. and Paris pulled up in front of the condo doing damn near a hundred miles per hour, certainly waking a neighbor or two. Paris slammed down hard on the brakes of her triple-black Chrysler 300M, causing the tires to come to a screeching, sudden halt. Leaping out the car before it came to a complete stop, O.T. ran up the walkway to see Kenya sobbing and another girl with her arm around her. By the time he got closer, the other girl raised her face, with its troubled expression, to meet his.

"What the fuck!" He had a puzzled look on his face as he turned back and forth, staring at both females sitting on the stairs. "Who the fuck?" O.T. shook his head in disbelief as Paris made her way to the group.

"Kenya? What the hell?" Paris, now totally bewildered, also questioned her best friend. "I don't understand."

"Yeah, who you telling? Me either!" O.T. raised his eyebrows. "This is straight wild!" The couple looked like they'd both seen a ghost.

Kenya stood up, wiping her face, leaving her twin sitting on the stair. "Hey, Paris. Hey, O.T. I know y'all confused and I'm gonna explain all of it later, I promise, but something awful done happened."

O.T., like Paris, couldn't take his eyes off of London. He was listening to the words come out of Kenya's mouth, but was in a daze trying to put two and two together. This was some *Twilight Zone*–type of bullshit to him.

"Y'all, this is my twin sister, London. She lives back out east in Detroit," Kenya quickly explained. "She's gonna stay with me and Storm for a little while."

"You got a twin? All this time and you didn't tell me? I thought we was way better than that!" Paris felt insulted and betrayed by her best friend. "What was the big hush-hush secret?" she asked, while taking her time giving London the once-over.

"Ain't this some shit! Do my brother know about this?" O.T. threw both his arms up in the air in a harsh rage. "Damn, Kenya! Your ass is straight-up out of order! You must be on crack or something! It's been one thang after another with you! And what's all this mess on you? Damn, you stank!"

London sat with a stern expression of amazement at the two strangers who were supposed to be helping the nerve-racking situation give her sister the third degree.

"Listen, O.T . . . I—" Kenya tried her best to defend her deceitful actions before he continued speaking, stopping her in mid-sentence.

"Matter of fact, I know motherfucking well this ain't the damn emergency?" He spit on the grass and raised one of his tan-colored, untied Timberland boots onto the step next to London's leg.

Kenya's filthy fingers rubbed her forehead before moving strands of hair behind her ear. "Damn y'all, I know I was wrong for not mentioning it, but—"

"But what?" Paris, like O.T. had just done, cut her off. "You forgot? It slipped your mind all the times we done hung out?"

London was also completely thrown off that her own identical twin sister had somehow conveniently chose not to acknowledge her very existence to these people whom she had been living with for months. She would surely deal with that hurtful issue later, but for the time being, London had enough of them beating up her sister with all the questions and stepped in to intervene.

"I'm very sorry that you two supposed friends seem to have some sort of a gigantic problem with her having family out in this big world, but I think there's a much larger dilemma that we all have to deal with back in there." Covered in smelly muck on her hands and face, she rolled her eyes, pointing toward the cracked front door.

London's first impression of Kenya's friends and so-called great life was not very impressive, to say the least. Ready to discover the real reason for the late-night call, O.T. and Paris followed the twins into the destroyed home. Pulling their shirts over their noses to shield the overwhelming, eye-stinging stench, they both started to sweat.

"What the hell happened in this bitch?" O.T. frowned as he reached in his waistband, snatching out his pistol.

Paris was stunned, staying close to O.T. when she saw the awful condition inside the condo that Kenya had just remodeled.

"Come on upstairs, O.T." Kenya sighed. "That's the real and true problem."

"What's up there?" he grilled before bracin' up on the grip of his shiny, chrome-handled 9 mm. "What other crazy stuff you got going on?"

"It's not like that!" Kenya begged her fiancé's brother. "Please, just come with me. I couldn't explain what's up there for a million dollars. Plus, if I tried you wouldn't believe me anyhow! So just come on."

O.T. turned to go with Kenya. "Okay, girl, let's roll!" Paris was right behind him.

"You should stay down here with me," London suggested to her, gently grabbing her by the arm. "It's nothing that you would want to remember."

Kenya sympathetically looked at her friend, urging her that London was 100 percent right. It would be much better for her to stay in the living room or what was left of it. Paris hesitantly agreed, standing silent next to London on the soaking wet carpet. As they watched Kenya and O.T. navigate their way up the staircase, London got a slight chill in the muggy living room in anticipation of what Kenya and him were about to encounter.

"What's up there?" Paris broke the ice out of curiosity, staring at London, then at the caved-in ceiling. "Can you at least tell me? Clue a sista in! And damn, y'all look just the hell alike!"

"Trouble!" London replied, glancing up toward the stairs, trying to remain calm. "A lot of trouble!"

"Okay Kenya, we up here. Now what in the hell is the big surprise you got for me other than the living room is tore up?"

"You'll see, O.T., just follow me." Kenya led him down the hallway into her and Storm's bedroom.

"Urggh . . . dang! The smell is getting worse!" Still holding his gun tightly, he looked down at his new boots that were now ruined from all the water.

"It's in there." Kenya had broken down into tears as she nodded toward the bathroom door. "Go see for yourself. I'll be out here. I can't go back in there—not now. And be careful. It's extremely slippery on that floor." She wanted him to go in there alone and check it out. There was absolutely no desire for her to want to see Deacon in that state ever again.

"Oh, shit! Oh, fuck! Hell naw!" Kenya could hear O.T. stomping his feet, yelling at the top of his lungs as the water on the floor splashed. "What the fuck happened? Oh, hell naw! Kenya! Kenya!" He ran into the bedroom, where she was standing with a face full of flowing tears. "Where's his fucking head! Who the hell did this to my peoples?" O.T. was confused and running around the room from side to side. "Where is my fucking brother? Tell me, Kenya! Tell me!" O.T. demanded, snatching her up by the collar. "Where the fuck is he at?"

Kenya was having trouble breathing as she unsuccessfully struggled to get loose from his strong grip. "You're hurting me, O.T.," she managed to say. "Let me go—please."

Shaking off his initial shock, he came back to earth and apologized. "Damn, Kenya, I'm sorry, but this shit is foul. I don't know what the fuck is going on here." He walked away from her and looked back in the bathroom once more to make sure he had truly seen what he thought he'd seen. "Where that guy's dome at and what about my brother? Is he in here too—in the house? Please tell me he ain't!" He dropped his head, swallowing extra hard, holding his gun down at his side as he paced. The wrong answer would cause him to bug all the way out.

"Naw, O.T., I haven't heard from him ever since I flew back home to Detroit. I've been calling his cell phone day after day and it keeps going straight to voice mail. That's why I kept calling you."

A relieved O.T. raised his face to look at Kenya dead on. "Do you know what went down here?"

"Nope—I don't. Me and my sister came home and the house was just like this." Kenya blew her nose with one of Storm's winter-white wife beaters that were lying across the bed. "The bottom was messed up and we heard water running. When we got up here to see where the water was coming from, I found Deacon's body in there."

"I can't believe this bullshit!" O.T. put his gun back in his waistband. "Whoever did that shit is ruthless as hell! Where's dude's hat rack at anyhow? Do you know?"

Kenya and he stepped out into the heavy-odor–filled hallway. "Go down there in the den and look in Storm's fish tank."

"Yeah, right!" O.T. frowned, dialing his brother's cell number. "Come on now, Kenya! I know you gotta be bullshittin'!"

"I'm not playing. I'm serious. Go see for yourself. I wouldn't joke about something like that—not now."

"This is wild!" O.T. took in all the damage done in the condo as he walked in the den door with his cell phone up to his ear. By the time he came out, he was sweating bullets and fanning his hand in front of his face.

Paris and London were waiting at the end of the stairs as Kenya and O.T. came into view.

"What was it?" Paris grilled her man, noticing he was look-ing overly distressed. "Is it bad? Tell me! What was up there? What did you see?"

"Yeah, shit is fucked—really, really fucked up!" He softly touched Paris on her cheek. "We gotta figure this mess out quick and get in touch with my brother!"

All the girls stood silent in anticipation of what O.T., a known screwup and hot-tempered personality, had in store. Out of the two brothers, he was no doubt the irresponsible one. That was pretty much common knowledge with anyone who came in contact with them both. Kenya knew firsthand O.T. was a flat-out fool, but for now, he was her only hope of trying to retrace Storm and Deacon's last few days. She and he took turns blowing up Storm's cell phone in hopes that he would pick up and shed some sort of a light on all this madness.

While they waited, hoped, and prayed, O.T. and the three girls sat down on the stairs of the porch, coming up with a scheme to try to get Deacon's body and head out the crib. Until one of them talked to Storm and knew exactly what the deal was, they thought it would be much better to keep Deacon's brutal murder on the down-low. If the shit hit the fan out in the streets that Deacon was dead and Storm was missing, it would be sheer pandemonium. The different crews around town would think it would be their chance to try to take over drug territory that Storm and his fellas had worked so hard to pump up.

O.T. had no thoughts of blessing them with that golden opportunity. That meant the four of them, a skeptical London included, would be on their own in this awful mess. Repeatedly getting her fiancé's voice mail was causing a red-eyed Kenya to have a nervous breakdown from worry as the anxiety built. Trying to remain positive, her heart broke a little bit each passing second he didn't call back.

"What could have gone wrong? This just ain't right," O.T. wondered out loud, as he had Kenya collecting every sheet and blanket she could find. "As soon as we get this body up out of here, I'm gonna call that ho-ass nigga Royce and see what he know. He was supposed to be with Deacon and Storm when they left town. I know that old wannabe pimp know something—he gotsta to!"

Taking matters into his own hands, he knew he had to do the majority of the dirty work. As much as fearless street soldiers he knew his woman Paris and Kenya were, a headless body and a chopped-off head of a dude they had just partied with would be too much for the average man to stomach, let alone two females. O.T. drained all the water out the bathtub as well as the aquarium. Deacon's torso was bloated, stiff, and waterlogged, making it feel almost three times its normal body weight. Putting on two pairs of the rubber gloves that Paris had ran and bought from the corner store, he tried lifting Deacon up by himself, but it was no use. O.T. then instructed an extremely reluctant London and an eager-to-please Paris to put on gloves to help him. They both quickly came to his aid, knowing this was no time to argue. He then yelled out for his soon-to-be sister-in-law, but by that time the usually scared-of-nothing Kenya was, understandably, of no fucking good to any of them or herself. The once good girl turned all the way bad, was curled up on the edge of the bed, rocking back and forth with one of her beloved Storm's shirts in her arms.

The newly formed trio moved on with O.T.'s plan, wrapping the body first in a sheet, then in two fluffy comforters. Paris luckily found several old telephone cords out of the utility closet so they could tie Deacon snug. London had located a box of heavy-duty Home Depot garbage bags, which she doubled up. Holding the bags wide open, she turned away as O.T. dropped the slimy, grotesque head inside.

Paris, the Bonnie to his Clyde, opened the garage of the condo, pulling her car all the way in, parking it next to Kenya's. When the door was shut and the coast was clear, London, Paris, and O.T. struggled to drag the freakishly heavy body out. On the count of three, they lifted Deacon, throwing him into the trunk. The weight caused the new car to bounce downwards to the garage pavement before slowly lifting back up. O.T. made the comment they should've driven his truck. Both Paris and London gave him the "as if you knew you were coming to remove a dead body, nigga, tonight" side eye.

"O.T., baby we need to get cleaned up and at least get this blood off of our clothes," Paris, thinking well ahead, suggested. "We don't want to get pulled over in this neighborhood with these clothes on."

"I've got nine motherfucking reasons none of these white Rodney King–ass-beating sons of bitches betta not fuck with nan one of us tonight!" O.T. raised his shirt up, revealing his pistol as well as his washboard abs that he spent hours working out to achieve. "But you right, I'm gonna go back upstairs and get some of Storm's gear to throw on. I'll grab one of Kenya's track suits for you."

"Thanks, boo." Paris leaned over, giving him a fast kiss on the lips. "Hurry up, okay? I don't want Deacon's blood and the rest of those fluids to leak through that blanket and stain the trunk carpet. You know how much they be charging to detail shit like that out!"

London stood back, amazed at the calm and coolness of the couple. It was as if they encountered this type of bizarre occurrence on a daily basis. *What has Kenya gotten me into? This is pure madness!* She pondered silently, wishing she was anywhere in the world other than where she was, doing what she was doing. *One day I'm at school, working toward my degree; the next, I'm tangled up in covering up not one, but two murders. God, this is so messed up—so wrong!*

After washing their faces and hands, getting themselves looking somewhat halfway decent, O.T. and Paris were ready to roll. With Paris behind the wheel, they cautiously drove off, trying to look as inconspicuous as possible. This was the one time, if any, that the gangsta love duo didn't need to get pulled over by the cops. The two of them would dispose of the body, while O.T. left his new partner in crime, London, in charge of getting Kenya's panicked, grief-stricken-ass together. Maybe London could get her sister to postpone her sudden hysterical breakdown and relax so that they could figure this strange mystery out.

Now was definitely not the time for any of the three to punk out and fold. If ever there was a night that a person had to think and react with their mind and not their heart, this, hands-down, would be that goddamned night.

Chapter Twenty-four

It Just Got Real

Kenya was all cried out. Full of emotion, she walked down the stairs to find her sister trying her best to salvage whatever she could from the lower level of the home. "Hey, sis," Kenya sniffed, pushing the redial button on her phone. "Is O.T. back yet? Have you seen him or Paris?"

"Oh, please, stop it! Don't you think you would have heard that loud, obnoxious Negro you deal with?" London barked, going from room to room, throwing stuff into a garbage bag.

"Girl, he's not that bad, girl!" For the first time since they had returned from the airport, Kenya gave her twin a slight grin, holding the phone to her ear. "You just gotta get used to him. He'll grow on you after a while."

"Well, I'm sorry. I have no intentions whatsoever of him growing on me. I feel sorry for his girlfriend and anyone else that has the misfortune to spend any more than ten minutes in his presence." London went on making wise comments pertaining to O.T.'s offbeat character. "He's a real jerk if I ever met one! She's a better woman than me."

Kenya held up her hand to shush London while she tried to leave another message in Storm's voice mail. However, it already was full, making that task impossible. Kenya was heated all over again, throwing her phone against the still-wet walls. Pounding her fist on the table, worry started once more to consume her thoughts. London, startled, ran from the kitchen to see her sister enraged.

"I swear to God I'm gonna kill a motherfucker if something done happened to him! I swear I am—I swear!"

"Calm down, Kenya!" London urged.

Just as Kenya finished ranting, Paris and O.T. returned.
London wasted no time in opening the door to let the pair
inside.

"Did you find out something?" Kenya rushed up to O.T.,
almost knocking him off his feet. "Did he call? Have you heard
anything? Tell me he called you!"

"Naw, baby girl," he regretfully hated to say. "But I did find
out that fugazy wannabe playa Royce's new number and shit."

"Well, was he with them? Do he know something? Where
did he say Storm was?"

"Kenya, pump ya brakes, will ya?" O.T. said, moving her to
the side so that Paris could get all the way in the condo door.
"His phone goes straight to voice mail too. I tried calling that
fool at least a good ten times—same thing—voice mail."

"Damn!" Kenya shook her head, desperate for any information to ease her fears.

"Relax, girl!" Paris spoke up, hugging her friend. "It's gonna
be okay. Storm is a soldier—you know that. He's gonna call.
Don't worry—you'll see."

"When I get you and your sister settled, I'm gonna shoot by
Royce's peoples and try to find out if they heard from him yet.
Just try to chill," he reasoned, obviously still worried himself.
"I'm on it!"

"I'm trying to be calm, but this whole thing don't make no
sense to me at all!" Kenya whimpered, not being able to hold
back another round of tears. "I need to stay here just in case
he come home!"

"Listen up, girl. Me and Paris done handled the Deacon situation for now, may he rest in peace, but I still don't think it's
safe in here. Whoever did all this and killed my manz might
come back. Y'all should just jet until we hear something."

"No damn kidding, Sherlock," London interrupted, ready to
be anywhere but there.

The tension in the air and dislike she was feeling for O.T.
was transparent and obvious to the entire room. Being a
career class-A asshole was second nature to O.T., so he was
used to people having an instant hatred of him. Brushing her
smart comments off as nothing, he finished his statement
without even missing a beat.

"Look, I'll fall through tomorrow myself and really clean up the bathroom and that nasty-ass fish tank with bleach and some of that strong-ass industrial-strength disinfectant that's down at the club. We can't risk letting anybody else inside here until we know what's what."

Everyone, even Kenya, agreed with O.T. that it would be for the best for the twins to vacate the premises, at least for the time being. Paris, loyal to the end, started to help London gather some of Kenya's things, so she and O.T. could take them to get a hotel room until they could get a handle on the real deal and sometime down the line get some workmen over to survey and repair the damaged condo. Besides, it was no way on God's green earth that the girls were gonna feel comfortable spending one night in a spot where who-knows-what had taken place.

"Come on, y'all got enough stuff for a few days."

"All right, O.T., we're coming." Kenya replied. After close to a hour of being in the house, all four of them emerged out onto the small porch. O.T. carried most of the bags to Kenya's car, while Paris grabbed the rest. London stood over toward the far side of the door as Kenya locked up, trying to secure the rest of her belongings even though crime almost never occurred in their secure community. In the midst of all the commotion that'd taken place since their arrival from Detroit, the overflowing of the flower-design mailbox was overlooked.

"Hey, Kenya, it looks as if you've got a lot of mail piled up in this box. You want me to get it?"

"Yeah, London—grab it out for me. Just throw all that mess in your bag. It ain't probably shit but a bunch of bills and catalogues. I ain't got time to give a damn about that junk now!"

Kenya double-checked the locks on the condo door; the same locks that failed to keep the intruders out. London stuffed all the mail, including a small-sized manila envelope, in her purse without even a second thought. She didn't take notice that a small parcel had nothing written on it front or back; meaning that more than likely, someone had to have left it in the mailbox personally.

***

After both taking showers, trying to unpack a few things and relax, Kenya laid across the bed dialing Storm's number once more, while London emptied the items in her purse onto the dresser in search of a comb and a brush.

"Oh, snap! What was that?" Startled, she leaped backward, almost tripping over her own feet.

"What's wrong, London? What is it?"

"Girl, there's something moving in this envelope."

"What envelope?"

"That one—right there," London pointed from afar.

"You bugging! Where did you get it from? And what you mean *moving*?"

"Stop playing with me, fool! It's the mail from your house, Kenya! That's where I got it from!"

"Well, who is it addressed to?" Kenya bit her lower lip as they both moved over closer toward the hotel door.

Bzzzzzzzz . . . The envelope vibrated once again.

"Go over there, London, and see what it is."

"Excuse me, Miss Kenya, but that's your dang-gone package, not mine! It came from your house—your mail! So you go!"

"Okay, but come with me," Kenya bargained with her sister.

As they slowly approached the dresser, the mystery mail buzzed once more. Kenya bravely reached over, carefully picking the package up with two fingers. Moving slowly, she walked over to the lamp on the desk. Taking a deep breath, she tried holding it up to the light, but couldn't make out its contents.

"Just open it," London insisted, knowing if it was a fragile bomb they'd both be dead by now. "It's not explosive, but be careful of poison."

"Okay, okay, okay!" Kenya tore open the envelope, dumping what was inside onto the bed.

"I'm confused. A silly old cell phone and an old burgundy-velvet ring box?" London casually asked, expecting something more. "Who would send you stuff like that?"

Kenya placed her hand over her mouth to muffle her scream. "That's Storm's cell phone! He's the only one who I know that has a neon-green antenna on his shit and an airbrushed tiger on the back! That's his phone!"

"Are you sure?"

"Yeah, London, I'm certain. This is definitely his!" Kenya snatched the phone off the bed, flipping it open. It said the words *Capacity Full* across the screen.

"What about the ring box, Kenya? Have you seen it before or what? What's in it?" the twin asked her confused sister.

"I'm still bugging out on this phone," Kenya told her sibling, holding it up in her hand.

"Well, I'm gonna open it." London leaned over, swooping up the small velvet box, shaking it slightly before peeking inside.

"What's in there?" Kenya waited before starting to go through Storm's phone for any clues to his whereabouts.

"Oh my God! Ugh!" London dropped the box on the carpet, revealing a small note and what appeared to be a severed piece of an earlobe with a diamond earring still attached. To Kenya's dismay, it was the same earring that Deacon was wearing; the same one that she also owned. It was Storm's. It had to be. Now it was proof positive that Storm was definitely injured badly, in danger or worse than that, dead.

Kenya, exhausted from grief, fell to the carpet, passing out. As her twin sister lay sprawled out on the hotel-room floor, London didn't know what else to do. Without hesitation, she rushed to the telephone, dialing the number that O.T. left for her. There was no need calling the cops for assistance. The way Kenya, Paris, and O.T. made it seem, they couldn't help anyhow.

Chapter Twenty-five

You Owe Me!

O.T. found the girls scrunched together down in the corner, near the door of the hotel room. "Where is it at?" He scanned the room with his eyes darting around.

"By the side of the bed." Kenya threw her hand in the direction of the small box. "It's over there."

O.T. swiftly bolted to the other side of the bed, bending down on one knee. London watched the cocky, perfect muscle-ripped, sagged-jeans, baseball-cap-backward–wearing thug, turn into melted butter as he held the evidence of his brother's apparent harm in his rough, seemingly strong hands. London could now for the first time since encountering O.T. somehow relate to his pain. Just like that, he now was a human in her eyes, instead of a beast, as he let his guard down, sobbing loudly.

"Please don't cry. We're gonna figure something out. I promise." London cradled him in her arms while her sister escaped to throw up in the bathroom. She had been in Dallas less than twenty-four hours and was already entangled in obstruction of justice and another murder. Including Swift, the hit man back home, that was two altogether.

"I'm tight, uhm . . . London." O.T. could barely remember her name with all the chaos that was going on that night. He wanted to call her Kenya, but he caught himself. He stood up first, reaching his hand downward to assist London to her feet. As they were standing face-to-face, O.T. leaned in close, moving London's hair out of her eyes. Her inexperienced romantic heart was working overtime. She shut her eyes and waited for him to kiss her. Feeling his body get closer, she held her breath in anticipation.

"Listen, London," he whispered in her ear. "We good, right? You ain't gonna tell nobody about that little punk-ass-faggot crying bullshit, are you? A guy slipped up on that female tip."

"What?" London was pissed, to say the least and disappointed that all O.T. was ultimately worried about was people knowing that he was normal and had normal reactions to abnormal circumstances. Her sudden compassion and fascination with him had come to a quick halt. "Is that all you concerned with—what people think?"

"Naw, but . . ."

Kenya came back into the room on the tail end of the conversation between them. "What's going on in here?"

"Nothing, Kenya," O.T. answered for both.

"Yeah, nothing!" London happily agreed.

You owe me and a phone number was written on the note that was stuffed inside the box.

"What does that mean?" Kenya rubbed both sweaty hands together. "*You owe me*? Owe who? Owe what?"

"We gotta call this number and hopefully we can find out." O.T. pulled out his cell phone, dialing the mystery person. After a few rings, what had to be an older-sounding man answered his call. Listening attentively, it was a voice that wasn't familiar to O.T. at all.

"Yeah!" the guy repeated twice before he got a response from Storm's brother. "I hope you're ready to listen? And pay attention!"

"This O.T., who this?" he finally blurted out, wanting some answers.

"Listen, let me make this perfectly clear, I'm asking the questions here, young man, not you. Is that understood?"

"Who the fuck is this?" O.T. was losing his patience with the man at the other end of the line.

"Tsk, tsk. Now, is that any way to address your elders?" The man also was growing seemingly frustrated of all the cat-and-mouse talk. "Didn't your project-living, three-part-time-job-working, two-different-baby-daddy having, now-crackhead mother teach you or your brother any manners?"

"Huh, what did you just say?" O.T. was thrown off his square as the girls looked on.

"You heard perfectly well what I just said and believe me, I'm not in the mood or accustomed to repetitious conversation!"

"Yo, nigga, how you know shit about my ol' girl?"

"Trust me. I know everything about your entire family. From your sorry excuse for a father, your brother murdered, to your third cousin twice removed on your mother's side—and by the way, I don't like to use the term *nigga*! I find it derogatory and barbaric."

O.T. was completely outraged by the stranger's overly blatant disrespect for him and his family. "Listen, dude! Where the fuck is my brother at? I swear to God, if you—"

The man cut him off, laughing. "You swear to God what? I'm not amused. Please refrain from making idle threats you can't possibly back up. I have come in the past not to appreciate them nor tolerate them. So now, if you don't mind, can we get to the business at hand, youngster, your brother's life or what's left of it."

O.T. was, for the first time since the call was placed, silent. He looked at Kenya and London, both sitting on the edge of the bed, anxiously waiting to hear any news.

The man started with the answer to O.T.'s original question. "This is Javier and your brother, Storm, is here with me. For the time being he is safe from harm's way. And trust, if all goes as planned, he will stay that way. You have my word on that much, but the outcome depends on you."

"How can he be safe, you lunatic?" O.T. grew more enraged staring at the ring box. "Ain't this a chunk of his damn ear and shit? You a sick-ass bastard for doing this!"

"What did I just mention about your mouth, young man? Any further outburst and name-calling will cause me to bring this call to an abrupt end—terminated. Are we clear?"

"Yeah, we clear." A once-again silent O.T. sat still after being scolded like a child.

"Now, as I was saying. Storm is here with me and alive, for the time being. If you have possession of this number, it is very safe to assume that you already have come in contact with your brother's business partner and associate, Deacon. Is this much true?"

"Yeah, if that's what you wanna call it." O.T. was being sarcastic and bitter. "Man, that shit was foul as hell! How could y'all do some old crazy stuff like that?"

"That's life in the game we all chose to play—you, me, your brother, and the recently departed Deacon. Now deal with it!" Javier chuckled before revealing some truths. "Your brother and his twisted personal life, has caused me and my various operations throughout the region major financial strains that must be satisfied."

"How so? I know for a fact he has never been short on a single payment to anyone on any package."

"Well, because of him, his ex-stripper girlfriend, and her do-good sister, I just have been made aware of my cash flow has been slowing down and that is not acceptable—not acceptable at all."

O.T. looked at the girls and felt a deep veil of hatred come over him. He now knew that it was because of them that his big brother was in serious trouble as he spoke. "What's the deal, old man? What you want?" O.T. wanted to skip straight to the point of their conversation. He wanted to know exactly what it would take to get Storm back safe and sound.

"Well, it seems London Roberts, his soon-to-be sister-in-law and her little group PAID, have been causing a few bumps in the road here and there," Javier spoke calmly in an even tone. "There was some confusion as to the identity of her and her twin Kenya, the dancer whore, at first, but that mystery has since been solved. A recently ex-employee of mine, a one Mr. Swift, ill-fatedly found out the hard way, but as the game goes it's always casualty in war."

"What?" O.T. asked, confused.

"So goes life," Javier coldly remarked.

"What the hell is PAID? And who is Swift?" O.T. inquired, as he attentively kept his ear pressed to the telephone receiver. "I don't follow you! What the fuck does any of that bullshit mean?"

"Listen, O.T., you have to ask your peoples any questions you need answers to. They can fill you in on their part in all this. My main concern right now is my revenue and nothing more. By my calculations, your brother Storm owes me approximately two hundred and fifty thousand dollars in lost sales. Although it's true he never has been late on his own payments, he is being held responsible for his peoples' actions, as it may."

"Two hundred and fifty thousand dollars! Are you nuts? That shit just ain't right, dude. What fucking people? What you mean?"

"Well, I guess that Storm's safe return doesn't mean that much to you." Javier still remained calm. "I'm sorry to have troubled you. I guess that this is good-bye and have a good life!"

"No, no! Wait!" O.T. stuttered, wasting no time reconsidering. "I'll get the money, I'll get it! But it's gonna take me some time. That's a helluva lot of bread to come up with just like that!"

"I'm aware of that and no one can say I'm not a fair man, so I will give you at least—shall we say—thirty days to gather it. Are we clear on the time frame or what?"

"Yeah, we clear. I'll call you as soon as I get the cash together. I swear to God I'ma get it, but how do I know Storm is even still alive?"

"You don't—not for sure. It's a gamble you have to take. And by the way, there's no need in calling this number again. I'll get back in touch with you when necessary," he vehemently demanded. "Thirty days youngster, no more."

And with that exchange Javier hung the phone up, leaving O.T. to explain to Kenya and London what was needed, not to mention get some of his own questions answered.

"What did they say? Where is Storm? Is he hurt bad? Is he coming home?" Kenya fired question after question. "Please tell me what whoever was on the phone said—please!"

"Well, bottom line is, thanks to you and this bitch right here, we supposedly owe Javier two hundred and fifty thousand Gs to get Storm back home. If we pay the dough, the old man claim he'll let him go fucking free." O.T. was pissed and made no excuses as he mean-mugged London for being the direct cause for the financial uphill battle he was now facing.

"What do you mean, two hundred and fifty thousand dollars?" Kenya was left puzzled by O.T.'s comments. "And why the fuck you calling my sister a bitch? What she got to do with Storm or Deacon?"

"What the hell is PAID?" he fumed, slamming his fist down on the nightstand, causing it to tilt over. "Can one of y'all identical bookends tell me that?"

London and Kenya quickly made eye contact with one another. It was now painfully apparent that Storm's sudden disappearance and Deacon's murder were all linked back to London's one true passion, People Against Illegal Drugs. The connection was all coming together.

"Damn frick and frack! Is one of y'all hoes gonna answer my damn question? Don't speak at one time! What is PAID?" O.T. was now on his feet, towering over the girls. "And who is this dead nigga, Swift? Y'all need to start talking quick!"

Kenya jumped up in his face. "Hold the hell on, mother-fucker. Me or my sister ain't gonna be anymore bitches or hoes, that's first of all. We can get that straight off rip!"

"What you just say?" O.T. spit out wildly, also caught in his emotions. "What you say?"

"You heard me, black man. I'm gonna explain everything and shit, but you not just about to come up here in our room and dog us the hell out. That ain't flying!"

"Oh, yeah! Is that right?" His nostrils flared and the veins in his neck were ready to burst.

"Yeah, it's right, O.T." Kenya suddenly pounced up and swung on him. "I know shit is real messed up right about now and we all upset and worried about Storm, but you got me all fucked up! You better act like you know, nigga!" With all her big talk, her punch missed its mark.

O.T. admired Kenya's off-the-wall crazy spunk and backed down to hear her explain. "All right then." He casually sat back in one of the chairs, folding his arms. "I'm listening and please don't leave shit out."

"I ain't!"

"Good! Then speak!"

London was preparing herself for all the fireworks that were sure to jump. She knew that she was gonna be number one on O.T.'s shit list, but so be it.

"Well, first off, PAID is an organization that my sister, London, and her roommate Fatima started back east in college."

"And?" O.T. was growing impatient. "Go on!"

"Damn! Calm down and let me finish."

"Go ahead, Kenya. I said I'm listening!"

"Like I was saying . . ." She rolled her eyes, clearing her throat. "My sister and her roommate were up at school and got together with a few other students to form a kids-against-drugs sort of a club."

London jumped in the conversation, clarifying what exactly it was. "It's called People Against Illegal Drugs, and FYI, it is more than just a small handful of my classmates, it's almost the entire campus of my university, as well as several other schools." She had her chest stuck out as she bragged about the strength of the group, not yet realizing the group was the reason behind the kidnapping and murder.

"Can you please shut the fuck up, London? Is you trying to make shit worse or what?" Kenya had to put her twin in her place. Even though London was busy trying to act all high and mighty, real talk, it was her bullshit that had Storm being held hostage and Kenya knew it.

"Yeah, London! Shut the fuck up!" O.T. cosigned with Kenya as he waved her off with his hand in a dismissive fashion.

London did as she was told and let her sister finish speaking, but gave O.T. the finger.

"Anyhow, the organization kinda spread out here to the South, I guess. I'm sure that's the group that Storm and Deacon were complaining about the other day. You know what I'm talking about, don't you?"

O.T. was disgusted as he stared at London. "You mean to tell me that all along your damn sister has been fucking shit up for our pockets?"

Kenya hated to admit to him that he was right, so she turned her back on him as she continued to explain. "I didn't put two and two together until a few minutes ago my damn self." She glanced over at London while running her fingers through her tangled hair.

"Okay, then. What about this buster named Swift? What's his role in all of this? Is that your ho-ass man?" O.T. directed his assault of questions to London.

"No, he's the man who tried to kill us!" she shouted out loudly for the whole world to hear. "In our own home, Mr. Know So Much. He tried to kill us! And right about now, I would rather be back in Detroit and take my chances with another lunatic murderer than be in this godforsaken town with you!" She sneered with contempt. "He was probably one of your dope-dealing cohorts anyway!"

London's boisterous outburst left O.T. and Kenya dumbfounded. It was the most words that O.T. heard come out her mouth all evening.

"Bitch, is you crazy? Who the fuck is you call yourself talking to?"

"Come on, y'all. We need to put all this petty junk on the back burner 'til we pony up on that loot and get Storm back." Kenya brought an immediate end to the heated exchange as she looked over at the small ring box and the tiny chunk of severed earlobe. "It don't matter what the fuck happened, the main agenda is Storm. The hell with that dumb shit, y'all two can fight it out later if you want. We ain't got time to waste. We need to see how much money we already have toward the two hundred and fifty Gs so we can get my man back home."

Kenya took a pen out her purse and grabbed the hotel stationery out the desk drawer. Calculating the ticket money from the workers in the streets, including the dope that they had stashed in reserves and the dough that Kenya had retrieved from the house floor safe, they were still very much short of their needed goal.

Much to London and O.T.'s surprise, Kenya announced that she was holding close to a little over a hundred grand in cash. She also made it clear that when she went to the bank to her safe deposit box, she planned on pawning the jewelry that Storm always insisted that she kept there. Lumped together with the cash O.T. had from Alley Cats, they still came up 135,000 dollars short. They had to devise a scheme to come up on the balance.

Kenya gave her twin a dirty look. She had only, just several months earlier, given London 15,000 dollars out the kindness of her heart, that she knew good and damn well that London was still holding on to that and all her other savings, for that matter. Here now, her identical twin sister sat on the edge of the bed, quiet as a church mouse, not even speaking up and volunteering to give the cash she was blessed with back to help free Storm and bring him safely home. From that moment on, Kenya knew things would never be the same between the two.

In a last-ditch attempt for London to jump in and have her sister's back, she spoke out softly in fear of the response, if any. "I also got some money coming in a week or so from the sale of my grandmother's house back in Detroit that I can kick in," Kenya said, sighing.

London still remained hush-mouthed, not offering her share of Gran's house, breaking Kenya's heart.

O.T. wrapped his arms around Kenya, who he could see had a game plan immediately in the works. "Don't worry. A nigga like me got a few more irons burning in the fire. We'll get it all by thirty days!" he reassuringly whispered in her ear. "I ain't gonna just let my brother's life go just like that if I can stop it!"

London watched the exchange of embraces from the two of them and felt strangely jealous for some odd reason. *Kenya gets every cute guy she wants.* She wanted to run across the room and rip her promiscuously rumored sister out O.T.'s arms and take her place. As the girls looked each other in the eye, London got a cold vibe from her sister. She knew Kenya like the back of her hand and knew that her twin wanted her to give up her share of the revenue from the sale of the house and give the money back she'd given her—just because. Without a second thought, there was no way in sweet fire hell that she was throwing her inheritance out the window on some lowlife drug dealer who she never had even met. *How could she put me in that position to risk losing my tuition money? What nerve! I see she still hasn't changed!*

Chapter-Twenty six

Da Grind

The days that soon followed were consumed with argument after argument between the twins. Each one of them was on edge for obvious different reasons. London missed being back on campus with all of her friends, trying to achieve her degree, while Kenya focused her entire mental and physical strength on getting her drug-dealer fiancé back home in one piece. London knew that her sister had an attitude with her about her reluctance to contribute revenue to the Save Storm Fund, but so damn what.

"How long are you going to stump around this room and not speak to me?" London finally inquired. "You need to grow up and handle things more maturely. I mean, none of this makes any sense."

"Excuse the hell outta me! Some of us can't go through bullshit and just blow it off like you. Everyone is not as frigid as you are!" Kenya cut her eyes, rolling them to the top of her head. "I'm trying to get this loot together to get my boo home, not that you give a damn! He's the most important thing in my life! Do you understand that?"

After clearing her throat, London fired back her own round of profound words. "Look, I truly care about you, not him. You best believe, if it was you that needed my money or my help, I would be right there, jimmy on the spot. Haven't I proved that to you time after time?" At this point she was all up in Kenya's grill, not giving her an inch to move. "If my memory serves me correct, wasn't I the one who just helped your funny-acting so-called friends carry a corpse to the car while you were busy putting on one of your all-too-famous drama queen roles? That was me doing all that!"

Kenya couldn't understand why her sister was being so callous and coldhearted, but didn't have the time to figure it out. It was only one thing on her mind, Storm. Keeping her eye on the prize, she finished getting dressed and left a disrespectful London in the hotel room to fuss, argue, and be judgmental by herself. O.T. had called earlier and wanted Kenya to meet him down at the club, so she assumed he had an update that he didn't want to share over the phone.

When Kenya drove up to the club, she pulled into her parking space. As she stepped out the cool, air-conditioned truck and into the sweltering Dallas heat, Kenya looked over to the empty space next to hers, also labeled RESERVED. *Don't worry baby. I'm gonna bring ya ass home where you belong,* she thought as she got the door keys to Alley Cats out of her purse and cautiously approached the entrance. Before she got a chance to unlock all the security doors, O.T. skirted up in the lot doing at least eighty. He had the music blasting as usual; straight foolin'. Kenya, on edge, was spooked by him burning rubber and almost took a shit in her panties.

"What's wrong with your crazy-ass, fool?" were the first words that flew out her mouth when he got out his pimped-out ride.

O.T. ran over to a visibly heated Kenya, picking her up off her feet and swinging her around. "I got some good news for you—real fucking good!"

"What is it? What is it?" She smiled, temporarily forgetting about his well-known idiotic actions. "Did you talk to Storm? Is he okay? Hurry up and tell me!"

"Naw Kenya, I haven't heard from him." He put her down, seeing she was getting the wrong impression of his news. "But I got us some more loot to throw in the pot, plus a line on a good-ass hustle that might push us over the top on that ho-ass buster, Javier's ticket."

Kenya was noticeably disappointed that O.T. hadn't gotten any more news about his brother; yet coming up with some more money would ease the load.

They both entered the club after disarming the alarm and got down to business. He informed Kenya that he was gonna set up a meeting in the club on Friday evening. He explained that he could double up on some good dope that he'd gotten a line on and possibly make all the money they needed. Encouraged, Kenya took her notebook out so that they could add up the new figures.

O.T. eagerly took 35,000 dollars cash out a shoe box that was behind the bar on the shelf and tossed it to Kenya. "Here you go. Add this."

Kenya reached for the stacks of currency that were crispy and smelled new. "Where did you get this from?" She was leery as she took another whiff, inspecting the bank-issued bands. "I hope your behind didn't do what I think you did! Please tell me you didn't!"

"Dig this here. Don't be so damn quick to always think the worse about me." He paused as he checked his brother's woman and opened up a beer. After two long gulps, he finally eased Kenya's mind, answering her question. "Your girl Paris done emptied out her bank account and pawned some of her jewelry. You know she's down on my team and yours and Storm's! You know she got your back!"

Kenya sat back on the bar stool, letting out a long, drawn-out sigh of built-up denial. She couldn't believe that her best friend Paris would kick in all her life savings and risk losing her jewelry, while her own flesh-and-blood twin sister couldn't care less. "Paris always is there when I need her. You better treat her right, boy! She deserves that!" Kenya pointed her finger at O.T., trying extra-hard to reinforce her words. "I ain't playing with you either, Negro. You need to make it legal like me and Storm is gonna do as soon as he gets home—get married and stop running these streets."

O.T. guzzled down the rest of the beer in the bottle and twisted the top off another. "Please Kenya, you know I'm a damn pimp!" He yanked at his manhood and chuckled loudly. "Matter of fact, where is that fat-ass big-mouth twin sister of yours at? Why she ain't roll with you down here? I got something for her!"

Kenya got up from the bar stool, stuffing the money in her purse. With her keys in her hand, heading toward the door, she laughed at his remarks. "Okay playa playa. You best to stick with Paris. She's the only one who will put up with your foul, crab-ass behavior you be dishing out. And as for London,

I think—naw, let me rephrase that bullshit—I know that she is a little bit out your reach, son. So you need to push on off that thought. My sister don't even get down like that, homeboy, so beat it!"

"Oh, yeah—okay? We'll see!" O.T. gave Kenya the side eye from across the club.

Kenya was pissed with London for being so cheap, but that still didn't stop her from chin-checking O.T. on his always reckless behavior. "Dude, go home to your woman with your ignorant ass and I'll see you Friday!"

O.T. was left standing in the club alone. Looking around, he started reminiscing about him, Deacon, and Storm playing pool and talking shit. O.T., feeling depressed, poured himself a double shot of yak, agonizing what the near future would bring.

The rest of the afternoon well off into the evening, O.T. sat in the back booth of the empty, dark, deserted club getting pissy drunk, smoking blunts. His thoughts were consumed with thinking about Deacon's decapitated body and, of course, getting up on the rest of the money he needed to get his brother home safely. Like the true dog he was, once or twice in the evening he even found the time to think about running up in Kenya's twin sister as a worried Paris blew up his cell phone, praying he was okay.

Chapter Twenty-seven

How Dare You

It was early Friday evening and Alley Cats was turned up on total bump. Everyone had come out for the club's most popular night, freak-out Fridays. They always had a couple more bouncers on duty on the weekends for all the extra crowd that would pack in. Paris and Kenya were out shopping one day and came up with the idea as a promotional gimmick to ensure they got the guys to stop in the club and spend a portion of their weekly paychecks with them before they took the rest home to their nagging wives and pesky kids.

O.T. was busy posted behind the bar, while Paris, was occupied with collecting the house fee from the dancers before they stepped on stage. Staying on top of the girls was always Kenya's job, but she was running late, causing Paris to fill in for her.

With the clipboard in hand she checked off the names as they paid.

"Will you hurry up, London? I've gotta get down to the club. We already late as a fuck and plus it's Friday night, so speed that ass up!" Kenya knocked at the bathroom door three times in an attempt to get her sister to rush things along. "Now come on and stop all that bullshitting around! We gotta bounce unless you staying here! The choice is yours!"

London was usually the one who was on time, but this was somewhat a special occasion for her. She was gonna come face-to-face with O.T. for the first time since that horrible night they met. London, for some strange reason, couldn't take her mind off of him. She kept Kenya up the night before asking question after question about his rude demeanor and if he was serious about Paris. Even though London tried her best playing it off, her twin was vibin' with her and could see right through her game. Kenya didn't have to twist London's arm one bit into going to work with her at the strip club she always said was so degrading to women. Especially when she found out O.T. was gonna be on the premises.

Paris was Kenya's best friend and it was no way on God's green earth that she was going to be a part of causing her even a moment's worth of pain. Blood ain't always thicker than water, and in this case it couldn't be truer. So if that meant cock-blocking her sister, then so be it. It would be done. After ten more minutes past by, London exited the bathroom with a brand-new bounce in her step and a huge grin plastered on her face.

"I don't know what in the fuck your slick-ass is so slap-happy about. Storm is still out there somewhere hurt and you all *hee-hee-ha-ha-ing*," Kenya agitatedly announced. "You act like you don't even care! Girl, let's go so I can make this money!"

"What?"

"You heard me! Stop smiling and let's go!"

"What, so it's against the law now to smile in Dallas until your drug-dealing boyfriend comes home?" London returned her sister's sarcasm, giving as good as she got. "Well, excuse me for living!"

"Listen here, Ms. Thang! While you being so smart-ed-mouthed and in the mirror primping, in case you have overlooked one damn thing, well, let me remind you, O.T. already has a wifey—Paris—remember her?" Kenya placed both hands on her hips and bucked her eyes. "So if you have any designs on him in any form or fashion, you better forget about it, college girl, and keep that shit straight moving. We clear? Understand?"

"Whatever, Kenya! I don't know what you're talking about. I don't like that lowlife, rude thug. That's more your style."

"Yeah, right! Whatever, my ass! Just don't forget what I just said." Kenya pushed London's arm. "He got a girl—my best friend!"

After the exchange the twin sisters finally left the hotel en route to Alley Cats, where it was destined to be one helluva long night.

***

"Hey, Kenya, how are—" With the twins standing before him, Boz, the head of security, couldn't believe what he was seeing, having the exact same reaction as O.T. and Paris.

"Close your mouth, Boz, before something flies in it."

"But—" He was stunned.

"I know, silly. This is my twin sister, London. Do me a favor and let her in the office through the back door—and oh, please don't mention her being here to anyone. Not to the other bouncers, the dancers, or anybody else on the staff. Okay?"

Boz's eyes were glued to London as he walked with her around to the rear of the club. He noticed that although she was indeed a mirror image of Kenya's face, their mannerisms were outrageously miles different. Kenya walked like a panther, seductively on the prowl for the weak, while London took each step with pride and confidence, head held high with an air of arrogance.

London, perceptive of her surroundings in light of recent events, glanced over, detecting his strange, silly expression. "Is there something wrong? Do I have a glob of snot hanging from my nose or what?" She winked, knowing he was another person in Kenya's life who failed to know about her existence.

"Oh, my bad. I didn't know the boss's girl had a twin, that's all." Boz laughed it off, showing his mouthful of gold-plated teeth. "It ain't no problem. It's just bugged out, that's all."

Going inside the strip club's doors and up the rear stairs, London caught a brief glance at the neon-lit stage. One of the dancers was hanging upside down from the brass pole, while others were sitting backward in men's laps grinding, simulating sexual acts. When settled down on the couch in the plush office, her mind began to wonder and she felt saddened. London realized that only a short time ago, her sister Kenya was one of these low-self-esteemed females.

"Hey, Paris. Sorry I'm late. How are things going so far? All these hoes out here paid?" Kenya found her friend in the dressing room going over some of the house rules for a new dancer named Jordan, who grew up around the way from Paris.

"Hey, woman! I was just thinking about where the heck your crazy-ass was at."

"Girl, you know I'm traveling with a little extra baggage these days," Kenya replied low-key, referring to her sister.

"Oh, yeah, Kenya, dig that."

"So, how things going in here so far? How we looking?"

Paris finished up schooling the new dancer on the dos and don'ts of the club and went into the hallway, followed by Kenya. "Everything's everything. We got a full house already and it isn't even eight yet. I already went in the kitchen and told them to get some more food prepped."

"That's what's up!" Kenya nodded, feeling positive. "We need all the cheddar that we can scramble up on. We definitely getting closer—especially thanks to you!"

Paris gave her girl a hug that was cut short by one of the dancers, Chocolate Bunny, who was walking fast, yelling out to one of the bouncers. Her manner was louder and much more ghetto than normal.

"Excuse me, Paris. Let me see what in the hell is going on with that dirty-black skank headed this way. You know she always got some drama stirring!"

Paris was glad that Kenya was finally there to intervene. If it was one female in the entire club that she despised, it was Chocolate Bunny. It was no secret to Paris or any other person that worked in Alley Cats that O.T. had fucked around with her back in the day. And still, every chance that Chocolate Bunny got to get close to O.T., she took advantage, at times rubbing their past "special friendship" in Paris's face.

Paris, a nutcase and street soldier in her own right, wanted to kick her black-ass on several occasions and had to be physically held back by some of the other dancers and a bartender. Feeling some sort of way, she often lobbied for Storm or Deacon to fire Chocolate Bunny's slimeball behind on the spot for her disrespectful antics, but she was one of Alley Cats's main attractions and made a lot of dough for the club. That meant that Paris had to suck it up for the cause, like it or leave it and be a big girl.

***

"What's the deal? What's wrong?" Pretending to be sympathetic, Kenya placed her hand on the drama-prone dancer's sweaty shoulder. "Calm down and tell me! What's going on?"

"Hey, Kenya!" Chocolate Bunny looked at her with blood in her eyes. "It's that old-ass wannabe pimp that y'all had us chillin' with before. Well, he must be nuts and got me messed all the way up!"

"Okay, slow down. Who are you talking about?"

I'm talking about that non-tipping, ancient-dressing asshole Royce!"

"Royce! Royce is in here? Are you sure? Where is he at?" Kenya excitedly scanned the room, hoping she and he could have words.

"Damn, yeah Kenya, I'm sure!" She pointed toward the rear of the club. "He's over there with his crew, talking about he about to buy Alley Cats and trying to get free dances. And you know a good ho like me don't play that free crap no matter who a nigga thinks he is or gonna be! I don't sell free ass this way!"

Before Chocolate Bunny could finish her statement, Kenya had abruptly walked away, leaving her standing alone with the bouncer. *Oh my God! Maybe Royce knows something about Storm. They was supposed to all be together when they left and O.T. ain't say nothing more about him.* Kenya spotted Royce dressed in one of his 1975 mack-daddy suits and several of his friends seated in the corner, just as Chocolate Bunny said. They had a few bottles of champagne and were surrounded by dancers falling for his weak lines.

"Excuse me, Royce. How you doing?"

"Well, well, well, if it isn't Ms. Tastey."

"Pardon me." Kenya assumed, without a doubt, that she must have been hearing Royce incorrectly.

Royce licked his lips. "Awww . . . Tastey, baby doll, don't be like that! Come over here closer with your pretty little self."

"What did you say?" Kenya felt her world shatter once again. What Royce had just said was hard to digest. No one in Dallas, outside of Storm, O.T., and Deacon knew her as Tastey, not even Paris—that was unless her man had told her.

"Come on now, sweetness. There's no reason to be shy with Daddy." Royce tried rubbing her hand. "I'll give you double if you give me one of your special dances or better yet, go hit that stage. I heard you extra good with a pole between your legs."

"I'm sorry, you must be mistaken. I don't dance. I just came over here to ask you a few questions if you don't mind." Kenya attempted her best to keep her fronts up, knowing she was shook to her soul.

Royce then brazenly pulled out a thick knot of money wrapped in a red rubber band. "You sure you don't want to come out of retirement and make this loot? Ain't nothing but hundreds in this roll and some of it could be yours for the asking, sweet thang you!"

"Listen up, Royce." Kenya was trying her best to remain professional as all eyes were glued on her. "I just need to ask you something in private, if that's okay. You can save the rest of that."

"Why, do you have a wire on you? Did the *feds* send you to fuck with me or something?" He stood up from the table with his glass in his hand. Everyone within ear range, drug dealers, dancers, and even the workingman, was quiet waiting for Kenya to respond to the old man's allegations of her working for the police in some capacity. "Now, tsk, tsk tsk. There's no need trying to act naive, young lady. I already know that you play for the other team, so to speak. You snitchin' little tramp! Yeah, I saw the picture. We all did!" Royce raised his left eyebrow, grinning, drink still in hand. "Your man Storm tried denying it, but we all knew. He wasn't slick and you ain't either!"

"What the hell are you insinuating? Storm knew what?" Kenya's violent streak and Detroit-born-and-raised temper was surfacing quickly. She had come to him respectfully, in peace, in hopes of gaining some information on Storm. Now he was calling her out—in her man's club, of all places. "Yeah, all right then." She promptly dismissed the dancers who were idly standing around, not making money but ear hustling. "Y'all girls can leave. This one and his entire crew on they way out the door."

Kenya's teeth were clenched tightly and her lips trembled as she summoned the dancers once more to move on to another customer. They hesitantly did as they were told in a slow fashion, trying to linger around for the shit to hit the fan. "Hurry the fuck up before I start sending bitches home!" That serious threat of being cut off from the crowd of stuffed pocket men made them speed their departure up. "Now back to you old man! How dare you insult me!" she feverishly lashed out, ready to kill. "All I wanted to find out is if you know anything about Storm. Why are you in here playing games with me? This shit ain't no joke!" Her voice was increasing with every infuriated word. "Are you crazy?"

An equally angry Royce quickly responded. "Pay attention, you little whore! I don't know shit about that coward Deacon or Storm . . . ask Javier, that's your best bet!" He stroked his unshaven salt-and-pepper beard, while straightening out his multicolored polyester suit. His crew were all hanging on every word that slipped out his past-tense jaws like he was spitting gold. "Matter of fact, here's a better option for you. Why don't you ask the coroner at the local morgue?" Royce boldly suggested, enjoying the growing tension that filled the room. "Yeah, get in touch with them. They probably could answer all your questions better than anyone else. After all, Tastey, Kenya, London or whatever name you're going by tonight, that is where snitches and bitches end up, ain't it—dead in the morgue?"

Kenya was straight bugging out and trembling in denial. Her past was coming back to bite her in the ass. She was completely drained from worry about Storm and sleep deprived. With her body temperature close to reaching boiling level from him exposing her private life to everyone in Alley Cats, her mentality started to further go off into explosive mode. On the other hand, Royce and his friends were taking pleasure in the sight of Kenya's high-and-mighty stuck-up self being brought down a couple of notches to where they felt she belonged. They were still holding their glasses in their hands and smiling, enjoying the show.

Kenya couldn't hold it together any longer. *These busters think I'm here to entertain them. Yeah, all right!* Kenya's mind was racing. Her palms were itching to smack Royce across his unshaven beard. She used her finger to nervously twirl her engagement ring as only one thought monopolized her brain: Storm coming home alive. Now Royce was putting shit in the game, making a scene. "The morgue! What? The morgue! Did I hear you act like you know something about my man? Is that what you doing?"

"You heard what I said, little girl!" With spite, he raised his glass as if he was making a toast. "Now your best bet is to get the fuck away from me before I kick your period on!"

The crowd was amused by Royce's brash words. Kenya was now borderline psychotic. *Five . . . four . . . three . . . two . . . one*—blast the hell off. Before Royce knew what was happening, Kenya socked him dead in his left eye, followed by several combinations of right and left hooks. He was thrown off balance, falling back into the booth, knocking all the bottles of champagne onto the club floor. Her attack caught his smug crew off guard as they watched Kenya pounce on top of Royce like a sick, deranged mountain lion.

"Motherfucker, you done earned this right here!" she shouted with each blow.

By the time one of his crew could snatch her off of their boss and get him back on his feet, Royce's face was scratched to the white meat. His lip was bleeding and his dentures were hanging sideways out his mouth. Showing no signs of letting up, Kenya wasn't done yet as she struggled to break free and continue showing Royce exactly who was boss in that motherfucker.

"Let me go! Let me go!" Kenya's piercing screams could be heard throughout the whole club. "Let me the fuck go!"

"I'm gonna kill you, slut, just like Javier killed that no-good snitchin'-ass man of yours!" he boasted once more. Royce's words were vindictive and sliced deep into her inner soul. "Matter of fact, they can bury you both together in a cheap wooden box!"

Kenya broke free of the guy's grip just as O.T. and the bouncers approached them. She stole on Royce once more, this time tagging the other eye. Her perfectly manicured nails had broken off into his face, causing him to scream out like a little baby.

"Don't fold now, old man! I ain't done. Let's do this! Boss the hell up!"

"Y'all better get that wild little whore!" Royce tried commanding his boys, "Before I kill her up in here."

Kenya was on the zigitty nut boom and close to practically foaming at the mouth as Boz grabbed her up in his chest. With Kenya's legs kicking wildly and arms still swinging, Boz caught some serious hell in dragging her up the staircase to the office door. He had easier times trying to throw a grown-ass, six foot two, 300 pound, drunk and disorderly man out of Alley Cats than he was having with his boss's girl.

"I'm gonna get you, Royce! I swear to God, I'm gonna lullaby that old, wrinkled-ass for good one day!" Kenya was leaning over the railing, yelling as an exhausted Boz still struggled. "I swear on everything that I love, just wait! You got that shit coming, Royce! On my parents' grave! That's ya ass!"

"Don't fret, Tastey." Royce was putting on a brave front for the club patrons. His ego was bruised, but he still continued to talk shit, trying his best to save face. "All right girl, I'll see you in them streets real soon and when I do, oh, my! I'll teach your pole-swinging-ass a priceless lesson of a lifetime, one that you'll never, ever forget!" Royce blew her a kiss and smiled in spite of the severe pain he was feeling. "I'll see you soon, little girl, real, real soon!"

"Say you promise! You old son of a bitch! Say you motherfucking promise!" Kenya managed to shout recklessly across the crowded bar as Boz finally pried her fingers off the railing and threw her in the office onto the couch, next to her terrified sister.

"Damn, Kenya! What was that all about?" London puzzled, not knowing what to think.

Chapter Twenty-eigth

Play Ya Position

Kenya confessed to London the real reason that she hadn't mentioned her very existence to her friends and employees. "It's simple. I know that you can't stand drugs or anything affiliated with them, so why would I even wanna get your name mixed into this world that I'm calling home? I mean, be serious, London, I already knew that any hopes of you accepting Storm and his lifestyle was little to none. I ain't stupid."

"Regardless of whatever, Kenya, we're sisters—family—blood. You act as if you're ashamed of me," London argued, feeling some sort of way. "No matter how much foolish stuff you've been caught up in the middle of in the past, I've never turned my back on you or even once thought about it."

"Yeah, you right, London."

"I know I'm right. So there's no reason to be up in here, feeling sorry for yourself. Things are gonna work out, you'll see. Now chill, Kenya, before you have a total nervous breakdown."

Kenya let her body relax and break back down to normal. However, her heart was still racing from her confrontation with Royce. "Girl, I think I better. That old bastard gonna make me hurt him."

"I was watching on that security camera behind the desk over there." London smiled, knowing how her twin could get when pushed to the edge or backed into a corner. "You are in some serious need of anger management. I'm telling you, Kenya, you are a straight-up nutcase."

"I know sis. I think I picked up some of your bad habits."

London hugged her twin, trying to ease her pain and worry. "You wish!"

Much to Kenya's surprise, during the course of their conversation, London announced to her that after long consideration, she'd reluctantly decided to at least return the 15,000-dollar gift that her twin had blessed her with.

"Thank you, sis. I knew that you wasn't gonna just leave me hanging like that. You best believe that I wouldn't even think about being an Indian giver if it wasn't a doggone emergency." Kenya was counting every penny she got her hands on, as a penny closer to Storm's release.

"Stop that kinda talk. I'll call my bank sometime tomorrow and get the money wired out here, okay?"

"Thanks, London."

"We're sisters, girl. I love you."

Meantime, O.T. was left to settle up and iron things out with a half-crazed, wounded physically and emotionally Royce. "Man, what the fuck did you say to piss her off like that?"

"What the hell you mean, what did I say?" Royce quizzed, hunching his shoulders, wiping the blood out the side corner of his swollen lip. "That silly once-a-month-bleeding bitch just went bananas for no good reason at all! She needs to be fucking medicated or put down!"

O.T. quickly studied the faces of Royce's crew as they listened to their self-proclaimed leader punk out.

"Damn, dawg, it's like that?" O.T. turned his fitted baseball cap backwards, getting in his zone. He cracked his knuckles while slightly smirking. Beads of sweat were swiftly forming on his forehead. "Please don't let me even imagine that your ass is truly gonna go out like this! I ain't trying to act no fool up in here and ruin none of these hardworking folks' night!"

The bouncers, ten deep, were all posted, ready to attack just in case O.T. needed backup.

"Come on now. What you talking about, youngblood? Where you going with all this?" Royce was shaking in his burgundy and yellow two-toned Stacy Adams as his crew put some cowardly space in between him and O.T.

When the shit jumped and the fists started to fly, it was more than apparent Royce was gonna be on his own on this one. This was potentially gonna be one stump down that his old-school-ass had coming. He had no business coming up in Storm's club, of all places, beefing with his girl, talking all that la-la-la mess. He'd crossed the line on number one of the player's code of ethics. Now, for real, for real, flat the fuck out, it was on! He had to pay up.

A bigger crowd started also gathered around the booth after the DJ stopped spinning music. Most of the dancers held their G-strings in their hands and had stopped giving private dances to eyewitness Royce get put back in his place. Even Chocolate Bunny's hard-hustlin' behind was waiting for the come on to come on and she wouldn't let the pope himself or Jesus slow her cash flow.

The entire town knew that O.T. was on lunatic status; a true, legendary madman when it came to clowning. And knew he was a few seconds shy of putting on a real show for all those who cared to see. A show so worthy that the streets would be buzzing about it for months and months to follow.

"Well, what's it gonna be, Royce? You plan on being a man and pulling your panties out your ass or what? How you wanna handle this bullshit? You gonna be a man or is we straight about to get gangsta with it?"

"Come on now, O.T., sit down and have a drink with me, youngblood. Can't we handle this misunderstanding like two gentlemen? I mean player to player, pimp to pimp?" Royce was trying his hardest to backpedal and talk his way out of the situation at hand.

O.T. had blood in his eyes as he spoke. "Listen here, pops, I wanna work with ya, but I ain't gonna be able to." He frowned as his cheekbone twitched and he posted up seconds away from attacking. "The question is still on the table. You gonna have some balls and 'fess up or what? Trust me, Royce! This is the final time a nigga like me gonna ask a ho-ass nigga like you! Trust when I warn you, you think my sister-in law Kenya whooped that ass, you ain't seen shit yet!"

"Okay, okay, okay!" Royce pleaded, throwing his hands up in hopes of buying a few more minutes, stalling a beat-down. "Just pump ya brakes, O.T., let me explain, but I guarantee you want to hear what I have to say in private. Please, man, for old time's sake? How about it?" Royce, having lost all pride, begged relentlessly.

"Yeah, okay then. I'm gonna hear you out and this shit better be good!" O.T. collared Royce up by his oversized lapels. "We can talk over there at my private table. Ya ho-ass boys can wait here or out in the parking lot! I don't give a shit!"

Royce was passed embarrassed, but still tried to save face and delegate some authority with O.T.'s huge hands firmly wrapped around his throat. "Y'all dudes can chill over here. I'll be back." Hopefully he would save himself the possibility of having to drink his food outta a straw for the next six months.

His crew, like everyone else in Alley Cats, had to laugh. Not only had Kenya and O.T. made a fool of him, now he was doing it to himself. It was official—Royce was a class-A idiot and all of Dallas knew it.

After nearly an entire hour of listening to Royce talk, explain, take a cop, and lie, O.T. was even more heated. He couldn't believe what he was hearing the old man claiming. Royce was right. This was the type of information that shouldn't be made public. Yet, in reality, he knew this was the first time Royce had probably repeated the outrageous story.

"Come on now, Royce, how many people you done told this story to? And try your best not to motherfucking lie!"

"To be honest with you, youngblood, only my boys over there know about it." He nodded toward their general direction. "And I've already told them to keep it close to the vest."

"Damn, Royce! Good looking out." O.T. was playing the game. He wasn't dumb. He knew good and goddamn well that if Royce hadn't already told the entire town of Dallas, he was well on his way; especially after tonight. After all, truth be told, if he or Storm had that type of dirt on Royce, you best believe that all bets would've been off.

"No problem, youngblood. We in this here game as us against the man. We gotta stick together."

O.T. was fed up with Royce's ass-kissing, but he was glad that he'd at least heard of what really went down with his brother, Deacon, and Javier on the island. However, not wanting to throw his own self under the bus, Royce failed to mention to O.T. that he was the first one to put his brother on blast. He conveniently left that part out of the story.

Royce went on to explain how Javier had both Storm and Deacon physically removed from the round table. He confessed that he and others heard a lot of hollering and commotion from inside the villa as he and the men were dismissed for the day. "Listen, real talk. I even tried reasoning with Javier, telling him that your brother wasn't like that and it had to be some sort of a mistake, but Javier wasn't trying to hear it." Royce threw that lie in the conversation, trying to throw O.T. off his scent of bullshit. "The next thing I can recall was two days later, Javier summoned us all back to the round table and dropped some knowledge on us."

"Oh, yeah, go on with it." O.T. was on the edge of the booth, listening in amazement.

Royce reached for a napkin to wipe the still slow-dripping blood off his lip that was continuing to throb as time ticked by. "As I was saying, Javier informed us that the hit man named Swift, or something like that, he sent out to Detroit to assassinate London Roberts, had the tables turned on him and he himself been murdered." Royce paused to catch his breath. "Apparently, not only is your brother's woman a straight-up crazed bitch living a double life, she's hooked up somehow with a radical group in Detroit that calls themselves the Motown Muslim Mafia. They must be powerful as hell with they shit, because one of their members who goes by the name Brother Rasul, had Swift's body shipped COD to Javier's front door with a note attached to his torso. I mean, that's the word that was floating around that man's compound."

Mentioning the Detroit-based hard hitters that Kenya and London were mixed up with caused O.T. to be silent, listening to Royce's deadly tale of what could possibly have been his big brother's last days on Earth. Royce could see the look of worry on O.T.'s face and decided to play his act for all that it was worth. He knew that he had to do a lot of fast talking and expert acting to convince O.T. to let him walk out of Alley Cats in one piece. Royce kept it coming.

"Now, I don't know what exactly were the contents of the letter word for word, but I do know that Javier stated that a horrible mistake had been made and asked us all to vacate the island by nightfall. He generously gave us each a half a kilo of his finest product uncut, having us to swear to keep the situation under wraps until further notice. That's it!" Royce grabbed for another napkin, trying to absorb the pouring sweat mixed with blood from his aging face. "No more was brought up about Deacon or Storm's whereabouts and who was I to question that man? A few hours later we were all put on a private jet and flown back to the States."

"Just like that?" O.T. sat, amazed at the wild tale he'd just heard.

"Sorry I couldn't have given you more encouraging news about Storm's well-being, but from where I stood, it didn't seem too pretty. But, one thing for sure, two things for certain, Javier seems to be very calculated about every single move he makes and words he speaks, so don't give up hope, youngblood. Anything is possible."

O.T. chose not to drop his hand, letting Royce's backstabbing-ass in on the fact that he'd already been in contact with Javier and if things went as planned, Storm would soon be returning home. Bottom line, you never let the left know what the right is doing. With authority, he then signaled to Boz to escort Royce and his entire crew to the door. Before leaving, O.T. made sure to make it perfectly clear that he was interested in buying some of that high-quality dope that Royce claimed he was sitting on. Royce quickly agreed, knowing that if he didn't, it would more than likely be an all-out open drug war in the streets of Dallas. His hands were tied tight.

Royce might have dressed like a clown and fight like a bitch, but he was a true businessman and it was to his benefit to make money, not mayhem. He really couldn't care less where the drugs were being sold at as long as he got his money off top. What did he care about—as far as he knew Storm and Deacon were both dead; so that meant he was about to rule the city one day soon.

Now O.T. was a hothead and extremely arrogant about his shit, vowing to die first before letting other crews violate the blocks that him or his big brother ran with iron fists. A fool would be signing their own death certificate if they ever tried. Always down for whatever it took, he didn't give a shit about it being only two or three burn bags that a dopefiend was trying to get off, O.T. always kept it gangsta.

Those blocks belonged to them, point-blank, period, end of fucking story! You feel me! Case closed!

Chapter Twenty-nine

Paid In Full

London and Kenya left Alley Cats that night, staying pretty much secluded in the confines of the hotel until the repairmen had the condo back in livable condition. O.T. delivered the profits from each night at the club and the loot that he made from other ventures here and there. Staying true to his ways, he made sure to flirt with London on every occasion he saw her. Kenya, not blind or naive, noticed an increasing change in her sister's behavior every time he'd stop by their suite. London was acting overly sassy and out of character.

On the day the girls finally returned to the condo, Kenya was a bit worried her home, which people once described as a masterpiece, would not be repaired properly. When the sisters originally crossed the threshold of the door, Kenya took a long whiff, trying to see if she could smell the scent of death in the air. She rubbed her chin, trying to figure out the difference between fresh paint and plaster and the everlasting, imaginary stench of Deacon's lifeless corpse.

Taking a tour around her home, inspecting the workmanship, left Kenya having flashbacks of her and Storm's once perfect life. The stainless-steel sink was clean and the kitchen cabinets were all freshly varnished. New appliances lined the walls. The floors had custom-made marble that reached clear out to the patio deck. With the brand-new living room set, along with the rest of the other overpriced furniture she charged on credit, Kenya was somewhat at peace.

It was bad enough that Kenya had to live with the feeling of being violated, by strangers being in her private sanctuary, but she had no intentions of keeping not one stick of butter they might have touched. Even though some of the condo contents could be salvaged, Kenya wasn't interested. She wanted no reminders of their trespassing presence whatsoever.

"Is everything okay?" London watched as her twin slowly made her survey.

"Yeah, I'm tight," Kenya sighed. "I was just thinking about the days that we have left to hustle up on the funds we need." It was eleven days and counting and they were still short by 48,000 dollars.

Although Storm preached repeatedly, time and time again to his baby brother, about hanging out, chillin' in the dope spots, and actually making hand-to-hand transactions, at that point it didn't matter. O.T. stayed in the streets slinging dope, night after night, sunup to sundown . . . he hustled. Everyone knew if you broke a package down and sold it, you'd make double, maybe even triple, what you originally paid. The risk was high, but the payoff was lovely.

Paris was missing her man, especially at late night when she wanted some, but she had her own task: holding Alley Cats down. Caught up in being an almost one-woman hustling army, she had drink specials running all night long, even letting the fattest, ugliest girls shake their asses on the big moneymaking days. As long as a chick could come up on the house fee, which was raised to a hundred dollars a night, they were good to go. Everyone was doing their part to get Storm, whether they knew it or not.

Paris's patience as temporary club manager was being put to the test on a daily basis by the increasingly arrogant actions of Chocolate Bunny, who ho-hopped around Alley Cats as if she owned the motherfucker or had stock. Lately, whenever O.T. came into the club, Paris would find him tucked away in some corner of the bar, whispering in Chocolate Bunny's big floppy ears. As far as Paris was concerned, she wanted her man to barely speak to the chicks who danced there, shaking they asses, then keep that shit moving. Breaking the house rules, to Chocolate Bunny, weren't by accident—they were more like a force of habit. Fighting back the urge to snap, Paris held her tongue for the good of Storm's safe return. Yet, she knew in the back of her mind as soon as he returned home, her claws would come out and she was gonna wax the floor with Chocolate Bunny's face.

Back home in Detroit, the real estate agent had contacted the twins, informing them that there was some sort of holdup in the transferring of the deed to Gran's house and there would be a thirty-to forty-five-day delay in the closing process. Sadly, any thoughts of relying on that cash revenue to push them past their needed goal were ceased. It seemed as if that house was cursed all the way around.

Just as Kenya put her hand around the brass-plated banister to go upstairs, her cell phone rang. "Hello."

"*As-salaam alaikum*, Kenya. Is this you?"

"Brother Rasul! Brother Rasul!" Kenya was elated as she smiled from ear to ear. "I'm so glad to hear from you. I wanted to get in touch with you ever since we got back in Dallas, but I knew better. Plus, so much been going on!"

"*Al hamd li Allah,*" Brother Rasul added to his greeting.

"Praise be to Allah," Kenya repeated to him, calming herself down.

London ran to her sister's side. "Is that your friend? Is Fatima with him? Is she?" She grabbed for the phone. "Can I speak to her?"

Brother Rasul heard all the questions. "Tell her that Fatima is back up at the university and sends her very best wishes. She wanted to call London personally, but I also explained to her that it would be best to lay low until I got to the bottom of all of this madness."

London was close enough to the cell phone to hear what the man who had saved their lives said. She believed in him for some strange reason. After all, Brother Rasul did put his own safety and freedom on the line for them and for that he forever earned her trust and respect. She was eternally grateful.

"I'm glad that you did as I told you and waited for me to get in touch with you," he praised her patience. "That was indeed the best plan of action."

"Oh, Brother Rasul, so much chaos has happened since we got here. We came home to find, Deacon, my fiancé's partner, dead in my house and some crazy son of a bitch is holding Storm hostage until we—"

"Until you come up with two hundred and fifty thousand dollars." Brother Rasul finished a shocked Kenya's sentence. "I was thoroughly informed pertaining that situation."

"Who told you? How did you find out?"

"Whoa, slow down, little sister. I told you I was gonna investigate the man-in-the-house situation and I did just that. Apparently, they go hand in hand with your present dilemma."

"Oh my God! Oh my God! Did you find out any information about Storm? Is he okay? Did you speak to him?" Kenya sobbed, shaking from nervousness. "Please say yes—please!"

"Well, yes and no." A calm-voiced Brother Rasul went over his conversation that just had taken place, less than a hour ago, between him and Javier. "It seems as if your friend's host, turned kidnapper, was first infuriated at the actions of Fatima and your sister London. Apparently, their widespread organization PAID caused a lot of financial downfalls for quite a few slimy lowlife drug dealers infesting the neighborhoods and killing our greatest resource, kids. The marches on drug houses caused many to shut down. It's one thing to sell drugs, but not to pregnant women and underage children. That's where me and my people draw the line"

"Oh, I see," Kenya interjected, feeling asha-med that Storm was one of the "anybody can buy" drug dealers that Brother Rasul was referring to. But nevertheless, she still wanted him home safe and sound. The world be damned about their point of views.

"Well, Kenya, after sending one of his henchmen, Swift, to Detroit to execute this London Roberts person, he somehow came to find out that Storm had been dating her. It seems as if Javier and everyone who was in attendance at this meeting, who saw the pictures being passed around for the first time, assumed it was you, Kenya, aka London Roberts. Do you understand what I'm saying?"

Kenya's mind flashed back to the altercation that she had in Alley Cats. At that point it didn't take a brain surgeon to figure the whole thing out. Kenya couldn't avoid the truth any longer, even if she wanted to. This was concrete evidence that Brother Rasul had gotten straight from the horse's mouth and it was crystal clear. *Now it made sense what Royce meant when he called me a snitchin'-ass bitch. Damn, that's why that fool called me London. Oh, fuck! He must have seen the pictures and thought that she was working with the police. I mean, he thought that I was. Damn!* She started to hyperventilate and wheeze when it hit her. The two worlds Kenya systematically did her best to keep apart, were now colliding. Then the next alarm rang in her head. *Oh, shit! If Royce's ass saw those pictures, then I know that Storm must've seen them too. Oh my God! I can't believe this! I know he must be going half out his mind. My baby probably thinks that I betrayed him. He must hate me right about now! Why didn't I just be honest and tell him from the get-go—why?*

London took the cell out of her panicked sister's hand. "Hello. Hey now, this is London."

"Hello, London. Where is Kenya? What happened?"

London glanced over at a blank-faced-looking Kenya and answered Brother Rasul's question. "I'm sorry, but you should know how she is by now. You know Kenya overreacts with everything she says and does. She's playing the drama queen right now, of all times."

"Come on, London. That's your sister. You have to realize that she's going through a difficult and trying time in her life now. So give her a break." Brother Rasul was acting as both peacemaker and therapist.

London listened to Brother Rasul's speech with growing anger, almost wanting to throw up in her mouth. The feeling of animosity toward Kenya and the whole mess was fueling her outburst. "I know she's catching it right now, not knowing if Storm is alive or not, but what about me? Who's feeling any sympathy for my plight?" London was visibly enraged as her impromptu rant continued. "I should be back at school with Fatima, working on my degree, not stuck here playing Inspector Gadget for some dope dealer!"

For the first time since being in Dallas, London was determined to make someone hear and understand her point of view. Playing the background dummy was over. It was her time to vent and get some things off her chest. Caught in her emotions, enraged, she went on and on, not giving Brother Rasul a second to get a word in edgewise. As London was almost out of breath from all of her screaming, O.T. entered the room. She saw him coming out the corner of her eye and decided to pour it on extra-thick.

"No one loves or cares about me! What about me?" she sobbed out loud, as the fake tears flowed, dropping the cell phone to the carpeted floor. "Who's going to look out for me and my future? I'm scared too! What about me?"

O.T. reached down, picking up the phone and yanking London into his body in one quick motion. "What's wrong? What's the deal, baby girl?" O.T. wrapped his arms around London's waist. "Tell me and what's wrong with your sister?"

London continued to play the weak role as O.T. finally spoke to the person on the other end of the phone.

"Yeah, hello! Hello!" He was impatient for a response as he kept a clinging, calculating London in his arms.

"Peace. Whom am I speaking to?" Brother Rasul remained, as always, even-toned.

"This is O.T., who this?"

"My name is Brother Rasul Hakim Akbar. I am a close friend of the girls."

O.T. loosened his grip on London, realizing who he was speaking to and the power that Royce mentioned that this man held. "Brother Rasul. I've heard of you."

"I trust that it was all positive and uplifting, but in all fairness I must admit that I don't know you." Brother Rasul was respectful, yet guarded, as he spoke to this stranger. He had no intentions of socializing with just anyone. "Can you please let me speak back to one of the twins? We have a bit of unfinished business that I need to inform them of."

"No problem, dude, but first I need to know if you know anything about my brother's whereabouts?"

"And just who is your brother?"

"His name is Tony Christian, but he goes by the name Storm. He's Kenya's man! I know you've heard of him!" O.T. was tired of all the formalities and went straight to it. "Look,

I already know you down with them Motown Muslim Mafia cats! I know y'all bodied that nigga Swift that tried to do Kenya and London." O.T. rubbed his hands across London's wet face and drew her back close to him. "Tell him I'm official, London. Tell him it's all good."

London leaned her cheek next to O.T.'s. "Hey, Brother Rasul. This is Storm's brother. He's been helping us and making sure that we stay safe." London made sure to mimic Kenya, trying to look sexy and seductive as she spoke. She softly bit the side of her lip just as Kenya often did to get her way with a man.

"Okay then, little one, I'll tell him what I wanted to put Kenya up on," Brother Rasul agreed.

O.T. was all ears. "All right, guy. You heard her, now please tell me what you know about my brother. Is he still alive or what? What's the real deal? Raw or not, I need the truth!"

"Well, I just got off the phone with Javier. He told me that he gave your family thirty days to come up with two hundred and fifty thousand dollars. Is that correct?"

"Yeah, that's right," O.T. huffed, "And that's some bullshit, straight-up extortion!"

"I know. That price is a little steep, even if Javier feels like he's been wronged somehow."

"Wronged how? Storm didn't know shit about all that PAID crap y'all keep talking about." O.T. walked to the other side of the room away from London. "How is he to blame? Tell me that much—how?"

Brother Rasul could feel O.T.'s intense fury over the phone. "Listen, brother, I'm not calling to discuss who's right or who's wrong or who owes who what. My organization tries not to get involved in the drug game on a daily basis. That's not our main objective. We have other concerns." Brother Rasul finally dropped the bomb, putting O.T. out his misery. "I just wanted to let Kenya know that I settled up the rest of the debt that Javier was strong-arming you all out of."

"What exactly does that mean, dude? Cut all the cloak-and-dagger out!" O.T. was confused and wanted some answers in plain English, straight to the point. "What you mean, *settled up*?"

"What it means is Javier has given me his word as a gentleman that in less than forty-eight hours, your brother Storm will be released and returned home."

"Are you for real? Don't be fucking around with my emotions!" O.T. blurted into the phone, causing Kenya to shake off her self-induced pity-party trance and run toward O.T., pushing London aside.

"Yes, Javier reassured me. And he knows that we as a whole don't take pleasure in being lied to," Brother Rasul snarled. "I know that you are overjoyed, O.T., but slow down, there's been some discomfort and pain that your brother has been made to suffer, so please prepare yourself, as well as Kenya."

"I know. That old, crazy dude sliced part of my brother's earlobe off."

"I was made aware of that. However, I'm afraid that it's a little bit worse than what you think."

"How much more worse?" O.T. hesitated asking, fearing the answer.

"Listen, the damage had already been inflicted before we got involved. It was nothing that I could have done or said to have prevented it. Just tell Kenya to remain strong and to call me if need be. Peace."

O.T. flipped closed the cell and led the girls into the living room, sitting them both down on the couch.

"Well, O.T., what did he say? Is Storm coming home soon? Has Javier changed his mind or something?" Kenya, acting extra, held onto his hand, squeezing it extra-tightly, jumping back up. "What did he say?"

"Sit back down, Kenya and pay attention. This shit here is deep."

"Yeah Kenya, damn, sit down!" London added, watching O.T. like a hawk. "Let him finish speaking, for God's sake!"

A bitter, yet thankful O.T. tried to the best of his ability to prepare Kenya for the unknown circumstances of Storm's arrival, even though he wasn't truly sure himself of what condition they'd get his beloved brother back. All he knew was he was still alive and that was good enough for him.

Chapter Thirty

Done is Done

"It's six hours short of the deadline that Brother Rasul said." Kenya anxiously paced the floor. "I wonder, should I call him back and see what the problem is?"

"Naw, Kenya, don't call him yet. He said Javier gave him his word, so let's just ride it out and see. We done waited this long, we can go another six."

"Okay, O.T, but one second after six hours and I'm calling, flat out." Kenya's palms were sweaty as she wore a path in the carpet from the door to the window and the window to the couch.

London, Paris, Kenya, and O.T. were all posted, congregated in the front room watching the wall clock move slowly. It was like sheer torture for the group, waiting and wondering what Storm's physical and mental condition was going to be. As the clock ticked, their fears increased, awaiting the unexpected to occur.

Kenya, having the most to lose, was on edge more than anyone else in the house. Storm was her life. She felt without him she was nothing. As the clock slowly dragged by, the tension could be cut with a knife. You could almost hear a tiny pin drop if you listened carefully. It seemed as if every fifteen minutes the silence was broken by O.T.'s cell phone constantly ringing. Even after turning it to vibrate it could still be heard in the midst of the quiet that surrounded the room. Each time he would look down at the screen and see the caller ID, he got more visibly agitated.

Paris and his arguing had increased a lot over the last few weeks, because she knew deep down in her heart, despite his denials, that he was up to no good. "I wish that disrespectful bitch of yours would stop blowing up the damn phone for once!" Paris blurted out with jealous malice. "Don't she ever sleep? All day and all fucking night!" she went on a long-winded rant. "Tell that cheap ho to get herself a life and go find her own man!"

"Look, girl, I already done told your silly, insecure-ass that I ain't fucking around with nobody else, so stop all that bugging." O.T. kissed Paris on her forehead as she pulled away. "So just chill the hell out, crazy. Ain't nobody getting Daddy's dick but you!"

"Whatever liar! Go on with all that game!"

Paris didn't believe him one bit, just as London, who felt jealous and somehow betrayed. It was bad enough in her eyes that he was claiming Paris as number one, but now she had some other uneducated loser as competition for his rotten affections.

Why is he doing this? He knows I like him. London's mind went over and over the reason in her head a million times as she watched, envious of the couple's twisted yet loving interactions. It was making her downright sick to her stomach.

"Can y'all all just shut the fuck up for a minute and put that stuff on the back burner? Y'all making me even more nervous, shit!" Kenya halted the heated argument between the two, with rage in her voice. "I can't think!"

"Yeah, can you two please be quiet?" London was quick to jump to her sister's defense, although she had her own secret, ulterior motives. "As much as I hate to interrupt your ex-change, this isn't the time or the place to discuss your intimate personal problems."

Everyone agreed as London turned the radio onto a jazz station she'd found, coaxing them to try to relax. She then dis-appeared into the kitchen to fix some coffee for the group that was all on edge. *Maybe everyone will calm down*, London thought as she ran some water.

She put the kettle on the stove, turning the fire on high. After getting some mugs out of the cabinets and rinsing them all out, London felt chills rush throughout her body as a pair of big, strong hands firmly gripped her waist. She could feel the warmth of O.T.'s breath in her ear as he whispered.

"Hey now, sexy. What you in here doing all by yourself?" O.T. devilishly smiled.

London's legs were growing weak as she tried to speak, but couldn't. Turning her body around with ease, O.T. pressed his tongue deep into London's mouth. His dick was hard as a rock as he shoved her up against the sink and started to slow grind. London was, for the first time, feeling raw-dog nasty-ass passion. Even though, thanks to the brutal rape she suffered at the hands of her devious college professor—meaning she was no longer a virgin—she still was unaware of what she was feeling.

Her pussy seemed to have a voice of its own and was calling out to O.T. to answer. London was feeling a true out-of-body experience and felt bigger than life itself. The fact that Paris and Kenya were merely yards away in the next room only added to the thrill and sheer excitement that the two were creating. The kettle was getting hotter and coming to a boil just as both of them were.

"I'm sorry about all that, girl, but I know that nigga is back fooling around with Chocolate Bunny's behind. They always be exchanging funny looks and notes and shit almost every night. My homegirl Jordan, from down at the club, said that black bitch has been going around bragging about some new buster that she done hooked up with." Paris seized the opportunity to gossip and fill Kenya in about her recent dilemma as soon as O.T. excused himself to go to the bathroom. "Jordan even told me that brain-dead cum-drunk Chocolate Bunny has been flashing a big-ass motherfucking ring somebody put on that bird's finger—I mean claw!"

"Shut the fuck up, Paris! Don't play with me, girl! I know that nigga ain't barebacking down with that wilded-out tramp again!" Kenya momentarily forgot about her own problems for a hot second and joined her friend in talking about O.T.'s known cheating ways. "That fool ain't lost his mind! He knows that ya ass will kill them both and then bounce!"

"Girl, he better not let me find out for sure they screwing, because if I do I swear I'm done! That's my word!" Paris's troubled relationship was in limbo and on the verge of ruin. Folding her arms in disgust, she sat back quietly, puzzling where she went wrong with O.T.

Kenya regretted the fact that her twin sister was attracted to O.T. and knew, given the right amount of time or the right circumstance, the two would probably act on that emotion. She was shocked that Paris, usually perceptive about these types of things when it came to her man, couldn't pick up on it. Her woman's-intuition radar must've been broken. Even Ray Charles on a bad day could see the way her sister and he carried on at all times. It was definitely a thin line between love and hate going on.

Oh, shit! Noticing O.T. was taking a long time returning from the bathroom, Kenya jumped to her feet and ran into the kitchen. Her intuition was working just fine!

The kettle started to whistle a long, piercing sound as Kenya abruptly entered the kitchen. "What the fuck are y'all doing?" She jerked her sister and her best friend's man apart. "Have y'all two lost y'all's mind or something? I know you are both aware that Paris is right in there." Kenya pointed toward the living room, trying her best to whisper. "O.T.! Why would you jeopardize getting caught and risk losing your woman? Is all this creeping shit you always doing worth it?"

Kenya, directing all her questions toward him, gave London a chance to remove the loud-sounding kettle from the stove.

"Dang, Kenya, why don't you chill with all that talk? You must want us to get caught up and shit!" O.T. laughed, placing his index finger up to his lips. Without any remorse, he headed back out to the living room. "I'll be in there with my baby, Paris."

Kenya was infuriated with London. That was the final straw. "Have you lost your damn mind? What the hell has gotten into your sneaky-ass lately? This kinda crap don't make any freaking sense! Do I have to remind you that Paris is my damn friend—my best friend at that?"

"No, Kenya, no you don't!" London was up in Kenya's face, fist balled on the verge of swinging. "That's all the hell I've been hearing ever since I got here in Dallas. Paris this and Paris that. Well, I'm sick of it! So there! Fuck Paris and you! Y'all can have each other—I'm good!"

Kenya was thrown off by the fact that her sister was cursing and all up in her face as if she was ready to attack a bitch. "Oh, it's like that now?" Kenya grinned, braced to swing back on her sister if need be. "I guess you's a big girl, huh? You wanna do big-girl shit—is that right?"

"Yeah, it's just like that!" London refused to back down this time as the twins stood toe-to-toe. "So now what are you going to do, Miss Drama Queen? I'm not scared or ashamed, so go ahead and do what you gotta do!"

Paris, as if on cue, walked in the kitchen just in time to stop the girls from coming to blows. "Hey, what's wrong in here? Y'all act like y'all about to throw down."

"Nothing," the twins answered at the same time.

Collectively, they put their family argument on hold as all three of the girls rejoined a smug-faced O.T. in the living room, waiting for Storm's arrival.

Kenya, tired of watching her sister and O.T. give each other the side eye on the sly, grew fed up and was about to explode and spill the beans, letting the chips fall where they may. "You know what?" she asked, looking at Paris with her eyes bucked and lips pouted out.

Before Paris got a chance to reply, there was a soft knock at the front door, causing everyone to pause and fortunately stopping an overly frustrated Kenya from busting on O.T. and her sister. Getting up, pulling his pistol out of his waistband, he put one up top. O.T. signaled over to his soon-to-be sister-in-law to get ready.

"All right, Kenya. Go ahead—open up the door!"

Kenya turned the knob on the door and cautiously pulled it open. She peeked out, barely getting a glimpse of the tail end of a black Yukon driving off as quietly as it apparently had driven up. Kenya looked down, receiving a happy, but sad, sight. Her man was home. It was Storm laid out on the front porch. His back was turned away from her, but Kenya could tell that it was without a doubt him. It was her Storm and he was home. Now things could possibly go back to normal and all would be well.

"O.T., hurry up! It's Storm! He needs help!"

Paris and O.T. ran out onto the stairs, leaving a hesitant London standing alone, waiting to come face-to-face with the all-so famous Storm. Even though she helped out in giving up her money for his safe return, she didn't know him, so it was hard for her to show genuine concern.

O.T. placed his hand on his brother's shoulder and took his time carefully turning him over on his back. "That mother-fucker! That old motherfucker!" O.T. mumbled with Javier on his mind. He was pissed to see his brother looking like he did. Paris, distraught, covered her mouth in total disbelief, while Kenya's already fragile heart skipped a beat and crumbled at the sight of her once strong, handsome, devoted fiancé all the girls wanted to be with and who all the guys wanted to be.

"How could they?" Kenya buried her face, sobbing into her hands. "Why would they—why?"

Storm's face had been somewhat mutilated and disfigured. Not only was his earlobe sliced, his entire right side of his jaw was bigger than both Kenya's hands put together. His once-perfect, kissable lips were cracked and dry as if he hadn't had water or any other fluids in days on end. Storm's overall body weight was decreased by at least twenty pounds since Kenya and O.T. last saw him. His left leg had a makeshift kind of medical bandage attached to a flimsy basement-made splint. And lastly, Storm was delirious and beyond dazed.

"Come on, y'all, and help me get him inside before the nosy-ass neighbors around here come outside," O.T. loudly ordered. "We have to get him on the couch and off this hard, cold concrete."

Paris let her anger with O.T. go as she bent down, position-ing herself to help lift an almost motionless Storm up. "Kenya, we need you to get on his other side so we won't bump his leg. Hurry up, because I'm losing my grip."

Standing frozen momentarily, Kenya swiftly snapped back to reality and took Storm's twisted leg in her arms. London could see that the trio was struggling, so she rushed over, swinging the door open wide as she could, praying to score points with O.T. for helping. When they got a semiconscious Storm on the couch, turning all the lights on brightly, they got a chance to fully take in the true harshness of the way that Storm was treated wherever he was being held captive at.

Storm's eyes were puffy, red, and watery. Almost swollen shut in the corners, they kept rolling in the back of his head while he was mumbling words that made absolutely no sense whatsoever to any of them. It was as if he was what the old people down south called "speaking in tongues" or "talking out the side of his neck," like he was insane. It was obvious he was half out of his mind.

Oh my God! This is bad! London thought.

Storm was drifting in and out of consciousness. The once-vibrant, outgoing young man wasn't aware of his surroundings or any of his family around him. Storm was messed up bad, to put it mildly!

"That fried-bean-eating motherfucker Javier is gonna pay for this! I don't give a shit how long it takes! Ain't nan son of a bitch alive walking this damn earth gonna do this type of bullshit to my family and live long to brag about it!" O.T. kicked the end table, causing the lamp to wobble. "I swear I mean it! I swear I do!"

"Listen, baby," Paris reassuringly caressed his back as she tried to soften his fury. "Now is not the time to trip. We should be thanking God that we didn't get Storm back in a body bag! Now we gotta call somebody and get your brother some medical attention. That's first on the agenda. So snap outta it and let's get it done!"

Remembering how Deacon made it back home, headless, London agreed with Paris as they stood on each side of O.T., watching Kenya down on her knees, kissing Storm's swollen face. "I'm so sorry, baby," she repeated as she wet his split lip with a moist rag. "So, so sorry."

"He knows already, Kenya," Paris now consoled her best friend also. "He knows, girl—he knows."

O.T. flipped open his phone and strolled down his locked-in contact numbers. He went down a long, long list until he found it. "Here it is!" he announced, happily glancing over at his injured brother. "Bernard Crayton." O.T. waited for the person to answer his call. "Hey dude, this is O.T., I need you to do me a solid. ASAP. It's an emergency—a serious one!"

***

"From the looks of things, without the aid of X-rays, it seems as if Storm's leg is broken. Now, considering the swelling and the color tone of the bruises on the lower knee area, I think it's already started the healing process, but honestly, in my opinion, if it isn't put in a cast and set properly, he might end up with a permanent limp."

Dr. Bernard S. Crayton had gotten to the condo in less than twenty minutes after O.T. placed the call to him. He was a regular fixture down at Alley Cats and on call 24-7 anytime one of the fellas would need him. He was shady as a motherfucker could get, but knew his shit. "Come on, let's move him to a bed and get him undressed so that I can examine him fully and get a better look at the damage."

As Kenya led the way, O.T. and Big Doc B carried the completely passed out Storm up to the bedroom.

"Lay him down here." She yanked back the covers and started undressing Storm the best she could as the guys talked over on the other side of the newly decorated master suite. Using scissors, she cut away what was too difficult to remove.

"You know that all this shit is on the hush-hush right?" O.T. focused in on Big Doc B's eyes.

"Come on now, how you gonna play me? You know me better than that," the doctor reassured him. "I know the routine."

"You my nigga!" O.T. smiled, placing one hand on his shoulder. "My motherfucking nigga!"

London and Paris were now left standing alone downstairs once again. It was much like the night that the two had first met, only this time the victim in the house was Storm instead of Deacon.

"I wonder what's going on up there? I hope he's all right." Paris put her hand on her chest. "I know Kenya is tripping out right about now."

"I know. I've been on my knees praying every night that Storm was safe." London was lying through her teeth as she tried conniving in intent to befriend Paris. "I know that O.T. is happy. Maybe now you two can stop all that silly bickering and live happily ever after."

Paris went and plopped down in the chair, feeling the brand-new soft, buttery leather. "Naw London, I'm afraid that it's a little bit deeper than just Storm being gone. Me and that man been and still do got bigger issues than that— much bigger!"

"Dang, gee Paris, I'm sorry to hear that." London smirked behind Paris's back. "Do you want to talk about it? I'm a good listener."

"Nope, I'm tight. I'm good. Besides, I ain't trying to start crying."

"Girl, maybe you should just get it off your chest!" London urged, continuing to smirk.

"Naw London, I don't want to bore you with me and O.T.'s problems. I'll just have to deal with him and that black spook Chocolate Bunny on my own."

"It's all right, Paris. We're friends, aren't we?"

"Yeah girl, but I'm gonna just sit here and think. Thanks, though."

London was disappointed that Paris choose not to confide in her, but she wasn't going to let that stop the fake compassion from pouring. She wanted O.T., thug or not, Paris's man or not—fuck Chocolate Bunny, Santa Claus, and the Tooth Fairy! They were all irrelevant to her!

If Gran was watching down from heaven, she would be ashamed at how London was behaving. Yet, London felt like the world had stepped on her for the last time. From day one she always tried doing the right thing and the only reward she got in return were several swift, hard kicks in the ass. Life for London was not fair in her eyes.

Her parents were both murdered when she was a baby. Gran was gone, the only one who truly loved her. Her favorite uncle, Stone, was killed. Her virginity was taken from her against her will. She had to suddenly drop out of school and now the only thing or person who she had left to cling to, Kenya, was slowly being snatched away by these strangers that her twin now called family. It was no way that London intended on that happening, no matter what the cost. Her vindictive alter ego had taken over and she didn't care who paid the price for her happiness.

What's taking them so long up there? London thought, staring at the stairs. *I hope that O.T. is okay. Maybe he needs me?*

Kenya had only gotten around to removing Storm's filthy, sweat-soaked shirt by cutting it off, when she noticed a huge-sized dirty gauze taped across his shoulder. She peeled it back. It revealed an ugly, open sore.

"O.T., my God, come here! What is this? What happened?"

The doctor ran over and investigated. "It looks like a gunshot wound to me. As far as I can tell, I think the bullet went in and out. I need to get a closer look at him. Hurry and flip him on his side."

O.T. did as he was instructed, gently handling his older brother. He held him in his arms just as their mother used to do when they were kids before she started smoking. Big Doc B rubbed his hands over Storm's back.

"Yes, here it is! Here's the exit wound. Yeah, I was right, it was a clear gunshot, in and out," he verified his earlier prediction. "And it appears as if it has been treated with bacterial ointment of some sort. There are no signs of infections. Someone seems to have cleaned it up pretty good."

"What the hell does that mean? Is he okay?" Kenya worried, confused. "Shouldn't we take him to the hospital?"

"We can't," O.T. cut her off. "That shit is out—no hospital!"

"Yes, Kenya, I'm afraid he's right, we can't risk doing that. You see, the doctors are sworn by law to contact the authorities when treating any gunshot wounds big or small," Big Doc B reasoned with her. "Besides, like I said, all in all, he's okay and healing just fine. Just let nature take its course. In the meantime, I'm gonna give you some morphine to keep him sedated and still. If he awakes in pain keep him calm and up the dosage slightly. I can also give you penicillin to fight off any of the remaining infections."

"How is he gonna eat?" Kenya inquired, having no idea how to care for Storm. "Or pee?"

"When he awakes, even for a few seconds, feed him warm broth, even if you pour a little bit down his throat, but the other part is on you. I sure hope that you're up to playing nursemaid for a couple of weeks. Storm's gonna need it!"

Kenya glanced back at Storm, who was tossing and turning and seemed to be gasping for air. The doctor had O.T. go out to his car and bring in a big, sealed cardboard box. After they got Storm comfortable in the bed, Big Doc B opened the box and pulled out ointments, syringes, penicillin, and plenty of morphine. He instructed Kenya in all the aspects of being the perfect caregiver to the badly injured Storm.

Storm was finally resting peacefully, back at home, in his own bed. With an IV in his arm, a slow-drip morphine keeping him doped up, and all his wounds treated, the doctor was finished for the night. O.T. escorted Big Doc B out to his car and paid him a nice chunk of change for the long, extended house visit and his agreed-upon silence.

Kenya stayed next to Storm's bedside, rubbing his forehead and begging for his forgiveness. Paris fixed some tea for them both and made her way upstairs also, deciding to spend the night and lend her best friend some much-needed moral support. That left O.T. and London all alone in a dimly-lit living room.

"Is she okay up there?" London whined, leaning her head on O.T. "You think Kenya needs me?" London would be first in line to receive an Academy Award for her acting performance, knowing in all reality she was starting to care less about Kenya's feelings.

"Naw, but I think I might need your ass. How about that?" O.T. had a long, rough day. Seeing his big brother and hero broken down had taken a heavy toll on him. "Come to think of it, I do need you."

O.T. rested his head in London's lap and in no time flat he was snoring, not once giving a second thought to Paris being in the same house. His brother was home and nothing else seemed to matter.

Things are about to be in my favor for once! O.T. said he needed me! Not Paris's stuck-up-ass and not that slut-bag Chocolate Bunny they keep arguing about, but me! London couldn't help but smile as she closed her eyes, finally dozing off to sleep herself.

Hopefully to avoid conflict, Paris and Kenya were upstairs doing the same. They had all had enough drama for the day and Paris catching her man cheating with her best friend's twin sister would only make the day end with a bang. No doubt about it, it was going to be a long couple of weeks for Kenya, Storm, Paris, O.T., and London.

Chapter Thirty-one

Da Game Ain't Fair

Several days passed and Storm was basically still out of his rabbit-ass mind. There was little to no change in his overall condition. The swelling in his jaw was, however, going down, but still had some very bad bruising. The gunshot wound was the only thing that appeared to heal quickly. Storm would move his bad leg from time to time in his sleep, when he would scream out in pain, like he was a small animal being hunted down, caught, and killed. Watching him in that state made a weary Kenya cry on the regular at his bedside.

The perfect brush waves Storm always sported were gone. His hair was growing daily and nappy as a fuck. His beard was thick and looked downright messy as hell. And even though Kenya kept his face washed, his once-brown, perfectly toned skin was dry and blemished. With all the weight that he had dropped since Javier first held him hostage, Storm was only a shadow of the man that he used to be. He stayed unconscious most of the time because of the intense pain he was suffering, making Kenya's job of getting even a tiny sip of soup down his throat almost an impossible task.

And then it was keeping the covers dry and clean, which was a bitch, seeing how Storm was pissing on himself and sweating like a motherfucker. Kenya refused to use the Depend undergarments that Big Doc B suggested. She felt like that was humiliating for her fiancé to have to deal with when he did come back to reality. When he would awaken, all Storm would do was moan and mumble about a lot of nothing that made no sense. Each day seemed to stretch out longer and longer before he would fully recover to his old self and things got back to normal. Kenya was exhausted, but was extremely devoted.

Big Doc B stopped by every other day to examine Storm and check on his healing process. Slowly, he was decreasing the amount of morphine that Storm was under the influence of. He didn't want to keep him sedated so long that he wasn't able to regain use of his leg without the aid of therapy. Big Doc B knew that with some of the excruciating pain, Storm would have to be a thoroughbred trooper and man the fuck up. It would be some hard shit to do, but nothing that Storm couldn't handle.

KENYA

"I don't know how much more of this I can take." Kenya was distraught and moving around like a zombie. Staying up late at night, waiting and catering to Storm's every need was breaking her down both physically and mentally. She was starting to truly look like hot death on a stick. It had been days since she had a long, hot bath or sat down to watch her stories on television. Her hair was standing on the top of her head and her face had forgotten what makeup was. Every moment that Kenya was awake, she spent posted by Storm just in case he opened his eyes and needed any little thing.

London would help her at times, but felt like it wasn't her duty or her responsibility to be a stranger's slave. Only when O.T. was around would she put on a front and act like she gave a shit about Kenya or Storm. Kenya had just finished changing the sheets and getting Storm settled when she heard her cell phone ring. She kissed Storm on his dry lips and went into the den to answer the call.

PARIS

"Why every day it gotta be the same old fake shit from you, O.T.?" Paris was in the bathroom, yelling at O.T. as he took his morning shower. "You just got in this motherfucker at four thirty in the morning, now you back out the door again! Nigga, I ain't slow or crazy. Ain't shit open that late at night, but the jailhouse and a stankin' bitch's pussy."

O.T. continued to let the hot water pound his body as he zoned Paris completely out of his mind. His hands rubbed the soap on his chest and let his imagination drift to thoughts of fucking the shit out of London. He had his fingers up inside of her tight, moist pussy and had sucked on her titties, but had never actually given her the dick. His thick, long manhood throbbed from his hands letting the lather work its way up and down as he stroked it hard. At that second O.T. would have spit in his dead great-grandmother's face if he could have had London bent over with his dick knee-deep up in her. He loved Paris as much as a man could love a woman, but her constant nagging was starting to turn him off. His motto was that there was nothing better than brand-new pussy. And London was his new target.

"Do you hear me talking to your half-nickel slick dumb ass?" Paris yanked back the shower curtain and rolled her eyes, immediately catching a serious attitude. "I'm trying to talk to you and you in here beating your motherfucking meat! You ain't shit!"

"Why don't you get out of my ear with all that ying-yanging and put your mouth to better use?" O.T.'s shit was about ready to explode, with or without Paris's help with it. "Now come on, girl. Come catch some of this cream!"

"Nigga, please. Why don't you get that bitch you was with last night to suck your little dick? That broken-ass cell phone of yours called me back after you hung up and I heard them bitches giggling and shit."

"Damn, Paris, stop tripping and come get on your knees!" O.T. let what his woman said come in one ear and fly out the other. "You know ain't shit little about this motherfucking monster I got in my hands! So why don't you come see Daddy?"

Paris was pissed off even more by O.T. ignoring the information she'd just confronted him with. "Didn't you hear what I said, with your trick-ass? I heard that slut talking about the ringer on her phone being 'Gold Digger'!" Paris pulled her robe tight and folded her arms. "What kind of real woman would have that bullshit on their phone? Don't fuck around and give me AIDS or something! You're a poor excuse for a man!"

O.T. had enough of her accusations and insults. This time he was innocent and didn't feel like all that drama she was bringing his way. O.T. was past running late for an appointment and still had to swing by a couple of his dope spots before he headed for his meeting. He was determined to get his nuts out the sand before he left and snatched an angry Paris into the shower with him.

Her hair was now drenched and her short, pink robe was soaking wet, causing her nipples to harden. In the middle of her struggling to break free from him, O.T.'s dick got harder than it ever had been before. He quickly turned her around, pressing her face on the wet shower wall, raising up her robe. He ran his hands down the crack of her ass and soon he had his index finger working her out. Paris was out of breath and gave in to her man as the steam filled the bathroom. He shoved all eight and a half inches up into her while he watched the water drip on her backside. Right before he was about to cum, O.T. shut his eyes, imagining that she was London. He tilted his head back and almost busted for what seemed like an hour straight past eternity.

"Now! Do that seem like a nigga been fucking around on your silly-ass?" O.T. blew Paris a kiss as he stepped out the shower, grabbing a towel to dry off. He splashed on some Armani Black Code and started getting dressed. Rubbing lotion on his face and brushing his hair, he double-checked the mirror twice, clipped his cell phone on his jeans, and got his wallet out of the nightstand. "I love you, Paris!"

Paris was too exhausted from the sexual beat-down that he had just put on her to even argue. "Whatever!"

"Here's some dollars for you to go get your wig tightened up for Daddy! And buy a new outfit." O.T. peeled off four or five hundreds and tossed them on the dresser before he left out the door.

"I need to talk to you," Paris yelled out, still weak in the knees. "I'm serious!

"I'll be back later, boo! Keep it hot for a nigga!"

Paris was left speechless as she heard him pull out of the parking lot and away from the apartment. "I know that bastard is cheating on me!" She had to vent and decided to call her girl. Maybe she could convince her to go to the hair salon with her. After grabbing the cordless phone, she dialed Kenya's cell and waited for her to pick up.

GIRLFRIENDS

"Hey, Kenya. Are you busy?"

"Naw chick, not really. What's really good with you?"

"Girl, I'm sitting over here mad as a son of a bitch. If I didn't have a lot of self-control, I think I would just put two bullets in O.T.'s cheating-ass and get it over with!" Paris stood in front of the mirror, brushing her wet hair back into a ponytail.

"Slow down, Paris." Kenya knew that her best friend was in pain and mentally tired of O.T. and his crap.

"Naw girl, enough is enough. I done about had it with him and his dogmatic ways!"

"Paris. You ain't making any sense right now. Tell me exactly what went on over there."

"First that fool had the nerve to slither his behind in the house at damn near four thirty this morning," she argued as her friend listened. "Even when I close the club at night that nigga will bug out if I'm more than five minutes late getting home, but he thinks he can fall up in the crib whenever! Girl, bye with all that—for real!"

"Dang! Where did he say he was? Or did he?" Kenya shook her head with disgust, knowing when it came to Storm's brother he could've been anywhere with anybody.

"You know that bullshit would be too much-like, right, but that ain't even the bad part!" Paris threw herself on the bed and put her feet up on the headboard. "His cell phone dialed me back by mistake and I swear to God I heard that tack-head Chocolate Bunny running her big mouth in the background."

"You lying to me!" Kenya was now also frustrated about the shit. "Please tell me you lying, Paris!"

"Hmph, I wish the fuck I was. And when I asked the two-timing dog he started playing the dumb role, then he had the audacity to flip the script and take the damn pussy!" Paris was shouting into the phone receiver by this time and was back on her feet. "If I didn't have an allergy to fucking prison, I'd kill him in his fucking sleep!"

Kenya couldn't understand why O.T. couldn't be loyal to one woman and was so damn ruthless. He was a bona fide ho! If she was dealing with a Negro like that, it would be no way that she would tolerate all the mess that Paris put up with. Paris was a way better woman than she was.

O.T. would stop by the condo every afternoon and sit by Storm. He filled him in on all the news from the club and the goings-on in the streets. The fact that Storm was doped up on morphine and didn't even realize that O.T. was in the room, never once stopped his brother from talking. O.T. had a split personality. He was like Dr. Jekyll and Mr. Hyde. He was sweet as pie one minute and the next, a beast ready to kill you at the drop of a dime.

"Kenya, I ain't lying. That boy gonna end up in a casket one day double-crossing a bitch like me!" Paris knocked a framed picture of him and her to the floor. "He got me twisted! Shit, I need a damn drink!"

"Girl, why don't you come on over so we can kick it in person? I can get London to cook us up some hot wings and fries," Kenya suggested, wanting some company other than Storm and her sister, both of whom were quiet.

Paris looked at herself again in the mirror, coming up with a better idea. "Why don't I just swing by and swoop your ass up? We can hit the Steak House, then the hair salon. How about it?"

"Girl, you know I can't leave Storm alone. He needs someone by his side constantly."

"You need to get out and get some fresh air. Your sister can stay home and look after him," Paris pleaded with her best friend. "I know you look a hot mess right about now."

Kenya noticed that three of her fingernails were in bad need of a fill-in and her polish was chipped. She then tried running her fingers through her hair, but was stopped by a few naps. "Yeah, I do need a touch-up and a manicure."

"Then it's settled. Let me get dressed and I'll come get you!" Paris was geeked to finally, even if it was temporary, have her road dawg back.

"Pump your brakes, Paris. I gotta go ask London first."

"Okay cool, but hurry up and call me back before I jump in the shower and wash O.T.'s good lying-ass off me."

"You silly as hell," Kenya giggled. "Just give me a minute to check and see what's up."

Paris and Kenya automatically assumed that London would be the perfect person to stay with Storm, considering the fact she didn't have a life of her own. Kenya's life and world had somehow swallowed it whole. The best friends never thought maybe London wanted to go out for lunch or get her hair done. She was also stuck in the house in a strange town with no friends. But that didn't stop Kenya from asking her for a favor just the same.

Kenya stopped in to check on Storm before going downstairs. He was quiet and seemed to be resting peacefully. Since the dosage was decreasing, he seemed to be in and out of consciousness more often. She kissed him softly and made her way to the lower level of the condo. When she got in the living room, she found her twin sister doing something that she'd never seen her do before. London was stretched out across the couch, feet up on a pillow, watching rap videos and even acting like she was enjoying them.

"No, you ain't! I thought you said videos were stupid and degrading to women? Now your butt sitting up here posted like a motherfucker!"

"Shut up!" London threw a pillow at Kenya. "I'm just looking at this ghetto trash, trying to understand exactly what everyone finds so interesting."

London was a lie and the truth wasn't in her. She had been keeping her eyes glued on the way the girls danced and moved their asses, to the way they dressed. She understood why O.T. liked Paris, who was smart, pretty, and always had his back. Paris truly had her shit together; that part was undeniable. Even if she wanted to hate, she couldn't find much. But that serpent Chocolate Bunny was altogether different. From what London had heard about her, she was no more than a dirty, unkempt gutter rat. Whatever O.T. saw in her, Paris, Kenya, and London were all hard-pressed to realize. Maybe all the wild, nasty videos would shed some light on the dilemma and help London to turn O.T. on. If it took being sleazy and a little hot in the ass to achieve the ultimate goal of having O.T. all to herself, then so be it, that's what she'd do.

"Listen, London, would you mind sitting upstairs with Storm for a few hours so I can run out for a little while with Paris? Please?"

London had been hoping and wishing that Kenya would leave the house so that she could be alone with O.T. when he would come over for one of his daily afternoon visits. Now was her time and to make shit even better, Kenya was hanging out with Paris. She would have O.T. all to herself.

"Yeah, sis, I'll stay here. No problem."

Kenya went and called Paris back, informing her that their plan was a go. She took a quick bath and got dressed. Meanwhile, London stayed downstairs and plotted her seduction game plan. Twenty minutes later Paris pulled up, blowing her horn.

"Don't worry about Storm. I'll make sure to check in on him every fifteen minutes and give him his medicine on time," London convinced her sister all would be well. "Go and have a nice time. He's in good hands. Take all the time you need."

"Say you promise!" Kenya hugged London.

"Yeah, I promise!" London walked her twin to the front porch, waving hello to Paris, knowing she was secretly scheming on stealing her man right from underneath her nose.

Chapter Thirty-two

Fuck Da World

O.T.

O.T. had the sounds in his car on bump as usual, causing all the other car windows to vibrate that he passed along the way. The long valet line at the mall's main entrance didn't matter one bit to him as he pulled up to the front and parked his ride up on the curb. He and his brother not only knew the parking attendants, they hung out with the lot's owners on a regular basis, making O.T. feel like he was above waiting for shit. He threw the guy his keys in case of emergency and walked inside.

He was already ten minutes late and wasted no time in going over to the designated meeting spot near the food court. It was always busy with people moving about, so he and his visitor would more than likely go unnoticed. It was no way that he wanted to draw attention to them. He looked around and didn't see the person yet, so he decided to order a large soda. By the time he reached in his pocket to pay the cashier for it, she was there.

"Hey babe, did you get me something wet to put in my mouth?" she flirted while sticking out her tongue to reveal the small gold ball pierced through the middle.

"Damn girl! You slick with your shit. I didn't even see your ass coming." O.T. ordered her a small soda to drink and fought the urge for her to lick the head of his dick just like she used to. "A brother better be careful dealing with your good creeping ass!"

"You know how I do, baby. Ain't shit changed since back in the day!" She sipped her drink slowly out the straw as she stared into O.T.'s eyes.

"I heard that," He took a large gulp of the soda and tossed the rest of it into one of the garbage cans. "But I'm trying to take care of some other shit today so I need to hurry the fuck up!"

O.T. took his time as he scanned his surroundings for signs of any trouble or unwelcome eyes on them. When he felt the coast was clear he pulled out a gigantic knot of money, big enough to choke King Kong, and slipped it casually into Nicole's oversized purse.

"Do I need to count it?" she playfully teased, pushing his arm. "Or can I trust you?"

"Come on, girl, act like you know! I don't make moves that ain't right or have you forgotten?" O.T.'s eyes shot down toward the huge print in his pants. "I'll expect to hear from your smart-ass tonight!"

"Yeah, yeah, yeah, I'll see you later at the club, don't worry." Nicole grinned, closing her purse. Being the true whore she was, she stood up, straightening out the ultra-short bright red sundress that was plastered to her thick frame.

"That's a bet, and be on time!" O.T. winked, getting a quick, glimpse of her two firm breasts, which were close to almost falling out of her clothes.

"Damn, I almost forgot. Can you keep a secret?" She put one hand on her hip and the other in his face.

"What is it?" He waited for her to answer.

Nicole leaned up and whispered in O.T.'s ear, causing him to smile. He then hugged her tightly and kissed her on her forehead before they parted ways.

"Okay, then drinks on me later," O.T. laughed as he walked away to the valet. "Or something like that, I guess!"

"You crazy boy!"

"Ain't that some foul-ass shit?"

Paris's homegirl and spy down at Alley Cats, Jordan, happened to be at the mall at the right time. She was busy spending the money that she made from doing a private party the night before and fucked around and got an eyeful of what was sure to be labeled the gossip of the year. Paris's man O.T. was giving

Nicole Daniels a gang of loot. After all the denying that he was doing to Paris about that tramp, he was out in public, in the middle of the freaking food court no less, tearing the bitch off proper style and to top it all, hugging her black-ass.

"Hell naw! I've gotta call Paris!" Jordan smirked as she whipped out her cell to put O.T.'s ass straight on blast. *It's gonna be a whole lot of crazy shit jumping off at Alley Cats tonight,* Jordan thought to herself as Paris's voice mail clicked on. She left her a message, "Hey girl, this is Jordan. Hit me back as soon as you get this. I need to put a bug in your ear about a little something. Trust me, you're gonna bug all the way when I tell you what I just seen. Call me back first thing first!"

GIRLFRIENDS

"Kenya, I'm so happy that you came out to hang with me." Paris had the air-conditioning on high and a mix CD pumping. "I miss your wild ass!"

"Child, me too. Now you know I love Storm like a mother-fucker, but a bitch did need some air. Plus, look at my nails and please, let's not even mention this tangled mess on my head! I walked passed the mirror this morning and scared the hell out of myself."

Paris and Kenya couldn't help but laugh until tears came out their eyes. It was just like old times.

"What about this crap?" Paris snatched one of O.T.'s baseball caps off her head. "If that nasty fool nigga wasn't so busy trying to take that pussy, my shit wouldn't be on the nut."

They had just finished up with a good lunch and a couple of strong drinks and were on their way to the hair salon. Hair In Da Hood was the most popular spot in all of Dallas when it came to getting your hair looking top-notch. It stayed packed with wall-to-wall customers who would often range from lawyers and doctors to freaks and hoes.

Charday was the salon owner and the main stylist that everyone wanted to do their hair. Her chair stayed full. Most of the time a person would have to make an appointment at least two or three weeks ahead of time. But of course, Ms. Charday, a true hustler, would always make exceptions for her special clients and her good friends. And since Paris and Kenya were known for being big-ass spenders when it came to tipping, they automatically fit into both categories.

Paris and Kenya were on a mission to pamper themselves for the day and that meant no stress and no drama or trauma.

"I've got a good idea. For the rest of the afternoon, let's make a pact not to bring up, mention, whine or complain about that pair of brothers we're linked up with." Paris stuck her hand out and waited. "Well, you gonna leave me hanging or what?"

"Naw chick, I got you!" Kenya gave her a play. "Bet it up for real!"

"Now that's what the fuck I'm talking about!" Paris yelled out as she adjusted the volume up as high as it could go.

The girls put their seats back as they floated down the highway toward the salon. Fifteen minutes later they were pulling up in a crowded parking lot, trying to find a space that wasn't eight doors down or around the corner.

"Damn! Is every trick in town up in that joint?" Paris frowned as she pulled her car into a tiny corner of the lot. "I hope our girl ain't too booked. I'd hate to have to smack somebody out the chair, but my shit is on emergency status." Paris looked at Kenya with a straight face like she was serious.

She turned the car's ignition off and reached for her purse that was on the backseat before she made her exit.

"Dang, you right, Paris." Kenya joined in on talking shit as she got out of the car. "Charday and them must be giving away free cheese, honey, and butter inside. I ain't never seen this motherfucker on bump like this either."

The girls swung the door open and stepped inside. Just as they figured, the salon was packed. Sable was the receptionist and was standing behind the desk, trying her best to reason with one of the many irate customers who were getting tired of waiting.

"Hey y'all!" Sable happily waved her hand in the air. "Long time, no see. Where y'all divas been hiding?"

"Just chillin' a little bit, that's all," Kenya replied.

"Yeah, Sable, we call our self letting our hair have a break from all the chemicals," Paris added, trying to play off their recent absence from the scene.

"I heard that," Sable responded, seeming frustrated at the phone that was ringing nonstop and the angry woman with conditioner in her damp hair in a plastic cap who kept coming back up to the desk to complain.

Kenya took a quick survey of the waiting room and asked the million-dollar question. "Hey Sable, how many customers do Charday have backed up in this tiny motherfucker and can she squeeze us in?"

"Well, let me check the book. I'm sure she can definitely work something out for y'all two." Sable grabbed the sign-in sheet and took the pencil out from behind her ear.

The lady who was standing there was pissed and sucked her teeth as she waited for Sable's answer. She had been there ever since 11:45 in the morning and still hadn't been rinsed or blow-dried. Same old story, once again as always, Charday had overbooked and had folks pissed.

"I'm gonna go speak to Charday myself and make sure." Kenya stopped Sable from trying to rearrange things. "I'll be right back."

Paris twisted her lip up at the agitated lady and let out a loud sigh. "Go ahead, girl, and see what's popping. I'll wait here and keep Ms. Thang and Sable company."

The woman took that as her cue to go back to her seat, shut the fuck up, and wait until she was called. It was either that or nine out of ten times get a quick double-trouble-ass beat-down from Kenya and Paris. When Kenya returned she had good news and bad news. The good news was that Charday could fit them both in, but they had to give her at least thirty minutes to finish up with the girl in her chair. The bad news was that she had to slip Charday a crisp hundred-dollar bill and promised her a bottle of new perfume for the deed. It was all part of being Storm and O.T.'s girls. They had to play the role—after all, no matter where they went, bitches hated. It came along with the territory being labeled "the shit."

Paris and Kenya sat down next to the angry woman who had pulled out a book and was totally engulfed in reading. She appeared not to even care anymore that she was still waiting as she turned page after page without once looking up.

Paris opened her purse and got out her cell phone to look at the time. "Shit, I didn't hear this thing ringing." The screen said *two missed calls* and had a small envelope in the upper corner indicating that someone had left a voice message. Paris stepped into the bathroom to listen to the message. It was much quieter in there. It was no women gossiping and the sound of the loud radio and television was muffled. *Jordan wants me to call her as soon as possible. What the fuck could this be about?* Paris wondered as she returned the call. On the first ring, Jordan picked up.

"Hey Paris, what took you so long?"

"Hey sis, I had my phone in my purse, what's the deal?"

"Girl, before I tell you this bullshit, you'd better sit down first."

"You too silly! Stop tripping and tell me what you gotsta say! What's going on?"

"Well, girl, I was just out at the mall jacking off some spare change and guess who the fuck I saw?"

"Who?" Paris's heart started pumping fast as she awaited the answer from Jordan. From the tone of Jordan's voice, Paris could tell that the name that was sure to come out of her mouth would bring automatic fury.

"I seen that slut ho Nicole."

"Nicole! Who the fuck is Nicole?" Paris tried to keep her now-agitated voice down.

"Come on, Paris, you know who I'm talking about, girl . . . Chocolate damn Bunny, that's fucking Nicole!"

"And? What's the big deal about that? Hoes gotta shop too!" Paris tried to crack a joke to ease the pain of what might be coming next.

Jordan didn't laugh as she gave her homegirl the lowdown. "Yeah, but she wasn't alone. She was at the food court all hugged up with O.T."

"What! What you say?" Paris closed her eyes, wishing she hadn't just heard what she thought she heard. "Are you for sure?"

"Yes, Paris, I'm certain," Jordan reassured her of what she had just witnessed. "He was wearing some dark-colored jeans, a Mavericks jersey, and Tims. That trick Chocolate Bunny had on a skintight red dress and was rocking a big Gucci bag. Knowing her fake-ass, it was probably bootleg!" Jordan vindictively added.

"It's all good in the hood. I'm gonna handle it." Paris pretended to be brave as her hand shook. "I got this!"

"Oh, yeah it's more. I even saw him give that tramp a nice-sized knot of cash! Hell, I wanted to follow that tack-head and rob her my damn self! With her stankin' no-good low-down dirty-ass! She ain't shit!"

"All right, Jordan, good looking on the info. I'll see you later tonight at the club."

Paris was heated as well as devastated. She went inside of one of the stalls and shut the door. When the tears started to flow she didn't want any of the women in the salon to see her at one of her weakest moments. After ten minutes of having an emotional fit, she splashed cold water on her face and went to fill Kenya in on the latest.

"What took you so long in there?" Kenya inquired. "I was about to send in a search party!"

"I was on the phone."

"Talking to who? And why are your eyes all red and shit? Have you been crying?"

Paris pulled her baseball cap down over her face in an attempt to shield any nosy bitches from noticing the same thing that Kenya had. "I called Jordan back. She left me an urgent message."

"Jordan from the club? What kind of message? Is everything going all right down at Alley Cats?" Kenya hoped that shit was in order. She didn't have the time or strength to go to the club and straighten out a damn thang.

Paris was agitated, trying her best whisper. "It ain't the club. It's O.T.'s no-good ass. Jordan just seen him at the fucking mall."

"What's wrong with that?"

"He was there with Chocolate Bunny." Paris felt like she had just been socked in the stomach as soon as the words passed her lips. "All up on that bitch—caking!"

Kenya was almost speechless. "Is she sure? You know how females like to start rumors—hatin'."

"Naw girl, she knew exactly what that cheating Negro was wearing from foot to fro." Paris sniffed, fighting back the tears. "The worst part is his ass is serving that black bitch up like a queen. Jordan said he gave Chocolate Bunny some dough like she was wifey or something."

"That trifling nigga must be smoking crack!" Kenya said with her hand on Paris's shoulder. "Something ain't right! O.T. and her?"

Less than ten minutes had passed in between the time that the best friends tried to figure out what was wrong with O.T.'s simple behind for doing that dumb shit to Paris and the five seconds it took Chocolate Bunny to prance her slap-happy-ass through the front door of the salon. She was dressed just the way that Jordan described over the phone—all the way down to her purse she was sporting, which, by the way, was definitely without doubt bootleg.

She proudly marched up to the reception desk like she owned stock in the bitch. "Yeah, I need Charday to tighten up my weave real quick!"

"I'm sorry, Nicole, but she's all booked up for the rest of today." Sable chewed her bubble gum and gave her a funny look. "What about tomorrow? She has a ten o'clock open."

Chocolate Bunny reached in her handbag and started flashing money. "Well, I'll pay a hundred dollars to any of y'all customers that wanna give up y'all spot with Charday!"

While she was showboating, Kenya was trying everything in her power to keep Paris in her seat.

"No, that bird ain't up in here spending my money. I outta go over there and knock her ass out!" Paris was fuming. "I hate the fuck out of her!"

"Listen, Paris, it is what it is! Don't let that girl or any other of these females up in here catch you off your square! Boss up—do you hear me?" Kenya was in Paris's ear, being the voice of reason. "Now come on and let's just jet before you embarrass yourself. We can deal with her later. Besides, you should at least give O.T. a chance to explain before you mess around and hurt somebody. Go out to the car and call him!"

Gathering her composure, Paris finally agreed. When the pair was almost out of the door, Chocolate Bunny spotted them and decided to do what she did best, make a scene and overplay her position.

"Oh, hey ladies! I didn't see y'all sitting over there. You two could have spoken or something." She was being bogus as a three-dollar bill. She knew that it wasn't no love shared between them. The only thing that they had up to this point in common was Alley Cats.

"Hey girl," Kenya said, nodding. "We kinda in a rush, so . . ."

"Okay, then damn, don't let me stop you," Chocolate Bunny giggled, rolling her neck. "Or you either, Miss Paris!"

Paris couldn't take it any longer. Her temper was on boiling status. "Listen up, bitch, don't even speak to my fine-ass! A ho like you ain't even in my damn league, okay! Now carry your messy behind the fuck on, before I give your family some arrangements to make for you!"

"Hold tight, Paris! Who you calling bitch, bitch! Is you insane or something?" Chocolate Bunny sucked her teeth, looking Paris up and down like it could and would be whatever. "And don't be threatening me either, Paris, I don't like that kinda shit! Me or my man!"

"Your man?" Paris flared up even more.

"You heard me! I said my man, ho—mine!" she repeated with certainty.

"Yeah, right! You got me all fucked up! I don't make threats, I make promises!" Paris pointed her finger in her face. "Fuck you and him! Believe that!"

Kenya stepped in the middle before either one got a chance to swing. The entire salon was staring at the group, waiting for a show. Charday, being the peacemaker, came over and asked them to calm down or leave. They were all good clients, but business was business and they were all tripping. The last thing she wanted or needed in her salon was a knock-down, drag-out.

Before Paris and Kenya could oblige to Charday's wishes and get out the salon door good, they heard the song "Gold Digger" playing. It was the ring tone that was on Chocolate Bunny's cell phone. Hearing that tune, Paris zoned out, having an instantaneous flashback to the other night when O.T.'s phone dialed her back and recklessly sucker punched the female in her jaw, causing her to fall to the floor smack down on her ass and at the feet of waiting clients.

"She was past due on that one!" Paris snickered as her and Kenya finally got in the car and pulled off.

Damn! Kenya thought as she drove away. *Alley Cats is gonna be on the nut tonight when Nicole gets there. I really gotsa go to the club now!*

Chapter Thirty-three

How, What, Why

O.T.

Driving down the interstate with the warm air blowing on his face, O.T. let the music take control of his mind. He was once again lost in thoughts of London's perfectly shaped ass. He secretly always wanted to fuck the shit out of Kenya, but considering the fact that she was Storm's woman, that made her off limits. Seeing how London was her identical twin, she was the next best thing to actually sticking the dick to his brother's girl. In his twisted mindset it would be like hittin' them both off at the same time.

As O.T. felt his hard pipe pulsate through his jeans, he smiled seeing his exit and quickly made the turn. It was now only a couple of short blocks to get to his brother's crib for his daily visit. His dick was stiff as a board. If he played his cards right, O.T. hoped he might get a few minutes alone with London, at least to feel on her titties or grab a handful of her ass. No matter what he did, she was with it.

Kenya always did her best to cock-block him when it came to her sister, letting him know that it was no way that she was being a part of any backstabbing conspiracy plotted against Paris. If London was in a room with O.T., you betta best believe that Kenya was in that bitch too. Day after day Kenya informed him that there wasn't a damn thing going down on her watch. Little did Kenya or O.T. have any idea that today would be his lucky day.

LONDON

No sooner than Kenya and Paris bent the corner, London ran back in the house and straight up the stairs. She tiptoed into her sister's room, past a sleeping Storm, and went into the closet. It was now time to select an outfit that would make O.T. lose his mind when he saw her. For days, she had taken notes from the videos and knew that with Kenya out of the house, she might finally have the chance to put her plan in effect. After snatching a short blue jean miniskirt off the hanger and a powder-blue T-shirt that was sure to fit tight, London headed for the shower.

She used some of her sister's favorite cucumber melon body wash as she felt the warm water hit her nude body. London then rubbed in plenty of the matching lotion after drying off. Slipping on Kenya's new shell-covered sandals, she pranced downstairs. She then admired her work in the mirror. London now looked exactly just like Kenya. Her once dull appearance was gone and the bait was now set for O.T. to get trapped.

I know that he's gonna want me now! If this doesn't entice him, I don't know what will, she thought as she hugged herself. *I just hope that he gets here at the usual time and Kenya stays gone. I don't need any obstacles getting in my way!* London went into the kitchen, getting one of Kenya's peach-flavored wine coolers out of the refrigerator. She hated the way that they tasted, but holding the bottle in her hand made her feel more mature and sexy. Plus, most of the females in the nasty uncut videos all had glasses in their hands as they danced around.

Where is he at? she wondered, watching the clock. Sitting down on the couch, crossing her legs, London held the remote in her right hand, clicking channels while tapping the cooler bottle with the left.

O.T. pulled into the driveway and turned off his car. He sat back in the custom leather bucket seats, leaning his neck on the headrest. O.T. had to collect his thoughts and closed his eyes briefly. Seeing his brother still suffering after all this time was causing him to have constant migraine headaches. As much as he tried being the strong person that all the people involved depended on, he was starting to crack from the heavy, stressed-filled pressure. When he sat up, opening up his eyes, O.T. saw Kenya standing in the doorway waving to him.

"Damn, I guess I should go ahead and go in," he mumbled as he unlocked the car door. Getting closer up toward the door, he busted out laughing. "Oh, shit, tell me I'm seeing thangs!" O.T. stopped in his tracks, folding his arms and started shaking his head. The jersey he was wearing showed off every muscle, his jeans sagged perfectly, and his Tims had the tongue stuck out with the laces loose.

"What's so funny?" London asked with her hands firmly on her hips. She had done her best to imitate Kenya and now O.T. was standing there laughing in her face. "What's wrong? You don't like it?" London stood still as she waited for him to speak.

"Ain't shit funny, ma. Ain't shit funny at all." He rubbed his chin, licking his lips. "I just thought that you was Kenya and shit. My mistake, don't trip!"

"I'm not tripping, but I don't want you making fun of me," London whined.

"Dig this here," he cut her off. "Where is Kenya at anyway? Is she up there with Storm?"

London stopped pouting and refocused back on her plan. "Naw, she's not home. She went somewhere with Paris. Don't you and your girl communicate?"

"Don't worry about my girl, okay? That ain't none of your business." O.T. got closer, kissing her on the lips.

"Well, what is my business?" she replied with a sarcastic, sassy tone.

"This right here should be your main concern right about now!"

O.T. put her hand on his dick and backed her into the living room. It was just like Christmas and his birthday all wrapped into one as his dick got harder and harder. He had his hands roaming her entire body. London's skirt was pushed up, exposing the fact that she didn't have any panties on. Her naked ass looked just as he had imagined; perfect, plump, and round.

After feeling on, across, and in every part of her body, O.T. was ready to get to the real deal. When he pulled his dick out of his jeans, London was amazed. His shit was long and thick. The head was lighter than the rest of it and was dripping.

"Come get this, ma, he wants to meet you." He motioned to her with one hand while slowly stroking his manhood with the other.

"Do you have any protection?" London wisely asked.

"Naw, I'm good. I ain't got no diseases!"

"I didn't say that you did, but I would feel a lot better if we used something." London spoke up as she broke free from his arms and ran upstairs to try to find a rubber in some of Kenya's belongings.

Five long minutes passed and London hadn't returned yet with the condom. An anxious O.T. sprinted up the staircase and bumped into London, who was coming out of Storm and Kenya's room. He held her tightly and began kissing her once again. She was breathing hard from searching the dresser drawers and was like a rag doll when he took his mouth off of hers. O.T.'s pants were still unzipped, making it easy for him to pull his semi-hard dick back out. He propped his body inside the doorway for support and pushed London down on her knees. Using both of his hands, he took her head in between them and guided her mouth onto the dome of his dripping stick.

"Give him a wet kiss," he urged.

"I haven't ever . . ." Her earring fell off from the force.

"Ever what?" He halted her words by rubbing his dick across her lips, making her taste his pre-cum.

The gloss that she had applied earlier was now on the head of his shaft. London tried to keep protesting, but was only met by O.T. placing his hand firmly behind her neck and the raw feeling of hard meat practically pounding her tonsils crooked. London was starting to make gagging sounds that only fired O.T. up more. The more that London fought to breathe, the harder he pushed in and out.

In all the erotic chaos that was taking place, the two of them failed to realize that for a few brief seconds, Storm had re-gained consciousness and reached out his hand toward them.

O.T. was at the point of no return and yelled out Paris's name, not London's, as he shot the mother lode down her throat, making sure that she swallowed every single drop. When he released her out of his strong-armed grip, London fell onto the plush, new-smelling carpet, gasping for air. Before she could regain her composure, O.T.'s phone chirped. It was Paris, saying that it was an emergency and to meet her at their house ASAP.

"I gotta go! Something's up and my baby needs me!" He stepped over London's body with his Tims still on to get a wet rag. O.T. then zipped up his pants on the way down the stairs, leaving a confused and emotionally drained and wounded London on the floor alone, whimpering.

"Please don't go," she quietly begged from the floor. "Please."

O.T. hadn't paid a second thought to anything that was being said. From the moment he got the call from Paris saying 911, nothing else mattered. "I'll be back to see Storm! And thanks for that head shot!"

London heard him slam the front door shut and the sound of the music from his car stereo fade out of ear range. After a short while she went to the bathroom.

London washed her face and brushed her teeth twice, trying to get the smell of O.T.'s thick, hot sperm out of her mouth. Every time she swallowed, it seemed like there was a strange aftertaste lingering. She couldn't believe that O.T. had the nerve to shout out another woman's name while they were doing something—well, at least while she was. London was totally pissed off, but not at him for that cold, callous display, but at Paris for interrupting them with her false problems.

London knew that Kenya would soon be on her way home, so she rushed to Storm's bedside to give him his medication and change out of her sister's clothes. She didn't want to hear Kenya's long, dragged-out arguing about anything tonight. She wasn't in the mood; besides, her throat was still hurting. The syringe was only one third of the way filled as London walked over to the IV bag that was hanging. She laid the needle down on the nightstand for a quick second to get one of the moist wipes out of the drawer and wet Storm's dry lips. Glancing over at the clock, she realized time was ticking and she still had to change back to her own clothes. As she reached over and started to touch Storm's face with the wipe, he suddenly raised his arm up, tightly grabbing her wrist.

"Kenya, how could you?" he managed to say through his dry lips.

"Stop—you're hurting me!" A stunned London tried pulling back. "Let me go! Let me go!"

"Why, Kenya—why did you lie to me?" Storm was now applying pressure to London's tiny wrist with every passing second.

"I'm not Kenya, I'm London!" she argued to no avail.

"Right, first you were Tastey, then Kenya, and now you're London!" Storm had tears swelling in his eyes. "I thought that you loved me? You said you did! You a liar!"

"I'm not Kenya I keep telling you! Now please let me loose." London tried prying his fingers off her. "You're hurting my arm, you monster!"

"You're not Kenya, but you're wearing the outfit that I picked out for her in Vegas. You smell just like cucumber melon, her favorite scent, and if you haven't looked in the mirror lately, you look just like Kenya!" Storm was heated as he confronted who he truly believed was Kenya. "Stop denying it. Your lies won't work anymore. Just tell me why?"

"Please, Storm, you're hurting me!" London continued to plead, trying to break loose.

"You hurt me too!" Storm argued. "And I see the shit ain't stopped. I woke up and called out to you and what the fuck do I see, but my supposed-to-be fiancée and the love of my life on her knees deep-throating my baby brother." Storm snatched London by her neck. He was furious and wouldn't listen to a word that was coming out of her mouth. "I outta snap this motherfucker in two. You ain't shit!"

London found the inner strength somehow and yanked away from him, stumbling to the floor. "You're crazy!" she screamed, running out the room. "You're crazy!"

Storm tried his best to get out of the bed and chase after her, but he couldn't. His busted leg wouldn't let him. "Kenya! Kenya! Kenya!" he kept calling out in vain. "Come back here! Kenya, come back!"

The echoing sound of his voice and the thought of what he had witnessed between her and O.T. was too much for London to bear. She ran out onto the front porch to escape his verbal wrath. Ten minutes later Paris pulled up, letting Kenya out of the car and drove off in a rush. Kenya casually strolled up the walkway and found London perched on the stairs.

"What are you doing sitting out here?" Kenya's facial expression changed when she got a good look at her twin sister. "And why the hell do you have on my fucking clothes? Storm bought me that damn outfit! Go take it the fuck off!"

As Kenya waited for her answer, London grew angry at the fact that everything always had to be about Kenya. She twisted her upper lip and grinned. "You always think that you and your girl Paris are so high and mighty, don't you?"

"What that got to do with why you wearing my damn stuff?" Kenya fumed at her twin, trying to change the subject. "Tell me that!"

"Whatever!" London ignored her sister, while trying to wrap her head around what had just happened between her and not one brother, but two siblings.

"Well, I'm waiting." Kenya tapped her foot as if she was a scolding parent or teacher. "Why do you have my shit on your back and my new shoes on your feet? Are you gonna answer me or what?"

London stood up, rubbing her sore wrist that was starting to bruise and let her twin have it full blast. "I'll tell you what, Kenya. I've got a bright idea for you. Why don't you get your uppity, stuck-up, trying-to-forget-where-you-came-from-ass inside the house and try answering some questions your damn self?"

"What are you talking about?" Kenya was puzzled by her sister's statement. "What do you mean? Stop talking in secret, cryptic code all the time and try being normal for once."

"What I mean is that you should stop worrying so much about your damn precious little clothes that I borrowed and go in there." London pointed over her shoulder back toward the door. "Your foolish-ass boyfriend, Storm, is wide awake and seems to be somewhat in his right mind. And if I'm not mistaken, something tells me he wants to see you. Now, how's that for being normal!"

"Oh my God! Move outta my way!" Kenya ran past London and up to her and Storm's bedroom. She could hear him screaming out her name louder with each step she took. It was now time for Kenya to face him, explain her ridiculous, unnecessary lies, and try her best to make shit right again.

Chapter Thirty-four

You Dirty Bitch

Kenya neared the door of the bedroom, almost coming to a complete stop. She leaned against the wall, taking several deep breaths. Her pulse was racing and a sudden feeling of jitters caused her to tear up. Trying to get herself together, Kenya's ears were filled with the echoing of Storm's enraged yells.

"Kenya! Kenya!" he ranted and raved. "Where the fuck are you at? Don't let me get out of this motherfucking bed! I'm not playing around with your no-good ass!"

She was frozen with denial. Kenya had never once, since meeting Storm, heard him even raise his voice at her. Now he was lying a few feet away, injured and laid up in the bed, sounding like he was ready to break his foot off into her ass.

Damn! I can't put this shit off any longer. It ain't gonna do nothing but make matters worse. After one more deep breath Kenya turned the corner going in.

"Oh, I see your stankin'-ass finally decided to come back, huh?" Storm's hands were clenched onto the thin blanket that was on the bed. "I know you heard me calling you!" Kenya was quiet, not believing the bitter and callous words that were flying out of Storm's mouth. She couldn't move out the doorway as he continued to go off. "If my leg wasn't fucked up it would be me and you, ho, and mostly me! Believe that!" Storm struggled to get up without success, finally resting his weak body back on the mattress. "Bring your no-good, dick-sucking ass over here!" he demanded, firmly fighting through the excruciating pain he was in. Kenya remained still as tears of pain flowed down her cheeks. Silent, she had no response to him and his insults. She felt guilty enough for what he was going through. In reality, Kenya had no true, solid defense, because if she'd only been honest from the jump maybe some—if not all—the crap that her man had to suffer and endure could've been avoided totally. "I said come here, bitch! I swear to God I ain't gonna ask you no more, Kenya—bring your ass!"

"Wait, listen, Storm," she finally got the courage to say. "Please, baby, I can explain everything if you just give me a chance to."

"We been together for months on top of months. You had all the time in the world to confess your double, rotten-ass life and now you wanna be calm and talk."

"But—" Kenya tried once more to speak.

"But what, bitch? What the fuck can you say?"

"Please, Storm!"

"Please Storm, what?" he lividly hissed as he pounded his closed fist into the mattress. "Please don't be mad that I'm a backstabbing little whore? Is that what you wanna say after all this time—is it?"

Once again Kenya grew speechless. Terrified by his behavior, she still hadn't got within reach of Storm's bedside in fear of what he might actually do. Staring down at the carpet as she cried, she saw one of her earrings on the floor. Noticing it was the mate to the one that London was wearing; Kenya made a mental note to check her sister later on, knowing damn well that this wasn't the time.

"I guess you playing the dum-dum role now. Well, I'll tell you what, Kenya, consider all the fake games as over." Storm swallowed slowly, trying to regain his self-control. "You ain't gotta say shit, after all, the writing is already on the wall. Just know that because of you and your scheming I damn near got killed. Look what they did to me because of your wannabe-police ass!"

"Wait, Storm, are you going to give me at least a chance to try to make you see my side in all of this?" Kenya held up her hand, trying to reason with him. "Please, Storm. I'm begging you. Just listen."

"What you gonna tell me, huh?" He managed to laugh as Kenya gathered up the nerve to get a little closer to the man who she loved with all of her heart. "You gonna tell me that you ain't know nothing about that PAID bullshit, right? You gonna tell me that you ain't trying to undermine my entire operation and shut shit down, right? Is that what you about to say Kenya—is it?"

Storm found some inner strength and reached out, yanking Kenya onto the bed with him. She didn't try to resist, feeling like if he kicked her ass and got it out of his system, maybe then he'd give her a chance to explain. Kenya was willing to make any sacrifice that it took to get things back to normal, even if it meant getting beat the fuck down in her own bed without putting up a fight. Storm tossed her around the king-sized bed with rage and fury as he kept the questions and harsh accusations coming.

"What's wrong, Kenya? I don't hear you telling me any more of those lies about you loving me so much!" he shouted as spit flew in her face. Yet Kenya didn't once scream or try to get away from the assault. "I guess you played me from the jump, huh?" Storm ripped Kenya's shirt off of her back, exposing her red-laced bra. The sight of her plump breasts usually excited him, but this time was much different. After seeing O.T.'s hands rubbing and feeling on them earlier as she sucked his dick, Storm wanted to throw up. Pissed at the sheer thought, he then smacked Kenya across her jaw with all his force. Not able to withstand the blow, she flew out the bed and hit the floor, dazed and dizzy. "Yeah, I guess you ain't London Roberts, either, with your good snitching rat ass?" Storm was enraged and out of control, as he threw the lamp off the nightstand at Kenya's head, "And I guess you wasn't just down on the floor swallowing my little brothers' dick damn near whole in front of my face neither, huh?"

Out of nowhere, the bedroom door flung open, causing both Kenya and Storm to turn and wait for the shit to hit the fan. The next round was sure to be worse than the first.

"Is that you, O.T.?" Storm asked as he wiped the sweat off his forehead. "Is it?"

Kenya planned on breaking the news about her twin sister, but the hell with it. She was now here to do it herself.

"No, it's not your henpecked little brother! It's me, London Roberts. The same London Roberts who was sucking his dick! Is that okay with you?" London stood with her hands on her hips, angrier than Kenya had ever seen her before in her life. "And if you touch my sister like that again I'm going to kill you with my bare hands!"

Storm's eyes seemed to be jumping out of their sockets. He rubbed them both, thinking that he must be hallucinating from the strong dosage of medication that they were keeping him doped up on. "I don't understand. What the fuck is going on?" He placed his palm on his forehead to check for a fever. "Kenya, who is she? I mean, which one of you is Kenya? I'm confused. What's going on? What are y'all trying to do to me? What is this?"

Storm started to hyperventilate from the shock and stress. He now was physically exhausted from struggling with Kenya. His body was still weak from his injuries and couldn't take the turmoil that was taking place. Without warning, he passed out cold.

It was a couple of hours later when Storm finally regained consciousness. O.T. was now sitting on the edge of the bed and laughing as his brother thankfully woke up once again.

"Open up your eyes, faggot-ass sleeping beauty. I ain't got all day to be waiting around to kick your pretty candy-sweet ass in the new Madden!" He teased as he normally did.

Storm was still slightly weak, but managed to sit up and get off into O.T.'s ass. "Later for all that. Man, where the fuck is Kenya at? I had one of the craziest dreams in the world, or should I say fucking nightmares. It was two of them bitches!"

"Hold up, dude, that wasn't no dream. It is." O.T. got his brother a cold glass of water to drink while he explained. "Your woman got an identical twin sister. Her name is London and trust me, you can't hardly tell them the fuck apart! Apparently, the girl been living back in Detroit all this time." O.T. shrugged his shoulders and rubbed his head. "Why didn't she tell you about her? I mean, that's wild. Kenya is straight out of order!"

"Fuck all that bull! Where is she at?" Storm asked loudly. "I don't believe all that twin stuff! Where the hell is she?"

"Who, London?"

"Hell naw, Kenya!" Storm frowned. "Matter of fact, yeah, go get both of them." He still didn't think that it could be possible that Kenya had a sister, let alone a twin sister. "Show me both of them side by side, then I'll believe that bullshit! Until then—"

"Yeah, all right then." O.T. left out the room and walked downstairs to inform the girls that Storm was awake. "Hey Kenya, he's up, but ol' boy don't think that it's two of y'all. He thinks that he was just bugging out on all that medication that Big Doc B got him hyped up on. He wanna see you and London, together."

"Well, too fucking bad! I don't want to see that no-good female-beating brother of yours!" London rolled her eyes as she kept a cold, wet rag pressed onto Kenya's swollen face. "After what he did to my sister I should call the damn police and press charges on him!" She leaped to her feet with anger.

"Bitch! I wish you would call five-oh on Storm!"

O.T. was now standing toe-to-toe with London, who wasn't in the mood for backing down. She still had a beef with him from earlier, but discussing that part would have to wait. Also sitting in the living room with a permanent grim expression was Paris. O.T. and his girl had been feuding ever since she stepped foot back inside their apartment. O.T., cold busted, had the nerve to try to lie about being at the mall with Chocolate Bunny. Even after Paris described stitch by stitch everything that the slut was wearing, just like a cheater, he still denied it.

Paris knew that her girl Jordan saw his ass, no doubt about it, but she wasn't gonna put her on front street or throw her up underneath the bus. Paris had just enough time to smack the shit out of O.T. and brace up to battle with his lunatic butt, when the call came in that Storm was awake and asking for him. The two promised to settle things up later that night as they put their differences aside and rushed over. Paris, fed up with his bully routine, got up in O.T.'s face, daring him to put his hands on London, Kenya, or her. O.T., feeling out-numbered, decided to try to reason with the hostile females, mainly Kenya.

"Listen, I don't know if all three of y'all is bleeding at the same time or what, but you gotta expect for Storm to be tripping right about now!" O.T. leaned over and looked Kenya in her eyes. "Don't none of us know what the fuck he had to go through and endure over there, do we? What the hell, that guy been shot, leg fucked the hell up, ear sliced, and almost starved to death, and you hoes wanna bug out because one of y'all got roughed up a little for starting all the bullshit from jump!"

Kenya was starting to feel remorse and guilt for having an attitude that Storm had kicked her ass without giving her a chance to talk. "I guess you're right, O.T." She removed the rag from her black-and-blue bruised jaw and got up off the couch. "Please, London, can you just go up there with me to see him for a minute?"

London folded her arms and turned her focus on the green grass and flowers that were right outside the huge picture window. She ignored her sister's request, acting as if the devil himself had asked for help burning Bibles on Easter Sunday morning.

"Get your punk-ass up them damn stairs before I drag you up there!" O.T. pushed London, who swung on him, but missed.

"Paris, I strongly suggest you get your coward so-called man before I say something that everyone will regret." London caught herself from falling into the sofa table. "Now that I think about it . . ."

Kenya remembered all the accusations that Storm made, including going down on O.T. and the fact that London owned up to it and even seemed proud. Kenya knew her twin's personality had turned foul and spiteful. She was in pain and sore, but knew that if London let that little cat out the bag, everybody in the house would be thumping.

"Please, London, I'm begging you." Kenya gave her the look, knowing exactly what her twin was only seconds from saying. "I'll do anything you want me to do. Just come on!" Kenya pulled her stubborn sister by the arm and led her up the staircase.

London turned back, giving O.T. the evil eye as she watched Paris start to argue with him.

The twins were almost at the bedroom door, when Kenya stopped and whispered in London's ear. "I know you and O.T. was fucking around this afternoon and that shit was rotten as hell. Me and you can kick it about that later tonight, but you got to promise me that no matter what, you won't go off on Storm. He was confused and he's still in so much pain, physically and mentally." Kenya held both of London's hands. "Please, London, be calm, for me!"

"All right—for you, Kenya I will and only you. I'll be on my best behavior, because as far as Storm and O.T. are concerned. I'm past being done!"

The twins joined hands as they slowly walked into the bedroom, making eye contact with Storm.

PARIS

"Damn O.T., why you always gotta go for bad all the time? Especially when it comes to females! Shit already fucked up enough without you trying to fight Kenya's sister because she don't wanna jump when you want her to." Paris was sick and tired of him and his wild ways. "I bet you don't be all mean-mugging and posted up in that nasty tramp Chocolate Bunny's face with that madness, do you?"

O.T. leaned back on the love seat and sucked his teeth like a woman. "I already told your ass I don't know what the fuck you talking about, so do me and yourself a favor and stop jumping to conclusions, blaming me for shit I ain't do before I really do backtrack and bang her black ass again!"

"You know what, you can do what the hell you want to do, but remember, two can play that game. It's nothing!" Paris took her purse off of the coffee table and nonchalantly made her way to the front door. "So think about that the next time your smart-ass goes missing in action!"

Paris started up her car and sped away, leaving O.T. looking dumbfounded.

"Kick rocks bitch!" he mumbled, walking upstairs.

Chapter Thirty-five

It's True

"Hi Storm," Kenya spoke in a low, soft tone. "O.T. told me that you wanted to see me—or should I say *us*." She pointed over to London.

Storm, still extremely sore from earlier, sat all the way up in the bed, wiping his eyes. "Come here, Kenya. Come closer so I can see." The twins held each other's arms, carefully approaching Storm, who was shaking his head in disbelief. He squinted as the girls came closer to the light. "Shit! What kinda game is this?"

"Storm, I'm so sorry that I didn't tell you about London," Kenya begged, getting on her knees at the edge on the bed. "I just didn't think that you'd understand."

"What? Why not? Have I ever given you a reason to fear me, Kenya? Have I ever tried to control you? All this mess could have been avoided!" He came to terms the best he could.

"No." Full of shame she dropped her head to avoid eye contact with him, letting her hair drape over her distraught, battered face. "Never once, Storm."

"Then why?" he asked, keeping his eyes glued to London as he questioned Kenya. "What was the big fucking deal? Can you tell me that?"

The sound of him raising his voice caused London to speak up and intervene on her sister's behalf. "It seems as if to me that you have some kind of anger management issues. That trait must run in your family," London sarcastically added. "My sister probably didn't tell you about me because she figured that you would disapprove of anyone who wasn't agreeable with your criminal behavior or lifestyle."

"Oh, yeah, is that right?" he fired back, not moved by her speech.

"It appears that way to me, especially by the looks of Kenya's face, you freaking animal!"

Storm had momentary forgotten about the harsh-ass kicking that he'd put on his girl. Remorsefully, he reached over, touching Kenya on her chin. "Look up at me." She obliged, hesitantly moving the hair out of her face, exposing the damage that would more than likely take days—maybe weeks—to heal. "Damn, Kenya! I'm sorry! I didn't mean to do all of that. You just caught me off guard." He then pulled her off the floor and onto the bed with him. "I'm sorry, baby girl."

"I know." Kenya nodded, accepting his apology. "I understand."

"Kenya! Please don't fall for that *I'm sorry* routine! If he hit you like that once he'll do it again! It might not be tomorrow or the next day, but it will definitely come again." London tried her best to discourage her twin from forgiving Storm.

"Why don't you try shutting the fuck up? It's your fault all this shit went down!" Storm barked, wishing he could strangle his woman's sister.

"My fault—are you sick in the head? I'm not the one out here running the streets, poisoning the damn community with drugs!" London yelled loud enough to wake the dead. "That would be you and your no-good brother who's guilty of that crime! You brought that wrath down on yourself!"

Storm tilted his head toward the side and had a flashback. "Oh, you mean the same brother who I saw you getting your knees dirty for earlier? Is that who you talking about?"

London was slightly ashamed, but continued her insults coming. "Yeah, that's him. He's also the same one that can get out of the bed and take a piss on his own! Not like you!" she teased with malice. "Damn bed wetter!"

"Oh my God, London, no!" Kenya tried intervening, not believing the low blow her twin had just dished out.

"Kenya, I want this troublemaking whore out my motherfucking house!" Storm tried to get up out of the bed, but couldn't.

"Why don't you get your crippled morphine-ass up and put me out?" London challenged, knowing full well he couldn't.

"Bitch, get the fuck out! I'm not playing around with your stankin' wannabe-the-police-ass leave!"

Kenya stood up and broke up the below-the-belt insults that were taking place between London and Storm. "Listen, London, why don't you go back downstairs and let me speak to Storm privately? And Storm, why don't you try to calm down before you fall out again?"

"Okay, Kenya. I'll be in the living room." London looked back over her shoulder at Storm with disgust. "Don't let this animal taint your mind!"

"Try being out on the curb, whore!" Storm screamed out as London made her exit.

Almost at the end of the hallway she met O.T., who was busy talking to himself. "Excuse me!" She bumped his arm.

"Why the hell is you bugging? I thought me and you was tight! What's the problem?"

London couldn't believe that O.T. was so dense in the brain that he was truly convinced that his cold, heartless actions from earlier in the afternoon were acceptable. She went straight ghetto ham on him. "Okay, Negro! I'll tell you what the problem is!" She pointed her index finger in his face as her voice got louder. "If you think that you're gonna just mess around and toy with my feelings and emotions, you've got another thing coming, buster! And don't ever push me again!"

"Whoa! Slow the fuck down!" He brushed her hand away from his face. "I had to go. You heard Paris chirp me!"

"And?" London waited, head tilted to the side.

"And what? My girl needed me and I jetted. What else did you expect me to do?"

"Maybe show some type of love or affection toward me!"

"Come on now, London. Don't act like me and you is in some type of real relationship." O.T. stepped back, throwing his hands in the air. "You knew that Paris was wifey from the rip! She's number one in my world no matter how much I mess around!"

London was hurt once again as reality spit in her face. "Whatever! Ain't nobody thinking about you like that anyway!" She marched passed O.T. and stomped down the stairs.

"All these bitches bugging out today!" he laughed out loud as he went to check on Storm and Kenya.

When O.T. peeped in the room he saw that she was next to Storm, holding his hand. They seemed to be in deep discussion, so he didn't disturb them. O.T. went into the den and laid back on the couch as he looked over in the corner where the aquarium once sat that served as a final resting spot for Deacon's head. *Damn, I'm gonna hate to tell Storm about Deacon!*

It was now dark outside. It had started to thunder and pour buckets of rain, making the night seem to drag by. Storm and Kenya had been talking for hours, trying to get their lives back on track. Everything that she was holding in about her former life, he was now aware of. From the first morning she skipped school, Ty turning her out on the dance game, and even the fact that she pocketed the money that he and Deacon paid to Zack after her uncle and his crew shot up Heads Up. Kenya's life was now an open book.

Storm had no other choice but to confess about shit that he was holding back on also. Kenya sat silent as he talked about his mother's crack addiction, which he never did before. She was stunned to learn that Storm had once did time in a juvenile facility for killing his stepfather and worse than anything else, he revealed that he, O.T., and Deacon had all slept with Chocolate Bunny at one time or another back in the day. Kenya knew that O.T. had fucked the bitch, but not Deacon, and certainly not Storm.

Her hands were tied when it came to getting mad or passing judgments on his past, especially considering all her lies and the chain of events they set into motion.

What could she say, after all the terrible secrets and scandal she was tangled up into? Kenya had to remain calm and be understanding, even though she couldn't wait until she bumped heads with Chocolate Bunny again. All the "try to chill" information that she always begged Paris to do was out the window. By the time they were finished, Storm agreed to let London stay temporarily until all the bullshit was done and over. Kenya knew that it was gonna be a lot of fussing and confusion, but she loved both of them and wanted them both in her life.

Storm wanted to talk to O.T. about Deacon because Kenya kept avoiding any and all questions that involved his partner's name. Kenya went in the hallway and called out for O.T., hoping he was still there. When he finally showed up, she informed him that Storm wanted to see him and was asking about whether or not there had been any information concerning Deacon. O.T. entered the room and delivered the fucked-up, devastating news of Deacon's callous torture and murder.

When it was all said and done, Storm was speechless.

Chapter Thirty-six

Mad Crazy

The months flew by and things only grew wilder and crazier by the moment. Storm was still in constant pain and hadn't stepped foot outside of the condo. He would have Kenya bring him home Tylenol 4's and Vicodin on the regular and kept a bottle of Rémy up to his lips, not being able to deal with his best friend's untimely murder. Even though Kenya would often beg and plead with Storm not to drink so much, especially while he was popping those pills, it was no use. He was obviously addicted and had started blacking out daily. His leg was still weak, so that meant that he was dependent on the aid of crutches, which messed with his mindset.

The fact that Storm was having trouble getting his manhood hard was also a major factor in his recovery. Most times he'd have to damn near beat his meat to death or choke and twist it to just make the motherfucker squirt piss. So him and Kenya getting it in like they used to was out of the picture altogether, driving him to drink harder.

Of course, London used that information to her advantage to taunt and tease Storm when he and she argued. What kinda comeback or response could any man have to that type of dis? Kenya, determined to make it work, would clean up behind Storm all day and manage Alley Cats at night. She was exhausted and drained each and every time her head would touch the pillow. She was nurse, maid, cook, and lastly referee between the still constantly-battling London and Storm. Her once-clear skin was now filled with pimples and dark bags were forming under both eyes.

O.T. and Paris were also still beefing. The shit seemed to never stop with them. O.T. was out running the streets harder than before. With Storm putting his own self on house arrest, that left O.T. to try to keep thangs pumping. That meant that every drop-off, every meeting, and every risk that went along with slinging dope was on his shoulders and his shoulders alone.

In between trying to be the self-proclaimed mayor of the hood, he still would squeeze in time to swing by and check on Storm. Those visits often would cause mad chaos to jump off at the condo when O.T. would see London. Kenya, knowing what she knew, was still on a strong mission to keep O.T. and London apart. She talked to a depressed and tearful Paris every night as she drove to the club. After the confrontation that she'd had at the hair salon with Chocolate Bunny, Kenya felt it best for the good of the club to let Paris go and get her head together. After all, it was only a temporary gig, so there were no hard feelings between the friends.

With O.T. gone so much, Paris would sit on the couch for hours at a time, watching old reruns of *Good Times* and stuffing herself full of candy, cookies, and chips, waiting for him to come back home.

London was having the time of her life as she sharpened her vocabulary skills Monday through Sunday, dusk to dawn, on an educationally disadvantaged Storm. They would find a reason to argue about rather the sun was shining at midnight or how many licks it really took to get to the center of a Tootsie Pop. All it took for the argument to be on was for the two to lay eyes on one another. For London, getting and remaining on Storm's bad side was second nature. She seemed to despise him no matter what he did or said. She even hated him when he was asleep.

Kenya felt that it was time for her sister to go back to Detroit or rather back to school, since the sale of the house was now final, but would never suggest it. Besides, they were keeping Storm's return kinda secret from the hustlers in the streets and with her and O.T. out and about, trying to hold things down, there was no one else that they trusted enough to keep somewhat of a watchful eye over Storm, especially with his blacking out from all the drinking.

FATE

It started off just like any other Friday night. Kenya was busy standing in the mirror, brushing her hair and getting prepared to head out to Alley Cats. She had on a pair of tight-fitting blue jeans and a blue and pink low-cut T-shirt with the words *Hot Shit* across the chest. Even with makeup on you could still see that she was worn out. Storm was lying, half asleep, in the bed with the television remote in his hand. An empty bottle of Rémy Martin was on the floor next to two 40-ounces of Olde English that were also bone dry. He was up to his usual behavior, getting drunk and passing out cold. Depressed and constantly belligerent, the once obsessed and overly attentive to his appearance man, hadn't shaved in days and as far as him taking a shower, that was almost an impossible feat.

The bedroom and the entire house, for that matter, smelled like a Texas roadhouse after a wild party. Kenya, never religious since Gran's death, prayed to God nightly that with time Storm would snap out of the destructive path that he was on and hopefully get his life back together and on the right track.

"Okay, sweetheart, I'm about to go down to the club." With the scent of cucumber melon lotion massaged deep in her skin, she lovingly nudged him on his arm. "Do you need me to get you something before I leave?"

Slurring, he reached out to grab her, almost falling out of the bed "Yeah, just you, Kenya! I want some pussy before you go!"

Kenya helped him all the way back up in the bed and played his request off, knowing that it had been months since he'd been home and his dick still couldn't get hard. Moreover, she had to go out and make the money and keep things going until her man got back on his feet and in his right mind. Kenya had no intentions on being late to Alley Cats because of one of Storm's pity parties that he was about to throw. "Look, I'll be back later. Why don't you go soak in the tub and chill out? I'll bring you a sandwich home from the club tonight—cool?"

"Naw bitch, why don't you bring me up another bottle of liquor and shut up your damn nagging?" He barked out orders like she was his slave and called her *bitch* so much she was beginning to think that was her name.

"Not a problem! I can do that." Kenya made her way into the den, yelling back to Storm. "I got you."

"Hey, London!" Kenya forced a smile as she saw her twin sitting at the desk, typing on the computer. "I'm about to leave and go to work. I know that this is asking a lot, but can you run to the store and get him something to drink?" Kenya pointed back toward her bedroom. "I'm late enough already."

"Don't you think that he's already had enough to drink for you, me, and the whole world?" London threw her hand up in her sister's face. "Your Prince Charming has turned into the village idiot, that much is obvious! He needs to get some help and you and his brother need to stop hand-delivering his poison."

"Sis, I know you're right, but I just don't know what to do. You know he ain't gonna humble himself and get help—well, not now anyways. So please, London, just this one time, for me?" Kenya begged, looking at her watch.

"Yeah, okay, let me get off Facebook with Fatima and I'll go."

Kenya, feeling like she had the weight of the world on her shoulders, walked passed the open bedroom door without as much as turning her head to say good-bye to Storm. *He's starting to get on my last nerve!*

London went into the kitchen to put away a few of the items that she bought from the corner store when she picked up a bottle for Storm. As she was bending down in the refrigerator to put the sodas on the door shelf, she felt a pair of hands snatch her body backwards roughly knocking her down to the marble floor. *What the—! What's happening?* Her head struck the corner of the oak cabinet, making her woozy and somewhat confused. *Argg! Oh my God!* When she regained her senses back she started to fight and struggle with a drunken, enraged, hallucinating Storm, who was now on top of her, licking her face. The more she wiggled, moving to get free, the greater pleasure he seemed to achieve.

"Don't fight with me, Kenya!" he drunkenly screamed in London's face with his nauseating, foul-smelling hot breath and scruffy beard rubbing against her cheek. "I told you Daddy wanted some, didn't I? Now give it to me!"

"I'm not Kenya, fool! I'm not Kenya! Get off of me! Get off!" she protested, trying to shove him off.

"I love you, girl! Why you acting like this after all I done did for you? Now give me some of that pussy you been holding out on!"

Storm ignored London's claims of not being Kenya and tried wrapping one of his huge hands across her mouth to silence having to hear anymore complaining or lies. London's eyes grew wide and bucked as her sister's fiancé held her down with the weight of his body. As he made use of his free hand to pull down his track pants so that his dick was dangling wildly between his and London's legs, she panicked. Her trying to knee him in the nuts was stopped by the force of him applying his total strength and body weight down on top of her.

"Are you crazy? Stop! Stop! Don't do this! Stop!" She fought until exhausted and out of breath from the struggle.

Storm was in some sort of a trance. It was like he was sleepwalking and totally unaware of his surroundings. His eyes rolled to the back of his head as he ripped London's shorts down and somehow shoved his hard dick up inside of her. It was the first, true 100 percent staying hard, can-bang-the-shit-out-of-you-all-night-long erection that he had since being back home and here he was on the kitchen floor, drunk as a son of a bitch with Kenya's sister's legs stretched wide open going in.

He acted like a madman as he went in and out of her overly moist pussy. All of London's outcries and claims of her not being her twin Kenya had come to a complete halt. She stopped resisting Storm and even seemed to start to enjoy what she was feeling. At one point she even closed her eyes and imagined that Storm was his brother O.T., making love to her. After two or three minutes of him having his way and doing his thang, Storm let out a yell as his body jerked and collapsed onto London's. After that, he passed out cold, not moving an inch.

Reality quickly set back in for her when the rotten-smelling musk of Storm's skin filled her nostrils. The ecstasy that she was just momentarily feeling had ended and now London wanted her sworn enemy the hell off of her. Somehow she managed to push his heavy body off onto the cold floor and got back up on her feet. The sight of Storm sprawled out, smelling like who done it and why, caused London to rush over to the sink and throw up all over the dirty dishes.

Damn! That felt good, but why did it have to be him? Stuff wasn't supposed to work out like this, London mumbled to herself as she stepped over his crutches that were blocking the door and walked out the kitchen to take a hot shower, leaving a snoring Storm to sleep his punk-ass on the floor. *But I sure see now why Kenya is putting up with all the crap that Storm is taking her through. I can't imagine what it feels like when he's sober.*

Chapter Thirty-seven

A New Day

The days that followed that night somehow brought about a drastic change in Storm's personality. He'd been woken up at four in the morning by Kenya returning home from work. He felt like warm, melted shit on a stick. Storm had no idea how he'd gotten downstairs, let alone on the floor. As he passed the huge oval-shaped mirror in the hallway, Storm caught a quick glance of himself and froze with disappointment at the sight. He saw a complete stranger staring back at him. It was then and there that he promised Kenya that he was gonna get his shit back right and 100 percent correct.

When he hugged Kenya his dick rose up, standing at attention, causing her to smile with excitement and anticipation of the possibility of what she'd been missing. The two of them made their way up the stairs and into their bedroom. Kenya turned the shower on hot as she helped Storm step inside. Having a new attitude, he spent what seemed like hours scrubbing months of built-up filth off his body. The combination of the soap and the hot water caused a mysterious deep scratch on the side of his neck to sting.

Strangely, when he closed his eyes, Storm kept seeing flashbacks of having sex with Kenya on the kitchen floor in front of the open refrigerator door. He knew that it must've been a dream, so he dismissed it out of his mind. No sooner than he was finished drying off, he pounced on top of Kenya, making love to her for the first time in months. She was in seventh heaven as he freaked her from head to toe. Kenya, unlike Storm who just had some pussy earlier, hadn't had sex in what seemed like twelve months of Sundays and was really feeling that shit. They went in 'til almost daybreak while London, having had a brief taste of Storm earlier, enviously listened to their loud moans from the other room.

For weeks and weeks Storm stuck to his word and stopped drinking altogether. The only fluid that was now constantly up to his lips were ice-cold water and the juices that flowed out of Kenya's forever wet twat. O.T. had helped him hook the basement up with weights and other gym equipment that he needed to get back right to his usual self. Dedicated, he spent every free moment and waking minute on getting his body tight. As the days past, he was slowly gaining back the pounds and muscle mass that he'd lost while being held captive, then bedridden. He was transforming into looking like the old Storm who Kenya first fell in love with.

Even, to Kenya's surprise, London stopped complaining so much and being judgmental. She was being much more tolerant and civil to Storm as well. The two of them weren't arguing as much and London was even sharing responsibilities, helping Kenya out with the housework more often. Yet poor, naive Kenya had no idea that the true reason London was lending a helpful hand was so that she could smell Storm's T-shirts and dirty underwear every chance she got. The high point of London's day would come when she'd carry the laundry basket in the basement to wash and get an up-close and personal show of Storm's perfect body pumping iron.

"Girl, thanks for looking out for me with some of this cleaning." Kenya hugged her twin, happy that things were settling down. "You know Gran blessed you with all the secrets in keeping a neat house, anyhow."

"Oh, it's nothing," London winked at her twin, being sarcastic. "What's yours is mine, so I wouldn't leave you hanging. Like I said, it's nothing."

"Yes, it is. I want you to know that you're really appreciated and that I love you, London!"

"We sisters, girl!" London gave Kenya a halfhearted smile and a hug, smelling Storm's scent on her twin's shirt. "You should know by now that I've got your back."

The two finished getting the condo together because they were having a special dinner later that evening. It would be Kenya, Storm, Paris, O.T., and London. Kenya trusted in the changes that were taking place in London when it came to O.T. It seemed just like a snap of the finger, London was no longer attracted to O.T. It would be days when O.T. stopped by to hang out with Storm that London wouldn't even come out of her room to even say hello. She stayed asleep most days, acting as if she didn't have a care in the world. She'd stopped talking about returning to college or Detroit altogether.

Whatever jumped off to keep the two of them from messing around again behind Paris's back, Kenya was overjoyed and didn't question it. She never did get around to having a long conversation with London about what really went down the day that Storm saw her and O.T. in the hallway, so Kenya let her imagination work for itself, then put it completely out of her mind. Putting two and two together was easy. But nevertheless, things were back on track all around, with the small exception of the ongoing Paris, O.T., Chocolate Bunny saga, which was a hot topic that raged on nightly at the club.

The table was set and everything was picture-perfect for the evening. Kenya, with London's help, cooked enough food to feed a small-sized army. The huge celebration feast consisted of everything from hot country fried chicken, pot roast smothered in homemade brown gravy and catfish, to fresh collard greens, candied yams, and black-eyed peas. The girls had outdone themselves just as their grandmother had taught them.

Paris and O.T. arrived to the condo on time. They planned on having an early supper because Kenya was due down at the club by eight that evening and couldn't be late. She tried to get someone to fill in for her, but had no success. She was the only voice of reason at the club and things had a habit of going crazy when she wasn't there. O.T. wasted no time disappearing into the basement where Storm was just finishing up his workout, leaving all three females alone in the kitchen area.

"Hey, Paris," London spoke as she inspected her sister's best friend's shape. Paris had packed on at least fifteen pounds or more since London had last seen her. "What have you been up to lately? Where have you been hiding?"

"Not much." Paris shrugged her shoulders. "I've just been taking it easy, trying to get my mind right."

"Oh, okay, it's just that I haven't saw you around here very much." London grilled her sister's best friend, still stunned by Paris's big physical change. "Is all well with you?"

Kenya saw the direction that her slick-mouthed twin was headed and jumped in to rescue Paris from all the questions. "Do me a favor, London." Kenya wiped her hands on the plaid-colored dish towel. "Can you go and call the fellas up while me and Paris start bringing the food to the table?"

"Yeah, I can do that." London happily left to go in the basement. If she was lucky, maybe Storm still had his shirt off. The aroma of the various foods was making her dizzy anyway, as well as the intense heat from the oven.

When London was clearly out of ear range, Kenya apologized for her twin sister being so damn nosy. "Girl, she didn't mean to be all up in your shit like that. She just was concerned, that's all. She don't know any better."

Paris grabbed one of the china platters with the chicken on it and headed toward the brightly-lit dining room. "Don't worry. I don't mind. I guess I do look like a mess with all this extra weight that I'm hauling."

"Stop tripping, you tight, girl." Kenya followed behind her friend with a big bowl of greens in her hands.

"You don't have to lie. I know that this fat shit ain't cute." Paris lowered her head in shame, on the verge of tears. "But I can't help it. That fool got me so messed up in the head I can't think straight half the time!"

"Stop being so down on yourself."

"I can't help it, Kenya! Do you know that O.T. hasn't touched me in over two and a half weeks now?" Kenya consoled her friend as she sobbed. "He barely even comes to the crib until daybreak. He claims that he's out hustlin', but I know that nigga is lying. He cheating with some ho!"

Before Kenya got a chance to hear the entire story, London returned with both guys trailing behind.

"Damn, that shit smells good!" Storm rubbed his flat-abs as he took a seat at the head of the long marble table. "I'm about to throw the hell down!"

O.T. followed his brother's lead and sat at the other end. After all the food was laid out and the girls sat down, Storm blessed the gathering before the first fork was placed to anyone's lips. Two or three seconds after that the shit was on! The guys acted like they'd never had soul food before as they devoured everything that they piled on their plates, getting seconds and even thirds of some dishes. The only dinner conversation that was taking place consisted of girl talk and the sounds of grunting.

It was close to seven and the group was just about done with eating. Kenya was bringing an apple pie to the table for dessert when O.T.'s cell phone started to ring, causing Paris to suddenly flip out.

"Damn! Can we have one day in peace when that ho of yours ain't blowing up your fucking phone?"

"Don't start with me, Paris. I ain't in the mood for that dumb shit now!" Fed up with her constant accusations, O.T. walked away from the table shaking his head. "I've got something to go handle."

"Yeah, right!" Paris reached back, trying to hit him as he walked passed. "You ain't shit but a cheating liar. We all know! The people at the club know! The people in the street know! Hell, even the old Chinese lady at the dry cleaner's knows you a cheating piece of garbage!"

Kenya leaned over and wrapped her arms around Storm's neck, who was still seated at the table. "Baby, oh my God, can you say something, please?"

"I love you like a motherfucker, Kenya, but I don't get in the middle of no couple's bullshit." Storm cut himself a piece of pie as he remained silent, watching his baby brother and Paris go at it. "And trust me, you don't need to either!"

London was especially enjoying the long evening observing both couples at each other's throats. At first she felt like a third wheel and out of place; now she was happy not to be either of the girls.

O.T. took Paris's car keys off the couch and trotted out to her car, leaving her stranded without a ride to get home.

"Damn, I hate him! I swear I do!" she huffed.

"Don't worry, girl. I'll drop you off on my way to Alley Cats." Kenya patted her friend on the back as she snarled at Storm, who was still nonchalantly stuffing his face with pie. "Just let me grab my purse and we'll be out."

Paris and Kenya left London and Storm home alone. On the ride to drop her off at her and O.T.'s apartment, Kenya was having a hard time trying to comfort an almost panic-stricken Paris. The loud, piercing cries from her were coming close to causing Kenya to swerve off the highway. She already needed a few aspirin for the headache she was suffering after her disagreement with Storm, but this was much worse.

"Why don't you go inside and try to get some rest? It's been a long day." Kenya tried her best to convince Paris to calm the hell down, go inside, lie down, and relax.

"You right, girl. I'm just gonna go in there and chill 'til his ass comes home—then trust, it's back on!"

Kenya blew the horn once as she drove off toward Alley Cats.

LONDON

"Dang, I guess this dinner party is over, huh?" Storm was polishing off his last piece of pie that was on his plate, not paying attention to a word coming out of London's mouth. "Are you listening to me?" London threw a napkin at Storm to get his attention. "Can you speak or what?"

"Dang, slow your roll, London. Can a guy eat his dessert in peace or what?" Storm pushed his chair back from the table and patted his bloated, full stomach. "Y'all females around here doing way too much for me tonight. Well, I might as well go in the basement and do a little cardio to work this shit off."

"Excuse me. Despite what all of you people around here think, I'm not the damn maid!" London grew infuriated that she was ultimately left the task of cleaning up.

"Where the hell is you going with this bullshit? I know your ass know for a fact that I ain't about to bust no suds for nobody." Storm stretched out his arms, yawning. "So, for real, if that's where you going with this conversation, you can cut that mess out right now!"

"Forget it! Just go work out with your lazy self!"

"Lazy? Wow, your ass is the one that needs to hit the gym. I mean, I ain't being in your business, but you is getting a little thick around the waist, London! You and that damn Paris both getting out of order and need to hit a gym."

"Just go somewhere, lazy Negro, while I clean up!"

"Come on now, London, is this the body of a lazy mother-fucker?" He lifted his shirt, exposing his eight-pack abs.

London controlled herself from leaping across the table and attacking Storm the same way he'd attacked her months earlier. "Whatever!" She looked the other way as quickly as possible and started removing the dishes, taking them in the kitchen. Once again, she started to feel dizzy and stumbled.

Storm felt sorry for her and grabbed a few of the dirty plates and followed in the kitchen behind her. When he turned the corner he saw London bending over in the refrigerator putting stuff away and had a brief flashback. "Damn! Why do I keep seeing that shit?"

"Did you say something?" London stood up, turning around to face him.

"Naw, I was just talking to myself." Storm shook off his strange thoughts as he rubbed the deep scar that was still on his neck.

"Does it still hurt?" London smirked, starting the hot dish-water in the sink. Her heart was beating double-time as she experienced flashbacks of her own. After all, they were back to the scene of the crime, so to speak. "It was pretty deep."

"What are you talking about? What you know about my neck?" Storm was puzzled that she'd even noticed him touching it.

"You can cut all the games out, Storm. It's been months and you see I haven't said a word to anyone. It's our little secret."

"Huh?" Storm was confused and his facial expression showed. "Stop playing around and tell me what the fuck you trying to say?"

"Come on now, are you serious? You don't remember?" London glanced down at the floor and raised her eyebrows.

"Remember what?" he asked again. "What the hell is your crazy-ass talking about now?"

"I've got to finish washing dishes." London laughed, still not believing that Storm had truly forgotten their sexual encounter. "We'll talk about it later—one day."

Storm left out the kitchen and headed toward the basement to try to figure out what his woman's twin sister wanted him to remember. *Whatever the hell it is, something tells me it can't be nothing good!* After months of being sober, Storm snatched a bottle of Rémy off the bar cart to keep him company and help him possibly remember.

Chapter Thirty-eight

I'm In Shock

Shit, it's crowded already. Kenya pulled around to the other side of the parking lot to make sure that security was patrolling the entire perimeter. She cut her lights off so she wouldn't draw attention to herself as she crept up. What she saw next made her headache start to pound worse. It was O.T. sitting back in Paris's car, talking to Chocolate Bunny, who was leaning in the window practically in the driver's seat.

After five minutes of her watching their every movement like a hawk, Kenya wanted to beat the shit out of Chocolate Bunny her damn self. Matter of fact, she wanted to stump O.T. in his fucking ball sack for playing with her girl Paris's emotions. She knew it was time for her to step in and do something about Chocolate Bunny once and for all. "This idiot gonna mess around and get AIDS one day," Kenya snarled under her breath, as she looked at Chocolate Bunny stuff some cash in her bra and wave to O.T. as he peeled out in Paris's car. "Flat out, I gotta get rid of that black no-good gutter rat."

"Hey Kenya, what's the game plan for tonight?" The head of security, Boz, was busy trying to get things straightened out before things really got off the hook.

"Same old same." She looked up toward the center stage at Jordan shaking her ass in front of a group of middle-aged customers who were posted on perverts' row. "Just make sure that all the girls circulate around the club and don't spend all night catering to one fool trying to slow pimp all his cash."

"You got it, boss. I'm on top of it!" he reassured Kenya. "Don't worry about nothing. I got you!"

Everything was flowing smoothly on the nightshift. Kenya sat on her favorite seat at the long bar and observed the crowd enjoying themselves. Most of the dancers were either up in VIP or humping on a guy's lap, doing something strange for some change. The DJ was working the high-priced light system and had the sounds spinning. It would definitely be a good moneymaking night for the club.

"If you fellas' nature stood tall and hard for that last honey that worked that brass pole, you'll love this next prime-time delight. Alley Cats is home base to this lovely dark meat. She's the warmest, wettest, freakiest thang walking around these-here parts." The DJ dimmed the lights low as he got the crowd going. "Chocolate Bunny, bring your wide twerkin' ass up on that center stage and do the damn thang!"

Kenya walked behind the bar and poured herself a small glass of wine. She studied Chocolate Bunny dancing and wondered what it was that made men like her. In Kenya's opinion she wasn't sexy or cute. The only thing that Kenya saw in the whore was that she had a big butt; a big butt that seemed to be spreading out a little bit more than normal for her taste, but the tramp was still bringing in revenue to the club and at the end of the day that was all that mattered. In her line of business, cash was king.

As Kenya sat drinking her second glass of wine, her opinion about the constant thorn in her and Paris's side started to change. *That tramp is gaining too much weight. Matter of fact, I'm gonna give her trick-ass a few weeks off to drop that shit or get fired altogether.* Kenya finally found a way, after months of plotting, to get Chocolate Bunny out of Alley Cats without Storm or O.T. feeling like it was being done out of spite. After all, rules were rules. Each dancer had to maintain a certain look to be on the schedule and it was plain to see Chocolate Bunny was no longer fitting that status. *As soon as she goes back to the dressing room to switch up on her outfits, I'm gonna break the bad news to her trifling butt.*

Kenya raised her glass to her perfectly glossed lips and slowly sipped the rest of her wine. After two more songs dancing on center stage, Chocolate Bunny was done with her set.

CHOCOLATE BUNNY

"I'm happy for you," Jordan lied with a straight face. "What are you going to name the baby? Is it a boy or a girl?"

"It's gonna be a boy. I'll probably name him after his big-head daddy." Chocolate Bunny was in the dressing room, bragging about being pregnant and the fact that her and her mystery man had just put a huge down payment on a new house.

She wasn't fooling everyone with all that top-secret hush-hush shit about the baby's daddy. All the girls in the club would see her all up in O.T.'s face day in and day out, laughing and giggling. They weren't blind or stupid. Jordan tried her best to pry the private information out of Chocolate Bunny or at least make her slip up and finally admit the shit, but wasn't successful. She was keeping that close to the vest.

"This week is gonna be my last grindin' up in this here motherfucker. My man wants me to sit on my ass and raise his son." Chocolate Bunny affectionately stared down at the tiny bulge that was growing and smiled. "I'm ready to retire out this game anyway and get my life back together. Maybe I'll go back to school or something productive like that."

Kenya was at the doorway ear hustling on the conversation that was taking place between Jordan and Chocolate Bunny. She felt like marching in the dressing room and knocking that bastard-ass baby the fuck out of the stomach of that man-stealing black-snake bitch, but what good would that really do? Paris would still be devastated whenever O.T. would be man enough to break the news to her. *He should've just broke up with her a long time ago and saved her the grief of all the drama.* Kenya eased away from the door, unnoticed, and sat back down at the bar. She had the bartender give her the entire bottle of wine and poured herself another glass. *This shit is fucked up,* was all that kept racing through her mind.

Kenya decided by her fourth glass that it'd be better to keep this baby-crap information from Paris as long as possible to spare her feelings. Considering the unstable, depressing state of mind and constant stress that Paris had been dealing with, Kenya was terrified what would be her best friend's response to all the madness that was going down. Luckily, this was gonna be Chocolate Bunny's last week dancing, so she claimed. But just in case she had any thoughts of prolonging her departure from Alley Cats, the sooner Kenya made it official and fired her low-down sneaky-ass the better. She'd call Chocolate Bunny right before her shift the next day and let her know what was really good.

"Last call for alcohol!" the DJ announced for the last and final time for the night.

It was damn near two in the morning and the strip club was slowly clearing out as the house lights came on. All the girls were going back to the dressing room to get changed and go home or wherever they planned on laying their head down for the night. Some had boyfriends waiting, some had husbands, some had tricks, and even a few had a bitch. Whatever the case was, everyone was hauling ass to leave out.

"All right, Addiction and Tight-n-Right, I'll see you ladies tomorrow." Boz held the door open and watched them to their vehicles.

"Hold up, Boz, I'm ready to jet too!" Chocolate Bunny yelled out while struggling with her duffel bag, followed by a loud-talking Jordan.

"Yeah, me too! I'll holler at y'all in a few!" Boz saw Jordan and her woman embrace, kiss, then drive off.

Chocolate Bunny seemed to be enraged as she threw her bag to the pavement. "What kinda jealous-hearted-ass ho done did some treacherous shit like this?" Chocolate Bunny fumed, looking down. "And Boz, where the fuck was security at?"

Boz walked over to investigate and found all four of Chocolate Bunny's tires slashed. "Damn, girl! Who the fuck did you piss off tonight?"

"You know how these bum bitches up here be hating on me because I clock major dollars up in this motherfucker!" Chocolate Bunny screamed across the parking lot to make sure that the rest of the dancers who hadn't left yet could hear exactly what she was saying.

"Fuck you!" one of them replied as they all laughed at her misfortune and went on about their way.

Chocolate Bunny whipped out her cell, rolled her eyes, and pushed number one on the speed dial. "Hey baby, it's me!"

"Where you at?"

"I'm still at the club!"

"Why you still there? I was waiting for you."

"One of these tramps done sliced my tires!"

"Well, just turn the sounds on and sit tight. I'm gonna send one of my street soldiers to find a nigga with a flatbed and come get you. I told you ya ass need to be done with that club!"

"Don't start with me, okay, sweetie? I love you!"

"I love you too! You and my son!"

"Okay, see you soon!"

Twenty minutes or so had passed and Chocolate Bunny was still sitting in her car, waiting. Boz was chilling on the hood, keeping her company as long as possible. Kenya finally appeared at the door and waved for him to come inside. It was time to pay the security detail for the night and close up, so he had to return to his post and finish up club business.

"You better come in the club and wait in there," Boz suggested as he opened the car door wide for Chocolate Bunny to get out. "I can't abandon your ass out here with all these perverts and stalkers roaming the streets!"

"Yeah, you ain't never lied. I don't want nobody to kidnap my fine black perfect ass!" she joked as they both walked back into Alley Cats.

Kenya was going over the paperwork and having each guy sign for his pay envelope. Boz had to do his job and verify each bouncer's nightly evaluation. As soon as Kenya was done with her part, she then focused on Chocolate Bunny, who was sitting at the other end of the bar playing one of the poker arcade games.

"Hey, girl, what's the deal?" Kenya interrupted her game, feeling like now was just as good a time as any to fire her.

"Nothing, just waiting for my sweetie to send a tow truck to come rescue me from them broke tricks slicing my damn tires! You know I'm off tomorrow, so I'll call the club in a few days to talk to you about something! It's kinda important."

"Well, I'm sorry about your tires, but this gives me the opportunity to kick it with you about something else. It's important too."

"Oh, yeah? Well, what is it, Kenya?" Chocolate Bunny smartly asked. "What the hell did I do wrong now? I'm dying to know!"

"Nothing, we just need to talk. Give me a minute to finish things up and send the fellas home so we can have some privacy."

"Yeah girl—whatever!" Chocolate Bunny put another quarter into the game to pass away the time waiting for the tow truck to arrive. She was gonna just tell Kenya over the phone she quit, but fuck it—now was as good a time as any. Fuck waiting any longer.

Boz and the rest of the guys gathered their stuff and left out with a few beers in hand. "Are y'all gonna be all right?" he turned back, asking before he started his truck.

"Yeah, we good," Kenya waved him off. "Go ahead and bounce. Go home to your family. I'll see you tomorrow evening!" Kenya shut the front door, making sure that it was locked. Ready to argue, she then took a seat next to Chocolate Bunny and braced up for round one. "Listen chick, I swear to God that I'm not trying to be twisted all up in your business, but I think what you been doing is seriously foul and wrong as a motherfucker."

"Excuse me, but what in the hell am I supposed to be doing, Ms. Thang?"

"Don't play silly mind games with me, Nicole. I was coming in the dressing room and heard what you said on the humble."

"And please tell me, just what do you think you heard?" Chocolate Bunny snickered as she leaned back on the stool, getting an earful.

Kenya was getting angry at the brazen and heavy-mouthed Chocolate Bunny. "So you about to have a baby, huh?"

"And so what? What's it to you?"

Before Kenya could answer they heard a noise come from the rear of the club. Both of them froze, looking at one another with a sense of fear, because they knew for a fact that everyone had left the building. Kenya kicked off her high heels and quietly made her way around to the other side of the bar, grabbing the pistol that they kept on the bottom shelf. Two seconds later she and Chocolate Bunny heard the noise once again.

"Whoever the fuck is back there, you about to catch some serious hot ones in the ass!" Kenya screamed out into the rear of the club. "I'm not bullshitting! You best to come out! We already done called the police!"

Chocolate Bunny and Kenya's mouths both almost dropped to the ground in disbelief when the person emerged out of the dark shadows and into the light. It was a red-eyed, worn-out, and exhausted-looking Paris. She had her nightgown and slippers on while a huge 9 mm pistol graced her side. Her hair was all over her head and her puffy face was full of tears. "It's me, Kenya!" She dropped the spare club keys on the bar. "Don't worry, it's only me!"

"Girl, damn! Why the fuck is your ass lurking like that?" Kenya, relieved, lowered her gun. "I could've shot you. And damn, why you dressed like that? And shit, why you here?"

"Damn, she's right. Are you crazy or what? Have you lost your mind?" Chocolate Bunny jumped in, confused also.

Paris's fingers tightly gripped the gun handle with animosity. "You don't say shit to me, man-stealing ho!"

"Who the fuck is you talking to like that? I 'bout done had enough of you tripping out whenever the fuck you feel like it! Not to mention putting your damn hands on me like at the salon!"

Kenya knew that Paris was out of her mind and didn't know what exactly she had planned on doing, so she did her best to try to defuse the situation before it got well out of hand. "Listen, why don't we all just calm down?" She raised her hands up in between Paris and Chocolate Bunny.

"Oh, I'm good!" Chocolate Bunny replied, as she looked Paris up and down, shaking her head. "I'm not the fool that's standing in a strip club in the middle of the night rocking pajamas with my wig tore up."

"Paris, why are you here anyway?" Kenya wondered, asking her friend. "And girl, why aren't you dressed? What's wrong with you? What happened?"

"I didn't have time." Paris was timid in her demeanor and response when talking to her best friend.

Kenya, tired of trying to figure her girl's motives out, threw her hands up in the air. "I'm confused as hell! I give up! What's going on? What's wrong? Tell me!"

"This whore right here is what's wrong with me!" Paris pointed at Chocolate Bunny with her pistol. "She's what happened!"

"Look, you lunatic, it'll be in your best interest to stop waving that gun around before it mess around and go off, then it really will be some shit!" Chocolate Bunny put her hands on her hips, showing no signs of fear of Paris and what she could possibly do.

Kenya stood back, realizing that her best friend was on some other type of shit and had totally and officially snapped. "Just tell me what happened? I thought that you were at home sleeping—relaxing?"

"I was at home doing what you said until Jordan called me!" Paris wept like a small child not getting toys on Christmas morning.

It then hit Kenya like a ton of bricks what the fuck this whole scene was about. Jordan must've called Paris with that baby bullshit getting in her head and getting her fired up. "Listen, Paris, I was gonna tell you, but I just found out myself—tonight."

"Look, y'all, I hate to break up this wild soap opera y'all living in, but I'll be out in my car waiting for my man's people," Chocolate Bunny blurted out. "Ain't nobody got time for you or you!"

"Bitch, I swear on everything I love, if you take one step that's your black-cheating-ass!"

"Yeah, okay Paris, can you just tell a girl, with your messy self, what the fuck this is all about, if you don't mind? I'm listening!"

Paris wiped her tears, gathering up her courage to hear Chocolate Bunny finally confess the truth. "So I heard you supposed to be having a baby?"

"Yeah, and?" Chocolate Bunny put her hand on her stomach. "What about it? Is that okay with you? Matter of fact, why do you even care so damn much?"

"Why the fuck would you think that the shit would be okay with my ass?" Paris hissed with anger and contempt.

"Girl, bye! I ain't gotta clear my personal life with either one of you two messy bitches. Y'all be buggin'!" Chocolate Bunny shifted her weight on one hip. "So deal with it! I'm having a baby—so fucking what!"

"So you ain't denying it?" Paris shouted nervously as her hand shook and her words echoed throughout the empty club. "You're pregnant?"

Chocolate Bunny started moving her fingers, acting as if she knew sign language. "Yes . . . dumb . . . bitch! I . . . am . . . going . . . to . . . have . . . a . . . baby!" She dragged out each syllable of each word while laughing. "Now . . . fuck . . . you!"

"Naw, fuck you!!!" Paris raised the gun up and started to cry hysterically. "I can't take this bullshit no more! I'm sick and tired of y'all playing me for a fool. Now you about to have his seed and throwing it up in my face!"

Chocolate Bunny saw her chance and took it, bum-rushing Paris, causing them both to tumble to the floor. Kenya watched helplessly while the two rivals fought and wrestled for the gun. She couldn't tell who was getting down the best and had no intentions on trying to get a closer look and maybe risk getting shot by mistake. All Kenya could do was clench her own gun tight and wait for the outcome.

"Now what, you crazy psycho bitch? Where is all them empty threats at now? Huh? Where they at?" Chocolate Bunny had come out on the top and now had possession of the gun. "Talk all that la-la shit now so I can bust a cap in your silly-ass! I'm tired of all your over-the-top antics!" She was trying to catch her breath with each passing word she justifiably screamed.

Paris was also out of breath from the struggle and her sorrowful crying had gotten louder. Kenya, out of desperation of what could possibly take place next, had no choice but to put one up top and point her gun at a now frantic, roughed-up and bruised pregnant Chocolate Bunny.

"I'm confused! Why is y'all hoes so worried about my son and me being knocked up, period? Am I making that much money for this club that y'all bugging out like that cause y'all gonna lose dough?" She panted repeatedly as a sharp, piercing pain unexpectedly shot throughout her lower belly. Chocolate Bunny then grabbed her side with her free hand and moaned out in agony. "His daddy is gonna—" Before she could get the words out another pain set in this time worse than the first.

"Son?" Paris whined, not believing what she'd just heard her sworn enemy say. "You having a boy—a son?"

"Oh, no! Oh my God!" Kenya pointed to the floor. "Look!"

Chocolate Bunny had streams of dark blood running down her leg. It had started to form a huge puddle right beneath the spot where she was standing. Her once-white skirt was not only dirty from the filth that was on the club floor, it was now soaked and stained with her own blood. Reaching her free hand up in between her legs, she felt her pussy. When Chocolate Bunny pulled her trembling hand back, it was covered in thick red and dark-burgundy mucus. Still having pain in her stomach area, the distraught mother-to-be smeared the foul-smelling clots on her skirt and instantly went the fuck off.

"You killed my baby! You killed my baby!" Her eyes grew wide with panic and death raged in her heart. "You jealous dirty rotten crazy bitch!"

Chocolate Bunny pointed the gun directly at Paris's head and was seconds away from pulling the trigger as Kenya quickly let off two rounds, knocking Chocolate Bunny off her feet, slamming her already battered body to the ground. The first bullet struck the pregnant female dead in the stomach, more than likely taking the baby out of the game for sure, while the other bullet found its mark in her collarbone.

Chocolate Bunny squirmed for a few good seconds, then moaned out softly. As she took her last breath and slowly released all her bodily fluids onto the strip club's floor, Kenya and Paris stood in disbelief, not fully grasping what they had just both taken part in.

"Oh, shit! I can't believe this!" Kenya lowered her gun, taking a long, deep breath. "That stupid girl made me do that dumb shit! She made me shoot her!"

Paris just stood in the same spot, not moving, mouth wide open. Kenya, still shaken, tossed her pistol onto the bar and went to get the other one that was still clutched in Chocolate Bunny's hand. Kenya then very carefully slid her finger off the trigger, placing it with the other gun.

"What are we gonna do now?" A dazed Paris finally spoke.

"We gonna get rid of this black bitch, that's what we gonna do now!"

"Okay, but how?" Paris was usually hardcore and a ridah, but lately she'd been punkin' out and scared of her own shadow.

"Listen, pay attention. Just go in the back storeroom and get me that big roll of plastic that the painters left and the jug of industrial bleach," Kenya ordered with authority. "And hurry up before this girl bleeds even more on my floor."

"Okay Kenya, I'm going!" Paris wasted no time as she ran toward the back of the club.

They rolled Chocolate Bunny onto the plastic and dragged her lifeless body over near the back door. Kenya had a scalding hot bucket of water and plenty of rags. Paris poured the strong bleach across the area and held her nose. It was supposed to be mixed with three parts water, but Kenya wanted it straight. Both girls' eyes burned as they scrubbed the spot Chocolate Bunny had taken her last breath in.

The club's floor was now spotless and there were no visible signs that a murder had just taken place. Kenya's car was already parked in the rear of the building in her reserved spot, so all they had to do was get Chocolate Bunny the hell out of there. It took ten long, hard minutes of tugging, yanking, and pulling to get her body stuffed and wedged behind the Dumpster that had just been emptied the night before. Paris took some of the plastic and balled it up, placing it in a bag.

On the way home she intended on disposing of it in someone else's garbage can on the other far side of town.

Kenya went back inside the club, grabbing both guns off the bar along with Chocolate Bunny's purse and Paris's set of club keys. Snatching the security camera tapes, she then put them all in a small bag and doubled it. After double-checking the entire interior once again for any other evidence they might've overlooked, she set the alarm system and jumped into the car with Paris. As they drove off in the other direction, they could see the flashing lights of a flatbed tow truck that was pulling into the club's parking lot.

"Damn, that was too close!" Kenya kept glancing in the rearview mirror to make sure they weren't being followed.

The ride to Paris's house was silent after that. Neither of the girls said a word to the other. They were about one mile short of getting to their destination when a police car got behind the two cold-blooded murderers. Kenya knew not to tell Paris that the cops were behind them because she knew that she would undoubtedly spaz out and get them flicked for sure. Luckily at the next traffic light the cops turned off, going on their way. When the pair finally got in Paris's driveway, Kenya turned to her and stuck her hand out.

"What?" Paris squinted her eyes at Kenya.

"Give me any more sets of them motherfucking keys you got stashed somewhere to Alley Cats, before your ass decides to come back in that bitch another night and lay another dancer to rest for messing around with that no-good cheating O.T.!" Kenya shook her head.

"Thanks, Kenya. You saved my life!"

"Can you just go in there and chill for the night? The shit ain't over yet—believe that! We gonna have to answer for this shit sooner or later."

FACE FACTS

The rest of the way home Kenya's conscience started to kick in and go to work overtime. In a short amount of time she'd been involved in dancing, transporting drugs, covering up Swift's murder, disposing of Deacon's dead body, and now actually committing the act of murder herself. "I don't know how all this shit jumped off in the first place. All I was trying to do was make a little extra dough and get out the hood!"

Pushing the remote, she parked in the garage. Kenya, nursing the worst headache of her life, found her way to the couch and plopped down. The condo was quiet except the on-and-off sounds of Storm, strangely asleep in the basement, snoring. Kenya assumed that London was asleep also because it was so late. When her sister came walking down the stairs wide awake, it shocked Kenya.

"Oh my God! I'm glad you're up. I need someone to talk to! This shit is important. Come in the kitchen with me."

London was thrown off that Kenya wanted her to come in the kitchen to talk. For some reason, she thought that the shit was about to hit the fan about her and Storm having sex on the floor by the refrigerator, so she sat at the table and braced herself for what was going to happen next.

Kenya set a plastic bag on the table and took her time pulling out the contents. The first two objects were both handguns. Especially alarming, one of them had obvious signs of blood on the handle. After what appeared to be a tape of some sort and a set of keys, the last thing Kenya quickly snatched out the bag was a designer purse.

"What is all of this?" London scanned the table, puzzled, as she watched her sister break down in tears.

Kenya went on to explain exactly what events took place earlier, from the moment she and Paris left the dinner they'd all shared together to now. By the time Kenya was finished with her confessional story, London was caught up in her feelings. She was pissed, infuriated, enraged, disappointed, and downright mad as a motherfucker at her twin for what she'd done in the name of friendship.

"Sis, why in the world would you do something so stupid?"

"Chocolate Bunny was gonna shoot Paris. What else was I supposed to do London, huh? You tell me."

"Listen, Paris had no business coming in Alley Cats acting all tough! That would have been on her! She brought whatever was gonna happen on herself!"

The twins' arguing went on and on until London, frustrated, got up from the table to make some coffee and slightly lost her balance, falling toward the stove.

"What's wrong with you?" Kenya suspiciously asked with her eyebrow raised. "You've been real clumsy lately. What's that all about?"

PARIS

"What took you so long to come home?" Paris screamed at the top of her lungs. "Was you out shopping for baby clothes and shit?"

"What in the fuck is your crazy-ass talking about now?" O.T. stood in the doorway, not in the mood for a shouting match.

"I already know about you and that trick having a baby, so don't try to deny it!"

"What female you talking about now, Paris—which one?" he asked, dismissing another one of her wild accusations.

"That lowlife tramp Chocolate Bunny, that's who!"

"You know what? I wasn't gonna tell you this bullshit cause it wasn't none of your damn nosy-ass insecure business, but you won't leave the shit alone!"

O.T., after months of being secretive about his late-night activities, filled Paris in. He explained the connection that he and Chocolate Bunny shared. Hearing the full and complete story left Paris in shock over what she and Kenya had done. Paris had no choice but to tell O.T. what had taken place and that Chocolate Bunny was dead, stuffed behind a Dumpster in the rear of Alley Cats.

His reaction was sheer anger as he sucker punched Paris dead in her mouth and left out of the apartment, telling her that he was never coming home or back to her trouble-making-ass again! A busted-mouthed Paris stumbled to the bathroom and opened the medicine cabinet. She twisted the top off a bottle of sleeping pills, swallowing a handful. After all the trouble she'd caused not trusting her man, O.T., she cowardly welcomed death, feeling that it was the only way out.

DAMN!

While Kenya poured the coffee in the mugs, London looked in Chocolate Bunny's purse to turn off her cell phone that kept ringing. There she found a thick, folded set of papers that were on the top and a few pictures. London read the first page of the legal documents, which were a purchase agreement for a house and couldn't believe her eyes. "I think you need to see this paper." She motioned to Kenya. "Now!"

"Oh, hell naw! It couldn't be! What the fuck did we do?" Kenya shouted out with remorse after reading the paperwork.

The papers were a deed to Chocolate Bunny's new house. They had her government name on them as well as another, Mr. Royce K. Curtis. The picture in her purse was an ultrasound that also had Royce's name on it. "All this time Royce's old ass has been the one she's been fucking around with? Why didn't she just say that bullshit? What was the big deal?"

Storm had waked up after getting a call from O.T and had been at the kitchen door eavesdropping and cut her off. "Because after the big fight you and Royce had down at Alley Cats about me, we thought it'd be better for you not to know that the old man was our new connect with some uncut product Javier had given him. Plus, it ain't really none of your business who Chocolate Bunny fucked with outside the club, O.T. or not."

"Storm, I—" Kenya tried to explain, knowing she had messed up once again.

"You know what, Kenya? From day one right off rip, I should've known that you was gonna be trouble. My little brother warned me about dealing with you, but I wouldn't listen. Now it's about to be a damn all-out street war because you and your sidekick Paris fucked the fuck up and killed that girl for nothing! The streets of Dallas gonna run red for this shit! I'm done with your ass for real this time! You costing me way too much!"

Kenya went into hysterics as she started throwing dishes against the wall and begging for Storm's forgiveness once again. Having no self-respect, the once Detroit diva was crawling on her knees, pleading with him not to leave her. London, stunned, was now pissed as she watched her own flesh and blood lower herself by this pathetic display.

"Kenya! Get up off that damn floor! His cheating-ass ain't worth humiliating yourself like this! Get up!"

"And as for you, bitch! I 'bout done had enough of your instigating-ass too! Why don't you pack your bags and get to stepping with her bad-luck-ass!" Storm ran up in London's face like he wanted to swing. "Get your funky-ass the fuck out my house!"

"Slow down, Storm! This is my sister's house too!" London fired back, standing her ground.

"Well, Kenya, you gonna tell this tramp to be ghost or what?" Storm waited with a smirk on his face. "It's me or her, and I'm not playing around this time!" It grew quiet in the room as all eyes were on Kenya, who was breathing hard, wiping the tears from her eyes. After a long pause she finally mumbled.

"What did you say?" Storm demanded to hear. "Speak up, we can't hear you!"

"I said, London, would you mind getting a hotel room somewhere until me and Storm figure all of this mess out?" Kenya, ashamed of what she'd just asked, failed to look at her twin sister. "Please, sis, it'll only be for a few days, I promise—until we work stuff out!"

"Naw—make that forever!" Storm shouted in response to Kenya's question to her sister.

"Oh, it's like that?" London was heated over what Kenya said. "I've put my life on hold for you for months and now you're taking his side over mine! How could you?"

"Please, London!" Kenya whimpered, not wanting to face or hear the truth. "Please!"

Storm started to laugh and couldn't help himself as he taunted his woman's sister. "You heard her now, didn't you? So go pack your shit and leave so I can get back to my life."

"Yeah, okay! Not at all a problem!" London headed up the stairs and to her room to gather her belongings. "You two deserve each other! I don't know how I stayed here in this madhouse this long anyhow!" she yelled as she tossed her clothes and a few personal items in a bag.

When she came back down Storm and Kenya were sitting on the couch talking. He was still dogging Kenya out, but stopped to sneer at London's seeming fall from grace. "Don't worry, I already called your silly, jealous-ass a cab so you can just go wait on the damn curb!"

Kenya was silent as London passed by and went into the kitchen to get something else before struggling to drag her bags to the front door. Just as she opened the front door the cab was pulling up and blew once. London looked back at her twin, giving her one last chance to change her mind. "You sure about this, Kenya? You're picking this slimeball dope dealer over me?"

Kenya lowered her head in embarrassment over what was apparently her decision. After all she and London had been through and stuck together, the sisterly love and bond they shared was now being torn apart.

"Okay, so you know what it is, bitch! Now kick rocks!" Storm held the door open. "And don't bother us again! Kenya will call you, so don't call her, you lonely ho!"

London was really overjoyed to leave. She'd suffered through just about enough of Storm's disrespectful mouth, not to mention Kenya's spineless demeanor. With all her bags on the porch she spitefully turned around to face her sister and the man she'd so easily chosen over their bond. Vindictively, London pulled up her T-shirt, exposing a secret of her own that would shut a boisterous Storm up once and for all. Rubbing her slightly pudgy stomach in a circular motion, looking down, London grinned, delivering the showstopping revelation of the evening thus far.

"It's all good this way. Don't worry about me. And trust, I ain't gonna be lonely for long, believe that!" London smirked as all eyes were on her, rubbing her belly. "Tell your *Aunt Kenya and Daddy Storm* bye!"

"I don't understand! What the fuck are you talking about, London?" Kenya broke her silence, running over to the door, following her sister out to the cab. "What you mean, *Daddy Storm*? What is you talking about?"

Getting inside the cab, London shut the door and rolled down the window. "Ask his ass what happened in the kitchen that night!" She pointed at the condo where Storm was standing, face buried in his hands, having a flashback. "He knows." London then instructed the cab to pull off, leaving Kenya and Storm on the doorstep arguing. Smiling, she opened one of her bags, which contained both guns and Chocolate Bunny's purse.

"Where to, Miss Lady?" the driver inquired.

"Yes, can you please take me to police headquarters—the Homicide Division? I need to drop something off!"

I guess blood ain't thicker than water!